Project Halfsheep
Or How the CIA's Alien Got High

Also by Susan Hasler

Intelligence

The Flat Bureaucrat

to Marty and Ann,

Project Halfsheep
OR HOW THE CIA'S ALIEN GOT HIGH

SHash

Susan Hasler

Bear Page Press • Asheville

Project HALFSHEEP

This is a work of fiction. Names, characters, places, brands, media, and incidents are either the product of the author's imagination or are used fictitiously. The author acknowledges the trademarked status and trademark owners of various products referenced in this work of fiction, which have been used without permission. The publication/use of these trademarks is not authorized, associated with, or sponsored by the trademark owners.

Copyright © 2014 by Susan Hasler.

All rights reserved.

No part of this book may be reproduced, or stored in a retrieval system or transmitted in any form or by any means, electronic, mechanical, photocopying, recording, or otherwise, without express written permission of the publisher.

Published by Bear Page Press, Asheville.

Bear Page Press and the Bear Page Press logo are trademarks of Zreil Global Marketing, Inc., or its affiliates.

Cover design by Susan Hasler

ISBN-13: 978-0-9965779-2-2

Second Edition: August 2015

*For Stephen White,
Janice Lierz, and the Owl*

Acknowledgments

Writing a novel is both a lonely and a crowded undertaking. I have many people to thank for helping me along the way. Janice Lierz, my writing partner, kept my spirits up and offered invaluable advice on multiple drafts of this work. Phil Richardson once again served as a wise and discerning reader. As always, I owe a debt to Judi Hill and the instructors at Wildacres for their generosity. Last, but certainly not least, I am grateful to my husband, Steve White, for his love and support—and for feeding my delinquent parrots when I was engrossed in writing.

Project Halfsheep

OR HOW THE CIA'S ALIEN GOT HIGH

PROLOGUE

The Security Control Uniformed Duty Officer, or SCUDO, checked their socials against his list and waved them through. The grey Honda turned down an unnamed road to a nondescript metal building, one of several comprising an unmarked facility in an anonymous suburb of an undisclosed city, about which you have no need to know. The car stopped, and two men got out, one white-haired and one bald. In concert, they spat, hunched their shoulders, and went inside. It was a Saturday, and no one else was there.

Llywelyn flicked on the light and squinted at walls of metal shelving stacked with boxes. He was the smaller and older of the two. They were retired contract employees, chosen for discretion and institutional knowledge. No one considered that some brawn might also be required to hoist the archived paper.

"Where do we start?" Llywelyn asked.

Chuck, the bald one, was taller by an inch and only a year younger. He was heavier, but the excess weight concentrated largely in a gut fabricated from beer and chips.

His florid face grew petulant. "I hate this, but nothing for it. The most sensitive ones are sealed with black tape. Go for those first."

Llywelyn didn't move. Despite his lucrative contract, he hoped the door would miraculously open and some senior official would rush in and yell, "Stop! Don't do it."

Chuck took a few slow steps down an aisle of boxes with unhelpful labels like "Special Sub-Project 37b" and "Background on BITTERPILL." He reached out and touched one. "Is Carnaby really going to hand the family jewels to Congress? I mean, everything?"

"Every last unsavory morsel." Llywelyn hooked a thumb under his belt and shook his head. "At least that's what he says. We'll see after he gets a good whiff of this stuff. We might as well close up shop and turn this intelligence agency into an insurance company. What's the point? We're already in hot water up to our balls."

"No help for it. Carnaby's boss. Last choice I would have made." Chuck thumped his palm against the box then pulled it off the shelf, allowing the end to come to rest on his gut while he changed his grip. He lowered the heavy burden to the floor with a grunt. "Gotta start somewhere. With luck we won't find anything too bad. Holmes had the worst of it destroyed."

"I hope to God he was thorough."

After four hours, the quiet grew oppressive. Llywelyn started to hear things—scratching noises high in the shelves.

"Chuck, listen to that," he said.

"For the third time, I don't hear a thing. Stop it. You're giving me the creeps."

"I tell you I hear something," Llywelyn said.

"I'll solve that." Chuck went out to the car and got his

wife's portable tape deck and a stack of cassettes. They weren't supposed to bring recording equipment into an Agency facility, but they were the only ones in the building. He plugged the tape deck in near the door and cranked the volume to high. Karen Carpenter's silken voice filled the dusty cavern of the warehouse. She sang about little white lies and nights with a thousand eyes.

By seven o'clock that evening, the Carpenters had given way to Paul Simon and *Kodachrome*. The men were coughing up dust. The sound of black tape being ripped off cardboard had frayed Llywelyn's last nerve. Chuck had washed down half a dozen aspirin with the cold coffee from his thermos, but his back still ached. Soon small bruises would bloom across his pale gut. They were two hours into time and a half.

Just as Paul Simon sang the line about handwriting on the wall, a dull crash brought the men up short.

"You can't say you didn't hear that." Llywelyn stumbled to his feet. Stepping over piles of paper spread out on the floor, he turned the cassette off.

"I think it came from over there." Chuck pointed to the north corner of the building.

Llywelyn found himself wishing he had a gun, but who could have anticipated that a day at the archives would require a weapon? He and Chuck moved toward the source of the noise, looking down each aisle as they went.

What they found at last was merely a box fallen from a high shelf. The brittle cardboard had split on impact with the concrete floor, spreading its contents in all directions.

"What made it fall?" Llywelyn whispered.

"Gravity, you idiot," Chuck said. "Somebody didn't put it up there right, and it finally fell. Maybe our music made it vibrate off the shelf. Do you think there are poltergeists in here? Get hold of yourself. I see black tape, so we might as well look at the contents." Chuck bent down to read the label on the box. "Project HALFSHEEP. Never heard of it."

Their generous contract put no limit on overtime. Good thing, because once they opened the HALFSHEEP vein, there was no going home.

For nearly an hour they read in silence, then Llywelyn held up a yellowed paper with an elaborate ink imprint. Seven knurled spokes radiated from a dark center. "What is this?"

Chuck looked at the paper; then the color drained from his face as his eyes focused on the floor behind Llywelyn. "It's the same as that." He pointed to a print in the dust, seven knurled spokes that matched the impression on the paper.

A drop of saliva slid from Llywelyn's drooping lower lip and ran down his chin. He wiped it away; then his hand swept over the boxes, which included army files, Mines files, and handwritten notes from the early 1950s. "My God, what is all of this?"

Chuck took off his glasses and rubbed his bloodshot eyes. "I'm hoping to hell it's a joke."

> "Officially, I didn't exist. I was a joke concocted by some clever Princeton grads in the Mines' earliest days. They told me that to my face, and their utter self-assurance almost convinced me."—Piyat

1

A SCINTILLA

If I were to indulge in the periwinkle prose, I'd say I fell from the depths of the universe and landed in a nest of spies. But only one of them, Lloyd, fit the traditional definition of a spy, and he wasn't a good one, according to his own account. Avery was a covert operator, or "loose cannon" in the common tongue, and Lee, a psychiatrist. They gave me spy fiction to read, but I found it silly. My favorite books were the first I ever read on earth: *Alice in Wonderland* and Webster's dictionary. I venerated Alice and Webster. If I could choose my own name, it would be Alice Webster. Unfortunately, the many names I've had—some quite rude—were chosen for me by others.

It is accurate to say I fell from the depths of the universe. I hail from Utorb, a planet smaller and more crowded than Earth. On Utorb, my life was blissfully dull and lacking in sudden shocks and inexplicable developments. It was also a big obese lie, but I was fond of it.

My journey here was a "directed assignment" as the humans would say. Humans and my kind are not as different as they would like to think. Utorbis, of course, are the older, more evolved race. So evolved that our initiative had atrophied, and we no longer had volunteers for hopeless missions. On Earth, the daring devils or fame harlots or heroical martyrs would step up to the dish and say, "I'll do it, pick me." On Utorb, all such beings had extincted themselves, and an excellent riddance it was. We, the evolved, shrank when the overseers looked our way, when they flicked drops of silver from their tongues. The rule was to look downward when they used the high language, to avoid contact through the eye, for it was treacherous. I would be the last to fracture that or any rule, for I was the shyest of a sheep-like race.

But on that crucial day, I was not paying attention. I was thinking about the latest IGM, or Introduced Genetic Modification, offered by the gene emporium. A simple injection would turn my flocculent butt whatever color I desired. I was trying to decide between two shades of pink—the one pallid and pretty, the other shockingly bright—when we were called for assembly.

This was not unusual. The sight of us gathered on the Grand Convocation Ground gratified the overseers in a way that made their scaly hides glow. They liked to speak at length, especially when the weather was foul. I allowed my thoughts to drift, lowering my eyes against a stinging wind, full of sand from the eroding mountains. I thought about those two shades of pink. That bright pink was lovely, but I feared an unprepossessing Utorbi such as myself couldn't pull it off.

I was unprepossessing but extremely hearty. That's the critical thing I didn't notice that day. I and all the other Utorbis assembled were among the heartiest of our race and also the most gifted in linguistics. I recognized many from my advanced language class. Usually, the overseers assembled us according to the erection in which we worked, not physical type or talent. If I had considered this, I would have been wary, particularly since I stood near the front of the crowd. If I had paid attention, I would have kept a firmer hold on my physical responses. I would have glued my eyes to the ground and the sand devils swirling around my lower limb terminals, which cannot be called feet, for they are more like a cross between a bicycle wheel and a toilet plunger (items pictured in Mr. Webster's dictionary).

Distracted, I allowed a scintilla to betray me. A drop of silver, still warm from the tongue of the large cheese, struck me on the tip of what humans would call the nose. I shall use the longer word "proboscis" to describe our larger, more sensitive facial protuberance. I shuddered and the drop took flight again. It glittered, slashing the fulvous murk of home. The overseer's eye rolled in my direction, and I looked up. His eye killed me. He volunteered me, and my old ignorant-but-happy, false-but-comfortable life was no more.

No one said goodbye. My friends did not fulminate or whimper. Who would be so muttonheaded even in a race of sheep? They averted their faces as the overseers hauled me off. I longed for them to look, but I knew they would not, for I would not have looked. That killed me, also.

They dragged me from one end of Utorb to the other and hoisted me above the whooping throngs. They took my humble name away and called me "Piyat," which in the high language means "brave one," and in the common tongue, "idiot." The overseers took my happy, dull story away and gave me another that fit so badly it pinched. My image—scrubbed clean of dents and blotches—flashed across every screen on the planet.

At long last, to a thunderous whooping from the crowds, they dragged me down a long, slanting chute. The gravel floor cut me. I cried out, and they lifted me higher, so my limbs no longer dragged. That was the first and the last bit of kindness that ever came from my overbearing asshole jailers. "Asshole" is a word I learned from humans, by the way. Utorbis have no such orifice in their nether regions.

But I digress. As we went deeper into the ground, the whooping grew muffled. At long last, we came upon a door. They shoved me through it and slammed it shut.

The room was full of mad shrieking, which came from my new roommate. In the blinding glare, I couldn't see him clearly. I curled myself into a ball covering all four of my sensitive aural organs, which are located on my limb terminals and not my head, as in humans. I rolled as far from the shrieking as I could. I sniveled, cried, and wondered why I, a lowly piece worker—a gene splicer who most assiduously performed my job without ever asking where the genetic material came from or where it was going—why I was plucked from my others and deposited here with what must surely be the most extreme fruit loop lunatic on the planet.

Sometimes the screaming was high and steady like a siren. Sometimes it turned into a panting gasp, or a mewling snivel, or a long, bleating sob. Occasionally I picked out words—always something negative, like "pain," or "kill," or "horror." I am ashamed to say that I, who never hated anyone, came to despise the screamer.

One day, he rose and went to the far wall. He seemed to gather himself up; then he launched himself straight into the opposite wall, falling forward at the last moment so his head struck hard. It made a thud that turned my stomach. I heard crunching gravel. My companion staggered to his feet and hurled himself against the opposite wall. All at once he was quiet. Amiable Utorbi that I am, I immediately forgave the screamer for the misery he had caused me. When the jailers burst in and dragged him away, I called out, "Most excellent luck to you. I hope you get a more agreeable assignment elsewhere."

Then I was alone. I'd never been alone, having lived my life in a cozy *uyut,* or hexicle, a more evolved version of a cubicle, with six harmonious sides instead of four. In my hexicle the translucent walls flickered with the silhouettes of my colleagues in neighboring hexicles. The hard, opaque walls of this room bounced harsh light back and forth, until images split and blurred. My head burned, and I couldn't keep my eyes open.

My jailers entered from time to time, wearing tinted goggles and masks with a breathing apparatus. Frightened, I leaped to the ceiling and stuck, an involuntary reaction. They brought flat-ended poles to force under my pods to break the suction. I fell. They rammed hoses up my proboscis, shined light into my eyes, and took small sample chunks of me with a device like a tiny melon baller.

I'd never been one to ask questions, for answers don't necessarily make one happy. Ignorance can indeed be bliss. But there was nothing blissful about my situation, so I asked them why they had taken me and what was going to happen. Always I got the same answer. It was a single word, muffled and unidentifiable through their helmets. I rolled it in my mind, trying to find its proper shape.

I listened to sounds I hadn't noticed during the screaming. During the day, the noise came from far above. Engine roars and booms that shook the ground. At night, the only noise was the sharp hiss of a valve in the ceiling. The hiss changed frequencies but never stopped. I sneezed until my sensitive proboscis puffed up. My jailers took the hose from my proboscis and attached it to my belly, where they dug a small hole into which to shove it. The sneezing subsided, the hiss changed frequencies, and the sneezing resumed.

Time shrinks, stretches, and warps. In that room, I couldn't tell if it was time growing smaller and then larger, or me growing smaller and then larger. On Utorb we didn't employ clocks in an effort to dice time. The humans think if they chop him small and give him a ticking sound, if they strap him to their wrists, they can understand time, but it is not so. He is not nor ever will be effable. Nor is he killable, no matter how they talk about killing him. So I could not judge the quantity of time that flew under the bridge before the hissing stopped. But it stopped, and there was no sound of engines from above.

My body went limp with relief. I melted onto the floor. It was brief, that happiness. All at once, I heard the faraway whooping of a crowd and the crunching of pods on gravel. My muscles clenched and propelled me to the ceiling. The door opened, and all the noises grew louder. A great sack of something hit the far wall. Then the portal closed, and the crunching of pods faded away.

I wasn't alone anymore.

2

BIG DISTRACTION

The first meeting between Deyahm and me was informal. We dispensed with the usual Utorbian civilities, to include the shaking of limb terminals and the jaunty waving of the proboscis. Deyahm was too dazed, and my proboscis was so sore from sneezing, I dared not move it.

I crawled to him and squinted. He was the most beautiful and oldest being I'd ever seen. Not old in the way of humans, with wrinkles and foul breath—we eradicated those on Utorb—but old in that his body came from a much earlier model year. His limbs were longer, and his torso shorter. His smooth skin had an amber tint, which appeared gold in spots. My scaly hide was gray. He had no mug wart on the shoulder, no webbing between the phalanges, no thick wool encircling his hips. Instead, he wore a garment that covered his nether region. His proboscis was half the size of mine and not fully prehensile. I'd heard whispers of such beings, but I didn't know any still lived. He looked so sad that I wanted to cheer him up.

"I'm not a screamer," I said.

He raised his head. Squinting and shielding his eyes with a limb terminal, he gazed at me as one would gaze at an idiot. He had lovely eyes. I never knew his real name. Deyahm was the name the overseers gave him. It meant "adventurer" in the high language and "doomed" in the common tongue.

At first, Deyahm couldn't speak because the hissing nozzle sent him into paroxysms of sneezing. I was only slightly less afflicted. The room began to whirl. Deyahm and I locked eyes to stave off vertigo, but soon we could only lie on our backs and sneeze and flop.

At the time, I still believed what the overseers had told us: that death had been eradicated on Utorb.

"Death" was the first word Deyahm said when the sneezing subsided, and the whirling ceased. He pushed himself up from the floor and blinked. His voice emerged threadbare. "Death," he said, "I would have sooner preferred."

"You remember death?" I asked in blinding ignorance.

Deyahm winced, drawing the dotted ridges above his brows together. "Do I *remember* it?" With difficulty, he moved himself into a more commodious position, stretching and folding his long, graceful limbs.

"Yes," I said, "do you remember it, back before it was eradicated?"

The dotted ridges arched. "And what do you think happened to your first roommate?"

"He stopped screaming," I said, "and they took him to a new assignment."

Deyahm's mouth opened and snapped shut on a word before it could emerge, damaging it beyond recognition. Squinting mightily, he stared me up and down. "Yes, I *remember* death. I remember too awfully much, which is why I'm here. And you?" he asked. "How did you come to be here?"

"I looked up," I said, and sadness engulfed me.

"Ah, an *iyusui*." Deyahm spoke in the high language with irony.

I nodded. In the high language *iyusui* meant "intrepid volunteer." In the vernacular, it meant "tool."

Deyahm's body sagged with exhaustion from the sneezing and whirling. His head fell forward, but he revived, blinked, and squinted at me. "You have no idea what's happening to us, do you?"

I shook my head. "I wasn't paying attention at Convocation."

Deyahm rolled his eyes. "I had too many students like you. Well, my little dunce, allow me to catch you up. We are intrepid volunteers for *Uyiquiti Ri Poi*."

"That's it!" I cried. "'*Uyiquiti*' is the word they keep saying to me. I don't know what it means."

Deyahm turned away. Finally he raised his eyes to mine and said, "*Uyiquiti* is the ancient word they have chosen as a name for our mission. In the high language, it means 'venture.' Venture with a sacred connotation."

"What does it mean in the common tongue?" I asked.

Deyahm gave a twisted smile. "Distraction."

"I don't understand."

The lights went dim. The words "*Uyiquiti Ri Poi*" flashed on the wall in front of us in elaborate script. Venture Number One. A burst of static erupted from speakers in the ceiling.

"Congratulations, intrepid volunteers Deyahm and Piyat, on completing the first phase of your training. Before we begin phase two, we shall review the illustrious history of Utorb so that you may understand your place in our history and the importance of *Uyiquiti Ri Poi*."

An image of Utorb from space filled up one wall. Familiar music played as green vapors swirled over yellow seas. Our Utorbian anthem has many verses, so many that our lower limb terminals would grow numb when we stood on the Convocation Grounds and listened. I will only translate the chorus.

> Utorb, Utorb, our mother orb,
> Oh land that conquered death.

After the anthem came a history of Utorb, illustrated with images of our outstanding ancestors, our tall buildings, and our colorful banners flapping over the Convocation Grounds. I had seen it all before, but it stirred a deep-seated pride. I felt my eyes glow. Then the wall went blank, and the speaker promised another lesson tomorrow. The lights went up. Far above, the booming and muffled roar of equipment resumed.

Deyahm moved closer to me and hissed under his breath. "You love the lies, don't you?"

"Lies?" I asked timidly. "Which part is lies?"

"The whole rotten lot, and keep your voice down," Deyahm whispered. "The noise only provides so much cover."

"I don't understand," I said.

"You understand nothing because you don't know your cycles," Deyahm said. "I was a teacher of cycles until they began to dictate lies to me. Then I went to work in the secret archives."

"Maybe I don't want to know," I said quickly. I'd never been the sort to insist on knowing what I was told I had no need to know.

Deyahm gave me a penetrating stare that made me want to curl into a ball. "Sorry," he finally whispered, "but wiping out ignorance has been my life's work. Be still and listen." He lay flat and rolled onto his stomach, placing his head on his arm as if he planned to nap. I copied his position.

"There was a time when death almost conquered Utorb. It was our own fault. We had befouled the necessary and exhausted the precious. We expired in droves. Our rotting carcasses sent up a fetor that brought the living to their knees. We would have all found death, if not for the Great Idea.

"The Idea was simple. If we had pushed Utorb so far we could no longer alter it, we must alter ourselves so that we could live with what we had created. We must evolve at a fearsome pace. Death must be purposeful, not random. The weak must die quickly, so that nourishment could go to the strong. To conquer death, the overseers harnessed it. Are you following me, Piyat?"

Not so much. I lifted my head to look at him. I could see the blank moon of my stupidity reflected in his eyes. So he said everything again slowly and returned to the words, "The overseers harnessed death." I still didn't understand, but he continued.

"First came selection, guided by geneticists who labeled characteristics as desirable or not. Then slaughter. They invented a machine for beheading that could grab and position a body and sever the head in seconds."

"Sever the head?" I said in surprise. "How do you live without a head?"

"You do not." Irritation crackled in Deyahm's voice. "That's the point. The machine was a highly efficient and relatively painless way to kill without damaging any of the parts intended for study. This was long before my existence. By the time I was born, the death chutes leading to the machines had been abandoned and filled in with gravel. In my role as archivist, I oversaw the excavation of one of them for historical purposes. The very one we descended."

"Death chute?" I felt a thump in my stomach.

"They herded undesirable Utorbis into the death chute, where they stood for hours, inching toward the machines. Placing the machines underground masked the noise and made it impossible for the Utorbis in the chute to escape. I uncovered writings scratched into the walls with gravel. The doomed wrote poems to the rhythmical squee and thump of the machine, the thud of heads hitting the conveyor belt that carried them to a facility for the extraction and study of genetic material, to the savory sharp smell of unused body parts burning, to the bitter juices that rose in their mouths. They wrote poems to the sound of their writing stones scratching the wall. I swept away the dust and read them all. They've since been erased." Deyahm clenched his limb terminals. "After the culling came the selective breeding, molecular cloning, and manipulation of genetic material. Utorbis mastered the art of controlled hyper-evolution, creating bodies that could breathe foul air and eat spoiled food. Proboscises got longer to filter out impurities, and livers expanded to do the same. And it worked." Deyahm spoke in the high language. "The cloying fetor of death cleared, and a new light illumined the sky—the lustrous dawn of a golden age. A vigorous new race of Utorbis was born." Deyahm closed his eyes. When he spoke again, his voice was filled with bitterness. "They could have stopped it then—destroyed the beheading machines, ended the breeding experiments, and left off playing with genes. Once the art of controlled hyper-evolution was mastered, however, it became an easy solution. Make the eyes bigger, so they can see in darkness, and there's no need to light buildings. Make a body that can survive on fewer nutrients, and you don't need so much food.

"Eventually, a movement arose against the beheadings. It came from everywhere at once, from all the classes. Utorbis were sick to their souls of the killing. So the machines were torn asunder, and the death chute filled in. We congratulated ourselves for raising civilization to a higher level. That was the 'Gleaming Age.' It was short, lovely, and filled with illusion."

"Why couldn't it last forever?" I asked.

"Because it was already too late," Deyahm whispered. "They had to start the beheadings again, this time in secret. It was considered a kindness. And a kindness it was, for the victims were suffering."

"Who were they?"

"Defective offspring. Controlled hyper-evolution had spun out of control horribly. At first only a small percentage of offspring were born with anomalies. Then came more with worse anomalies. Soon there were offspring who couldn't move, who suffered wrenching pain with each breath. These were beheaded with all possible speed and kindness. The new machines played music and emitted puffs of anesthetic. Instead of long conveyor belts, the heads were caught in soft baskets and covered with beautifully woven cloth before being taken for study. The horror was not much reduced by such measures. As the anomalies and beheadings increased, more Utorbis became aware of it, although it was not spoken of openly. Sorrow shadowed the Gleaming Age until it was extinguished." Deyahm's voice faded.

I'd seen only one live offspring, and this from far away, through whooping crowds. Her name was Luyeel. I had images of her on my desk. We all had these images in our hexicles.

Our hexicles. I shut my eyes tight. In my head, I took all of the things from my hexicle and put them in the empty space in front of me until I felt I could reach out and touch them: my bright pictures of Luyeel and the tiny gel chambers, pipettes, and magnifiers I used in my work. I would go back to my hexicle. Somehow, after *Uyiquiti Ri Poi*, I would go back.

I sighed and opened my eyes. Deyahm pointed to the valve, which continued to hiss, but no longer made us sneeze. "Do you understand what that is?" he asked.

"A hissing valve." The question was annoyingly obvious.

"But do you understand what it is?" he said.

The valve pumped air into the room. The sneezing was connected to the valves and the change in frequencies. It had been some time since I had sneezed. Suddenly, I understood the function of the valve. My throat clenched. I struggled to force out the word "conditioning."

"Indeed," Deyahm said softly, "Drugs come through the tubes to enhance our bodies' ability to adapt. We've been conditioned to breathe other air. And what does that mean, Piyat?" Kindness and necessary cruelty hid behind his words.

"It means," I said, "we can no longer breathe the air of Utorb. We cannot go back to our hexicles." As this horror sank in, another idea came to me. "My eyes. I can open them wide and see everything now. So--"

"So even if you returned to your hexicle and could

breathe the air, you would be blind because your eyes have been conditioned to a new level of light." Deyahm delivered this news in his softest voice.

"Could they reverse the conditioning?" I asked.

Deyahm regarded me sternly. "Best not to think about your hexicle, where you will not recur. You need your wits about you or you will not survive. If you care to survive." Deyahm's long phalanges slowly opened and closed like a flower. "For me, not so much."

Uyiquiti. I still didn't understand what it really meant. Deyahm anticipated the question. "You remember, I said *uyiquiti* meant 'distraction' in the common tongue?"

"Yes."

"So what do you need to know before you can truly understand what *uyiquiti* means?"

The answer lit on my proboscis. "I need to know what they're trying to distract us from." I raised my eyes to Deyahm's.

"Haven't you figured it out?" he said.

I had not because I was still an idiot, despite his attempts at education.

"Utorbis have started asking questions. Why can't we contact people who have been sent away on new assignments? Why are the historical cycles no longer taught in the schools?"

"Why?" I asked.

"Because our race is dying." Deyahm pronounced these words with such sadness and exhaustion, I feared he would expire before the end of the sentence. He rallied and continued. "With all our skill at genetic engineering we no longer have the will or imagination to fix it. The overseers have tried many ways of distracting us from the truth. They introduced the hot silver tonic, which is both stimulating and intoxicating. They began a wave of Introduced Genetic Modifications designed to satisfy and distract: first the mug wart on the shoulder to hold and heat the tonic and later even sillier things. A small injection or operation, and voila, you grow flocculent bloomers." Deyahm laughed. "I see you went for everything offered."

"What's wrong with my bloomers?" I looked down at the thick, curling skirt of wool that ringed my hips. "They allow me to sit comfortably without cushions or even the necessity of shifting my buttocks. The mug wart allows me to work and drink my tonic simultaneously. My bloomers protect my lap against spills of hot tonic, which, as you know, are the primary source of injury on Utorb."

Deyahm shook his head. "As your enthusiasm demonstrates, the effort to distract the population enjoyed some success. Such as you lapped your tonic happily from your mug warts as you worked. But questions remained. The overseers distracted us by sending volunteers to all the six moons, but Utorbis have grown bored with that. Now the overseers hope a glorious mission across the Bitter Sharp to another planet will cover the signs that our race is dying. Perhaps we could even build a new home there. They hope to inspire Utorbis to new ideas and great undertakings, to inspire them to solutions to the problems that are killing us. Everyone will watch our launch."

"Launch? What launch?"

"Piyat," Deyahm said, "Do you think this is our mission? To sit in this room? No, we're going far away."

"And coming back?" I asked weakly.

"Of course not," Deyahm said. "The purpose of this mission is to see if we survive the trip and can live on the target planet. We're expendable. Later they'll send more highly trained 'volunteers.' Come, Piyat, how could you not know what's been happening? Why have you never asked about the great clattering, the sounds of digging, the thunder of sheets of metal being bent, the whining drills?"

The next day, our memory and language training began. The video wall gave us exercises to strengthen our brains. It trained us to memorize bursts of made-up language and then to decipher them. It taught us to recall sensations, to order and store events. We did well in these exercises. Deyahm surmised that drugs designed to enhance our ability to store information were flowing into our bodies through the tubes.

"This is your charge," the speaker told us. "Go forth and build in your memory box a record of all that you see, hear, and smell. Others will come after you and will need to hear your story."

There are things in my memory box that are like hot coals. They burn when I touch them. Even after all this time, the pain is undiminished. Of all the unkindnesses visited upon us by our jailers, this was the most profound.

3

LAUNCH

After the memory drills ended, the words "*Uyiquiti Ri Ga*" flashed on the screen in elaborate script. Venture Number Two or The Second Distraction. The wall speaker told us that another mission would follow ours. Equipment on our rocket would allow us to communicate with them as they approached. In case our equipment didn't survive the landing, they had implanted tracking devices under our skin so that the second expedition could find us. The sensors would glow, growing brighter as they got closer. We would brief the second expedition on our findings and help them with their mission, whatever that was.

After that, the video wall grew quiet. The sound of machinery died out.

In my dream, I burned. I awoke to a fearsome roar and vibration strong enough to blur my vision. Deyahm's mouth gaped. I screamed, but I couldn't hear my voice above the terrible white roar.

When it was over, Deyahm and I lay on the floor, unable to speak for some time.

"That was the engine test," Deyahm finally said.

"Will they do it again?"

"Not until we are atop the rocket."

Now, I understood the screamer and said a silent apology to him. I screamed myself. This time I could hear my voice, like something outside of me, alive in and of itself, screaming without my volition. It bounced around the room, demented and uncontrollable. I tried to escape from it. I raced in circles and caromed off the walls until I collapsed in a quivering heap.

Then Deyahm was above me, holding my mouth shut. "If you scream again," he said, "I will thwack you senseless." I tried to shake him loose, but he tightened his grip as the screams rose inside me. I rolled and bit, but he stayed with me. Old as he was, he was strong and intransigent. We fought the day through, scrabbling back and forth across the floor. Deyahm fought me from the outside, and the screams fought me from the inside. At last I was spent and fell into a stupor.

For days, we said nothing. Deyahm had saved my life, for the screaming would have killed me as it did my first roommate. The silence grew and sickened us. All we could do was contemplate the thing that would at last break the silence.

The crunch of pods on gravel began softly, coming from far above. I cried until Deyahm's face blurred, and his eyes were a smudge of lavender. I rolled into a ball and pushed myself into a corner.

The crunching stopped. The door opened with a bang and an oath. Two Utorbis grabbed me and scraped the wool off my butt with a blade. They stuffed Deyahm and me into stiff black garments. They forced helmets over our heads. Our jailers cut off the light, and we were blind.

I heard more Utorbis crowd into the room, enough to surround us on all sides. I called out to Deyahm, but my voice bounced around inside the helmet and could not get out.

They led us back up that long chute. I couldn't see the scrubbed walls. In the darkness, the poems of the doomed rewrote themselves. In my head, I could hear the scratch of the stones. I wanted to grab a stone from the floor and scratch my own poem on the wall so there would be something left behind of Piyat, who used to be Beyal before they took her name away.

We heard the throngs whooping long before we reached the surface. I had attended moon launches. The overseers would serve tonic and hand out flags decorated with images of "volunteer" space travelers. I always thought it must be happiness to be the face snapping and smiling above the crowds.

Images of Deyahm and me must have waved all around us. My old friends were somewhere in the crowd. I wouldn't see their faces again, nor would I see the absinthe-colored clouds of Utorb, the winking crystalline rocks on the western horizon, or the choppy yellow sea to the east. I had loved the Utorbian landscape for its beauty. But Deyahm had told me that the clouds were the venom left by factories. The towering crystalline rocks winked in the light because they had been drilled away on the inside by miners. Once there were many more of them, but now they crumbled one by one like rotten teeth. Phosphorescent creatures, both beautiful and edible, once swam the yellow seas, but they were long gone. Somewhere to the north was the structure that housed my hexicle, with my pipettes and my pictures of Luyeel, the last Utorbian offspring. She was also dead, according to Deyahm. He told me that she never acquired adulthood, that her organs failed painfully, that—as a kindness—they beheaded her shortly after the pictures were taken.

When we reached the top of the chute, the crowd caught sight of us. "There they are! There they are!" I thought the brutal butterflies in my belly would kill me. Deyahm managed to slip his limb terminal over mine and squeeze.

We had to walk a long, swaying bridge above the crowd. I remembered it from earlier launches as a beautiful thing, painted all in gold with winking blue lights. In my blindness, it was a horror of motion. My pods were covered in cloth and couldn't make suction. I slid and came near to toppling more than once. Each time, my jailers yanked me upright. I lost Deyahm's hand and feared that he had fallen away.

Because of our violent weather, Utorbian rockets are launched out of the ground. The humans think that aliens fly in saucers, but our rockets are not so different from theirs. Our laws of physics are the same. The rocket must be pointy to pierce the atmosphere and get out into space. At least I think that's the reason. I was never good at physics.

The saucer part of our rockets is just below the nose. It's all that's left after the nose falls off, and the fuel in all the other stages of the rocket is spent. The saucer is like one small slice of a long cylinder.

All the truth Deyahm told me about Utorb had caused me pain beyond description. But if he hadn't destroyed the false, happy Utorb in my head, I couldn't have survived the launch.

The butterflies beat inside my belly. I feared the noise and heat of the engine below. The fear made me struggle when nothing could be gained by it. Even Deyahm struggled, which surprised me. To my left, I could feel him writhing against our jailers.

We fought for the same reason: we could not make it easy and convenient for them to tuck us inside a great horrific rocket and launch us into the Bitter Sharp. Otherwise, they would go home happy and content that they had done their jobs. So we fought to pierce their bubbles of contentment, so they would feel a draft of the Bitter Sharp before they condemned us to it forever.

It angered them and understandably so. For who would relinquish their stupid happiness willingly? It angered them, but they couldn't be too rough. They must tuck us into the rocket without killing us and without letting the crowd know we were unwilling. So our jailers closed around us, unfurled more flags, and hid us from the throngs.

When we reached the rocket, Deyahm and I fought fiercely, but they wrapped us with brawny straps and stuffed us into a space smaller than my hexicle. They tightened the straps, so our limbs couldn't move. I realized that they would not loosen them again and that we could not loosen them ourselves.

Our jailers stuck tubes in our bellies and slammed the portal shut. Abruptly, the noise of the throngs disappeared, and the darkness allowed us to see a large, hooded window, which would reveal the Bitter Sharp when the nose of the rocket fell away. It was such a small space between my proboscis and that window. Inches. Here we would be flung into space and yet have no space to ourselves. We shivered and waited for the great searing noise.

It came from below, starting small and quickly reaching an unbearable pitch, obliterating everything. The world trembled. I thought we were dying in a great explosion. Along with the terror of it, came a queer euphoria. I waited for the brawny straps that held us down to dissolve. I waited for release, for blazing manumission, for some incomprehensibly large freedom.

Instead, our rocket began to rise. For some time, I saw nothing but blackness. I slowly came to understand that I was alive and still bound by restraints and that it was probable that this condition would never change. Gradually other truths began to reveal themselves: my butt stung and ached, my limbs had cramped, and my proboscis was perhaps broken.

From Deyahm, I heard nothing.

4

THE BITTER SHARP

Time is a duplicitous bastard. Humans, who think they have his number, ought to take the trip I took across the Bitter Sharp. Instead of one big, warm-hearted star peeking over the horizon at unvarying intervals, I had a billion stars, all with their disparate ideas of time. I encountered tailed fireballs, extinguished chunks, glittering dust, and assorted celestial gewgaws. The sky was both up and down, instead of being in the one understandable "up" direction only, as it is on Utorb and Earth. You can see how somebody like me—a mentally below-average Utorbi—could become severely disoriented. Even now, I can't answer the simple question: how long was your trip?

Long enough that all the fiery stages of our rocket burned and fell away.

Long enough that the wool grew back on my butt.

Long enough that I almost went mad.

The worst part of the trip was not knowing whether I sat next to Deyahm or a corpse. Held fast by the restraints, I couldn't see him. My helmet allowed only a view straight ahead. Mostly I kept my eyes shut because the big dazzling things and small glittery things moved towards us at great speed. When I did open my eyes, I flinched like an alien on the dissecting table, sure something was about to hit me. It never happened. The rocket must have possessed a collision-avoidance system.

I fought against my restraints, but heard nothing from Deyahm. I called out and met with silence.

I strained to move my eyes toward my left, where he sat. At last I noticed a fuzzy dark spot in the corner of my vision. I determined that it was Deyahm's limb terminal strapped to a rudder, a false rudder, which didn't move or cause anything else to move. It was for show. They had a camera on us, beaming our images back to Utorb for the distraction of the populace. Utorbian cameras recorded images in great detail and also rendered smells—although most of us turned that function off.

I didn't care about the camera. I only cared for that spot in the corner of my vision. I forced my eyes to stay open, despite the stars flying in my face. I watched to see if it would please move.

I remembered what Deyahm said about death and putrefaction. I sniffed. I couldn't smell anything, but that might have been because of my helmet, which was attached to a hose for breathing. So I was both together with Deyahm and alone, not knowing if he lived or decayed.

As my wool grew back, I began to itch so severely that I forgot everything else. In all the universe, the only thing I wanted was to scratch my butt.

Anger was the next stage of my trip, after itching. I grew to hate all Utorbis who weren't on that rocket. I despised the helmet that restricted the movement of my proboscis, the window so close to my eyes, and every blasted scrap of space crap that flew at me. I looked into the camera and mouthed the most obscene Utorbian insult I knew. I said it over and over until the camera turned its eye from me to look out the window. Evidently the overseers no longer considered me suitable viewing for the public. I felt satisfaction.

I began to fight against my restraints, pulling and punching until I tired myself out enough to sleep. When I awoke, I started again. One day, a sleeve tore. I worked harder against the cloth and my restraints. The restraints would not tear, but they did stretch enough to allow a greater range of movement. Eventually, I could reach up to my head. One day I was able to touch the helmet. Then I was able to grab the bottom of the helmet and pull at it until it broke and fell away from my face. I felt the pain of approaching death as my pulmonary sacs collapsed. I grabbed the hissing nozzle that had been inside my helmet and stuck it up my proboscis. I could breathe again.

I gathered my courage, such as it was, and turned to Deyahm. His face behind the visor was stiff and staring. Lavender eyes had faded to gray.

I felt the cry rise up with the searing force of a rocket launch. It tore from my mouth with a burst of pain and bounced about inside our capsule. Then a miracle. Deyahm blinked, and the lavender in his eyes stirred and bloomed.

I fought my restraints until I could grasp his visor and pull it away from his face, almost damaging his head in the process. He began to gasp. I quickly stuffed the hissing nozzle up his proboscis. He sneezed once, dislodging it, but I stuffed it in again.

"Talk," I begged. "Please, talk."

He gaped and struggled. When they came, the words were quiet as a sigh. "Death," Deyahm said, "I would have preferred."

When I first met Deyahm, he taught me about death with words. In the last part of our trip, he taught me without words. I learned that there is alive and "alive," and that the two are not the same. Deyahm was "alive," but not the way he had been on Utorb. He said nothing more, not one sweet word.

I beseeched, but it was useless. Deyahm sometimes blinked, but more often, he looked away or closed his eyes, which faded again to gray. He lived, but he was not alive. I could have borne sad, bitter, or cruel words better than none at all. The absence of words was an exile's exile.

Despair was the final limb of our trip. I gave up. I opened my eyes to the terrible stars rushing at my face, and I keened. I wished our ship would collide with something and cease to exist, so there would be no doubt as to what was alive and what was "alive." I howled at the collision-avoidance system. Then it occurred to me that I could destroy it if I could figure out where it was. Our cockpit was full of knobs, buttons, dials, and levers. I started pushing and twisting them, but after a short time, they crumbled. They were as fake as the rudders. They were for the camera.

I looked down at the feeding tube that sprouted from my belly. If I pulled that tube out, I would starve to death eventually. Death did not bother me, but I found that "eventually" worrisome. I considered the tube stuffed up my proboscis. I could pull it out and expire faster, but I remembered the pain in my lung sacs between the time I broke my helmet and the time I put the nozzle back in my proboscis. Could I stand that long enough to die?

A thought came: how would Deyahm feel riding next to a corpse? I didn't know that he would feel anything at all but suppose he did? I couldn't abandon him to that.

I howled some more. Then the answer arrived, and it made me cold in a way that my clever temperature-regulating body couldn't handle. The howl died in my gullet. I must kill both of us. The worst part was that I would have to start with Deyahm, because the other way around wouldn't work no matter how I turned it in my head. I would have to remove the hissing nozzle from his proboscis and then my own. I must somehow be brave enough not to put the nozzle back when the agony of dying came. My agony and his agony, which I would have time to witness.

I pushed the answer away. Again and again it returned with the screaming stars that rushed my face.

Perhaps Deyahm would die without my intervention. This was a happy thought—a measure of how grim my existence had become. It came to me one day when my gullet was too sore for howling. I glanced at him from the corner of my eye. He stared as always, with his head listing to the left. I pressed his *hackuhl*, the green pulse point between his eyes, and felt a light thrum. I tried to judge whether the thrumming was less than it had been before.

I began to check the *hackuhl* at shorter intervals. All the while, I wondered if he knew what I was doing. Did he guess that I wanted him to die?

But he would not die.

The stars rushed, Deyahm stared, and my linear journey circled back again and again to the same conclusion:

I must kill my friend and myself. I determined how to do it in a way that couldn't be undone, no matter how great the pain. If I took the hissing tube out of my proboscis, it would be too easy to stuff it back in again. The thing to do was to pull it out of the control panel. The tube was attached at the very bottom of the panel. Even though my restraints had stretched, the glass of the window made it impossible for me to lean forward enough to replace the tube. So I would die. With luck, sooner than later.

I planned to pull out Deyahm's breathing tube first, and then my own. I thought everything out most carefully. Then came the time to do it.

"I'm sorry," I said to Deyahm, "but I'm going to kill you and me both." I waited, hoping that he would say something to stop me. "So that was your warning," I said, "so if you want to say 'stop' now would certainly be the time." I waited. "Because if you don't say something, you and I will be dead soon. This will be irreversible." I waited a long time. "Well," I said, "this is it. Time to die. You may experience some agony. If you want to avoid that, please say 'stop' now." I waited, but there was no response. I pressed his *hackuhl* in the hope that he had expired, but no. He thrummed. I only had two choices, to wait forever or not.

I grabbed his breathing tube and yanked hard, but it didn't come out. I pulled and kicked at the tube until I exhausted myself. I rested briefly, then drew myself up for one more big effort. I gathered my strength, closed my eyes, and pulled.

A siren went off with a piercing woo woo woo.

I presumed the siren to be part of the breathing apparatus, but Deyahm was not gasping and dying as would be appropriate in the situation. I opened my eyes and looked at the control panel and saw his tube still attached. Then I became aware of a largeness. I looked at the window and saw a great blue orb. *We will collide and be done with it*, I thought. I felt relief and fear. Then I realized that our ship was slowing down. A word lit up on the panel in front of us: *situsyu*. In the high language, it meant "destination," and in the common tongue "crash."

5

TRUDIE IN JULY OF '47

Trudie found *Pride and Prejudice* gutted on the floor—it was like discovering the mangled body of a pet. Earl had fed the pages to the fire. Her stomach kicked. She pressed her hand to the rough adobe of the fireplace and thought she might be sick. Her husband had chosen a favorite book, a gift from her late mother, to make the act sting.

It was bitter to admit her marriage was a mistake. In school, Trudie Pilcrow excelled in every subject. Yet she had made the most boneheaded error of them all—falling for a good-looking man full of flattery when she was a homely girl with a big inheritance coming. Her father had pushed for the wedding because he wanted a man who could run the ranch some day. His son, Lloyd, had opted for college and a career.

A few months after the wedding, Trudie's parents drove into the path of a cattle truck under blackout conditions. They left their daughter land rich, cash poor, and bound to a man now free to express his contempt in a thousand large and small ways.

Trudie's father, Hiram Pilcrow, had demanded absolute control over everyone and everything in his domain, from the Hungarian wife he had acquired in World War I, to his children and hired hands, to his mongrel dog. Trudie thought his death might give her some freedom, but old Pilcrow had extended his control beyond the grave by giving Earl power of attorney over decisions concerning the land. He didn't want Trudie to sell the place and do something foolish like go to college.

When the marriage went south, Trudie had consulted a lawyer to see about getting a divorce. "Does he beat you?" the man asked. When Trudie said no, he raised his brows until they pushed furrows into his greasy combover. He fingered his bolo tie, adjusted his glasses, and fixed her with a look that put her on the same level as a prostitute or ax murderess. "You'll lose everything and, frankly, you deserve to lose everything. I thought you were a good Catholic girl. Your mother would be heartbroken. Go home and thank your lucky stars you found a man willing to marry you."

No, Earl didn't beat her. He wasn't an intelligent man, but he was smart enough not to give grounds for divorce. He didn't sleep around. *Laziness*, Trudie thought. Out here in the New Mexico ranch lands, it would be work to find a woman and a half day's drive to get to her. Earl could satisfy his sexual needs more easily with Trudie and kill two birds with one stone by humiliating her in the process. Certain places on her body—hipbones, the flesh above the knee, and the breasts—bore the bruises of his passionate contempt. She wished she were delicate, rather than big-boned and strong. Then Earl might accidentally break an arm or a leg, and she might get some sympathy from the legal system.

Trudie hid the remains of *Pride and Prejudice* behind some books on the top shelf in her father's old study. She had a full day. She ought to get on with it, but she stood frozen atop the ladder. From here she saw the room at a different angle than usual. It struck her as a stage set for someone else's life. The adobe and dark timbers of the Pueblo style house were imposing, but full of cracks that needed repair. The furniture was massive and uncomfortable. From the grave, her father forced her to live in this high-maintenance pile of dried mud. It was her job to extend his dream beyond his death.

Trudie wasn't the type of woman to cry or throw up her hands when there was no solution. Nor was she the type to live caged and miserable. She reached up and took a leather-bound volume off the shelf. It was lighter than it looked, for it was hollow. Earl knew nothing about it. Inside was the brass key to a safe hidden behind a landscape of the Jornada del Muerto Desert. The safe held her mother's emerald necklace and her father's silver-plated, ivory-handled pistol, which he had polished more often than fired. Trudie could have used a shotgun, but she wanted an elegant weapon.

That night, Trudie lay on her back at the edge of the veranda where she could see the sky. With one hand, she swept her frizzy blonde hair away from her neck and fanned it out above her head. She often slept here in warm weather to escape Earl's snoring, but tonight she'd brought no bedding. She arched her back and pushed her knotted shoulder muscles into the coolness of the terracotta tiles. Then she assumed a corpse-like pose with her hands folded over her stomach. The occasion seemed to warrant it.

Not that she was maudlin. No, she considered this a more or less practical solution to an intractable problem. The only other out would be to shoot Earl, and that would raise a host of moral and legal issues she hadn't the heart to tackle. No one else would see him as a monster. All she had to show were small bruises. Like stains on a shirt or wax buildup on the kitchen floor, small bruises were something a mid-century wife was expected to handle.

Sleeping on the veranda was a habit Trudie had begun in her teenage years, when she would ask the constellations for extravagant and absurdly detailed favors, like an east coast education at a school with ivy-covered brick, sidewalks shaded by flaming orange sugar maples, and a campanile with a carillon that tolled on the hour. She didn't ask stars for favors anymore.

Trudie reached for the pistol and laid it on her chest. She ran a finger over smooth ivory and silver engraved with running horses. She picked up the weapon and positioned the barrel against her temple. A calico cat appeared, then a white one, then a tabby gray. They pushed their heads into Trudie's body, purred, then settled against her. *They'll be fine*, Trudie thought. The cook would feed them. Hell, if they wanted to snack on her body, it didn't bother her. She had no one to hold her back. She was barely on speaking terms with her brother—she hadn't returned his phone calls in months. Thanks to backbreaking work and rough handling, her body no longer housed a fetus.

Trudie had collected quite a few books on astronomy, so she knew what she was looking at as she stared into the sky. She could name every visible constellation and recite the story behind it. She was a studier, a collector of proper terminology, an avid reader, and a woman who liked to think deeply about the most common of things. That had been her salvation, but it couldn't keep her soul alive anymore. Her finger found the trigger.

Then Trudie saw something she couldn't name. She had observed meteor showers, eclipses, comets, and other astronomical phenomena. Two years earlier, just before sunrise, the eerie flash and rumble of Trinity, the first atomic bomb test, had shaken her faith in solid earth and left her with a lingering unease. That was to the south. What she saw now was to the north. It bore no resemblance to any celestial phenomenon she had ever seen, and it engendered wonder, not fear. It started off as a small, citrine light and quickly grew in size and intensity, bouncing and throwing off sparks of turquoise and coral. The sky pulsed with the color, then a flash that blinded her. When her eyes adjusted, the heavens had returned to normal.

Trudie thought she had dreamed it, then Earl came to the open bedroom window and yelled, "Jesus Christ, what was that godawful racket?"

The visual display had been so magnificent, that Trudie hadn't noticed the noise.

"It was thunder." Trudie had no desire to share anything special with Earl.

He swore and disappeared. Trudie looked deep into the sky. Perhaps this was a sign that a miracle could come to even the most stagnant life. She laid the pistol aside for now.

6

SITUSYU

If *situsyu* meant "destination" in the high language and "crash" in the common tongue, then I would say that both meanings were correct in our case. It wasn't appalling initially. Our spacecraft slowed as we approached the blue orb I now know as Mother Earth. She was attractive, both in the sense of beauty and gravity. I could feel her embrace, and it took my breath away. Then our landing became appalling.

The cockpit grew warmer as the accumulation of space dust on our window burned away under a writhing sheet of blue and white flame. Utorbis are designed to withstand a greater temperature range than humans, but I feared I would roast. The flame burned itself out, but this didn't improve our situation. Mother Earth grew overweeningly possessive and grabbed us to herself roughly. A trio of engines on our rump was supposed to fire lustily and simultaneously to slow our descent. They fired, but neither lustily nor simultaneously. The first engine erupted with less a roar than a fart. It sent our spacecraft tumbling so that the earth was sometimes above and sometimes below. The second engine farted and jerked us in a different direction. I grabbed Deyahm, and he made a cry, which would have cheered me if not for our impending doom. The farting of the third engine coincided with our impact with earth. Then came a booming, bouncing, crashing, rolling, rollicking, and things coming apart, accompanied by red sparks, yellow dust, flaming balls, and a feces load of pain. I may have the order of that wrong, but it doesn't signify.

When it stopped, I opened my eyes and then shut them tight against smoke and stinging grains of sand. The upper part of me swung back and forth, but I could not move my stinging lower limbs. My head felt extremely heavy. Then I misplaced my consciousness.

When I awoke again, the smoke had cleared. I saw a thin slice of moon. I looked around, but there was only the one, all by itself in the middle of the sky. The Earth moon is similar to Utorbian moons. It is brighter and lonelier, but otherwise it waxes and wanes the same. It heartened me, despite the pain. As my vision cleared, I saw two circular shapes not far from the moon. When I realized that these shapes were my lower limb terminals, I became agitated. I was upside down. My head was swinging free while my pods were immobilized. Any attempt to move them caused severe pain. I was terrified to discover that the restraints still wrapped around my pods were stuck with spikes attached to a green monster. Subsequent research has revealed that the monster was a vicious sort of plant known as a cactus or, to be more precise, an *opuntia imbricata* or tree cholla.

This was my first encounter with a plant. Botanical creatures were rare on Utorb, and I concluded that this was a good thing, which should have been celebrated. The cactus was vile and malicious. As I struggled to break free, it hung on to parts of me, including bits of hide and wool. I panicked, struggling until I broke off the monster arm and fell to the Earth with it. I landed on my back, still tangled in my restraints and stuck to the broken arm of the cactus. In a panic, I crawled away from the horrible monster and hid behind a rock. I peeked out and saw that he did not follow me, so I took the time to pull the spikes from my hide.

Then I remembered Deyahm. I must be brave and find my friend. Perhaps the crash had awakened him so that his was alive, rather than only "alive." With hope in my cardiovascular ticker pump, I crawled out from behind the rock.

Hope faded when I saw our spaceship scattered about in smoking chunks. Sometimes a brown bouncing thing, which I now know to be a tumbleweed, would blow across some wreckage and burst into flame.

I didn't think anything alive could emerge from that horror, but then I was alive, so there was hope. I limped to the nearest chunk of debris. It was blackened and cone-shaped. One of the farting rocket engines, I believe. I limped further and found other chunks of twisted metal I couldn't identify. Still, I was convinced I would find Deyahm alive. Surely I deserved a happy ending.

The sky had begun to lighten when I saw a dark shape nestled in a scrubby plant creature. The brutal butterflies awoke in my belly, and I didn't want to look closer. What else was there to do? I looked and saw that it was a fake rudder, with Deyahm's upper limb still strapped to it.

He could still be alive, I thought. *A Utorbi can live without a limb.*

But not without a head. I found that behind the bush.

It was embedded in a chunk of melted glass from our bubble window. His flesh had burned, but the imprint of his gentle physiognomy was visible in the glass. It bore such a ghastly expression that I knew he had gone from "alive" to alive before he died. In my head, I heard Deyahm's voice. "Death," he said, "I would have preferred."

Well, death he had gotten.

But maybe not? We Utorbis were healers. It was something the genetic engineers had devised. We had about us a way of gathering green energy and focusing it on a wound, speeding healing greatly. I had never seen this done with someone as badly off as Deyahm, but I had to try.

I gathered up the parts of him. It took time, for they were spread far and wide. Some still smoldered, and others were almost liquid, but I continued until I considered I had the most of him. Then I arranged the parts on a large flat rock with the glass-encased head at one end, and a mangled lower pod—I could only find one—at the other. Betwixt the two, I laid out the other parts in roughly the correct configuration, although poor Deyahm was as full of question marks as flesh.

Then I sat down and laid my limb terminals on him and began to thrum. I say "thrum" because that is the closest human word. The sound was both lower and higher than a human humming, and it could penetrate bone. The thrumming mustered the green energy around me, concentrated it, and transferred it through the conduit of my sensitive pods to Deyahm. It should have mended bone and made the flesh grow over it. It should have filled in the blank spots. It should have made his humors to flow and knitted up torn muscle. I thrummed through the heat of the local star and the chill of the night. For a long time, I wouldn't open my eyes. I felt no change through my limb terminals, but as long as my eyes were closed, I could imagine my friend returning to life.

But he was, as the humans say, "too far gone." When I finally opened my eyes, it was to a sight every bit as atrocious as before. My thrumming had healed the wounds in my flesh but done nothing for Deyahm.

I felt bitterly sad for myself, but not for my friend. Death he had preferred.

I said goodbye and raised my eyes to the emptiness of the desert. As I've mentioned, Utorb is much smaller and more crowded than earth. Our seething green sky is low overhead, and the thick air does not allow for long vistas. Here, the great stretch of barren land and the hollow, glaring arc of the sky all but sucked me dry. I cursed the overweening overseers who had adapted my body to earth conditions well enough that I did not die immediately, but not so well that I thrived. I was sure would die eventually, and attaining that eventually promised to be miserable.

I wandered over rocks and through brush. I wandered under the blazing local star and the lonely local moon. I wandered until my flesh desiccated, my stomach shrank, and my body grew weak with hunger. I could find no *yot* nozzles anywhere among the rocks and malicious plants. *Yot* was the only thing we ate on Utorb. It had been generations since fresh plants and animals thrived, so our scientist-chefs had devised this crunchy edible, which was offal mixed with spicy chemicals and infused with air. Every hexicle featured a *yot* nozzle. One had only to press a button, and foam collected at the end of the nozzle. It dried in seconds, and could be broken off and eaten. Everyday *yot* was the color of human flesh of the Caucasian variety.

On holidays, it was dyed in festive hues. Our Utorbian hot silver tonic served as the perfect accompaniment to *yot*.

Earthly deserts did not feature anything resembling *yot* or silver tonic. Utorbis don't need much nutrition to live, but they do need some. I began to starve. I tried consuming random things, on the chance they might be edible. I found that Earth rocks are neither chewable nor digestible. Deyahm had said that Utorbis once ate plants and animals.

All of my experiments with this ended regrettably. Tumbleweed was not palatable and scratched on the way down. I broke off a bit of cactus and forced myself to consume some of the green goo on the inside, but it disagreed with me. My belly vociferated until I regurgitated the green goo and found that it was now many times more disgusting than it had been before I ate it. Earth plants were too rich.

I thought Deyahm must have been mistaken about eating animals because I couldn't imagine how it might be done. The animals scampered or slithered away from me, but sometimes they paused to look at me before they ran. They had eyes, which made me feel less lonesome. I couldn't imagine how one would get past the eyes.

So I starved until I was no longer able to drag my stubby carcass from place to place. I curled up under a shrub and thought about Deyahm and how I, also, would prefer death. I waited for it to come.

7

THE INOPERATIVE OPERATIVE

Lloyd peered at the long line of people waiting to board the bus in Memphis. More eyes, ears, and voices to crowd the narrow space and unsettle his fragile equilibrium. He took a breath and released it slowly. He moved his briefcase off the seat and put it between his feet. He had clothes at the ranch, so he carried nothing else except for the stuffed bear intended for Trudie's soon-to-arrive baby. The bear's legs stuck out from the overhead rack. He hoped everything was okay with her pregnancy. Trudie hadn't answered his letters for months and hung up on him when he called.

Lloyd considered whether or not to get something to read from his briefcase. It held the latest issue of *Foreign Affairs* with George Kennan's article on the Soviet threat. He had already read it at work in telegraph form and thought it underplayed the threat. It was too full of academic circumlocution to sound a proper alarm. Few people knew the nature of the threat better than Lloyd.

He turned back to the window. Young men with cardboard suitcases shuffled in line. Probably veterans, still drifting two years after the war. He knew the feeling. Too many of them had been demobilized, way too many, way too quickly. How naive of the country to think that an end to the war meant peace. Lloyd should be back at work, but that wasn't an option.

This trip was no vacation. They'd given him three weeks of administrative leave and told him to get himself together. The army doctor who examined him said, "Rest, Lloyd, that's an order. We don't want to see you back here before mid-August. Make an appointment for the day you get back. We'll reevaluate then."

Lloyd's face, already florid with heat, turned a deeper shade as he remembered his recent erratic behavior. Erratic—the last word anyone would use to describe the old Lloyd Pilcrow. Steady, dependable, dedicated. Perhaps a little boring. Those were his words, and he was content with them. They were perfect for an operative. He hadn't been the sort of person anyone would notice or remember. But now he had become erratic. People did notice and remember. He could feel their unbearable attention tickling at the nape of his neck. The well-dressed man on the opposite side of the aisle had been eyeing Lloyd since he boarded in DC. What did he see? Lloyd slowed his breathing and shut his eyes.

His eyes popped open at the sound of a young female voice rising above the din of boarding. "Don't fuss. I'm right as rain. This is the commonest condition in the world." The driver rose to help her up the step. She was well into her third trimester. Her round baby face was slick with sweat, but she was calm and self-possessed. A young man walked behind her, gripping a tied-shut suitcase in his right hand, while the left hovered solicitously near her shoulder, ready to steady her if necessary. The man wore his wedding band on his index finger, the only digit remaining on that hand. Scars ran up his arm. Another veteran. The couple scanned the bus in vain for a seat together.

"Here," Lloyd said. He waved them to his seat, grabbed his case, and moved next to the elderly man in the seat behind.

"Thank you, kindly," the woman said and gave Lloyd a smile so full of gratitude, it made him weak-kneed. As he settled himself into the new seat, he felt he ought to turn his eyes away from her for the sake of decency, but he couldn't. This is what he wanted: a wife with a baby on the way. Was that so much to ask? He was thirty. In the imaginary life he had mapped out for himself, he became a father at the age of thirty. In real life, his wife was barren, and his marriage was rotting, thanks to his erratic behavior.

Erratic men couldn't be operatives and perhaps they couldn't be husbands either.

When the bus got underway, the young veteran looped his injured arm around his wife's neck. "You sure you feel okay, Lucy? The bus fumes ain't making you sick, are they? We shoulda made this trip sooner."

"We couldn't afford to have you away from the shop that long. Everything will be fine. I'm healthy as a horse," Lucy answered.

Everything will be fine for them. Lloyd fought back a wave of jealousy. *I can't think this way. It will drive me crazy.* He mustn't get upset because that might cause the demons to come out.

Demons. Lloyd would have been the last man on earth to believe in demons, but he had seen them. The first time was in a jail cell on Andrassy Street in Budapest. He thought they were the result of the hellish noises he heard in the night: screaming, moaning, the thud of rubber truncheons striking naked flesh. He'd heard one phrase shouted over and over, but couldn't make out the words. He had nightmares about it, but still couldn't make out the words. As an American, he got special treatment. They did nothing to him that would leave marks, physical marks at least. The torture was the noise. They had rolled up his whole network of assets—spies—the same night he was arrested. In jail, he listened for their voices in the cacophony. He saw one hung by the neck in the courtyard.

By the time the US military mission secured his release, the demons had taken up permanent residence in his brain. They would be quiet for days or even weeks, but then they would crawl from the walls and scream obscenities. Lloyd pushed them out of his mind. Thinking about them sometimes attracted them. He turned his attention back to the couple.

The young husband's anxiety wouldn't let him be still. He spoke gently. "Lucy, honey, your face is red as a beet. You sure you're feeling okay? I don't know why we couldn't take this trip after the baby was born."

"Carl, this is my first baby, and I want to be with my mama." Lucy's voice was firm and serious. "Hush, you're making me nervous. Look around, every single face on this bus is flushed. It's ninety degrees. And your arm is making me hotter."

Carl moved his arm reluctantly.

Lloyd wanted to be that young man taking care of his pregnant wife. He wanted to have visible, comprehensible scars from the past and a visible future in the curve of a woman's belly. Lloyd pushed those thoughts aside. If he indulged them, they would make him crazy. Crazier.

If he couldn't be a father, then at least he could be the world's most attentive uncle. Lloyd was on his way to visit his elder sister, Trudie, whether she wanted to see him or not. She would be in her eighth month of pregnancy by now. Maybe his administrative leave was a good thing. He might even be around for the birth.

The baby ought to have someone happy to welcome him. Trudie had cried bitterly when she found out she was pregnant. She and Lloyd had argued over that. Even though they'd been close growing up, they did nothing now but argue. That last blowup was the worst, but he'd never known her to hold a grudge. He was worried and he needed to talk to her. Besides, if anyone could help scare his demons off, it was Trudie.

But first he had to make it home without incident. If the demons came out while he was on this bus what would happen? Would he be arrested? Since Budapest, he had an inordinate fear of incarceration. Would they lock him away in an asylum? Lloyd remembered he had purged his wallet of everything but his fake identification papers before he had left for Hungary. Did he ever put his real identification back? He didn't remember. Lloyd pulled out his wallet and opened it to find a driver's license with the name James Wellborn. The photo showed Lloyd with a dark brown beard and a prosthetic nose. In the past, he would never have forgotten a critical detail like this. Merely having these items in his possession in this country was a security violation. He felt something give way in his mind as he realized he wouldn't be ready to go back to work in mid-August. He might never be ready.

The elderly man next to him had fallen asleep. Moving slowly so as not to awaken him, Lloyd pulled his briefcase onto his lap. He used it as a desk to write:

> Lloyd Pilcrow
> 62 Wilson Circle, Alexandria, Virginia.
> Emergency contact: Colonel Brian Turner

Lloyd was relieved to find Turner's number in his memory. He took it as a sign of sanity. He jotted it down and folded the note in half with the print side out and stuck it in his wallet. He took out the fake driver's license. Glancing around to make sure no one was looking, Lloyd tore the license into tiny pieces. What to do with them? He didn't want them on his person. He popped a stick of gum. He rested his chin on his hand and slowly fed the pieces of the license into his mouth, chewing until he was sure that gum and paper had melded into an inseparable mass. He took it out and leaned across his sleeping seatmate to toss it out the window.

Lloyd picked up a sharp movement in the corner of his vision. The man across the aisle had turned his head to look, and then quickly turned it away. The man was watching him and didn't want him to know it.

I'm getting paranoid, Lloyd thought. *Spy games are in limbo for now*. He was between intelligence agencies. The end of the war spelled doom for the Office of Strategic Services. The new president distrusted Edward "Tiger Ted" Sullivan, the head of the OSS, so he had disbanded the organization, farming out its functions. Analysis went to Department of State while clandestine operations went to the Army. That was how Lloyd came to work for Turner, but the situation was temporary.

Rumor had it that things would change within days with the creation of a new civilian intelligence agency. Whether there would be a place in that agency for an erratic operative was another question.

Lloyd couldn't think about that now. Too upsetting. He had thought it would help to put miles between himself and Washington, but it didn't. He felt like he was about to suffocate and he couldn't blame the heat.

As if she shared his thoughts, Lucy took a couple of deep breaths. Lloyd watched alarm ripple through Carl's body.

"Are you okay?" He put his arm around her again.

"I'm fine. I told you, your arm makes me too hot."

Carl withdrew his arm. She leaned her head out the window and closed her eyes. The rushing air pulled strands of dark hair loose from the pins crisscrossed at the back of her head. Lloyd focused on her profile with its freckled, upturned nose and prominent brow.

Carl leaned closer. "Honey, are you—"

"That's enough," Lucy snapped. "Leave me be."

Lloyd sat up straighter. Something in Lucy's voice worried him. Carl stared at his wife with pure panic.

"Don't look at me like that, I'm fine. Take a nap," Lucy said. Her voice sounded better now, strong and reassuring.

As if the order were directed at him, Lloyd closed his eyes and let his head fall forward. He hadn't slept well for a long time. Now, he slept in that uncomfortable manner one sleeps in moving vehicles, with frequent interruptions to adjust body position and shallow half-waking dreams that had the bus rolling now through Eastern Europe and now through Hell.

In reality, the bus was rolling through Arkansas. It was climbing a hill when a cry woke Lloyd.

"Carl, my water broke."

The old man next to Lloyd picked up his feet, and Lloyd looked down to see a rivulet coming under the bus seat.

Carl screamed, "My wife's having a baby, you got to stop this bus."

The driver yelled back over the din of alarmed passengers. "I can't pull off the road here. There's nothing but a ditch. Can she hold on twenty minutes? There's a hospital in the next town. Any doctors on board?" Lloyd felt the bus accelerate.

The passengers looked around. Finally, a man near the front of the bus stood. "I'm a veterinarian."

"Close enough," said the driver. "Get on back there and help the lady."

The veterinarian pulled his bag from the overhead rack. "Hell, what's one more species? At least I reckon I won't get kicked." He hurried down the aisle, lurching with the movement of the bus. Arriving at Lucy's seat, he cocked an eyebrow at Carl and gestured with his thumb. "You, go sit in my seat. I don't need no hysterical husband hanging over my shoulder."

A woman across the aisle took Carl by the arm and dragged him away. "There, there," she said. "She don't need you for this part."

The veterinarian took off his straw boater and handed it to Lloyd. "Hold this, will you?" Lloyd took the hat, and the man held out his hand to Lucy, "I'm Dr. Bill Jenkins."

"Lucille Hartley," she said in a quaking voice. "Pleased to meet you."

Dr. Jenkins' handshake seemed to calm Lucy. He sat down and in a low voice asked a series of questions, nodding with each answer as if it was exactly what he'd expected. Then he got up and had her lie down on the seat, legs sticking into the aisle. "I need one calm, strong lady who's been through this a few times," he announced.

"That would be me." A woman in her mid-forties stood up. She had sunburned arms and a worn, flowered dress straining at the bosom.

"Good. Your job is to hold her hand and make sure she don't roll off the seat." Dr. Jenkins had her squeeze into the tight space between Lucy and the seat in front of her.

"All the rest of you folks," the doctor said loudly, "look out the window."

Lloyd stared at the doctor's hat. His cheeks were aflame, and he felt a silly urge to put the boater over his face. Trudie once called him a world champion blusher. It was true. All it took was a mild double entendre to turn him vermillion. Now a man was cutting a woman's underwear off in the seat right in front of him. Through sweat and cigarette smoke, he could smell something more intimate. He heard her groan. Lloyd clutched his chest and for a moment thought he was going to have a heart attack. He shut his eyes tight.

"Hang on," Dr. Jenkins said. Lloyd thought the man was talking to him. He almost answered, but Jenkins spoke again. "Don't push yet. It's not time. With luck, we'll make it to the hospital. If you want to scream, go on. If you want to cuss your husband, that's fine too. My wife did, and I don't hold it against her."

At the next contraction, Lucy screamed. Lloyd opened his eyes to reassure himself that he was on a bus in the United States and not in a prison in Hungary. He counted slowly to ten, to twenty, to a hundred.

Lucy's next scream shattered the small pocket of calm the counting had created. Lloyd began to tremble and sweat dripped off his nose onto the veterinarian's boater. He'd rather endure torture than listen to screaming. He began to count again.

"I don't need a timekeeper," the doctor said.

Lloyd hadn't realized he'd been counting out loud. He bit his lip until he tasted blood. Lucy screamed and swore.

On Andrassy Street, Lloyd was sometimes taken into rooms that smelled of blood, urine, excrement. It gave him an uncomfortable intimacy with the prior occupants. The odors broke him down more effectively than all the blows from the guards.

Lloyd felt the gates to Hell crumbling now. It started with afterimages. Dr. Jenkins moved his arm, and it trailed a yellow light. Lloyd gripped the edge of his seat. They were coming, bubbling up out of his blood. Lloyd bit his tongue. He opened his eyes and saw the clothing of his fellow passengers dissolve to reveal mottled green flesh, the color of oxidized bronze. After a few seconds, he could no longer pick out individuals. He saw rib ladders stretching to the sky, twisted torsos, arms folded over heads. Facial features melted. The mass of flesh flailed, curled in on itself, fought, and copulated.

And screamed.

Lloyd had no idea he was screaming himself. The writhing green flesh covered him and pressed him into the small space between the seat and the floor. Someone clamped a cloth over his mouth and nose.

Lloyd awoke in bed. Heavy straps crisscrossed his body. He laughed out loud and then stifled the sound because it wasn't a normal laugh. Even before he could put together a reasonably clear memory of what had happened on the bus, he understood that the appearance of sanity was the most important thing now. More important than sanity itself. He could worry about that later. The priority was escaping these straps.

They smelled musty. They must not get many crazy people here in … wherever the Hell he was. Somewhere in Arkansas. He felt sluggish and nauseated. He had no idea how much time had passed since they'd taken him off the bus. It was still daytime. He looked around and saw glossy green paint on the walls, a spatter stain on the ceiling, and scarred furniture. On the table next to his bed was a hand-lettered sign on paper folded into a tent. It read, "The call button is broke. Holler if you need help." The paper had yellowed. Lloyd guessed he was in an underfunded county hospital. He felt strangely calm. The demons had receded.

He didn't hear the nurse until she was in the room. She moved as silently as an operative. "Hello, Mr. Pilcrow," she said as she reached for his chart. "How are you feeling?"

"Constricted," Lloyd said.

She nodded. "Straps will do that. We didn't want you to hurt yourself. I feel terrible we had to do that to you, considering you're a hero. Oh my Lord, the things you did. I can only say thank you."

"What?" Lloyd asked.

"We called the number in your wallet, and your boss told us everything. He said he sent you out of town because you were suffering from exhaustion from serving your country. Then he told us about how you took that machine gun nest single-handed."

"Never mind that." Lloyd didn't want to hear what lies Turner had told. "Could you thank me by undoing these straps? I need to get back on the road. I'm on my way to visit my sister who's expecting a baby …" A look of annoyance passed over Lloyd's face.

"What's wrong?" the nurse asked.

"Nothing. I just remembered I had a stuffed bear for the baby and I left it on the bus. It doesn't matter." Lloyd remembered Lucy. "There was a woman in labor on the bus, Lucille Hartley. Do you know how she is?"

"She and her baby are fine," the nurse said. "The little girl was born fifteen minutes after the bus got here. The whole hospital is talking about nothing but that bus and how it come tearing up to Emergency with a pregnant lady and a man out cold. My friend Shelley saw it. Said the man was driving that thing like it was a sports car."

Lloyd interrupted her. "I'm sorry, but could you please undo these straps?"

She clutched her chest and looked genuinely distressed. "Oh sir, I'd like to help, but the doctor has to give the word. We're going to have to keep you overnight, just to make sure you're back to normal. Won't be another bus until tomorrow, anyhow. Is there anything I can get you? Coffee or tea or juice?"

Lloyd's face flushed. At least the nurse wasn't a young one, but still it was hard to ask. He sputtered, trying to get the words out. "I have to …"

"Make water? Sure I can help you with that. Don't be embarrassed. I'm honored to do anything for a brave boy like you."

8

CREOSOTE HILL

Lloyd didn't know what Turner had said, but the hospital staff treated him like he was Audie Murphy. The doctor released him from the restraints, apologizing profusely. He told Lloyd he would drive him back to the bus station personally. The next day, the staff assembled to see Lloyd off. They had pooled their money and bought him a stuffed bear to replace the one left on the bus. It was huge, with mustard yellow fur and crazy eyes. Carrying it made him Lloyd feel painfully conspicuous.

The doctor got out of the car with him at the bus station and whispered to the driver as Lloyd struggled to jam the bear into the crowded overhead rack. One other passenger boarded the bus. He had a beard that seemed wrong with his complexion and wore clothing that was cheap, but brand new. He sat down a few rows behind Lloyd.

The rest of the trip was uneventful. Lloyd sweated. Periodically his face flushed red as memories of his send-off floated to the surface. He supposed he should thank Turner for saving his ass, but the unearned adulation had been excruciating.

Lloyd's neck itched. Surveillance always made his neck itch. He was sure the man with the beard was the same as the well-dressed stranger he had noticed yesterday. Why would anyone follow him here? But then why wouldn't they? If the Soviets had targeted him for recruitment, they would follow him on a trip like this, just like a coyote would target a calf separated from the herd. Out here in the middle of nowhere, it would be safe for them to pitch him.

Lloyd's memories of the demon incidents were usually sketchy, but now he remembered the cloth that had been pressed over his nose and mouth. Chloroform. He sat up straight in his chair. It wasn't the doctors who had put him out. The nurse said he was out cold when the bus arrived. Could Dr. Jenkins have chloroformed him? Would a veterinarian carry chloroform? Lloyd wanted to turn his head to look at the man with the beard but he couldn't. It was best not to reveal his suspicions.

The town of El Claustro, New Mexico boasted one of everything a body could desire: one school, one bank, one grocery, one general store, one movie theatre, one gas station, one motel, one doctor, one diner, one laundromat, and one bus terminal. Why would anyone need more than that? If a young person left looking for more, in the town's opinion he was up to no good. So when Lloyd got off the bus in El Claustro, the first person he saw, Ed Vacaro, gave him a look of disapproval.

"Well, if it ain't Lloyd Pilcrow." Vacaro nodded at the gaudy stuffed bear under Lloyd's arm. "That the kinda game you hunt back East?"

"Don't make fun, Ed, he put up a hell of a fight."

Vacaro snorted and continued on his way. Lloyd watched him, but out of the corner of his eye, he kept track of the man with the beard who had gotten off the bus right behind him. The man must know Lloyd would be on to him by now. What was he after? Lloyd jangled the change in his pocket. He took out a handkerchief and wiped the sweat off his face and neck. The man with the beard crossed the street to the diner and went in.

Lloyd propped the stuffed bear against the outside of a sun-bleached wood phone booth. He entered and slipped his coin in the slot. The sound of it falling made his stomach turn over. He spoke to the operator calmly. While she put through his call, Lloyd's eyes wandered over the numbers, initials, and crude drawings on the wall of the booth. He took out his penknife to scratch through some of the worst.

Earl picked up. "Hello?"

"It's Lloyd. Is Trudie handy?"

"She don't want to talk to you."

Lloyd was expecting this. "I'm in town. I came out to see her, so could you come get me? I have a right to visit." Lloyd sank onto the butt-polished seat and listened to the buzz on the line.

"One of us will be there to pick you up directly." Earl hung up without saying goodbye.

Lloyd resumed pacing and jangling his change. The wind picked up. He stopped, closed his eyes, and imagined the desert heat sucking the moisture out of him: the damp of the Hungarian winter, the summer humidity of DC, his wife's tears. It wouldn't be a loss to anyone if the heat reduced him to a carapace, and the wind blew him away. As soon as this thought crossed his mind, he remembered twelve-year-old Trudie standing over him, shaking her finger at her crying little brother. "You're being *lugubrious*, Lloyd. Stop it."

Trudie and Lloyd had been close until Trudie's marriage to Earl Bucknam. Lloyd couldn't think about it without mouthing the words "tragic mistake." He was sure Trudie felt the same, but she refused to talk about it. It created a barrier between them that grew with each passing year.

The marriage had happened quickly. Lloyd suspected his father had gone out and hunted down the best-looking man in the county to hire on as a ranch hand. Lloyd was with the OSS in Europe at the time. He wished he had flown home to prevent his sister from marrying.

Lloyd felt a measure of guilt for the way things had turned out. If he had stayed home to run the ranch, it never would have happened.

When the family truck pulled into the terminal, Lloyd was shocked to see Trudie in the driver's seat. He cursed Earl for making her undertake the long drive in her condition.

"Get in," Trudie yelled out the window. She didn't cut the motor.

Lloyd picked up his briefcase and covered the distance to the truck in a few long strides. Whatever the circumstances, Trudie's face was a sight for sore eyes. Lloyd pulled open the door, stepped onto the running board, and dropped his briefcase. It sprang open as it landed on the pavement.

"Pick up your stuff, Lloyd," Trudie said.

Lloyd stepped down and bent to retrieve the case. A few sheets of paper fluttered away, but he didn't go after them. He snapped the case closed.

"Get in," Trudie said. "I can't park here."

Lloyd climbed into the truck and shut the door. It didn't latch on the first try.

"You have to slam it," Trudie said.

Lloyd opened the door and yanked it shut so viciously, a chunk of the cracked window broke off entirely.

"Now look what you've done."

Lloyd settled himself in his seat and stared straight ahead. "You're not pregnant."

"No, I am not." Trudie put the truck into gear and pulled out onto the road.

Lloyd put a hand on the dashboard to steady himself. He glanced back toward the terminal and saw the crazy-eyed yellow bear leaning against the phone booth. Lloyd tried to run the math in his head, but his brain was spinning. "Did the baby come early?"

"I lost the baby months ago." Trudie's voice was flat.

"How?" The word came out like an accusation.

Trudie kept her eyes on the road. "I miscarried."

Lloyd said nothing more until they left the paved roads. The rattling of the old truck sounded in his bones. He felt like he was coming apart. Twenty miles out of town, he said, "You didn't do anything to lose that baby, did you?"

Trudie stomped down on the brake, throwing Lloyd forward as the truck skidded to a halt. She cut off the engine and stared at her brother, blue eyes burning through her bifocals. Lloyd stared back, determined not to break the gaze first. Their dust settled on the road.

"No," Trudie said.

"I'm sorry." Lloyd looked away, and Trudie started the engine and drove another five miles before she stopped the truck again, gently this time. But the eyes she turned on Lloyd were harder than ever. She leaned over and grabbed his tie, crumpling it in her hand and holding it in front of his face.

"Look at you, wearing this uncomfortable thing on a bus cross country in the high heat of the summer. You were always such a damned goody two-shoes." Trudie let go of his tie and slammed the heel of her hand down on the truck horn. She let the sound die out. "I'm sorry. I'm angry all the time now, but I shouldn't be angry with you. You're the only family I have left."

Lloyd lay awake long after midnight, trying to think how he could make his sister's life better. If he sent her money, Earl would confiscate it. If he sent her gifts, Earl would find a way to ruin them. He had to talk to Earl.

Lloyd didn't relish the thought. He didn't get on with his brother-in-law. Earl was arrogant, thick-headed, and filled with contempt for his fellows. What could Lloyd say to make Earl appreciate his sister? The man resented her intelligence and wit. The only thing Lloyd and Earl had in common was a love of horses. The thing to do was go on a long ride with the man and have a heart to heart. Yes, that was the only thing to do. Then maybe he could have his heart to heart with Trudie. He needed her help as much as she needed his.

9

SOUNDS LIKE A DUCK

Lloyd couldn't get the conversation started. Every time he brought up Trudie, Earl would ride off to investigate a gully, rock, or clump of brush. It didn't help that Earl had saddled the ranch's most unreliable horse for Lloyd. Lizard was a high-strung, hard-mouth, barn-sour filly who danced sideways, shivered, and tossed her head, distracting Lloyd from what he needed to say. *Damned erratic beast,* he thought.

"Earl," Lloyd finally said, "I need to talk to you."

"Well, I don't need to talk to you," his brother-in-law said.

Lloyd was about to push it when they heard a singular sound—not an especially loud or alarming sound, but one that was out of place. A quack. Lizard reared. Earl grabbed for his gun and said, "What in Sam Hill is a duck doing out here?"

"Can't be a duck," Lloyd said as he got Lizard back under control.

"There," Earl pointed. "Something moved under that creosote bush. I'm going to shoot it."

Lloyd held up his hand. "Wait, Earl, that's not a duck."

They heard the sound again.

"Hear that? If it sounds like a duck, it's a duck." Earl aimed and fired. Lloyd saw something larger than a duck jump and then fall back into the bush. The strange, oily smell of broken creosote branches filled the air. The creature tried to run but foundered.

"You're right, that ain't no duck," Earl said.

"You wounded it."

"I didn't hit nothing but brush." Earl aimed the gun again.

"Wait, I want to see what it is." Lloyd urged Lizard into Earl's line of sight. He didn't like the idea of shooting something before he knew what it was. He wiped his glasses on the tail of his shirt and put them back on. The creature rose as if to run, and then tripped over its own feet. Splayed on the ground, it stared at them with eyes unlike any Lloyd had ever seen. *It's a demon out of my mind*, he thought. His body stiffened. Sensing the change in her rider, Lizard bucked, but Lloyd kept his seat.

"What the hell is that?" Earl said. "Looks like a coyote got hold of a sheep. A sheep with lizard eyes and a dick for a nose."

Lloyd exhaled. Earl saw the same thing he did; it must be real.

"Jesus H. Christ," Earl continued. "If that ain't an abomination. I'm going to shoot it." He raised his gun.

"Stand down," Lloyd said. "It's some rare animal. I need to get a better look." He dismounted and handed the reins to Earl. He slung a coil of rope over his shoulder and grabbed the bag that Trudie had packed him for lunch.

"Take your gun," Earl said.

"No."

A sour look of contempt uglified Earl's handsome features. "Now that's the difference between you and me. Foolish optimism. I say shoot it, and then look at it."

"Some zoo might want to study this."

Earl snorted. "What is a zoo going to do with it? You couldn't show that thing in public. It's obscene."

"It's nature."

"Most unnatural-looking piece of nature I ever saw."

Lloyd approached the creature and stopped. It was pitiful, nothing but scaly skin and bones with patches of wool. It trembled, and its huge eyes darkened. *Australia*, Lloyd thought. *They have some strange, big-eyed animals there, but how did it get here?* "Looks like it's got a harness," he called back to Earl. "Maybe it's somebody's pet. It hasn't run away."

"Maybe a Coyote got it," Earl said. "Half the wool is tore off and something's wrong with the feet."

"I'm going to see if I can get closer." Lloyd started walking again.

"Suppose it's poisonous or rabid?" Earl said.

"I'll risk it."

"You may be educated, but you got no sense." Earl spat, and Lloyd saw the creature turn its eyes away as if disgusted. This was exactly what Trudie did when Earl spat. Then he thought, *no I'm anthropomorphizing it.* He was now quite close. He stopped and held out his hand with the palm down. A strange look came into the creature's eyes. *If that thing were human,* Lloyd thought, *I'd say he was offended.* He moved his hand closer and spoke softly. "Go ahead, boy, sniff. I'm not going to hurt you."

The creature stood up on two legs. It was maybe three feet tall. It folded its bony arms across its chest. Something in its stance reminded Lloyd of a kangaroo. It wrinkled its trunk-like nose as if it smelled something bad. Again, Lloyd had the impression that it was offended.

"Come on, boy," Lloyd said. "I'm not going to hurt you. Come and sniff my hand."

The creature looked down at Lloyd's hand, and then he reached out and shook it as if he were a Wall Street banker and not some stray, exotic pet.

"Will you look at that?" Lloyd called to Earl. "Somebody taught him to shake. Good boy."

"Watch or that thing will bite your hand off."

"It's tame, I tell you, and it's starving. I wonder what it eats?"

Earl frowned. "Jesus, you're not going to feed it? We'll never get rid of it."

Lloyd slowly withdrew his hand and reached into the lunch bag. "Steady, boy. Sit. I'm going to see what Trudie packed. Here's an apple. Let's try that." Lloyd cut off a piece of it with his pocketknife. "Look at this." He placed the fruit on his palm and stretched it slowly toward the creature. It showed no interest. Lloyd ate the slice himself. "Um, um good. Here, you try some." He sliced another piece and offered it on his palm.

The creature took it in its bizarre paw and sniffed delicately.

"Don't it just give you the willies the way he moves that nose," Earl said.

"I think he's going to eat it," Lloyd said.

But the creature handed it back to Lloyd.

Earl laughed. "Maybe it would rather eat your hand."

"Let me try the some chips." Lloyd opened the bag with his teeth and took out a single chip. The creature took it, sniffed, and tasted it. It seemed to agree with him, for he chewed it thoughtfully and swallowed.

"You like that, don't you, boy? Have some more." Lloyd poured several chips into his palm. The creature accepted them and began to eat greedily. Lloyd took advantage of his preoccupation with the food to grab him and hog-tie him. "Sorry, boy," he said as he pulled the knot tight, "but this is for your own good. I'm sure whatever coyote tore half the wool off you is still out there."

The creature began to make its odd noise.

"Don't that thing sound just like a duck?" Earl said. He dismounted and approached cautiously.

"It sounds like a duck cursing," Lloyd said, and they both laughed.

Earl didn't like the idea of taking it back with them, but Lloyd insisted. "I have to find out what kind of animal this is. You take Lizard." He threw the creature over the saddle of Earl's horse and mounted behind it.

"What are we going to do with it now?" Earl said when they got back to the barn.

"You have an extra stall?" Lloyd asked.

"Yeah, but it ain't been mucked out in a month of Sundays."

"He doesn't look particular." Lloyd lifted the bundle off the horse.

"What sex is that thing, anyway?" Earl said.

Lloyd flipped it upside down and pulled aside the wool. "I can't find a gonad anywhere."

A nasal squeal issued from the creature's trunk.

Earl looked over Lloyd's shoulder. "I don't even see where it shits."

"Let's untie it, put it in the stall and let it calm down. We can get a closer look tomorrow. I'm starved."

10

MARTIA

When Lloyd said of me, "He doesn't look particular," he couldn't have been more mistaken. Utorbis are a clean race. Due to the extensive and thorough digestive system designed by our genetic engineers, we had no need to commit excrement. This upgrade was introduced before my birth. I'd never encountered any form of feces before I landed in that disgusting stall. I panicked when I sank into the noisome muck. My muscles clenched, and I sprang to the low rafters above the stall and clung there, gagging.

Sometime later, three voices approached. Two belonged to Lloyd and Earl. The third was light, lacking in bluster, guile, or other unpleasant additives. It belonged to Trudie, who would turn out to be my favorite being in all the universe.

"If I can get a good view of it," she said, "I can look it up."

Earl answered with sarcasm, which I recognized because it was a prominent feature of the Utorbian common tongue. "How are you gonna look it up if you don't know what the thing is called? What you gonna look under in the Encyclopedia: D for don't know what the hell it is?"

"I didn't mean an encyclopedia. I meant Linnaeus' guide, *Systema Naturae*. I'll look it up according to its characteristics."

"Oh," Earl said, "one of your Greek books."

"Latin, you—"

Lloyd interrupted. "Trudie, you may find the appearance of the creature offensive. I don't think it's dangerous, but stand back when I open the door. It can jump."

"I'm going to get my gun," Earl said.

I'd begun to comprehend the meaning of a few critical words, "gun" and "shoot" being first among them. I began to quake.

"Earl," Trudie said, "forget the gun. If I can handle stallions, I can certainly handle something that you tell me is less than three feet tall. I mean it, leave the gun be. Open the door, Lloyd."

"Don't give me orders." Earl's voice had a growl that made my hide crawl.

"Earl, stand down," Lloyd said. "We don't need the gun. Now, Trudie, I warned you, its appearance is indecent." Lloyd slid the door open, and a bright round light shone in and crawled over the stall.

"Did it get out?" Lloyd said.

"Shine the light up there on the ceiling," Trudie said. "I think I saw something move." The harsh beam found me. "My word." Trudie let her breath out in rapid, throaty gasps. As I had never heard human laughter, I thought she might be sick.

"Shut up, Trudie," Earl said.

Trudie spoke with difficulty through her laughter. "I know now why you don't like him, Earl. You're jealous.

His nose is bigger than your—"

"Trudie, shut up." Earl's voice was surly.

Trudie's laugh faded. A recklessness sneaked into her words. "How could anybody be afraid of such a pitiful creature? He's trembling. Why did you put him in this filthy stall? No wonder he's on the ceiling." She pushed past the men and stuck her head in the half door. Her words were gentle and sweet—precious after my long exile from kindness. "Don't be scared. Come down and I'll feed you." She motioned for me to come to her. I didn't want to touch the feces again, so I crept along the ceiling. I climbed down and perched on the bottom door. I quivered and tried to wipe my filthy pods off on the wood.

"He doesn't like being dirty," Trudie said.

"Keep your distance. I don't want to have to run you to the hospital and pay a fortune to get you patched up after that thing bites you," Earl said.

"If he doesn't like being dirty, if he wipes his feet, then he's more civilized than most men I know." Trudie held her hand out to me. "Here, let's go get you something to eat."

"Don't you bring that thing into the house." Earl's voice held a threat.

"Hush, you're scaring him." Trudie took me by the hand and helped me down. "Did you name him yet, Lloyd?"

"It's not a pet," Earl said.

"Well it might be," Lloyd said. "It's got a harness, and it knows how to shake hands."

Trudie settled on her haunches to examine me. Her face featured a yellow curtain, which humans call "bangs"—the same word they use to describe the sounds that come from a gun. Even after all the time I have spent on Earth, the idiosyncrasies of the language confound me.

Trudie took one of my restraints in her hands. She bent it this way and that, scrunched it, stretched it out, smelled it, and held it up to the light. Then she looked me up and down. "You're right about one thing, Earl. He isn't a pet. He's a space alien. Perhaps a Martian. He's probably smarter than all three of us put together. You would have to be to figure out how to travel so far."

Earl laughed, but it was an unpleasant sound. "Space alien. You've been listening to too many radio shows."

Trudie held out my restraint to Lloyd. "Look at the material. Feel the texture. See how it refracts light? It's not cotton or wool or silk or linen. It doesn't have the smell of a synthetic fiber. I've never seen a weave like that. It's not something you could buy at Woolworth's or McCrory's. Look at his face. Those eyes are intelligent. I think he understands a little of what we're saying. He understood when you said 'gun.' He nearly jumped out of his skin. Think back to your taxonomy, Lloyd. Where would you classify this creature? Linnaeus never came across anything like it."

Earl and Lloyd bent and examined my frayed restraint, then me. They tilted their heads this way and that. Weary of their lack of manners, I stared back at them. When they tilted their heads, I tilted mine. I copied every expression I noted on their physiognomies.

"Well, I do believe there's some intelligence there," Earl said, "but I don't think he's no alien."

"I don't know," Lloyd said. "Trudie may have a point. He doesn't resemble any animal I've ever seen, and I've been halfway around the world. And that harness is an odd piece of work."

"You know, I do believe it's a she, not a he," Trudie

said. "She's delicate in her mannerisms. I'm going to call her Martia."

"For Christ's sake, don't name it." Earl spat on the floor, and I turned my head away.

"I don't like it when he spits, either," Trudie said to me. "Come along, and let's get you fed and cleaned up."

"Trudie—" Earl reached for her arm.

"Earl," Trudie said, "Martia is a guest. I don't treat guests like farm animals. If you don't like it, you can sleep in the barn."

"I ought to shut you in that stall with the alien," Earl said.

"Enough," Lloyd said. "Suppose his planet is preparing to attack us? Suppose this is a scout for an army?"

"All the more reason to treat her as a guest. Maybe they'll decide we're decent beings and not attack us," Trudie said.

"This is an issue of national security," Lloyd said. "I'd better call it in."

"No, you're not going to call in the spies," Trudie said.

Lloyd glared at Trudie. "I'm a civilian employee of the Army."

Trudie rolled her blue eyes. "Right. And I'm a ballerina. It's getting chilly. I'm taking Martia to the house."

※

"Hold up a minute, Earl," Lloyd said. He put a hand out and laid it on his brother-in-law's brawny arm.

Earl turned halfway and looked down at the hand with undisguised hostility. "What do you want?" he said.

Lloyd had observed the interaction between Trudie and Earl with unease. "Are you treating my sister right?"

he asked. Lloyd felt a shudder of muscle under his hand, but he didn't break his gaze.

"I don't hit her if that's what you're talking about," Earl said. "Maybe you should talk to your sister about how she treats me." He broke away and headed toward the house.

11

RITA HAYWORTH

Trudie was the only human who never hesitated to touch me. She took my upper limb terminal in her hand and led me down a dark, dirt path. It had been a long time since I had felt so safe. Ahead a white erection caught the moonlight. Its windows glowed yellow. Before we went in, Trudie showed me how to wipe my pods on a mat, and then she opened a heavy wooden door.

The interior divisions of this erection were rectangles and not hexagons as on Utorb. I found ninety-degree angles cramped and confining in comparison to our expansive 120-degree angles. Despite this, my first impression was pleasant. The brightly patterned rugs were soft, a vast improvement over the grainy surface of the desert. Effort had been made to make things clean and pretty. Soon, however, I noticed a static that set my chewing ridges on edge. I saw wounded things: a scarred wall, a cracked glass, a chair with a broken limb. I saw strange and curious objects that I wanted to touch, but I did not wish to be construed as overly forward. I was anxious not to offend Trudie.

She examined me closely in the bright interior light. Her curiosity held so much good will that I didn't find it offensive. "First," she said, "You need a bath."

"You're not going to wash that thing in our bathroom." Earl had just come in the door, and his presence soured the atmosphere.

Trudie ignored him. "Come on, Martia." She led me into a small room with extraordinary shiny white furnishings, the function of which I could not fathom.

"Do you know what a commode is and what it's used for?" Trudie asked. She watched the blank moon of ignorance rise in my eyes. "I was afraid of that. This will be awkward for us both, but you can't stay inside unless you know how to use a commode. She pointed to a strange white vessel against the far wall. Trudie opened the lid, and I peered into it to see water, a rare and costly substance on our planet. I had never seen it in such a large amount. This must be a wealthy family. On Utorb, overseers built handsome fonts for water called *yudulyai*. They were considered sacred.

"You're not getting the idea, are you?" Trudie said. "You see on Earth, we don't pee or poop on the floor." I didn't understand her words back then, but if I had I would've been quite surprised and gratified after my experience in the noisome stall. "We don't pee or poop on the floor," she repeated, "We do it in one of these things."

I was flummoxed.

Trudie shook her head. "I hope you are a she." Then she did a disturbing and astonishing thing: she lifted the hem of her garment and then lowered another garment to reveal a column of *yot*-colored flesh. She sat atop the font. Presently I heard a stream of liquid fall into the precious water. Trudie wiped herself, stood, and rearranged her garments. She pointed to the font, and I looked in to see that the water had been fouled. I could detect an unpleasant odor. Trudie pushed a silver lever. The water circled and disappeared. Then more clean water appeared. "Now do you understand?" Trudie asked.

I nodded yes, even though I hadn't the smallest notion of what had occurred. Nothing in my life had prepared me for such a bizarre, sacrilegious demonstration.

"After we pee and *especially* after we poop, we wash our hands." She walked over to a square vessel, which protruded from the wall. "Here's a step stool. I'll push it over here, and it will help you reach the sink." She turned a silver knob, and more water came out. More water! Trudie picked up a rectangular pink object and rubbed it on her hands. They foamed up like *yot*. My stomach rumbled. Trudie held her hands under the water. She turned the knob again, and the water stopped flowing. "Now that I've washed my hands, I dry them on this white towel. Not the little towel with the lace. That's the guest towel. You're a guest, but I would thank you if you didn't use it. It's for pretties. Now, that wasn't so hard was it?"

I felt like I was back in my Utorbian physics class, which I'd failed three times. This must be the human version of physics.

"Do you need to go now?" she asked.

I didn't answer as I had no idea what was required.

"Fine," she said, "then we'll give you your bath." Trudie turned to an enormous, empty rectangular vessel. "This is the nicest bathroom in three counties. My father wouldn't waste money on frivolities like a female's education, but he did have a taste for premium plumbing. What a person spends their money on says a lot about them, doesn't it?" Trudie sucked her lips in, and then she said, "I'm not being fair. I can't say I don't like having this bathroom. And if it weren't for Daddy organizing the local electric cooperative, we might all be sitting in the dark right now."

Trudie turned first one, then another silver knob. A great, astonishing stream of water poured out. "A bath is a luxury here. I don't like to strain the well, but you need to soak. Our water is a bit alkaline, but I'll add bubble bath. It can make even the homeliest girl feel like Rita Hayworth." She took a pink bottle and poured some liquid into the stream of water. The most glorious scent wafted up, and I almost swooned from joy.

"You're the most interesting visitor we've ever had," Trudie said. "I saw you arrive a few weeks ago. You lit up the sky like the northern lights. Not that I've ever seen them, but I've read about them. Look at the two of us together in this bathroom. I've never been anywhere, and you've been farther than any being on Earth." Trudie squatted down and examined my restraints. "While the water's running, let me get that filthy harness off you." She extracted a double-bladed weapon from a drawer. I curled into a ball.

"You do that just like a pill bug. Don't be afraid. I won't hurt you." She spoke in her most mellifluous voice. I uncurled myself and allowed her to cut the restraints. When they fell away, they took some of the horror of the trip with them.

"Now, climb in." Trudie moved the little stool next to the tub and helped me crawl over the side. I sank into water for the first time in my life. On Utorb, we cleaned ourselves with chemicals—much like the earthly process of dry cleaning. The fragrance of the bubbles was delightful, but their taste was bitter.

"Oh, honey, don't eat the bubbles," Trudie said.

I dipped my proboscis under the water and blew bubbles into the air. Trudie laughed. She showed me how to soap up my flocculent butt and helped me pick out the burrs and sticks. I didn't want to leave the tub, even after the water had grown dirty and cold, and my hide had wrinkled. Trudie pulled out the small cylinder that held in the water. I bent over and watched as it disappeared down the drain. I had been briefly wealthy and was now miserably poor again.

"Don't look so sad." Trudie fit a rubber hose onto the end of the faucet and turned it on. Water sprayed out the other end. She rinsed away the bubbles. Then she wrapped me in a cloth, rubbing until my wool crackled with static. Finally, she brought out a small blue bottle with a pointed gold cap.

"You seem to like pretty smells, so I'm going to put some of this on you. It's called '*Soir de Paris*,' or 'Evening in Paris.' A friend sent it to me from France. Hold out your hand." She opened the bottle, put her finger over the opening, and turned it over and back swiftly. She took my limb terminal and dabbed her moist finger on my wrist. I jumped. My proboscis shivered with pleasure as I picked up the sublime fragrance. I held out my other limb terminal, and Trudie dabbed a little there, too.

"I would put some behind your ear if I could find it. I think that's enough." She set the bottle down. "I ought to put some clothes on you for decency's sake, but that wool tutu covers up the plumbing. What's on your face, though, might be misinterpreted." She disappeared and returned with a curious item called a "hat." It had a veil, which made my proboscis less noticeable.

Earl went out on the veranda to smoke, while Lloyd paced the front room, jangling his change and turning the idea of an alien over in his mind. It wasn't a hallucination. Earl and Trudie saw the same thing that he did unless he was imagining their reactions. Maybe he was imagining everything. Maybe he wasn't even in New Mexico.

Lloyd reached up and touched the rough wood of the lintel. His fingers found the familiar wormholes and gouges. No, this was his home. He didn't feel the way he usually felt when a hallucination was coming on. As bizarre as it was, the alien was real.

It galled him that Trudie—who had had no training in analytical thinking—had figured it out first. Now Lloyd's training kicked in, and his mind began to generate implications, most of them dire. The creature could be a source of incurable alien disease. The white man's diseases had nearly wiped out the Indians. Surely introducing diseases from another planet would dwarf the impact of introducing diseases from another continent. Mass death. The creature could be a scout for others to come. Spaceships could be circling the earth at this moment. Trudie was right, his race must be more advanced or they couldn't have sent him so far. What was their intent?

Lloyd couldn't handle this alone. The situation called for experts and secrecy. Public panic could be dangerous. He recalled the *War of the Worlds* broadcast. He must call in someone from the government. Colonel Turner would know what to do.

Lloyd took out his wallet and counted out enough money to cover a long distance call twice over. He fanned out the bills and tucked them under the doily on the phone table in the hall.

He repeated his story a half dozen times, and still Turner said, "Are you sure of this?" Lloyd had to explain again how this wasn't a hallucination. Finally, Turner seemed convinced. "It just so happens that an associate of mine is in your area. I'll give him a call. Meanwhile, don't tell anyone, and I mean *anyone*, about this. No local authorities. You got that?" Lloyd hung up and went to change clothes.

Trudie finished her efforts to adorn me and stood back to assess. "Much better. You look sophisticated. Now let's go get you some food."

I went out feeling quite joyful until I saw Earl.

"Good God," he said, "it looks like an ugly church lady and smells like a French whore."

"Her name is Martia, and I will thank you not to call her 'it' or use foul language. A guest is a guest," Trudie said.

"Not for long." Earl crossed his arms over his chest as he spoke. "I reported the alien to the Sheriff, and he called Alamogordo Airfield. The Army is sending some people over first thing tomorrow. In the meantime, we're to keep the alien under lock and key and not say a word to anybody."

"What the hell have you done?" Lloyd stood in the doorway. "I've already reported this to the government, the government in Washington."

"Shut up, both of you!" Trudie said. "Did anybody consider asking me what I thought? Why did you call the sheriff? Much less the federal government. What has

Martia done to you?"

Lloyd held up his hands, "Now Trudie, you need to be an adult about this. It's a serious situation. We should minimize contact with the alien immediately because it might pass on an incurable space disease."

"Space diseases!" Earl yelled as he backed away from me. "Trudie, I told you not to bring the goddamn thing into the house."

Lloyd reached for his wallet. He unfolded it and removed green papers. On Utorb, we didn't use physical objects as currency. Instead, we employed bursts of white energy, which is a difficult concept to explain to people so unevolved as to still be committing excrement.

Lloyd said, "I'm going to have to make another long distance call."

"Take back your thirty pieces of silver, Lloyd, I don't want any part of it."

"Now, Trudie, don't get upset," Lloyd said.

"Upset? I'm furious. You didn't ask me first. What is the government going do with Martia? Did they tell you that? No? I didn't think so. They probably won't ever tell us. They'll take Martia away and do God knows what to her, and we'll never find out what happened." Trudie was yelling. I balled my limb terminals into fists to cover my aural organs.

"Trudie, you need to calm down and think straight," Lloyd said. "This is a matter of national security. It must be handled by professionals. You act like I'm sending it to the slaughterhouse. I'm just sending it to the US Government."

"I don't trust the government."

Lloyd spoke in a soft voice. "I understand that, but this is a dangerous space alien. We have to let professionals handle it. It's too late to call them back. They would come even if I told them not to."

Trudie collapsed into a chair and covered her face with her hands. Her body shook. She keened.

"We have to get it out of the house right now before we all catch an alien disease," Earl said. "We'll lock it in the stall."

Trudie raised her head. "Martia will stay in the guest room."

Earl's voice filled up with gravel. "I've had enough lip from you. I won't have you put us all in danger."

"The alien should stay under lock and key tonight," Lloyd said. He tried to say more, but his voice sank under Earl and Trudie's. Their voices grew by tens of decibels. Lloyd tried to talk, but nobody listened, and he grew silent. I backed into a corner and curled up, covering my aural organs by drawing my limb terminals into fists.

12

A RESTLESS NIGHT IN NEW MEXICO

As they argued, I made mental notes on their behavior, as I had been trained to do. Arguing made humans stupider. The more hotly they argued, the further they drifted from a sensible solution. This was exactly how things worked on Utorb. I took a deep breath and allowed the air to escape slowly through my proboscis, producing a doleful soughing. Clearly Earth was also doomed, and I had crossed the Bitter Sharp for nothing. I could be comfortably awaiting annihilation in my hexicle, instead of cooling my pods in the middle of a vehicular horse park in the desert with these irrational humans with their tempting, *yot*-colored flesh.

I slept on the veranda. Trudie brought quilts and pillows. Her boots cruelly stomped the tiles, and she hurled the bedding to the floor as if to knock the last breath from it. Earl stayed in the house. Meanwhile, Lloyd tethered me to a column with the same rope he used on the vehicular horse.

"Shameful," Trudie said to him. "If flying saucers attack Earth, it's your fault."

She had brought bedding for two and was about to lie down next to me, but Lloyd grabbed her arm. "No. We should limit our exposure to avoid contagion."

Trudie tried to pull away. "Did it ever occur to you that fear is not the most intelligent reaction to every new phenomenon in the universe?"

Lloyd spoke softly. "There are plenty of instances when a little caution could have saved a lot of lives. Please, Trudie. You're my only family. We have our differences, but there's not another human being on Earth I value as much."

Trudie squinted at him. "What about your lovely wife?"

Lloyd lowered his eyes. "You were right about Faye. My marriage was a mistake. We Pilcrows are smart at everything but choosing partners, aren't we? I'm trying to make it work, but I'll never be able to talk to Faye the way I can talk to you. So please, humor me on this one. Martia will be fine out here."

Trudie relented. She left me with a large bag of potato chips. "Since this is the only thing you will eat," she said with a note of accusation.

They all went back into the house, and the yellow lights blinked out.

I sniffed at the delightful fragrance of *Soir de Paris* on my limbs as I consumed the crunchy edibles. Now and then I poked at my flocculent bloomers, which were clean and springy.

I thought the humans had settled for the night, but I heard a movement inside. A small light went on. Through the window, I saw Lloyd pick up the phone. My vehicular horse tether allowed me just enough play that I could creep over, reach my limb terminal up and touch the glass, pressing my webbing tight against its surface. Now I could hear Lloyd's voice, even though he spoke softly. I stored the words until I could divine their meaning.

"I have an update," Lloyd said. "This wasn't my doing. My idiot brother-in-law called the sheriff." I heard nothing for a while, then Lloyd said, "I know. I can't tell you how sorry I am." Another pause. "At least the sheriff called the Alamogordo Army Airfield ... But why don't you want? ... I'm sorry. Not telling him wasn't an option. He was there when I found it ... Of course. I'll do what I can. Goodnight." Lloyd placed the receiver back on its hook and made his way up the stairs in the darkness.

I sniffed my *Soir de Paris* and drifted toward sleep. Then I sensed a furtive movement nearby. I heard growling and saw a shadow to my left. A strange and complex ululation erupted near my head. It was answered from the other end of the veranda. Then a pair of glowing yellow eyes appeared. "An overseer. Do not make contact through the eye," I told myself, but I was powerless to lower my gaze.

The eyes blinked, and the creature crept closer. It had four legs and was not large, but when it opened its maw, I saw two rows of sharp, white points. I pulled against my rope, but Lloyd had tied it securely. I feared I would be torn apart and ingested. I turned over onto my belly and covered my head.

I peeped out, and one of the creatures, a black one, strode boldly across the veranda and sprang upon me. In my terror, I swooned.

To my surprise, when I came to, my flesh had not been ripped from my bones. A gentle thrumming soothed my aural organs. I felt a light, rhythmic massage in the area of my flocculent butt and a gentle, intermittent swishing against my limbs. I opened my eyes and looked into yellow eyes with vertical pupils, like those of the overseers on Utorb.

The creature peered back, turning its small head this way and that. It butted its head against mine and thrummed. Its fur was soft, and its intentions seemed not only benign but genial. I carefully twisted around and saw that my carcass was covered with these creatures. One had settled deep into the wool of my butt, pummeling it gently with furry phalanges, while others lounged along my limbs. The gentle swishing came from their twitching tails.

Now, I know these were cats. I didn't know what to call them at the time, but after my terror had subsided, they proved fine colleagues. We slept together contentedly.

※

I dreamed about a motor high above my head. I was back in that bright room on Utorb, and the digging machines were coming closer …

I awoke when my feline colleagues tensed up. As one, they stared at a spot high in the air. I followed their gaze into the rosy gold morning sky. I saw something floating. It was white and round on the top, with veins converging onto the smaller section at the bottom. Only when it had drifted further down, did I realize that the bottom part was human.

It landed not so far from the house, frightening some vehicular horses, who lounged nearby. The round white part flattened abruptly, and my feline colleagues dug their claws into me before quitting the veranda, leaving a few tufts of fur floating in the air. I wished I could disappear, too, but I was bound fast.

The human untangled itself, shed its outer skin, and began to walk toward the house.

13

THE PARACHUTIST

Lloyd didn't sleep, and that was worrisome. The demons were more likely to come out when he was tired. He finally got out of bed and paced, wearing only his boxers. He paused by the window. The sky above the mountains was growing lighter. He had almost convinced himself that he had imagined the events of the previous day when the sun broke the horizon, and he saw a fragile-looking plane approaching from the east. He watched it drop two parachutes near the house, one with a man and the other with some piece of equipment.

Now, what? Lloyd thought. He pulled on a shirt and trousers and crept out into the hall. He passed Trudie and Earl's bedroom and heard them snoring. He mouthed a silent thank you and tiptoed to the front door. Lloyd stepped out onto the veranda and looked to his left, not sure if he would see an alien or not. It was there in all its comical strangeness. Its odd nose waved slowly from side to side as it watched a man fifty feet away shed his parachute and walk toward the house.

Lloyd didn't want the man yelling and waking Trudie or Earl. He hurried down the veranda steps and broke into a jog. He bent and slipped through a barbed-wire fence with the ease of one who has done it a thousand times. He approached the visitor.

The man extended his hand and said, "Avery Stanton."

Lloyd was about to shake Stanton's hand when he drew back. He had seen this face before, in altered form. Mentally he drew a beard on it. "You're the man who was following me on the bus."

Stanton broke into a dimpled grin. "Very observant," he said. His hair was pale blond, with only a small purplish stain at the neck to indicate the recent dark rinse. He had fine, aristocratic features with an aquiline nose and high, arched brows.

Lloyd recovered himself enough to shake the proffered hand. "I expected you to have a Russian accent."

The visitor laughed. "Sorry to alarm you. I'm not from the USSR; I'm from Donovan and Cornwall."

"A lawyer?" Lloyd asked. "Why would a lawyer be following me across the country?"

"You have something against lawyers? Actually, I'm about to officially vacate my Wall Street office and return to the good fight. For now I'm just moonlighting."

The phrase "good fight" was a euphemism. "You were OSS?" Lloyd asked.

"I worked with Elliot Ludden."

"Of course," Lloyd said. Ludden had headed OSS operations out of Bern. He had come from Donovan and Cornwall, bringing along a few bored Wall Street wunderkinds. This must be one of them. The spy service had been full of these wealthy dilettantes. Lloyd had no use for them.

"Why have you been following me?" Lloyd asked.

"Why for god's sake did you arrive by parachute?"

Avery ignored the first question. "I had to beat the Army here—and I like to make an entrance. No more questions. Just listen."

Lloyd started to speak but bit back the words.

"Where is the purported alien?" Avery asked.

Lloyd pointed toward the house. "Please be quiet. My sister and brother-in-law are asleep, and it's better if they stay that way as long as possible."

"We're agreed on that." Avery followed Lloyd to the veranda. When he saw Martia, his blue eyes grew round. "My God, it is real," he whispered. "I had serious doubts." He approached the alien slowly. "You tied it to a pole? This is how you secure a potentially dangerous creature?"

"It's docile," Lloyd said.

Avery tilted his head as he looked the alien over. "Ugly, isn't it? If it's not a space alien, then I don't know what it is. Let me get some quick photographs." He took a camera from a bag on his back and began to click it in the alien's face. The creature blinked its large eyes and curled up like a pill bug, leaving them with a view of its woolly ass and little else. Stanton poked it with a toe in a vain effort to get it to uncurl. "Thanks to your brother-in-law's inability to keep a secret, a twelve-vehicle convoy is headed in our direction—nothing subtle about the Army. I saw it from the plane that dropped me."

This brought up a question that had troubled Lloyd since his phone conversation the night before. "Why all the concern about the Army taking possession of the alien? Turner was apoplectic when he heard the sheriff called Alamogordo. Turner and I work for the Army. I don't understand."

"Because the National Security Act is going through,

and Turner and you and I will all be working for a new intelligence agency by the end of the month. The new agency should have the alien, not the damn Army. But thanks to you, they'll be here in less than an hour. We'll have to let them take the alien for now while we secure the crash site. Here's the plan. You're going to go back to where you found the alien and track its steps until you find the crash site. Radio in your location. The field radio landed behind your barn.

"Meanwhile, I'll be Lloyd Pilcrow for the day and lead the Army on a merry ride through the desert in the opposite direction. I didn't believe there really was an alien, but just in case I prepared a fake crash site—nothing elaborate given the time constraints. We simply stuffed a thirty-pound incendiary bomb into a washing machine and dropped it from the plane on the way over here. Not elegant, but it will keep the Army busy while we exploit the real site."

"This is crazy," Lloyd said. "What airfield did you fly from?"

"A little semi-private operation you have no need to know about."

"Can you even ride a horse?" Lloyd asked.

Avery drew himself up straight. "I excelled at dressage at Groton."

"Well, don't ask my horse to dance or he'll toss you in a cactus. What are you going to do about my sister and brother-in-law while you're pretending to be me?"

"Not to worry. I'll take care of it."

"How?"

"I'm not giving you a choice, Pilcrow. This was decided above your pay grade."

Lloyd shook his head. "How do I explain—"

"We don't have time for discussion. Are you going to do your job?" Avery slipped a hand into his pocket and pulled out a small gun. "Or do you need encouragement?"

Lloyd rolled his eyes. "You're pulling a gun on me? Are you serious?"

Avery raised the gun higher. "When I make a point, I like to underline it. No, I wouldn't shoot, but if you don't get moving, I'll make a world of trouble for you."

As Lloyd stared at the gun, it began to spark with green light. A wave of panic made it difficult to breathe. The demons were coming at the worst possible time. He didn't want to leave this man with his sister, but if he stayed … Lloyd had a vision of being clamped into handcuffs by the Army as he screamed like a madman.

"I suppose I have no choice," Lloyd said.

"Excellent. Help me stow the chutes and let's get this show on the road."

※

The humans left me tied up as they made themselves busy. I saw Lloyd leave on one of the vehicular horses while Avery went into the house.

The door had barely shut when I noticed something on the road, a cloud of dust that grew slowly larger. Soon I could see a line of what I at first took to be motley beasts and later realized were vehicles. They came to a halt, and humans spilled out. One of them yelled while the others swarmed around the veranda. Like my gentle colleagues, the cats, they began to hide. They ducked behind rocks and vehicles and other such large objects as they could find, with their firing limbs bristling out.

Avery came out onto the veranda and hailed the one

who appeared to be the overseer. He held up his hands with palms facing forward. "This is overkill," he yelled. "It's gentle."

"Stand down," yelled the overseer. The firing limbs lowered. Unlike the ones who had scurried behind the rocks, this man walked in a stiffly upright position. He approached and stopped a few feet away from the veranda, took off his hat, and snapped his body into rectitude. "Major Emory Estep."

"Lloyd Pilcrow," Avery said.

"Where is it?" asked Major Estep.

I ducked my head.

"Right here." Avery pointed to me. I tried not to make contact through the eye, but I knew it was too late. I'd already been volunteered, and, as the humans would say, my gander was fried.

"You were supposed to secure the alien under lock and key," the major said.

"He's tied down," Avery said.

"Tied down? You tie a dangerous space invader to a pole like he was a poodle? When the US Army gives you instructions, you follow them to the letter. This is unacceptable. Go inside while we secure the alien. Then you're going to show us the crash site."

"Yes, sir. I'm happy help in any way I can, sir."

The overseer turned and barked at the men behind the rocks. They raised their firing limbs and approached from all sides. Someone grabbed me, cut the ropes, stuffed me into a bag, and dragged me over bumps and rocks. They hoisted me through the air, and I landed on a metal surface. A door slammed shut, and all was dark.

Motors roared, and my jail began to move. I had no idea where we were going, I just knew that I was getting farther and farther away from Trudie, the fragrant bubbles, and my congenial feline colleagues.

※

Everyone thinks I crashed in Roswell, New Mexico, but that's not true. Roswell was where the army pretended to find me because they didn't want uncleared humans to discover the real crash site, which was not the real crash site, but rather the one devised by Avery. For their fake crash site, the Army welded together salvaged parts from a B-45 Tornado that had crashed in the desert and a 1940 Chrysler Saratoga that had also crashed—I believe these were two separate accidents. They sprayed the resulting object with silver paint and dropped it from a plane. It landed near Roswell and was found by a local rancher. Then the Army fabricated an "alien" out of rubber. They didn't make it look like me because my proboscis was "obscene" and my flocculent butt "ridiculous." Then they dressed a private in a white coat, laid the rubber alien on a table, and photographed the "alien autopsy."

I found all of this out years later when I discovered the boxes sealed with black tape.

14

LABYRINTH

Lloyd rode off in search of the crash site with deep misgivings. What did Avery mean when he said he would "take care of" things? The man had about him a reckless, I-can't-believe-the-government-pays-me-to-do-this glee. Lloyd had seen it often in the Office of Strategic Services, especially among the rich boys, the ones who were doing covert actions and "special projects" rather than straight-up espionage. They didn't have the patience for the tedium of traditional operations. They would do any hare-brained, high-risk thing just for the hell of it.

He would have stayed, but with the demons and the Army approaching, it was better to ride out into the desert where no one could see him. He chose the ranch's most phlegmatic and trustworthy horse, a twelve-year-old Appaloosa mare named Belle, in the hope that she wouldn't run off and leave him if he started acting strange.

As Lloyd rode, the visual effects grew more pronounced. Every time he moved his head, objects left trails of light. The light had a sound to it—nothing alarming, just a gentle whining. He could still function. He could even appreciate the strange beauty of it. Belle flicked her ears but didn't seem alarmed. Lloyd counted slowly. The light trails diminished but didn't disappear.

Despite the visual displays, Lloyd found the creosote bush where they had first seen the alien. He dismounted to look for the creature's tracks. They weren't hard to find. They were circular with seven radiating spokes. It seems the creature had done plenty of foot-dragging, thrashing about, and running into things. Lloyd followed the trail on foot, leading Belle. The tracking got easier when the footprints began to glow with an orange light. Was that real or a misfire in his brain? How would he define "real" in this circumstance? Real light generated by the real footprints of a real alien? Other people saw the alien so he must be real. But this light? During the war, Lloyd had witnessed things that seemed unbelievable: a building swelling and coming apart before his eyes, a headless body walking—a whole range of pyrotechnic wonders and physical improbabilities. His concept of reality had stretched to accommodate those things. But now it was about to break. The light from the footprints grew stronger and began to pulse. Then the pulsing took on the sound of a croaking frog.

Lloyd looked back at Belle. Her eyes were calm and focused in the distance; her ears were angled to pick up the small sounds of the desert. She didn't see what he saw or hear what he heard.

Lloyd felt a scream expanding deep in his throat. He mustn't let it out. He focused on Belle, and she turned her eyes on him. Nothing but gentle sanity in those eyes. They gave him strength. He had helped foal Belle when he was in high school. They had an old connection. Lloyd buried his face in her neck and breathed in the horse smell. She reached around to nuzzle his shoulder. He mustn't frighten her; she might bolt and leave him here.

It occurred to Lloyd that being around horses again might be the thing that could bring his sanity back. He could quit his job and stay at the ranch, at least for a while. He could make sure that Earl treated Trudie right. He could ... Lloyd shook his head. No, he could do no such thing. He had a wife in Virginia.

Lloyd patted Belle's neck and turned his attention back to the trail. It was a winding, drunken path that often coiled in on itself. It made no sense to him. No creature moved across land like this. Sometimes the tracks zigzagged up the sheer face of a rock or went straight into a ditch. Was the path itself a hallucination or the manifestation of the pointless wandering of his mind?

After a while, the croaking died out. The round footprints quit glowing. Lloyd continued to follow them throughout the day until his brain had calmed, and he was reasonably certain that the world all around was real. Then he looked up and saw the crash site with its charred and twisted metal.

Lloyd stared, then turned his back and radioed in his location. He waited for the plane carrying Avery's colleagues. By the time they parachuted in to secure the site, the sun had set. Fortunately, a full moon had risen, providing more than enough light for Belle to find her way back home.

15

UNRELIABLE

Three days later, Lloyd was back in El Claustro, staying in the town's one hotel and trying to put his ragged memories in chronological order. He shifted an ice-filled towel against his forehead, sending a drop of cold water into his ear. He shuddered, and shards of light sparked across the back of his eyelids. He lay on a sour mattress, imprisoned in the striped shadow of blinds that wouldn't close. The Hotel El Claustro did not indulge in regular maintenance.

He'd fled Creosote Hill because he couldn't answer any of Trudie's or Earl's probing questions. They didn't remember what happened the day the Army took custody of the alien. They slept through it and awoke in the afternoon headachy and nauseous. Avery Stanton had slipped upstairs and chloroformed them. That was how he "took care" of the situation. Then he left Lloyd to figure out what to say to them when he got back to the ranch. Lloyd guessed that Avery went out of his way to find excuses to chloroform people.

Returning home from finding the crash site, Lloyd

had endured tears and a vicious tongue lashing from Trudie. Earl threatened to get his gun and blow somebody's damn fool head off. Feeling the demons approach, Lloyd had locked himself in his room and then curled up on the floor of the closet under quilts to stifle his screams. The next morning Trudie told Lloyd to get his things ready. She drove him back to the bus station without saying another word.

The migraine started on the ride from Creosote Hill. Lloyd's vision squeezed in until he was looking through a porthole. He didn't let Trudie know what was happening, even though he was nearly blind by the time he got out of the truck. He stood still until she drove off, and then stumbled across the street. He got a hotel room and waited for the pain that would come when the tunnel vision wore off.

Lloyd carried spare underwear in his briefcase, but he hadn't bothered to wash or change into it. He lay on the thin mattress in grimy boxers and undershirt and allowed himself to ripen in the heat. "Wallowing," Trudie would call it. He felt empty when he realized he'd come all the way out here and hadn't had a chance for a good talk with her.

When someone knocked on the door, he thought it might be his sister. But then he heard the refined, bored voice of Avery Stanton. "I know you're in there, Pilcrow, open up like a good boy."

"Last person on Earth I want to see right now, you gilded frat brat," Lloyd muttered under his breath. "Go away," he yelled and winced at the pain this exertion caused.

"I'm as persistent as Poe's raven. I shall leave you nevermore."

Lloyd cursed. Declaiming poetry was another of the intellectual affectations favored by the OSS society boys.

Avery tried the knob and found the door unlocked. He stepped inside. "A good operative always locks the door, Pilcrow."

Lloyd didn't bother to get up. "I'm not an operative anymore. I'm quitting as soon as I get back to Washington." He had made this decision on the ride from the ranch.

"Quitting is not an option for you. By the way, you work for me now." Avery shut and locked the door. He turned on the battered radio to the agricultural forecast. He crouched by the bed and said in a low voice, "I pulled some strings. You and I are two of only three people with access to a compartment we shall call HALFSHEEP, which contains all information pertinent to the alien."

"Who's the third?"

"Elliot Ludden," Avery said.

"Don't I have to agree to a thing like that?" Lloyd sat up. The towel began to leak profusely.

"I agreed for you. You're welcome." Avery went to the window and tried to shut the blinds all the way.

"They don't close." Lloyd stood up unsteadily.

Avery spun around and raised his voice in exasperation. "Why didn't you make them give you another room? Most of the rooms in this fleabag hotel are vacant. I despise suffering stoics." He wrinkled his nose. "Especially smelly stoics. Is this how you dress for a meeting with your boss? I'm going to have to insist on more decorum."

"I'm going to have to insist on prior notice of your visits." Lloyd carried the dripping towel into the bathroom and dropped it in the sink. He put his hands out and braced himself on the counter to let a moment of dizziness pass. He opened his puffy lids and looked into the mirror to see his chin disappearing into three days' worth of ginger stubble. He squeezed his eyes shut then opened them wide. The sclera were shot with red vessels and a yellow tinge of paranoia. Lloyd allowed anger to creep into his voice. "And I insist that you not chloroform my family again. Is that too much to ask?"

"Yes, far too much," Avery said cheerfully. He pulled a small screwdriver from his pocket and began to remove the cover from a light socket. "Chloroform is something of a specialty of mine. I'm quite good at it. Haven't killed anyone yet that I know of. But in deference to my new employee, I'll make a sacrifice and refrain from using it on your family." He paused. "You're welcome. My god, this room only has one socket. What a dump." He crossed the room to the one chair, a musty, bile-colored wingback. He looked under the cushion, scowling at a dark stain. "I repeat, what a dump."

Lloyd scooped his pants from the floor and put them on. Bending over intensified the pain in his head. He collapsed into the rejected chair. "I'm going to have to check you out with Turner," he said.

"Be careful what you say over the phone," Avery said. "Tell him you're calling in reference to the small compartment. He'll say 'the deal is done.' Those exact words."

Lloyd felt his heart congeal. He had no doubt the conversation would go as Avery said. "Do I have a job title?" he asked.

"Special projects officer." Avery picked up the bedside lamp and turned it over to examine the underside.

Lloyd winced. Avery had pulled that title out of his ass. It was vague enough to cover a multitude of sins. "I know I'll regret asking this, but what does a special projects officer do?"

"A little of this and a little of that." Avery made a dismissive gesture with fine, manicured hands. "Why the pouty face? I hand you a plum, and you act like it's a lump of shit. By the way, I moved you up a grade. You're welcome."

Lloyd rubbed his hands over his eyes and spoke quietly. "I can't do this. I'm not up to it. I haven't been well lately."

Avery approached the wingback and squatted down to get a better view of Lloyd's face. He tilted his head to the right, then to the left, peering as if he could see straight through Lloyd's skull to the seething gray matter underneath. "If you're talking about your recent erratic behavior," Avery said, "I know all about that."

Lloyd looked up in surprise. "You do?"

"Turner and I have been discussing you since you returned stateside. Evidently the fucking Commies slipped some exotic drugs into your gruel while you were in prison."

"If that's true, then why didn't anyone tell me this?"

"The existence of such drugs is compartmented, and you're not in the compartment," Avery said.

"But the drugs are in me." Lloyd felt something like carbonation in his veins. He turned his palms up and stared at the blue branches in his wrists as if he could see the bugs crawling in them. "What are these drugs? What do you know about them? Will they ever go away?"

"I don't know."

"I thought I was losing my mind."

Avery shrugged. "You may be. We don't know that yet either."

Lloyd struggled to process this information. "Is that

why you followed me from Washington?"

"We couldn't let you go wandering off unattended. For all we know you could be primed to do the bidding of Soviet masters."

"That's ridiculous. No one is controlling me."

"Really?" Avery said. "Can you say that you've had control over your own mind lately?"

Lloyd's hands began to shake. He pressed the palms together.

"Prayer won't help you now," Avery said.

Lloyd forced himself to look into the man's face. The slate blue eyes revealed nothing. He might as well be staring at a dead fish. "Is Avery Stanton your real name?" he asked.

"Do you think I would trust you with my real name? I—we—don't trust you with anything. There are some who would be happier if we could terminate you, but you're one of us, and that counts for a lot."

"Why didn't you have me locked up?" Lloyd asked. "Surely you could trump up some charges."

"That wouldn't be a problem," Stanton said, "but, again, you're one of us. Also, we wanted to see what you would do. We've been looking for any sign that you might try to gain unusual access to people, places, or information."

"I haven't."

Avery nodded as if approving the actions of a small child. "No, you haven't."

"How long have you been following me?"

"A while. I have an enormous interest in any drugs the fucking Commies might have developed." Avery stood and began to speak with grand gestures as if addressing a roomful of people and not one rancid, broken operative.

"Think of it. Think how useful such drugs would be to our operations. Face it, a fair percentage of the information we collect is shit. Some of it is gold, but half the time we can't tell the difference between the two. Imagine what we could do if we could eliminate the unreliability of the human factor. A guaranteed trustworthy asset. Isn't that the holy grail of operations?"

"There's nothing reliable about me right now."

"Agreed. Clearly, the fucking Commies have some bugs to work out. I don't think you're much of a threat." Avery went to the window and peeked out the blind. "I was getting pretty bored with you. I was planning to stay here to keep an eye on the bus station, but it was such a dump, I decided to take a side trip to a friend's ranch. He's the one who flew me to your place in one of his planes."

"One of his planes? How many does he have? Was that his bomb that you dropped on the fake crash site?"

"He's a man of many and varied hobbies. But enough about him. To continue, I had grown completely bored with you, and then I got a call from Turner, saying you had seen an alien. Of course, neither Turner nor I believed it, but I thought I'd better check up on you. I was going to drive out in the morning, but then I got the second call. After you told him that your brother-in-law got in contact with Alamogordo, Turner checked up and found that it was true. He began to think there might actually be an alien. So at that point, I ordered the preparation of the fake crash site to divert the Army and packed my chute. Still, I was shocked to find an alien."

"Why do you want me to work for you if I'm so erratic?" Lloyd asked.

Avery smiled. His white teeth, dimples, and inexorable cheer roused a fresh wave of loathing in Lloyd. "Several reasons," he said. "Number one: I want to observe every nuance of your behavior. Number two: I want to keep an eye on you, so you don't do anything damaging to the organization while you're in one of your erratic phases. Number three: I need some help and I don't want to read anyone else into the HALFSHEEP compartment."

"What kind of help?"

"Help retrieving our ugly little friend from the Army."

"Avery, I work for the Army."

"No, you work for me. Moreover, your intelligence unit is about to be folded into a new civilian intelligence agency, so you won't be working for the Army in any case."

"Since when are agencies of government supposed to work against each other?"

Avery gave Lloyd a penetrating look as if he were evaluating the man's sanity. "They're not *supposed* to, but who can deny that they do? One of these days, you should buy our old chief Ted Sullivan a drink and get him talking about J. Edmond Bissell and the FBI. We would still have the OSS if Bissell hadn't planted his nasty stories in the press."

Lloyd shielded his eyes with his hand in a vain effort to shut out the persistent light in the room. "Why do you want this alien so badly? Isn't the Army better equipped to handle it?"

Avery's face took on a look of pained astonishment. "How can you even ask a question like that? In the space of a decade, we've had the COI, the OSS, the CIG, et cetera, et cetera. A host of competing intelligence agencies. We're about to get a new one, the CIA. Who knows if it will last or whether it's merely the latest acronym to float up from the alphabet soup. I want the organization to succeed, to become the premier intelligence agency. Lloyd, what do you think an intelligence agency needs to do to establish itself?"

Lloyd expelled a sigh. "I would like to think the answer is 'a superior job of gathering and analyzing intelligence,' but I have a queasy feeling you have something different in mind."

Avery laughed indulgently. "You're such a lamb. Let me explain what we're about here. What an agency needs is a mythology, an aura. What faster way to that goal than to be the one agency in Washington with its own alien?" Avery brought his fist down on an invisible surface. His eyes glittered, and his sunburned face grew redder. "Even if only a handful of the most powerful men in Washington know about it, others sense it. It's something past the common understanding, and whoever possesses it has the power."

"Like the Holy Grail?" Lloyd meant to be facetious, but Avery pounced on the comment.

"Exactly! It's the Holy Grail, and the Army doesn't deserve it."

A thought occurred to Lloyd. "You spent some time in the Army, didn't you?"

Avery's face clouded over. "Yes. I volunteered when the war began, but I found I don't take orders well. Had to pull a lot of strings to get out of it with an honorable discharge."

Lloyd allowed his eyelids to droop shut. "And how do you propose we get the alien out of the Army?"

"I worked my contacts and found out they're moving it from Alamogordo next Wednesday. They're preparing a quarantine facility up north."

"Where?"

"A Top Secret underground facility near Gilman."

Lloyd frowned. "I haven't heard of any military facilities in that area. The only thing up there is logging."

"What does 'Top Secret' mean, Lloyd?" Avery asked. He took a crumpled map out of his shirt pocket. He unfolded it and spread it out on the bed, for lack of a cleaner surface. "Hoist yourself out of that chair, old man, and get over here."

Avery was perhaps five years older than Lloyd, but he had about him a boyish mischief while Lloyd, at the age of thirty, was sliding into a premature middle age. He rose from the chair slowly to save his aching head the shock of a rapid change in altitude.

Avery turned back to the map. "Okay, next Wednesday at dusk two convoys will leave Alamogordo Airfield. The larger one will go first, heading towards a small facility just about here." Avery's finger traced a route north, ending in an empty spot on the map west of Oscuro. "That's the decoy. About an hour later, a smaller convoy will leave, headed for Gilman." Avery's finger traced a much longer route west and then north into the Jemez Mountains.

"What's your source of information?" Lloyd asked.

"A very highly-placed individual and reasonably close relative by marriage. By the way, can you drive a large truck?"

16

A SPECIAL PROJECT

Lloyd waited in the dark cab of a deuce-and-a-half, drumming his fingers on the wheel and pondering the origins of the vehicle. Did Avery steal it? Where could you borrow one of these things? What did it cost? Certainly enough to put it in the category of grand theft. How many years of jail time for being an accessory to grand theft? No, more than an accessory. Avery would undoubtedly escape prosecution altogether, and Lloyd would take the blame and do the time. He had a feeling that the unwritten job description for Special Projects Officer was "scapegoat."

Maybe the deuce came from Avery's rich friend who also owned several small planes and at least one incendiary bomb. He must be running some type of paramilitary training facility.

Even if Avery hadn't stolen the deuce, there were other illegalities. Lloyd fingered the material of his fatigues. Impersonating army personnel. If his memory served, that was a felony.

Suppose he accidentally hurt someone during this

operation? Avery had supplied him with a gun, telling him it was only for show. Lloyd had already made sure it wasn't loaded. Even so, he guessed that mere possession of the weapon would increase his prison sentence. Lloyd grabbed the gun from the seat and flung it out the open passenger window. He didn't hear it hit. The ground here dropped off steeply to the Guadalupe River below. His truck tires were inches from the edge.

Lloyd laughed at himself. Why should he worry about accidentally injuring a soldier? Soldiers had guns with real bullets. They were trained in hand-to-hand combat. Lloyd had double-majored in International Affairs and Finno-Ugric Languages.

Avery had promised Lloyd wouldn't have to overpower any soldiers if the scheme played out as planned. Lloyd figured the odds of this at a hundred to one.

With any luck, Avery would be wrong, and the convoy would go somewhere else. *I'm not a lucky man*, Lloyd thought. *Damn your full-grain hide, Avery Stanton.*

So far, the man had been right. Two convoys had left Alamogordo Airfield on Wednesday. The longer one left first, heading north. Later, a shorter convoy headed north then cut west. In the days before interstate highways, convoys moved slowly, giving Avery and Lloyd plenty of time to prepare.

A few months earlier, this road had been an abandoned feeder line for narrow-gauge logging trains. The rails had been ripped out. Now the road carried trucks to the new sawmill at Gilman. And to a secret underground military facility, if Avery was right. Why would anyone put a facility up here? It didn't make sense, but then the state of New Mexico was pocked with secret sites. Why would anyone put a secret site at Los Alamos?

The single-lane road snaked along the shear side of the Guadalupe Box Canyon. Lloyd's deuce-and-a-half sat on a pull-out after the first of two tall, narrow tunnels.

Lloyd's front shirt pocket held a crude sketch of Avery's plan, depicting the seven vehicles in the convoy as rectangles. The deuce-and-a-half carrying the alien, indicated with an X, was in the middle of the convoy. Parallel lines breaking the road represented the tunnels. A few small circles above the first tunnel indicated rocks. Avery and Lloyd had spent the day clinging to the face of the cliff above the first tunnel preparing a small rockslide that would be set off by the movement of a precariously placed timber. A rope tied to the timber led down into the tunnel. A series of arrows on the sketch showed how the scenario would play out if everything went as planned.

Lloyd growled low in his throat remembering the confidence and condescension in Avery's voice as he explained the sequence of events.

"It couldn't be any simpler, Lloyd. Stop being negative." Avery sketched an "A" on the schema. "That's me. I'll be up where I have a clear view of the road. When I spot their lights, I'll move down into the first tunnel." He drew an arrow. "I'll let the first half of the convoy go through." More motion arrows. "As soon as the deuce with the alien passes, I yank the rope, sending the rocks tumbling down in front of the next vehicle. The driver of the deuce stops and steps out of the cab to see what's going on, and I'm there in a flash with my chloroform. I overcome the driver and take control of the vehicle."

"There will be a passenger," Lloyd said. "They always

have a backup driver."

Avery's face showed impatience and contempt. "Not a problem, I can handle two. I'll take control of the vehicle, flash the lights once—that's your signal—and drive the deuce out of the tunnel. You be ready to pull out onto the road, because I'm going to move right into your spot. The switch has to be fast. By the time they clear the rocks, and the rest of the convoy comes through the tunnel, I'll have my deuce camouflaged, and you'll be driving with the convoy. I'll get the alien out of the back of the deuce, bag him, and carry him to my car, which will be hidden in the brush not far away. Meanwhile, you continue driving with the convoy until you get to the pull out here." Avery pointed to a spot just off the paper. "Get out casually, like you're going to take a dump behind a rock. Then clear out of there as fast as you can."

"And go where?" Lloyd asked.

"Over the edge of the gorge. Cling to some rocks. They probably won't find you in the dark. Then you can hike out."

"You're leaving in a sports car, and I'm hiking out at night over treacherous rocks?"

Avery sighed. "You're such a complainer. I'm doing the real work. I limited your role as much as possible, because, frankly, you aren't all that reliable. By the way, if you start acting crazy, I'll shoot you. Now, buck up and stop complaining. Did you think you were signing up for a tea party?"

"I didn't sign up for anything. You signed for me."

"You're welcome."

The growling in Lloyd's throat grew louder. For a moment he thought the demons were coming, then he recognized the sound of engines. The convoy. He twisted around and stuck his head out the window. A branch caught him in the eye. Lloyd pushed it aside with an oath and listened. Tears welled up in his injured eye. His heart thumped and rolled in his chest. He held his breath until dots swam before his eyes, then he let it out and gasped. The convoy had yet to reach the entrance of the first tunnel. Lloyd felt rather than saw the black mouth of that tunnel. Time was playing tricks. Surely the convoy should have reached the tunnel by now. He could hear it getting closer and closer, yet it didn't arrive. Alarming things took place in Lloyd's chest: irregular thumps and gurgles. Lloyd turned away from the tunnel and gripped the steering wheel. He thought of driving away, but he shook it off. The engines were close, and then they were in the tunnel. Lloyd shrank back into the cab as he saw the lights of the first vehicle. A jeep emerged, followed by two trucks. The alien was in the fourth vehicle. Lloyd heard the sound of rocks sliding down the mountainside. He started the motor and peered through the darkness toward the tunnel. He watched for the flash of headlights indicating that Avery had taken control of the deuce with the alien. A stinging drop of sweat ran into Lloyd's eye. He rubbed it and waited. Nothing. Then he heard a most unexpected sound: laughter. Rolling, raucous laughter. And it wasn't Avery.

Lloyd sat for a minute and listened. All of the motors cut off—from the vehicles up ahead and those behind. The laughter died away in the tunnel. The dead silence of a windless night set in. Lloyd waited. He would have to go find out what had happened to the stupid bastard. He would probably be arrested. He pushed the door of the deuce open and fought his way out through the branches they had piled on the vehicle for camouflage.

    Lloyd was sorely tempted to walk away. He couldn't change anything that the Army had done or would do to Avery. He could stay out of sight and hike back down to where they had hidden Avery's car. The key was in the ignition. If he drove the car back to Avery's motel room in Los Alamos, it would hardly count as theft. He would be a free man.

    But that would be dishonorable. Of course, Avery was a completely dishonorable man, but Lloyd couldn't abandon him. What did his mother used to say? "Lloyd, the world isn't fair, but I insist that you be fair." Lloyd squared his shoulders and entered the tunnel. All headlights had been turned off, and it was black as pitch inside. He scraped his fingers along the rough sidewalls to keep his bearings. He knew other men were in the tunnel, and their deliberate silence unnerved him. He tried to move noiselessly, but his army boots crunched small stones. Did he hear whispering? He paused and listened, then continued walking as random thoughts flickered through his brain: *What is happening here?*

    A sudden searing light caught Lloyd in the eye. He sank to his knees and covered his face with his hands. The light moved on, settling on the ground a few feet in front of him. Lloyd blinked away the after images, trying to make sense of the long, pink lozenge lying in the road. His brain firmly rejected the truth at first, but as his vision cleared, he could no longer deny that this was Avery's naked body. Nor could he deny that the nakedness disturbed him more than the idea that Avery might be dead.

    "Is he dead?" Lloyd asked the invisible men behind the light.

Laughter erupted. When it died out, a deep voice said, "No, just chloroformed. When he wakes up, tell him two things. Number one: his methods are getting too predictable. Number two: a man who cheats on his wife shouldn't consider her brother a reliable source of information. The alien is safely in his quarantine facility, and you two are up shit's creek."

"There's no military facility up here, is there?" Lloyd asked.

"Hell no, why would anyone put anything up here?"

Thankfully, they didn't arrest Lloyd, but they stripped him and left him standing in the road beside Avery. They took the deuce. Lloyd listened to the convoy turning at a wide spot in the road just beyond the tunnels. Then they all drove past again, waving and laughing.

Lloyd hoped the sports car was still in its hiding place. He left Avery and walked down the road. His bare feet were raw by the time he located the car. He got in and found the leather seat cold. He was slightly cheered knowing that the thought of his bare ass in the driver's seat would irk Avery to no end. Lloyd drove back up to the tunnel, inching the car forward until he saw Avery in the headlights. He was sitting up.

"What happened?"

"Long story. I'll tell you on the way back to Los Alamos. In the meantime, let me summarize by saying never trust a goddamn brother-in-law."

17

QUARANTINE

Red-lettered signs marked the place called Quarantine. No one spoke to me there or uncovered their faces. They wore white hoods with visors and bulky white garments with gloves. They were as afraid of me as I was of them.

My room in Quarantine was similar to the one where Deyahm and I stayed before our appalling launch, except that it had four sides, not six. Harsh light bounced off the walls without cease. An observation window framed frowning, squinting human faces. Hooded jailers entered periodically, causing me to spring to the ceiling. They whacked me with a broom until I fell. They took small sample chunks of my flesh.

In Quarantine, they thrust many and varied substances down my maw, but the only one that did not resurface was potato chips. They experimented with a variety of liquids, to include, of all unlikely things, water. My visceral response left my jailers splattered and astounded. They tried wrinkled strips of a reddish savory, a curdled yellow gloop, and a gummy gray mass studded with debris. Later, after my studies in human anthropology had advanced, I learned that these substances were called, respectively, "bacon," "eggs," and "chipped beef over toast" or, in the common tongue, "feces on a shingle." They were consumed by humans the first thing in the morning. I could see how this would make humans mean after a while.

My jailers were swabbing my regurgitated breakfast from the floor when I heard a knock on the observation window. I looked up to see a man holding up a round container. He pointed to it and shrugged. One jailer left the room and returned with a small bowl of dark liquid. My proboscis quivered at the smell. He set the bowl on the floor and pushed my face into it. I sputtered and blew bubbles, but a few drops hit my tongue. I tasted a bracing astringency, not unlike the delightful silver tonic served on Utorb. I grabbed the bowl and poured its contents into my mug wart. My tongue darted out and curled into a tube. I closed my eyes and sucked the liquid with deep contentment.

The next day my jailer brought a bag I took for more potato chips. I turned away because my mouth had grown sore from the sharp chips. He grabbed me and turned me roughly back around. He poured the contents of the bag onto the floor. My proboscis quivered at the spicy, chemical bouquet. I leaned down to get a closer look at the pile of orange, vermiform dinguses. I picked one up and crumbled it. It was as light and lacking in substance as *yot*. I tasted a piece—divine. From that day forward, Cheezees and coffee comprised my diet in its entirety.

Quarantine was not interesting and not appalling. I was bored and lonely. I frequently glanced at my right upper limb, to the place where they had implanted the tracking device. I felt the lozenge-shaped lump and strained my eyes to see if I could detect a glow, a sign that the *Uyiquiti Ri Ga* was on its way. Sometimes I dreamed that they came, greeting me in the beautiful Utorbian language that I had not heard for so long. But when I awoke, I was alone.

Late one night a ruckus erupted in the outer room where my observer usually sat with a clipboard, a frown, and coffee. I crept up the wall and peeked through the window to see a man in white garments and visor standing behind my observer. Moving quickly, the man clamped a cloth over the observer's nose, and then stood back as he fell to the floor, limp. He noticed me staring through the window and gave me a sign consisting of a fist with the opposing digit jauntily raised.

Surprise mutated into alarm when this human entered my room. He removed his visored head gear, and I recognized him as the golden-haired one who had floated down to the pasture next to Trudie's house.

"Avery Stanton," he said. "You may remember me. I'd shake your hand, but I find it disgusting." He took a cloth from his pocket and clamped it over my proboscis.

After that, I remember nothing until I woke up amidst a great clattering of metal. The sound reverberated painfully inside my head. It was dark. As I hadn't been in darkness for some time, I was blind. I tried to stretch my limbs but found myself confined in a noisome cylinder. I tried to cry out, but my mouth wouldn't open. I issued a loud, resonant honking through my proboscis.

"Halt! Open that trash can."

"Gun it, Lloyd." I heard a door slam shut, a motor start, and vociferous shouting. A vehicle leaped to life beneath me and moved erratically. My cylinder fell over and rolled, first one way then another. My sensitive proboscis suffered as it made repeated and violent contact with metal. I heard shots. Then my situation deteriorated sharply. My cylinder became airborne. The clattering briefly stopped, then there was a boom and accompanying jolt so severe it nearly dislodged my head. I became airborne again, and the process repeated itself.

※

Many years later, when I had the opportunity to read my official army file, I discovered this account under the heading "Intelligence Summary: Attempted Abduction of Alien by Suspected Red Communists."

> The following events have been reconstructed with the help of eyewitness accounts and physical evidence. At zero four hundred on the morning of March 17, 1948, two intruders dressed as an Army corporal and a private approached the base from a southerly direction driving a Morris CDSW. Two guards, 2LT Masters and PFC Jackson, were manning the front gate. The driver presented what appeared to be correct documentation, and the truck was allowed to pass. It parked behind the Alien Isolation Facility (AIF), where the passenger unloaded a garbage can and entered the AIF reception area through an unlocked window. It is unknown why the window of an isolation facility was unsecured. The intruder proceeded to the changing room, where he donned biological isolation garments. He entered the AIF observation area (AIF-OA) and overpowered CPT Lorton, utilizing chloroform. Lorton's feet and

hands were bound with duct tape. Red cloth was stuffed into his mouth and secured with duct tape. Upon inspection, the cloth bore a tag with Cyrillic lettering. It appeared to be a scarf like those worn by Soviet Young Pioneers, a Communist organization for indoctrinating youth. The intruder proceeded to the alien isolation cell (AIC), where he chloroformed the alien and taped its mouth shut. This proved to be a critical error, as the alien was still capable of emitting loud sounds through its trunk-like nose. The intruder then removed his biological isolation garment and placed the alien inside the metal garbage can, securing the lid with duct tape. He loaded this into the back of the Morris CDSW. The alien regained consciousness and emitted a loud, bugle-like sound through its nose.

SGT Sloane, patrolling nearby, ran to the scene and ordered the intruder to halt. The intruder jumped into the cab of the Morris CDSW, failing to properly secure the trash can containing the alien in the back of the truck—another critical error. The vehicle took off at high speed. SGT Sloane comandeered a jeep and pursued the truck to the front gate, where sentries attempted to stop it. The truck swerved and drove through the perimeter fence. At this point, one of the sentries, 2LT Masters, attempted to shoot out the tires of the vehicle. The other sentry, PFC Jackson, jumped into a truck and joined the pursuit. Roughly two kilometers from the gate, the CDSW went over a bump, ejecting the garbage can from the back of the vehicle. The can was still airborne when it was struck by SGT Sloane's jeep. The can bounced over the hood, landing on SGT Sloane, who lost control of the vehicle. The jeep ran off the road and overturned, coming to rest in a ditch. SGT Sloane broke his collarbone and left arm, and received lacerations to the face and shoulder. Meanwhile, the trashcan bounced into the path of the vehicle driven by PFC Jackson. PFC Jackson applied his brakes too abruptly, causing the vehicle to spin off the road. The private was thrown from the vehicle and suffered numerous injuries, including a dislocated shoulder, broken leg, and two broken ribs. The truck driven by the intruder escaped. The alien was recovered from the battered garbage can. It was shaken and confused, but miraculously uninjured.

All personnel exposed to the alien, including emergency medical personnel, have been ordered into quarantine in the AIF for the next three months. All base personnel will be required to take two new training courses: Detection of Counterfeit Documentation, and Defensive Driving and Accident Avoidance. All windows in the AIF have been permanently sealed. On no account is the above occurrence to be discussed or referred to in conversation with persons outside the Alien Observation Unit (AOU).

(Signed)
Lieut. [Blacked out]
Intelligence officer, [blacked out]

Lloyd and Avery assumed the alien was dead. How could it survive being struck at high speed by two vehicles? It didn't occur to them that the little creature was far hardier than a human being.

Avery flew Lloyd back to Washington in a Piper J-3 Cub borrowed from his mysterious friend. Lloyd studied the muddy footprints on the floor, pondering the identity of the previous passengers. In the pilot's seat, Avery sipped a whiskey sour from a cocktail shaker. Lloyd considered saying something about the drink, but then he thought, *If we crash, we crash.*

Once they were back in the new agency's temporary quarters on the Washington Mall, Avery closed the HALFSHEEP compartment. He and Lloyd stuffed their notes into a box, sealed it with black tape, and sent it to archives.

"Now, what do I do with you?" Avery said. They sat atop wooden desks in a room that had no chairs. The new bureaucracy was not exactly humming yet.

Lloyd shrugged. "Have you lost interest in me?"

"Yes," Avery said. He lit a cigarette and gave Lloyd a penetrating look. "You're not erratic in any interesting way. Sure, sometimes I see you looking at things that aren't there, but that gets old quickly. I want to go back overseas where things are happening. You, on the other hand, can't go back in the field."

"Agreed," Lloyd said. He had come to that conclusion long ago.

Avery picked up the phone receiver. "I have a friend who went into analysis after the war. I could see you as an egghead. Maybe even a good one. That will keep you where we can observe you. I'm going to have them assign a psychiatrist to your case."

"Is that necessary?"

Avery put the receiver down and fixed his cold eyes on Lloyd. "Do not expect to walk around unattended ever again."

18

A HISTORIC OPERATION

The attempted kidnapping at Quarantine rattled my jailers. After they had determined that I was not infectious, virulent, or communicable, they fell into the habit of moving me frequently, always in the night. They devoted a special truck to me, which they called the "Martianmobile." Outside it looked like any other unattractive brown army vehicle. In the back under the cargo cover, it had a locked steel cage inside another locked steel cage inside yet another locked steel cage. The innermost cage was so small that I could not stand or stretch my legs.

One Army base looked much like the other, but one place I will never forget. I arrived in the middle of the night in my Martianmobile. They plunked me into the usual brightly lit room, but this time they strapped me to a table. A woman entered, the first I had seen since Trudie. She wore white from top to bottom. Her mouth puckered in distaste as she took a blade and scraped off my flocculent bloomers. Then she swabbed my skin with a cold liquid that ignited the scrapes she had just inflicted. Two men used white tape to secure my limbs even more tightly to the table so no part of me could move. They pried my mouth open, rammed a tube into it, stuffed it with gauze, and ran tape from one side of the table, over my proboscis, to the other side. A man wearing a white mask began to push my table. In my worst nightmares, I remember the rolling. I rolled under a series of bright lights that flashed by with rhythmic regularity. A pair of doors opened, and I came into a room with brighter lights, and several humans wearing masks. More eyes stared down from windows above.

I couldn't always tell who was talking behind the masks. Their words floated over me. I understood some and put the others into my memory box. I hoped and feared that there would come a time when I would understand.

"It makes me uncomfortable to do this without anesthesia," one of them said.

"It doesn't feel pain. Besides, it's not human so we have no idea what the anesthesia would do to it. I don't want to kill it."

"We might kill it anyway, Dr. Stone."

"We'll do our best not to. Nurse, scalpel." I heard the slapping noise of the weapon hitting a gloved hand. Then Dr. Stone spoke into a microphone held by a nurse. "We don't know what we're going to find when we get in here. This is a seat of the pants operation. Our goal is to lay it open, photograph it, and close it up—hopefully before we kill it."

Of those words, I understood only "pants," which was a garment for the nether region, and "kill," which was a frequently abrupt way to separate the spirit from the carcass.

Dr. Stone continued. "I will cut from the upper torso

and down to the pubis. We've taken samples of the skin and determined that the epidermis is thicker than that of a man—almost as thick as an elephant's skin. Maybe they should have called in a veterinarian." He laughed.

He held up his weapon. "This scalpel was custom made to pierce the thick skin of the alien. The creature appears not to be diseased. We believe it doesn't carry pathogens harmful to humans. Nevertheless, this room has been sealed. Who knows what may be released when we cut into it? At this point, I would like to thank the brave men and women who volunteered to attend at this procedure. You deserve the gratitude of your country."

Someone whispered, "We didn't volunteer."

Dr. Stone continued. "If, at any point, we have reason to believe that toxic substances have been released, one of us will pull this red lever." He pointed to the wall. "You will hear a warning siren. Observers in the gallery should exit immediately. I understand that you've been briefed on the sensitivity of this operation and have signed the nondisclosure agreement?"

"They have," another voice said. "Perhaps we should get on with this before it dies of fright on the table."

"This is a historic occasion," said Dr. Stone, who was hot and quick with the joy of hearing his own voice. "It must be introduced with all due ceremony."

I heard another whisper near my head. "Asshole."

"Are we ready, then?" Dr. Stone asked.

I cannot bear to describe in detail what happened next, so I will summarize. The asshole slit me from end to end and peeled my hide back and pinned it fast so that I felt all the pain in the universe. It shimmered over me like a sheet of burning light crackling over my surface, furling and unfurling. I felt it from the smallest molecule of my carcass to the wholeness of my being. Then came the searing flashes as they photographed my raw insides from every angle.

I went in and out of swooning.

And through it all the voice of Dr. Stone rose in pompous pronouncements, strutted over high-sounding words, danced with itself in an ecstasy of unrestrained ego. I heard fragments: "extensive intestines," "rectal dead end," and "confusing sexual organs."

And through it all was the other voice, which was quiet but increasingly urgent, saying "hurry" and "get on with it" and "close him up, please."

Then they folded me back up and stitched me together. They rolled me under the rhythmic flashing of the bright lights, back to the white room.

For many hours, I didn't try to heal myself with the green energy. My soul wanted to leave my stinging and devastated carcass. Then the door of my room opened, and one of the humans came in. He looked at me with light blue eyes, almost as nice as Deyahm's lavender eyes and almost as full of pain. With only a slight bit of hesitation, he put his hand on my upper limb terminal. It was the first time someone had touched me without wearing a glove since I had left Trudie. When he spoke, I recognized the quiet, urgent voice that had requested Dr. Stone to hurry.

"I'm so sorry."

I understood those words immediately.

※

I hummed up a cloud of green energy and healed myself. The cruciform wound closed. The scars disappeared, or at least the scars on my carcass. Energy had no influence on the addled and seething contents of my head. I curled into a ball and refused to make contact through the eye with anyone. I wouldn't cooperate in the linguistic experiments that followed, even though they weren't painful. I sealed up my maw.

Presently my jailers grew bored with me. The poking, prodding, and photographing grew intermittent. I ate my Cheezees, drank my coffee, and thought about Deyahm. I remembered the doctor's words: "It appears not to be diseased."

It's ironic that my human captors were so concerned that I might harbor disease. Our Utorbian genetic engineers had defeated contagious disease long before my existence. Deyahm told me about it as we waited for our appalling launch. I'm ashamed to recall my stupid response. "That is truly delightful."

"Yes and no," Deyahm had said.

I protested. "How could there be a no?"

"Unintended surprise upshots," he replied. "To keep Utorbis from contracting diseases, evolution facilitators worked on strengthening the body's defenses. Proboscises expanded to incorporate more membranes to filter germs. Our hide thickened. We developed more energetic antibodies. Then antibodies became too energetic and began to attack each other." Deyahm curled his phalanges into hooks and knocked them together. "A million tiny wars erupted inside our bodies. Many Utorbis died in anguish before evolution facilitators fixed the problem. Nearly an entire generation perished."

"But they fixed it, and now there is no more problem?" I said, still searching for my happy ending.

"No more of *that* problem," he replied.

I had felt a hot flush of resentment as if Deyahm were responsible for the problems. I hated him for assaulting my happy ignorance. But that was before doctors assaulted my innocence with scalpels.

"I'm sorry, my friend," I said to the wall.

19

THE MINES

Lloyd and his colleagues called the new agency "the Mines." Located in a warren of temporary buildings on the national mall, it had a cloistered, underground feel. No one said the real name out loud. They were under the thrall of the Threat with a capital "T." They lived in the shadow of its crossbar. It separated them from outsiders, those who didn't understand the country was still at war. They felt pity and no small condescension toward those uncleared, uninitiated, uninformed outsiders.

Lloyd felt more comfortable at work than anywhere else. If he suffered an "incident," his colleagues would gently shuffle him off to the "Episode Room," a closet-sized space furnished with a mat, a plastic water pitcher, and paper cups. If it happened at home, his wife who would cry and call her mother. He fell into a pattern of working late and stealing into their bedroom after Faye had fallen into the delicate, one-position sleep dictated by face cream and curlers.

Lloyd worked for the Office of Human Ecology. Most of his colleagues were doctors. Lloyd had no medical degree, but he had fluent Russian and Hungarian, and the ability to read Polish. The doctor's found Lloyd's language and research skills invaluable. They were trying to determine what advances the Soviets had made in psychotropic drugs, truth serums, induced amnesia, brainwashing, hypnosis, sensory deprivation, and other subgenres of mind control. Lloyd's desk was so covered by Russian psychiatric journals and monographs that he resorted to using his briefcase as a lapdesk—until Security caught him. A stern young SCUDO (Security Control Uniformed Duty Officer) pointed out that the imprint of Lloyd's writing was clearly visible in the leather of the briefcase. Lloyd tried to argue that it would be impossible to extract anything legible from the mishmash of imprints, but they confiscated the briefcase. Lloyd got a security violation and a personal lecture from the head of Security. He never saw that briefcase again.

Fortunately, Lloyd's boss didn't hold the violation against him. He liked Lloyd and admired his work ethic. Seeing that his star analyst was upset, he procured a typewriter for him. At the time, only the secretaries had them. Lloyd immediately fell in love with the imposing hump of the steel-gray Remington. Of course, he still had to remove the platen each evening and lock it in the safe.

Lloyd had a minder, a Dr. Basil Prine, an up-and-comer straight out of Johns Hopkins. He and Lloyd didn't get on. The first time they met, Prine took out a small spiral-bound, government-issue notebook and began to scribble as he asked questions about Lloyd's mother. Lloyd pulled an identical notebook out of his pocket, labeled a page "Basil's Asinine Affectations," and listed them: pipe, monogrammed silver lighter, silk pocket hankie, tweed, pencil mustache, exaggerated diction, excessive use of jargon, Briticisms, and the word "precisely."

"Precisely what are you writing?" the psychiatrist finally asked. Lloyd handed Prine the notebook and watched his baby face pucker as he scanned the list. A few months later, Dr. Prine secured an overseas assignment and left without saying goodbye.

Lloyd's victory was short-lived. The following Monday, he glanced up to see a woman standing at his door. "May I help you?" he asked. His eyes drifted back to his work before he finished speaking.

"Lloyd?" the woman said. It was customary to use only given names in the Mines, even on the first meeting.

"Yes?" Lloyd responded reluctantly. He raised his eyes again, took a closer look at the woman and saw that she was wearing trousers and a crisp white blouse. He didn't approve of masculine garb on a woman. Trudie wore overalls, but she rode horses and she was, well, Trudie. Lloyd couldn't keep the irritation out of his voice. "I wasn't aware that we were getting any new secretaries."

"I'm Dr. Lee Ogilvie. I'm a psychiatrist. I'm here to judge your mental stability and fitness for classified work. Do you have any chairs that aren't covered by debris?"

Lloyd jumped up to move a stack of journals from a straight-backed chair. He stepped on yet another stack of journals on the floor and took a wild slide into a file cabinet. Dr. Ogilvie raised her arched brows but didn't break a smile. Lloyd righted himself, cleared off the chair, and motioned for her to sit.

"I apologize for the mess, and for mistaking you for a secretary." Lloyd's voice sounded stiff and hostile to his own ears. He tried again. "I promise to cooperate fully."

"Relax," Lee said. She was in her mid-thirties, Lloyd guessed. She had an arresting face, fox-like in its alertness. Her piercing, chrysolite eyes took in every nuance of expression on Lloyd's face. He blushed purple. Lee crossed her legs and rested her elbows casually on the arms of the chair. Lloyd sensed calculation in her movements, as if she had studied body language and deliberately chosen gestures that conveyed an inviting openness. He found this irritating.

"I hope you'll last longer than Dr. Prine," Lloyd said. This was insincere. He wished Dr. Ogilve and all her kind would take a flying leap off the nearest pier. "You don't plan to run off overseas, do you?"

"I would if I could, but the new office policy is not to assign female psychiatrists overseas. They say this as if they had more than one female psychiatrist. I suspect the only reason I was hired was that they looked at the top of my application and assumed I was a man. That's why I legally dropped my first name, Brenda, and replaced it with my middle name, Lee. I added a new middle name, Cabot. Having a last name as a middle name added that upper-class touch that means so much here. Sometimes simple ploys work, especially when brand new agencies are looking to fill their employment rolls quickly." Lee smiled. Her teeth showed white against aggressively red lips.

Lloyd settled back into his chair and tried to regain his poise, but his voice came out brittle. "It must be a disappointment for you to have to work with me, instead of flying off to evaluate some double agent."

"I've learned to reject disappointment and make the most of what's in front of me. It's the only way to get ahead. You're my assignment. You were given drugs that interest me greatly, so I look on this as an opportunity." As she spoke, Lee continued her unnervingly close observation of Lloyd's face. He began to regret scaring off Dr.

Prine. How could he not have recognized the advantages of having an idiot for a psychiatrist?

"You're what Hippocrates would call a melancholic," Lee said. "Pavlov would say 'weak inhibitory.' Your personality type affects your reaction to psychotropic drugs. Melancholics are quicker to reach a state of fear paralysis. The circumstances under which you receive the drugs also affect your reaction. Given that you were in a hellish prison, it's no surprise that you're still suffering after effects."

"Do you think I'm under the chemical control of handlers in Moscow?" Lloyd asked.

Lee laughed, a sound that spiraled up and rained down. "I know there are some in the Mines who believed the Soviets have progressed that far. I doubt it. Opinions are split. Some think that it might someday be possible, but only after intensive research and experimentation. Others think that the human spirit will always overcome such efforts."

"Which side are you on?" Lloyd asked.

"The people who say something can never be done are often proven wrong."

Lloyd was disappointed in her. "I'd rather be on the side of the human spirit." His eyes fell to her hands and those fiery fingernails. He would soon learn that in the office she always dressed in black or charcoal, with a white blouse ironed and starched within an inch of its life. The only color she indulged in was red, the burning red that she applied to her nails and lips.

Lee procured the office next to Lloyd's so that she could observe him more closely. Late one evening after everyone else had gone home, Lloyd went into that office to search for clues to Lee's personality. He thought it only fair. She knew way too much about him.

But she had left no clues: no family pictures, funny cartoons, or potted plants. She stored her books and monographs neatly on shelves and left nothing on her desk but an electric fan, a plain glass ashtray, and a clean white coffee mug. Her notes and files were locked in the safe. Lloyd sniffed and caught no whiff of perfume, just a faint, powdery smell.

The next morning Lee came into Lloyd's office with a steaming pot. "I made you coffee," she said.

"Why?" Lloyd asked.

"I know I make you uncomfortable. I'm just trying to make amends."

Something seemed off about the gesture, but Lloyd pushed his coffee mug across the desk and Lee filled it. She left, and Lloyd went back to the monograph he was reading. He typed his notes on the Remington. After about forty minutes, however, something went wrong with the machine. The keys frosted over, turning white and breaking off one by one. It was the last clear memory Lloyd had for twenty hours.

＊

When he opened his eyes, Lloyd was stretched out on the mat in the Episode Room. Lee sat beside him on the floor, her long, trousered legs folded under her rump. She smoked a cigarette as she scanned a tract on hypnosis.

"What did you give me?" Lloyd asked. Everything was fuzzy, but his crisp, black anger.

Lee looked up and snuffed her cigarette in a tin ashtray. "Good to see you awake. How do you feel?"

Lloyd spoke deliberately, as if a careless word might send him tumbling into the abyss. "I feel like killing you."

Lee looked into his face. "How does this experience compare to Hungary?"

Lloyd took an unwavering look into those piercing eyes and said, "How could you do this to me?"

Lee patted his hand and spoke softly, "I will never give you anything I haven't tried on myself. I took the same substance in the same amount last weekend and I had a glorious, transcendental experience."

"I feel like I'm drowning in cherry soda," Lloyd said.

Lee took a damp cloth from a bowl by her side and dabbed at Lloyd's forehead. "Don't you want to know what they gave you? How will we ever find out if we don't experiment?"

20

FIRST LIGHTNING

Lloyd found out about it weeks before the public announcement. Whispers spread through the Mines until the buildings hissed. Those who knew were grim-faced and withdrawn.

In terms of his own reaction, Lloyd could only compare it to the sudden violent death of his parents in that head-on collision. Before their death, mortality was something off in the distance. Afterward, it loomed close and undeniable. Now the issue was collective mortality. The new Threat overshadowed everything, changed everything, even morality. Surely the end justifies the means if the end is saving the country from annihilation.

The stink of betrayal hung in the air. Who? Someone at the center of the nation's most closely-held secret was a traitor. All of the elaborate and expensive security measures had proved useless. Someone who had been vetted and determined trustworthy was not. That someone still hid deep inside the system. The knowledge changed the way people looked at each other. For Lloyd, it magnified the paranoia engendered by the drugs in his system.

Sometimes, he wasn't sure if this new threat was real or whether his drug-addled brain had created it.

Then came the day when a SCUDO arrived in Lloyd's office. "Come with me. Leave your briefcase here." He took Lloyd to another building, to a small room with two straight-backed chairs. He didn't invite Lloyd to sit.

"I'm sorry, but we're temporarily revoking your clearances until we can re-evaluate your reliability." The SCUDO's voice was full of regret, even kindness.

"Why?" Lloyd asked. "What did I do?"

"Nothing, but you have a security watch on your file. The Boss of Mines has ordered everyone with a security watch to be reevaluated. It may take weeks. Don't worry, your pay will keep coming." A smile lit the SCUDO's boyish face. "If it was me, I'd take the wife on a vacation."

Lloyd stiffened. The thought of unbroken blocks of time with his wife was unbearable. How would he explain this to her? She wasn't cleared to hear the particulars. Lloyd's hand trembled as he slipped off his Mines security tag and handed it to the SCUDO. He shuffled out of the building like an old man and blinked in the steamy glare of late-summer. He felt off balance without his briefcase.

The public announcement came in late September, 1949. The president's words were bland, calculated to reduce panic. "We have evidence that within recent weeks an atomic explosion occurred in the USSR."

The public would teach their children to duck and cover. They would dig holes, fill bags with sand, and stockpile water, Civil Defense All-Purpose Survival Crackers, and tins of Spam. They would furnish their fallout shelters with bunks, radios, sealable receptacles for human waste, and board games to pass the time while waiting for the roentgens to dissipate. They chose Sorry, Parcheesi, and the free-market favorite Monopoly, passing over Chinese Checkers as too goddamn Red Communist.

They would allow the atomic threat to alter them in ways large and small.

21

THE PROVING GROUND IN 1951

A Clutch of humans entered my room. I recognized the overseer, referred to as the "full bird." I could have identified him even without the bird on his shoulder, because of his rectitude and unpetering oral effluence. He began to bloviate with great vigor and small specks of saliva that sprinkled down upon my head, like our rare and slimy Utorbian rain.

I had learned some human words, but could perceive only the barest outline of what he said. I stored phrases in my memory box: "experiment on blast effects," "extraterrestrial," and "Stallion, the second shot of Banger-Beeswax." I knew than an "experiment" was something done to me that none of them would have done to themselves. "Extraterrestrial" was one of their many names for me. Others included: "alien," "creature," "Dick Face," "subject," and my codename for traveling, "Gas Mask One." I could not decode the term "Stallion, the second shot of Banger-Beeswax."

The full bird said, "He's the perfect test subject. Virtually indestructible and no relatives on this planet."

They stuffed me into my traveling costume, which differed from the garments humans wore in that it had no sleeves or other separate facilities for limbs. Nor did it have an escape hatch for the head. It was similar in configuration to what the humans called a "garbage bag." They threw Cheezees in with me and closed my traveling costume over my head. Then they hoisted me up, toted me outside, and threw me into the triple iron cage of the Martianmobile.

I disliked these excursions because I bounced, hurting my proboscis and crushing all of my Cheezees. I couldn't see anything but darkness.

Then I could see something. My eyes caught the barest, citrine glow. It pulsed and grew stronger. I looked down at my left upper limb and saw that the glow was coming from my tracking device. I squealed with joy. Even as the Martianmobile began to travel a particularly rough road, I laughed, too full of joy to mind the bumps.

The trip was long. By the time I arrived, I was contused and covered in orange dust, but the pulsing citrine glow was growing brighter. When the Martianmobile stopped, I clamped a limb terminal over my tracking device. I didn't want the humans to see it.

They unlocked each of the nesting cages and dragged me out. They unpacked me. The local star had not yet stolen a gander over the horizon, but the moon offered enough light to make it clear that I was not on the usual military base. I was in the middle of the desert. I could see a few sheds and military vehicles parked about, seemingly at random. A tall, metal tower sprouted a few thousand yards away. For the only time in my life, I saw the flocculent creatures called sheep. They were tethered to a pole. I saw no humans other than the ones from my Martianmobile. The rest of the convoy was gone.

"Everybody else has been banned from the site until we get him secured. Hurry up, it's D minus two hours, and after we're done, they have to get the troops into their trenches."

"How far away are the trenches?"

"Seven thousand yards from ground zero, or two thousand yards further than this point."

"Stallion is the largest shot of the series, isn't it?"

"Yep, if it doesn't fizzle, it should rattle a few windows in Vegas."

They clamped a metal ring around my lower limb terminal and dropped me into a deep hole, barely wider than my body. The sides of the hole were dirt, but the bottom was concrete. A metal ring with a short, heavy chain stuck out of this crude floor. Two men held onto the legs of the third as he lowered himself down into the narrow space to secure me to the chain. As they pulled him out, he said, "Keep your head down, Dick Face. Fair warning."

"He doesn't understand what you're saying."

"Then he'll end up blind."

I waited until they drove away to uncover the tracking device. It glowed even brighter than before. I stood up and looked at the sky, or what small part of it I could see from the bottom of the hole. They were coming closer. My fellow Utorbis were approaching. And for some reason, the humans had tethered me out here and abandoned me. How could I be so lucky? My Utorbian colleagues would find me easily. I practiced what I would say. I listened to the words, *"Alamiyi mavi"* or "Welcome, friends" bounce off the walls of that narrow hole. I could barely contain my joy.

Then an unbearable thought floated up. Suppose *Uyiquiti Ri Ga* crashed, just as *Uyiquiti Ri Poi* had? But surely our clever Utorbian engineers would have improved the landing rockets. Engineers were always making improvements. They never built one rocket exactly like the previous one.

Joy swelled in my breast as the pulsing light of my tracker increased rapidly in brightness, so that the walls of the hole glowed citrine. Straining my eyes into the dark sky, I caught a glimpse of a small disk shining faintly to the west. At first I wasn't sure, but then it grew larger, approaching swiftly. It would arrive in seconds. "*Alamiyi mavi!*" I screamed.

I tasted metal. Then a flash brighter than a thousand local stars. Roaring, searing heat. Darkness.

22

SOLITARY PLUS ONE

The nuclear test blinded and burned me. Despite my weakness, I hummed up a batch of green, healing energy. I was desperate to see whether the tracker still pulsed with citrine light. When they removed the bandages from my eyes, my vision had returned, but the pulsing light was dead. I concluded that *Uyiquiti Ri Ga* was also dead, vaporized by the bomb.

I fell into despondency. When hunger drove me to it, I ate a few Cheezees and drank coffee. When they came to move me again, I was too disheartened to care where I was going. To quarantine? To vivisection? To another nuclear bomb test? Whatever. I allowed them to stuff me into my traveling costume and I calmly munched Cheezees as the locks clicked shut.

I arrived same as always. Boots crunched the ground beneath me, then clumped on a hard floor. Then things began to differ. We stopped moving. Something banged shut. The floor descended, screeching and squealing like a creature in agony. We went down a long way. I could feel the depth and hollowness of the place. Sounds caromed off hard surfaces. I smelled the reek of fuel and machinery.

By the time we got to the bottom, my lethargy was gone, and I was rigid with fear. I'd been in a place like this before and exited atop a burning rocket. When the elevator stopped, they threw me into a small room.

I found out only later that this was not a missile silo as I'd feared. It was a different sort of underground facility, the function of which I didn't have a need to know.

They gave me easy, painless tests involving colored cards with pictures. A man with a puffy face and dark spectacles would show me a card and record my reaction. At first I gave him little to record. He got himself a cup of coffee and sat back down. "Easy duty," he said to the guard.

His attitude—and the fact that didn't offer me any coffee—rankled me. When he showed me the next card, I squealed as loudly as my six lung-like sacs could manage and jumped to the ceiling, startling Puffy Face into spilling his coffee. He cursed as the private poked me with the end of his rifle to get me down. I dropped to the floor and waited. Puffy Face wiped his crotch with his handkerchief and swore under his breath. Then he scribbled furiously in his notebook. At last, he put down his pen and showed me the next card in the pack. I made my eyes huge, grabbed my chest, staggered backward, spun on one lower limb terminal, and fell to the floor in a sham faint. More cursing. More poking with the rifle. I pretended to recover. Puffy Face made copious notes. I could see the hesitation in his face as he lifted the next card from the deck and turned it around. I pointed and laughed so hard I fell to the floor and began to roll back and forth. Puffy Face scribbled.

The stack of cards was high. It took creativity to find new gestures and reactions for each one, but it turned out to be the first pleasant day I had enjoyed in some time. At the end of it, when Puffy Face left exhausted and angry, a new thought cheered me. Surely there would be *Uyiquiti Ri Bo*, a Third Glorious Mission. Why would they stop with two?

After they had finished testing, they put me into a smaller room with one very bright light, which was never turned off. They gave me a scratchy brown cloth they called an "army blanket." A toilet stood in the corner. An observation window in the door was large enough for me to see a pair of staring eyes and nothing more. A speaker in the ceiling played the same words over and over:

> You are in the custody of the United States of America. You will never return to your planet. Your people don't know where you are. They can't help you. You will never see them again. You depend on Americans for everything. You belong to the United States of America, body and soul.

Twice a day, the eyes briefly disappeared, and someone shoved a tray through a slot at floor level. The tray held Cheezees, a pot of coffee, and a tin mug. I left them untouched. I did this to upset the humans, rather than to starve myself. I planned to eat something before I died completely, but I wasn't close to that yet.

One day, the speaker fell silent. I heard a knock. I ignored it. The door opened slowly. I remained under my blanket.

"Hey there. You alive?" The voice was not unpleasant,

peremptory, imperious, or presumptuous. I chose to ignore it, however. "Hey, little feller. No reason to be scared of me. I'm nothing but an unmotivated private with no aptitude whatsoever. Least that's what they tell me. Name's Jimmy. I'm worried you ain't eating. I got a nice pot of joe for you and Cheezees, too. Shame to waste it."

I said nothing, but Jimmy didn't leave. He considered me at length and said, "If you don't eat, I have to report you to the base doctor, and, myself, I hate goin' to that doctor. He uses rectal thermometers just for the meanness of it."

I knew the word "doctor," and it terrified me. Fortunately, I didn't know the term "rectal," or I would have become unhinged.

"You moved!" Jimmy cried. "Thank the Lord. I don't know what they'd do to me if you passed. I'm going to bring this tray right to you in case you're feeling too poorly to come get it."

I heard him set the tray down.

"I ain't supposed to be in here," Jimmy continued, "'cause they're experimenting to see what long-term solitary does to a body. Anybody with any sense ought to know it ain't going to do nothing good. Can't imagine what a poor critter like you done to score time at the bottom of this bunghole. Me, I like critters, even ugly ones. Had a pet possum once."

As this gentle stream of words washed over me, I relaxed. He was chatty like Trudie. I felt a pang of loneliness and stifled a sob.

"You okay in there? I'm gonna take a peek under your covers to make sure everything's copacetic."

He raised the corner of my blanket. I felt harsh light on my face, but I kept my eyes closed. "Whoa Nellie," he said, "you make my possum look like Betty Grable. You are plug ugly. But we're all God's critters, so I don't hold it against you, Mr. Plug. But I will have to hold it against you if you don't eat."

Jimmy held a Cheezee under my proboscis, and a rumble rose from my sunken belly. I tried to keep my proboscis still, but it followed the treat as Jimmy waved it back and forth. Then he put the Cheezee between his lips. Abruptly, he grabbed my proboscis with one hand and my lower mandible with the other. He pried my maw open and blew the Cheezee into it. I sputtered. Jimmy rubbed my throat, forcing me to swallow.

I sat up and used my foulest language to tell him what I thought of the indignity perpetrated upon my carcass.

"Dang, if you don't quack just like a duck," Jimmy said. He issued a spasmodic sound that made me laugh.

"Now you sound like a duck on helium." He slapped his thigh and made the sound again. I realized it was laughter. The human and Utorbian laughter echoed off the concrete walls until I grew weak.

"You look done in, Mr. Plug. How 'bout some joe? I made it fresh. Hope you like it strong." Jimmy took a towel off the pot and poured the coffee into a tin cup. I almost swooned from the aroma. My willpower gave way, and I grabbed the cup and dumped it into my mug wart, which heated it to a temperature that would have scalded a human. I curled my long tongue into a tube and sipped. It was the strongest, best coffee I had ever tasted. I finished it and ran my tongue around the empty mug wart.

"If that don't beat all." Jimmy picked up the pot. "There's more if you want it."

I twisted so that my mug wart was closer to Jimmy. He filled it and poured Cheezees onto the tray. I took one and gestured for Jimmy to do the same.

"Why, thank you, Mr. Plug. Don't mind if I do."

We sat companionably on the floor of that tiny concrete room until the Cheezees were gone and the pot empty. All the while, Jimmy talked. The words soothed me. I was sad when he said, "The night guy comes on duty in half an hour, so I reckon I better git. When he comes, I'll turn the speaker back on. You pretend nothing whatsoever happened." He left.

After the door had closed, I waddled over to the toilet. I looked in and saw my countenance staring back at me. Except that it was changed. Instead of a flat gray, it was tinged with a radiant orange. I wiped at it, to see if the color was merely dust from my Cheezees. It was not dust; it was me. The essence of the Cheezees had tinted me from within. I held up my limb terminals. They remained gray, but I saw hints of the color higher on my limbs. I felt a bubble of happiness. I had heard the humans call me "butt ugly," but I was orange, and orange was beautiful. I gazed, now and then gently touching the surface of the water with my pod and watching the ripples shiver my Cheezee-hued countenance.

Jimmy sat with me every day, talking until I understood him quite well. One morning, he pulled a book out from under his shirt. "If anybody saw this," he said, "it would ruin my reputation. But I thought I could teach you to read so's you'd have something to pass the time."

The book was entitled *Fun with Dick and Jane*. It was not fun. No, it was not. Not fun fun fun. Not at all. No, Dick. It was not fun. Easy to understand? Yes yes yes. But no, it was not fun. After Jimmy had read it to me, I shook my head sadly, depressed at what it told me about the cultural attainments of the human race.

Realizing he had insulted my intelligence, Jimmy brought me better books. He's the one who gave me *Alice in Wonderland*. "This one was my little sister's favorite growing up," he said. I fell deeply in love with Alice. Her courage in the face of the shocking and perplexing phenomena visited upon her small person was truly inspirational.

My ability to understand the human language increased as I listened to Jimmy read and watched his index finger follow the words across the page.

Jimmy also brought me *Gulliver's Travels*, and then Webster's Dictionary, which he allowed me to keep hidden under my blanket.

One day, he brought a pad of paper and a pencil. "Thought you might want to try writing," he said, "although I ain't sure if you can hold a pencil with those pie plate hands."

I stretched out an upper limb terminal and showed Jimmy that the webbing between my phalanges was retractable. It was an Introduced Genetic Modification that allowed significantly more functionality. I could use my upper limb terminals as suction cups, as a container, or I could roll back the webbing to free my phalanges to perform tasks requiring great manual dexterity. "Damn," Jimmy said as he watched. I took the pencil from his hand and discovered that it was not difficult to maneuver. Nor were English letters hard to master. Soon I was writing notes to Jimmy, telling him all about Utorb.

Jimmy loved my stories about Utorb, but he burned them with a lighter and flushed them down the toilet when he was done.

"Don't let on to anybody you can write," he said. "If you tell the Army where you come from, they'll just go bomb it. Talk about a bunch of people who can't leave well enough alone. If it was me, I wouldn't tell 'em anything at all."

I thought of *Uyiquiti Ri Ga* and resolved to follow Jimmy's advice.

Jimmy explained many things to me, the most useful of which being the arrangement of power in the Army. I had already figured out the order of the ranks and general protocol, but Jimmy introduced to me a host of useful subtleties. He sat cross-legged on the floor, drinking coffee from his battered mess cup and elucidating the finer points of terminology. "Now there's a difference, see, between an ass kisser and a brown noser. The brown noser is in deeper. He don't even try to hide it. He's got no shame. He don't understand why it don't get him ahead. He's too obvious. The brass would be embarrassed to promote him. Brown nosers get bitter.

"Now an ass kisser, on the other hand, is more subtle. He can move pretty far up the ranks, particularly if the people above him is ass kissers, too. His problem comes when he ends up working for somebody smart with some common sense. Believe it or not, the Army's got those, too. The Army's got more kinds of brass than a marching band."

Jimmy described the characteristics of each species in detail. "It ain't important what rank is on a man's shoulder, what matters is what rank he is in his head. First, you got what I call the 'minus ones.' Their minds is one rank below. Their men hate 'em, because they're always trying to do their jobs for 'em. Meanwhile, minus ones don't have a clue as to how to do the job they got.

"The opposite of the minus ones is the 'starry eyes.' They don't think a private is human. They're movin' up, and they got no time to notice how many heads a man's got. They got a golden glow. They ain't mean. To be mean to a man, you got to notice him."

I nodded. I had seen both types on Utorb.

"Now you know who you really got to watch out for? That's the 'third timers.' They've been promoted too far. They're in over their heads and goin' down for the third time. They're looking for somebody to grab hold of and take down with 'em. You gotta steer clear of them."

I pointed to Jimmy.

"Me? I'm the type that does his damnedest to lower expectations to the point where it ain't no trouble to live up to them." He laughed. "Play it right, and it's a sweet life. You make it look like you're trying your best. You got to have a happy, dumb grin—I got that down pat. You got to be the most mannerly, good-natured old boy on the base. Helps to forget every bit of grammar Mrs. Smiley ever taught you in the ninth grade and play up the accent, because up here in the north, they look down on southerners. I got it down to the point where they're thrilled with me if I can figure out how to peel a potato. Hell, I even learned to enjoy peeling potatoes. I do it real slow and careful. I pay attention to every lump and bump in that spud and take the peel off thinner than any man in the whole damn US Army. They don't have the heart to yell at me because I try so hard. I lowered their expectations to the point where they're happy if I don't try to stuff the spud up my nose.

"That's how I got this job. They said, 'Private Hildebrand, this assignment is so simple, even you can't screw it up.' Here Jimmy laughed until he started to cough. "All you have to do is open the bag and pour some of these Cheezees on a tray. You make a pot of coffee and put that on the tray, too. You slide the tray through this opening. Then you watch him through this little window. Do not make any contact with the alien and do not speak to him, because he's in solitary." Jimmy continued to laugh. "I made them show me three times how to make coffee."

※

One day, Jimmy came in walking strangely. He said, "Funniest thing happened last night. You know a Mr. Avery Stanton?"

My proboscis shriveled as I remembered flying through the air in a garbage can. My body jerked with the memory of how first one, then a second vehicle crashed into me.

Jimmy watched my reaction intently. "Looks like you don't like him much."

An amusing understatement, but I didn't laugh.

"Tell you the truth, he didn't look trustworthy to me, either." Jimmy poured my mug wart full of coffee, but he didn't sit down as usual. "I took in a movie last night—good one with Tracy and Hepburn. At first I didn't notice the guy watching me. He wasn't obvious about it, but I got up to get popcorn and saw him sitting three rows back. He'd slouched down in his seat, trying not to call any notice, but he stuck out like a sore thumb. Money and attitude. You can't hide 'em. Especially out in the bare-ass middle of nowhere.

"After the movie, he followed me outside. I turned around and asked him what he wanted. He said, 'Just a few moments of your time.' I laughed in his face. When somebody says that, believe you me, they want a lot more. Know what he wanted?"

I started to shake my head, but then I considered and pointed to myself.

"Right you are. Offered me good money, too. Had a cockamamie plan to sneak you out of here hidden in the dirt and rock they bring to the surface. Sounded all kind of dangerous to me, so I said I didn't want his dirty money. Then he offered to pay me to keep quiet about ever meeting him. I did take that. It's enough for plenty of beer and movies with some left over to send home to Mom. I got you a present, too." Jimmy undid his buttons, and I saw why he was standing so strangely. He had a long, flat box inside his shirt. "It's called chess," he said, "and it's my favorite game. I'm right good at it, but I wouldn't let anybody in the Army know that. I'm going to teach you how to play."

※

We were playing chess one day when we heard a sound at the door and saw eyes, angry eyes, at the peephole. Jimmy leaped to his feet, scattering the pieces. He executed a salute as a full bird broke into the room.

Jimmy had told me about this full bird, a Colonel Rodney Crocker. He was what Jimmy called a "Dead-Ender," someone who had gone as high as he ever would. Crocker looked mean to me. A bony ledge of forehead jutted out over small, glittery eyes. The snub nose left an uncomfortable amount of space between his nostrils and his thin upper lip. I watched that lip tense.

"Is this how you take care of a prisoner in *solitary* confinement?" the colonel yelled. "Do you know what the word 'solitary' means, soldier?"

"Yes, sir," Jimmy said. "It means all by your lonesome, sir."

"And is the prisoner alone?"

"No, sir."

"Who is with the prisoner?"

"I am, sir," Jimmy said. He blushed and added, "But I ain't nobody, sir."

Colonel Crocker's head appeared to expand. "I came here to check on the progress of this important operation and I find that it must be started all over again." He noticed the chessboard. "You're playing chess?" he asked.

"I call it horse and people checkers," Jimmy said. "You play it just like checkers only with horses and people."

"Who put this idiot in this job?" Crocker turned. Officers of lesser rank stood just outside the door.

I didn't hear the answer, for Crocker began to scream obscenities. I shut my eyes and didn't see what happened next. The door closed, and all was quiet. I opened my eyes, and Jimmy was gone. I never saw him again.

The speaker in the ceiling crackled.

> You are in the custody of the United States of America. You will never return to your planet. Your people don't know where you are. They can't help you. You will never see them again. You depend on Americans for everything. You belong to the United States of America, body and soul.

23

LLADRó

Lloyd spent most of his time at the office. It was winter of 1953, and the temporary suspension of his clearances had been long forgotten. Even Faye had stopped throwing it in his face. She had quit nagging him about his hours. Perhaps he had finally convinced her of the seriousness of his job. Lloyd envied men who had wives working at the Mines. They didn't have to conceal the largest part of their lives from their partners. A mixed marriage—one spouse cleared and the other uncleared, one at war and the other convinced the world was at peace—was bound to be shaky. But perhaps his marriage had weathered the worst of it. When Lloyd went off to a three-day training session in the Maryland hills, he missed Faye's pretty face.

When he returned, he was alarmed to find uncollected mail cramming his box. He carried it inside and dumped it on the table. He caught sight of Faye's handwriting on a pale pink envelope. The truth didn't sink in until he had read the letter twice. Faye had stopped nagging him because she no longer cared. While he was away, she had fled to the M Street townhouse of a senior official of the United States Postal Service.

Lloyd should have known, but it hit him with the force of a stroke. He collapsed into a chair and stared at the letter, addressed in her swift, neat hand.

She'd fallen in love, she wrote, noting that her new amour was a GS-18 and lived downtown, which was where she wanted to be. Lloyd was "more than a little strange" and "no fun anymore." *I'm less fun than a GS-18 postal official?* Lloyd thought. Faye still considered Lloyd a "dear friend." She listed the furniture, knickknacks, and dishes she wanted. "It's only fair that I get these things," she wrote. "Please use lots of newspaper to pack my angels."

Does she think I'll roll over and give her a divorce? Lloyd had rolled over and given Faye almost everything she'd asked for during their marriage. Well, this time he wasn't going to cave. No divorce. Not now. Not ever. Lloyd balled up the letter and threw it across the room. It hit the nasty pink and green trellis wallpaper he'd hung only a few weeks ago. She must have been planning to leave him then. Why did she insist he do it?

Lloyd stared at the wallpaper until it blurred and darkened around the edges. Another migraine was coming on. A strong cup of coffee might temper the pain, but he didn't have the energy to get out of his chair and make it.

An hour later, Lloyd's vision returned to normal, and the pain set in. He stretched out on the couch with an ice pack and tried to will himself into a state of nonbeing.

An odd idea floated up out of the pain. He could call Lee, and she would come take care of him, give him some drug that would alter his consciousness for a day or so. He quickly dismissed the idea and shivered at the wrongness of it. They had developed an odd relationship over the past few years, almost Oedipal in its sensitivity and complexity. She watched over him like a mother—although she would be appalled at the comparison. She took care of him during incidents and, from her own soft hand, gave him pills that sometimes had a pleasant effect. He had grown dependent. He resented her, almost hated her, almost loved her. He struggled to put her out of his mind.

When the phone rang on the nightstand next to his head, it jangled every nerve. Lloyd grabbed the thing to keep it from ringing again.

"Hello," he said.

"My, aren't we grumpy today." It took a few seconds for Lloyd to place the voice. When he did, he almost hung up. But Lloyd's mother had hammered politeness into him from an early age. He sank back down onto his pillow and said, "Hello, Avery."

"You can call me boss."

Lloyd sat up abruptly, and his head punished him with a shooting pain. He fought through it and made his voice firm. "No, absolutely not. I will not work for you again."

"Have I ever mentioned that I'm a close personal friend of Elliot Ludden?"

A pall of inevitability closed over Lloyd's head. "Repeatedly."

"Ludden would like you to work for me. Unless you want to try to get an appointment with him and talk him out of it, I suggest you get used to the idea."

Lloyd pressed his palm to his forehead and wondered whether it would be possible for a man to crush his own skull. It would be worth trying.

"I got you another promotion," Avery said. "You're

welcome. I'll be at you house in twenty minutes so we can discuss the particulars. I don't need directions. I know where you live."

"Leave me alone," Lloyd said. "I have a migraine. I like what I'm doing now. I—"

"See you in a few minutes." Avery hung up.

Lloyd opened the door to a smiling Avery. The man had a few new creases around his eyes, and his golden hair was thinning, but he still had that blinding, movie-star polish that made it difficult to guess what he was thinking.

"You look like grim death," Avery said.

Lloyd pointed his guest to a chair and sat back down on the couch, clutching his ice bag to his head. "I still have nightmares about you. What foul wind has blown you back into my life?"

Avery's eyes wandered the room. "Your place is precious. I see someone likes adorable angel figurines. You?"

"My wife," Lloyd snapped. "The one who just left me. Don't mention her again or I'll bean you with a Hummel."

"I'm sorry for your difficulty," Avery said.

Lloyd opened one eye and saw that the leer had faded from Avery's face, replaced with a look akin to genuine sympathy. "I heard about the Albania operation," Lloyd said quietly. Word of the colossal failure had spread through the Mines the year before. "You have my sympathies, as well."

"If I don't get to mention your wife, you don't get to mention Albania," Avery said coldly.

Lloyd nodded. "The work I'm doing now is important. I have extensive knowledge on the subject. It would be a loss to my office if I left."

"I know you're with Goldfarb and the Human Ecology Staff, but I don't know what you're working on," Avery said.

"At the moment, Beria."

Avery considered this. "Worthwhile, but not as important as my project. Don't worry, your knowledge won't go to waste."

"I hate to ask," Lloyd said, "but what is your project and why do you need me?"

"I'll answer the second question first. I need you because you're read into HALFSHEEP."

Lloyd started. "That compartment died with the alien."

"Our hideous little friend is still alive."

Lloyd shook his head. "Impossible. No creature could have survived that crash."

"No earth creature. Our mistake was underestimating him." Avery plucked a delicate Lladró angel from the coffee table and turned it in his hands as he spoke. "I found out he was alive a few years ago. My brother-in-law let it slip. It took me a while to discover where he was being kept. It's an underground facility in the Nevada desert."

"Do I have to remind you of the last piece of intelligence you got from your brother-in-law?" Lloyd recalled the excruciating night at the Gilman Tunnels.

"I found another source and confirmed the alien's location. They're running an experiment on the effects of solitary confinement on the brain. At the end of it, they plan to give our alien a series of tests, and then dissect him."

"Kill him?" Lloyd was appalled.

"He's a hearty little fellow, but I doubt he can survive

having his brain sliced like a salami. They would have done it already except that they found out that the private responsible for feeding him was playing chess with him. So they had to start the period of solitary over again."

"The alien can play chess?" Lloyd asked.

"What surprises me was that the private could play chess. He was a real yokel. A while ago, I tried to bribe him to help me kidnap the alien, but he refused. Odd man. I dropped the matter because I had to go back overseas."

Albania, Lloyd thought.

"Last month, I remembered that it was about time for them to dissect the alien, so I took the issue directly to Ludden. He came up with the most ingenious plan."

"How many felonies will I be required to commit?" Lloyd asked.

"None."

The idea of saving the alien appealed to Lloyd. It was something he could do for Trudie. Their relationship remained distant, but when they did speak, she always asked if he knew what had happened to Martia. It would be wonderful to tell her that Martia was fine. That would be a security violation, but for once he was willing to break the rules if it made his sister feel better.

"Okay," Lloyd said, "I'm on board. As if I had a choice."

"You don't, but I like volunteers. By the way, are you still acting erratic?"

"The after effects of what they gave me in Hungary have subsided. But my damned Mines psychiatrist still gives me drugs that leave me worthless for a day or so."

Avery's face grew keen. "They've been giving you more drugs?"

"I don't want to talk about it."

"Fine." Avery held up the slender Lladró angel. "You

obviously feel like hell. You're seething with anger, and rightly so. No wonder your head aches. So why are you taking it out on yourself while allowing these fragile idiocies to exist?" Avery handed the figurine to Lloyd. "I have to be going. I'll contact you in four days. If memory serves, that's how long it takes for one of your migraines to wear off. I'll see myself out."

When the door closed, Lloyd hurled the Lladró angel across the room and watched it shatter against the wall. The pain in his head eased a bit. It occurred to him that the porcelain would be so much easier to pack in pieces.

24

THE MOST WONDROUS THING

The bus stopped at a light about a block from the terminal. Lloyd swiped a gloved hand over the glass to clear the frost. He saw her pacing in front of the building, bent into the wind with a long, determined stride. She would prefer the bitter cold to the cigarette haze of the waiting room. She wore their father's old sheepskin coat. The familiarity of it caught in his throat.

When Lloyd hugged Trudie, he smelled horses in her hair. It made him cry, or maybe it was just her presence. Growing up, when he was hurt or upset, he ran to Trudie. Lloyd pinched the bridge of his nose hard. That was his way of getting tears under control.

Trudie's voice was firm but kind. "I'm sorry she hurt you, but I'm not sorry she left you. Her character was flimsy as a dime store chair. It was bound to give way on you. Get in the truck. You can curse her cheating tail all the way home."

Lloyd threw his briefcase in the back of the truck and pulled the heavy door open. The smell of manure, dried blood, damp wool, and sour milk washed over him. It obliterated decades, a world war, a cold war, a betrayal. It brought the tears back to his eyes.

Trudie apologized. "I meant to clean up. Just knock that stuff on the floor. No, let me do it. You're wearing good clothes." Trudie pushed past Lloyd. She grabbed a bloody chain and cane and stuffed them into the space behind the seat. "Would you believe Belle dropped a filly this morning? This time of year and at her age? I had to give her considerable help."

Lloyd felt a moment of panic. "Is she okay?"

"Right as rain. She's a tough old girl. Like me."

Trudie went around to the driver's side. Lloyd climbed in and sat down on an old horse blanket that covered the split seat. He set his feet down carefully on a wooden box of veterinary equipment that nested on the floor in a welter of yellowed newspapers.

Inhibited by the presence of buildings, traffic, and people, Lloyd said nothing. It had been a year since he had seen Trudie. From the corner of his eye, he looked for changes in her, and he knew she was doing the same with him.

She appeared not so much older as rougher, more windburned and chapped. The Pilcrows' pale complexions didn't bear the elements well. In the winter, Trudie wore her thick, crimped hair about her shoulders for an extra layer of warmth. It saddened Lloyd that his sister, who had grown up aching for an East Coast education, would look as out of place on one of those campuses now as a coyote walking down Constitution Avenue. He looked for some sign of happiness or sadness, some hint of how things were going for her, but all he saw was determination on her face.

When the truck left El Claustro for the open road,

Lloyd finally spoke. "I don't mean to dump my troubles in your lap," he said, raising his voice above the noise of the ancient engine. "I came to tell you some good news."

Trudie's eyeglasses had a queer way of jumping on her nose when she raised her brows. The sight gratified Lloyd. It had been a long time since he had brought her a good surprise. He smiled. "You always say I'm such a goody-two-shoes, but I want you to know I'm committing a felony by telling you this."

"What?" The eyeglasses jumped again. "My little brother doesn't break rules."

"I've finally realized that rules don't guarantee fairness, or safety, or goodness or anything else. They're just rules."

"Took you long enough."

Lloyd turned to look out the window. He found comfort in the frigid emptiness of the landscape. In Washington, he had to be intensely careful about what he said. He had altered his speaking pattern to include pauses to review all the usual questions. What was the listener's level of clearance? What was the source of the information he was about to impart? Did the listener have a need to know? Out here, in the face of a fierce wind that eventually eroded everything, it was hard to remember why such things were important. It didn't matter that Trudie had no clearances; she had a need to know. He took his glasses off and wiped them on the tail of his coat. "I'm going to work on a special project. The Mines is getting Martia back from the Army. I'll be on the team that will work with her."

Trudie sat up straight in her seat, and her hands gripped the wheel tighter. "Martia? My alien?"

"The same."

The opaque determination dissolved to reveal clear blue eyes full of happiness. "My god, my god, my god. Sometimes I look back on that and think I dreamed it all. Then I get depressed because that was the most wondrous occurence of my life. How is she? Have you seen her yet? Do you know what condition she's in?"

"I haven't seen her, but as far as I know she's healthy. I'll see her in two weeks."

"Where is she?"

"I can't tell you that. I play more loosely with the rules than I used to, but I try to limit myself to one felony a day." Lloyd smiled, a thing that made him almost handsome. The years had tempered his awkward features with tolerance, kindness, and a rueful bemusement that became him. "I would appreciate it if you wouldn't say anything about this to Earl," Lloyd said. "I know married couples shouldn't keep secrets, but—"

"Don't worry," Trudie said. "I don't tell Earl anything."

The opacity came back into Trudie's eyes. Lloyd opened his mouth, then thought better of doing something profoundly stupid, like asking Trudie how things were between her and her husband.

"After you see her, will you come back here and tell me how she is? Every detail?" Trudie turned her beautiful eyes on her brother.

"I promise."

※

Lloyd reached up to hang his coat on the old rack made of horn. It was gone. He gave Trudie a questioning look.

"Earl broke it," she said. "I threw it out."

"I wouldn't think you could break that thing with a

sledgehammer." Lloyd's eyes scanned the room.

"You'll find a lot of things are broken," Trudie said. "I'm sorry if any of them were yours."

"He hasn't hit you, has he? You tell me the truth because if he has—"

"No, Lloyd."

"Trudie—"

"I can take care of myself and I won't discuss it with you. I'll put your coat in the closet."

Lloyd had never been able to win an argument with his sister. He handed over the coat and made a note to himself to talk to Earl.

"If you talk to Earl, it will only make things worse," Trudie said.

Lloyd shook his head. "After all the years I've spent in my line of work, you shouldn't be able to read me like that. I must be practicing bad tradecraft."

Trudie made a noise in her nose. "Some of the things you men call 'tradecraft' are what we women call 'things we were born knowing.' Come in the kitchen. I'll fix you coffee while you tell me why you're still wearing that damned wedding ring."

Lloyd felt like a little boy again. "You never tell me anything about problems in your marriage, why should I tell you why I'm still wearing this ring?"

Trudie gave him a look that took him back to his grade school days. "You will tell me because I insist. It's not healthy to hang onto things that should be released. Are you going to refuse that woman a divorce?"

Lloyd crossed his arms in front of his chest. "I am. I took a vow. She took a vow."

"What happens when you corner an animal?" Trudie asked. "It strikes out. It gets dangerous. Every critter deserves a way out, even your cheating wife. Give it to her, Lloyd."

That day, Lloyd stalked off to his old room but two weeks later when Trudie dropped him off at the bus terminal, he took her hand and dropped the ring into it. "Payment for good advice," he said. "Sell it and buy yourself something nice."

25

THE STENCH OF A DYING LIVER

I hadn't seen the local star since I descended into the ground. I had no concept of how much time had passed since Jimmy left. I knew from Mr. Webster that a year comprised twelve months; a month, four weeks; a week, seven days; a day, twenty-four hours; an hour, sixty minutes; and a minute, sixty seconds. Because I had no idea of what a "second" might be, however, I was left in blinding ignorance. I guessed that years, months, weeks, days, minutes, and seconds had passed—enough time for me to memorize Mr. Webster's dictionary and learn the limitations of circular reasoning.

I was reading my dictionary when the door opened. I sprang to the ceiling and clung next to the bare light bulb. Mr. Webster clattered to the floor.

"Get it down. I don't want it above my head."

"Yes, sir, Senator McAffey."

One private knocked me to the floor with a broom. Another dragged me to the outer room, which was full of visitors: two privates, Colonel Crocker, a three star, and three men in gray garments.

"Are you sure it's not dangerous?" Senator McAffey asked. His garments were gray, but his hide was colorful. It had a yellow cast and was marbled with red veins, especially on the upper cheek and dented bulb of his nose.

A bullet-headed three star spoke up. "Yes, Senator. Its temperament was mild throughout the study and experimentation phase."

The senator squinted at me. "It's orange," he said in a way that suggested he didn't appreciate the gorgeousness of the color.

"Yes, sir," said the three star. "Its diet consists entirely of Cheezees and coffee. It turned orange over the years since it crashed. Originally it was gray."

"Male or female?" the senator asked.

"That has not been determined, even though a surgeon opened it up to take a look. It has confusing sexual organs," said the three star.

"Questionable gonads, you say?" The senator screwed up his eyes. "Make it walk."

The three star motioned for the privates to let go of me. I didn't move, so one of them gave me a shove. I walked to the other end of the room and back, feeling self-conscious about my dwarfish limbs and protuberant belly.

The senator's facial muscles twitched. "It's a goddamn *homosexual*," he pronounced. "See the way it minces?"

The visitors leaned away. Their eyes narrowed, and their nostrils flared.

Then I noticed the odor that hung about the senator. It grew stronger when he was agitated. My proboscis shrank from the smell. It was partly alcohol—a reek that often lingered on the breath of army personnel—but it was also something I had smelled on Utorb. I remembered the screamer who shared my room before the launch. He had given off the sour scent of fear, desperation, and impending death. I shuddered to recognize the same scent now. The senator was, to use Jimmy's phrase, a third timer. I trembled.

The senator spoke in a voice seething with vexation. "A *homosexual*. How can it be that no one in the US Army figured that out?"

The three star spoke with hesitation. "Well, Senator McAffey, the alien has never exhibited—"

Rage contorted the senator's face. "It's not an alien! Do I understand you correctly that the US Army has never figured that out?" He looked around. "Anyone? Is it a safe statement to say that no one has figured it out?"

The muscles in the three star's neck began to jump. "We have photographs documenting the crash site," he said.

McAffey stared at the three star. "Do I understand you to say that you have no *real* evidence that the vehicle came from outer space? Is that right?"

The three star squared his shoulders as his color rose. "Sir, there is not another creature on Earth like this one."

McAffey clasped his hands behind his back. "Let me ask you this: Have you been everywhere on Earth, General?"

"No, of course not, sir."

"Specifically, have you ever been to the Soviet Union, General Perkowski. Perkowski is a Russian name, is it not?"

"Perkowski is a Polish name, sir, and I have never been to the Soviet Union."

The senator seemed to take these words as an affront.

"There is no substantive difference between Communist Russia and Communist Poland. He pointed a finger at the three star. "Let me ask you again, have you ever been to the Soviet Union or any of its Communist satellite states up to and including Poland?"

"No, sir."

"Not even Poland?"

"No, sir, I was born in Wisconsin." The expression on the general's face did not vary, but the color of his cheeks and neck was in constant flux between white and red. I felt his confusion, for the lines of authority—which were generally quite clear in the Army, forming straight verticals and horizontals that met at clean ninety-degree angles—were here askew, and not at all what they seemed.

The senator continued, "If you have never been to these enemy states, then you don't know if they have creatures such as this, do you?"

"No, sir, but—"

"But what?" asked the senator. "I haven't heard a straight answer out of you yet. Are you intensely loyal to the United States of America, General?"

"Yes, sir," the general said. "I served under Patton in North Africa, sir. I lost three toes."

"And do you think three toes are an adequate sacrifice for your country?" the senator asked.

The general opened his mouth to reply, closed it, swallowed, and opened it again. "I would have given more had they been required."

The red vessels in the senator's face grew more prominent. "The important thing here, General Perkowski, is that this is no alien." He pointed his finger at me. "Do you know what it is?"

Resignation showed on the three star's face. "No, sir."

The senator turned to the man who stood behind him. "Mr. Ludden, would you like to tell him or should I?"

I had taken little notice of Mr. Ludden, for he was quite still. Now I saw that he had a square jaw and round glasses. Behind those glasses was a pair of eyes as shrewd as Deyahm's, but lacking the kindness. Then I saw that the man standing behind Mr. Ludden was Avery Stanton. He winked at me, and my heart stumbled.

"You do the honors, Senator," Mr. Ludden said.

McAffey made a huffing noise through his nostrils. "The damn thing is obviously a Soviet spy. Don't you see? They've taken an adolescent example of one of their shorter races—say an Uzbekistani—and surgically altered him. Elliot, I want the CIA to take over for the Army."

General Perkowski allowed a thought meant solely for the interior of his head to burst out. "But you don't get along with the CIA."

McAffey scowled. "Elliot and I have come to an understanding." He turned to Ludden. "We'll make it happen. I want a team of your best doctors, your best technical experts, and your best operatives to evaluate this thing. I'm not pleased with the way the Army has handled the situation. Not at all. Once your boys have done the initial evaluation, Elliot, you can transfer it to the CIA."

The three star protested. "The Army has plans to dissect the alien's brain next month. This is part of an experiment that has been years in the making."

"How are you going to interrogate it if you dissect it?" the senator asked.

"We can't interrogate it. It doesn't understand English," the general said.

"O course, not," McAffey said. "Have you tried speaking to it in Uzbekistani?"

"No, Sir."

"Well, there you go. Elliot, do you have Uzbekistani speakers?"

"Two Uzbek speakers," Elliot said. "What about funding, sir? We'll have to prepare a special facility—"

"Whatever you need, Elliot. I'll make sure you get it."

Elliot executed the subtle, closed-lipped smile of a man who has gotten what he wanted all along. I realized that the confused lines of authority in the room were not confused at all. They radiated from this man. Ludden was Earth's Supreme Overseer, and I was about to fall under his control.

26

THE UZBEK

My toilet font imparted a feeling of wealth and security. In my loneliness, I befriended him and named him Sir Cheshire because, like the teeth of Alice's feline, he gleamed perfect and white.

I was about to lose Sir Cheshire just as I had lost Trudie and Jimmy.

I stared into his water, blowing air and watching ripples crease my orange reflection. Suddenly the infernal speaker, which had blared non-stop since Jimmy's departure, cut off on the word "custody." The door banged open, and I leaped to the ceiling. A private scraped me down with a broom. They dragged me into the outer room where Colonel Crocker waited.

More people flowed in on furtive feet and hovered on the periphery. They wore unmatched garments lacking stars, stripes, birds, or other fandangle. Civilians. I was about to get a lesson in human anthropology.

Colonel Crocker cleared his throat. The army men snapped to attention while the civilians slouched and exchanged looks. "In preparation for the transfer of the alien, the US Army has compiled guidelines for its care and handling." Crocker held up a sheet of paper. A sour glance rolled around the periphery of the room. The colonel read, "Number one: the Army agrees to provide protection for the Agency team during the evaluation phase. Private Harper and Private Jensen will—"

"No, they will not." Avery Stanton stepped forward. "The CIA does not agree to have army personnel in the room during the testing."

Crocker held up a hand, "For the safety of the Mines team, it is necessary—"

"It's the size of a three-year-old. We'll take our chances." I looked up when I heard the laughing female voice. She wore trousers like the men, but everything else about her was more deliberate and defined. Her upper garment was crisp and white, and her claws and lips were sharp and red.

"Ma'am," Crocker said, "with all due respect—"

Avery cut the colonel off. "What are the rest of your rules? I'd like to get underway. Please summarize."

Crocker scowled. "Suit yourselves, but the Army takes no responsibility for accidents. In the closet, you will find a leg irons and chain. You'll notice iron rings in the floor there, there, and there. We suggest that you keep the creature chained at all times. I can have Private—"

"Not necessary," Avery said. "We'll handle it. Continue."

"The alien is fed twice daily," the Crocker said. "In the closet, you will find—"

"Cheezees and coffee. We can handle that."

Crocker's jaw clenched. He relaxed it enough to speak. "Coffee is poured directly into the vessel-like growth on the alien's shoulder. At no time should any other utensil be in this room while the alien is out. Lock them in the closet. I see you brought a lot of gear with you. No furniture or equipment should be brought into the room unless the alien is secured to the floor. It must be kept well out of its reach."

"Gotcha," Avery said. "We can read the rest for ourselves. We have a few rules of our own. This is a Top Secret compartmented operation. You, sir, are not cleared to know the name of the compartment. At no time should army personnel enter this room. Those are the conditions agreed to between Elliot Ludden and the Secretary of Defense. I have a paper signed by both." He pulled an envelope out of his coat pocket, extracted the paper, and handed it to Crocker.

The colonel's jaw muscles wrestled with each other as he read. Then he came to something that pleased him. "It says here the Agency has agreed to conduct the follow-up tests that the Army was planning to do."

"Yes, except for the dissection of the brain," Avery said.

"But the dissection is the most important part," Crocker protested.

Avery smiled. "Yes, but it will ruin the alien." He held up a hand. "Correction: it will ruin the Uzbek spy."

Crocker scanned the sheet. "When will you turn over the results of your tests?"

"Nowhere on that paper does it say we have to."

Crocker adopted a wide-legged stance and placed his hands on his hips. "Well, we don't have to give you our results either."

"We already have them." Avery's face glowed pink, and I thought he might giggle. "Colonel Crocker, I suggest you get a better negotiator next time you deal with the

CIA."

Red blotches marched across Crocker's face. "Mr. Stanton, I will leave you with these instructions." He handed his sheet of paper over. "The Army has had custody of the alien since 1947. You should take advantage of our experience."

Avery took the sheet. "Thank you, Colonel Crocker. I'll read this avidly. Now if you will excuse us, we would like to get underway."

Crocker left, followed by his underlings. As soon as the door closed, Avery crumpled the sheet of paper and flung it toward the door. The others stood quietly and listened as the steps faded away. The female bubbled up with laughter. Then they were all laughing.

Avery squatted to get a better look at me. "You haven't gotten any lovelier over the years. What do you think, Lloyd? Has the orange improved its appearance?"

Lloyd? I looked up, and there he was, frowning down at me.

"Bizarre," he said.

"They say you are what you eat, and this thing has had nothing but Cheezees since it landed," Avery said.

"Do you want me to go get the chains?" said a young, eager-looking human.

"No need, Carl. Let's get moved in. Put the folding table by that wall and set up the polygraph. Lights and camera go over there. Lee, dear, make a pot of coffee; it's going to be a long day."

"I don't make coffee." Lee's words pricked like needles. She busied herself unpacking a case.

"You don't know how to make coffee?" Avery asked.

"I know how. I don't make it on principle. I'm your colleague, not your wife or your mother. If I make your coffee, soon you'll be asking me to do your laundry. I don't make coffee. That is non-negotiable. I'm here as a psychiatrist." She slammed the case shut.

The men's eyes rolled in their sockets.

Lloyd spoke up. "Trust me, you don't want Lee making the coffee unless you want to take an unscheduled trip to Hell."

Avery seemed amused. "Her coffee is that bad?"

"She only makes coffee to hide drugs in it."

Avery squinted at Lee, and she returned the look without flinching. "Henry," he yelled, "make the fucking coffee. After this, everyone will take turns making coffee, except for Miss Ogilvie."

"It's Dr. Ogilvie." She began to lay out stacks of brightly colored cards. I recognized them from the army tests.

The team set to work in earnest, hauling cases into the room, opening them, and pulling out gizmos, doohickeys, utensils, and apparatuses. I crawled into the smaller room and hid behind Sir Cheshire.

Chairs scraped, hinges squeaked, and metal tinked against metal. Voices called back and forth. "Anybody bring a Phillips screwdriver?" "Check in that box." "Can you hold the other end of this while I adjust the height?" "No, turn it in the other direction." "Have you swept for bugs?" "I'm doing it now."

I lost interest in the conversation. I was drifting off to sleep when I realized that it had gone quiet in the other room.

"It's time," Avery said. "You want to do the honors, Lloyd?"

"Sure."

Someone rattled a bag of Cheezees. "You want some of these to lure it out?"

"I don't think that will be necessary," Lloyd said. He came in and knelt by Sir Cheshire. "Martia," he whispered, "please come out."

I hesitated, but I loved the name 'Martia' and had not heard it for a long time. I took Lloyd's hand, and he led me out.

"Well I'll be," Avery said. "Lloyd, you do have a way with alleged alien Communist homosexual Uzbekistanis."

"Alleged alien my eye," Lloyd said. "I saw the one crash site that wasn't fake."

Avery nodded. "Why don't you tell us about finding the crash site. Henry and Vince will monitor the alien's responses. That will give us an idea of whether or not it understands what we say. It doesn't look that smart, but then it comes from a race intelligent enough to build a rocket and send it into space."

"Maybe it's not a member of that race," Lee said. "Perhaps the dominant race sent a member of a less dominant species just to see if it would survive."

Avery shrugged. "I suppose that's a possibility. Pour me a cup of black, dear."

Lee poured a cup, added two white squares from a box, and stirred it with a spoon. She took a sip of the coffee and turned her back to Avery. "Pour your own, I need to go over the army test results. I was selected for this team as a psychiatrist, not a waitress."

Avery rolled his eyes. "I didn't select you. You were foisted upon me against my will, because you're Lloyd's babysitter and because the psychiatrist I requested is under investigation by the Inspector General."

"For what?" Lee asked.

"He accidentally killed somebody. Try not to do that."

"I don't plan to do that accidentally or on purpose.

Thank you."

Avery poured his coffee. My proboscis wriggled at the smell.

"Maybe we should give some to the alien," Henry said.

"No," Avery said, "we'll give it to him as a reward when we're done. I don't want caffeine to interfere with any of our experiments." Avery held up the pot, "Do you need some coffee before you start, Lloyd?"

"No, thanks."

"Then bring him over, and we'll hook him up."

Lloyd held out his hand to me again. "It's all right," he said, "nobody will hurt you. I promise."

He didn't convince me, but I gave him my upper limb terminal. What else was there to do? There were six of them, each twice my size, which made it roughly twelve to one, I believe, although mathematics was never a good class for me. Henry led me to a large chair. He motioned for me to sit. I had to climb into it.

Lloyd stepped back, and Henry moved in holding a long, curly, black wire. "This goes around its chest to measure its breathing. Vince, are the lungs in the usual place?"

Vince, a scrawny human with red bumps on his forehead, held a dark sheet to a light. "I have the X-rays from the Army, and photographs from the vivisection, but damn if they aren't a bitch to read. He has more pulmonary organs than a human—at least six lung-like constructions, including those sacs on the side of his nose."

"The things that look like testicles?" Avery turned to Lee. "Excuse my language, dear."

"Thank you, but they told me all about testicles in medical school," Lee said. "I even dissected a pair."

"Somehow that doesn't surprise me," Avery said. "Vince, where should Henry put the sensor coil?"

"I'd tape it down over those sacs on either side of the nose. Although the idea of touching those things gives me the willies."

"I'll hold the coil in place, you tape it down," Henry said.

The men stood over me, pressed the black coil down over my face, and affixed it with white tape. Vince's breath smelled like a rotten carcass I had come across in the desert.

"Now," Henry said, "let's see if we can get a reading." He bent over the machine on the table, making adjustments. "Well, the stylus is moving, but this isn't the pattern you would get from human breathing. It's going to take a while to figure out how to read this. Let's hook up the heart monitor. Vince, where's the heart?"

The doctor shook his head. "Strange circulatory system. He pointed to a light blob on the Xray. "I think this is the heart. It's located higher in the body than the human heart."

Once again Vince and Henry, accompanied by their appalling halitosis and body odor, bent over me. By the time they had finished with the tape, I couldn't move my upper limbs. This recalled my vivisection, and I grew agitated.

"Done," Henry said, "Now how do we monitor blood pressure?"

Henry and Vince began to press their oily human fingers on various places on my body. I cried out in protest.

They laughed, except for Lloyd, who looked depressed. Carl said, "Damned if it doesn't sound just like a duck."

"I think that's its new name: Duck," Vince said, pleased with himself.

"Duck it is," Avery said.

Vince and Henry chuckled as they resumed pawing me. Vince ran his fingers lightly over my face, stopping on my *hackuhl*. I squirmed.

"There, feel that green spot," Vince said. "There's the pulse."

"Bingo," Henry said. "Finally. Let's tape a sensor over that sucker and get this show on the road."

Henry bent over the machine on the table and began to adjust the styluses. Presently he said, "Go ahead Lloyd, tell us about the crash site."

Lloyd sat on a chair with his legs outstretched and crossed at the ankles. He folded his arms over his chest and lowered his head. "I rode out to the place where we found the alien. There wasn't much to see, just a creosote bush in a gully. The trail wasn't hard to follow, but it twisted back on itself. I couldn't decide whether I was tracking a creature who was highly intelligent or highly stupid. The windings of the trail had an almost deliberate complexity, like a labyrinth. I followed it for the better part of the day, but it was so convoluted; I only went about four miles as the crow flies.

"The crash site was in an arroyo. I saw multiple impact sites. The largest was the initial hit. The craft left a round, black imprint. It evidently bounced. I found four more impact sites. It hit up against a solid rock wall and broke up with burning pieces flying in all directions, leaving black trails radiating out. Like somebody had drawn a spider with a blowtorch. That crash must have lit the place for miles." Lloyd looked at me. "I don't know how anything could survive. There was glass that must have been part of a window. It was partially melted. A charred alien's skull was embedded in it. You could see the imprint of the face before it burned. Spookiest thing I've ever seen."

Lloyd closed his eyes and continued.

"This had been moved, dragged onto a flat rock. Other pieces of this alien's body—a limb with a sort of hand attached and part of a shoulder—had also been dragged there and arranged as if someone had tried to put him back together. A wilted cactus flower lay next to it."

One big tear grew in the corner of my eye until its weight dragged it down, and it rolled over the white tape half covering my face.

"That's about it," Lloyd said. "I radioed in the location, and before long I heard a prop plane. Avery's friends dropped like dandelion seeds. They took over the site, packed everything up, and carted it off, to the last grain of blackened sand. Later it was reported that an alien crash site had been discovered near Roswell. That was the Army's diversion. The so-called photographs of the scene were obvious fakes in no way resembling the real crash site."

"Interesting," Avery said. "The alien does appear to understand some of what you're saying."

"Where are the artifacts from the crash site?" Lloyd asked.

"At the Archives. We'll have access," Avery said. "We'll have anything we want. Ludden is behind this one hundred percent."

"Why?" Vince asked. "I don't understand why Ludden got involved with this in the first place. He knows this thing isn't an Uzbek. And why he would kowtow to someone like Jordan McAffey is beyond me. I thought the Mines was the one institution in Washington that wouldn't let McAffey paw through its underwear drawer."

"You underestimate Elliot Ludden," Avery said. "He wanted the alien. McAffey was a convenient and particularly malleable tool. Ludden invited him to his office and told him about an 'alleged alien' being held by the Army, hinting that the Army didn't understand the true nature of this 'alien'—using air quotes to pique McAffey's interest. He led the senator to the conclusion that Duck might be a Communist plant. It didn't take much to move McAffey's rum-addled imagination into high gear."

"But how can he trust a sot like McAffey not to go to the press?" Lloyd asked.

Avery leaned back and laughed. "Picture the story in the Post. 'Senator Jordan McAffey alleged yesterday that an alien held by the US Army since 1947 is a Communist plant. The senator explained that the alleged alien is actually a surgically-altered Uzbek adolescent' and so on. Everyone in Washington knows McAffey's a drunk."

"I see your point," Lee said, "But why did Ludden want the alien so badly in the first place? You can hardly argue that an alien landing on US soil is Mines turf. According to the National Security Act—"

Avery interrupted. "Ludden doesn't give a crap about jurisdiction. Possession is nine-tenths of the law." Avery fixed Lee with a look of contempt. "I wouldn't expect you to understand."

"I'm the group's psychiatrist," she said. "If anyone here has a prayer of understanding you, Avery, it's me."

He turned away from her. "Our job is to find out as much about the alien as we can while doing nothing to piss off McAffey. Until further notice, this is Duck, the Uzbek."

They stuck the long paper from the polygraph to the wall and scowled at it. "I've never seen anything like this," Henry said. "No pattern. Completely random. I don't see any sign of comprehension here."

"He understood everything. I could see it in his eyes," Lloyd said.

Henry indicated the paper with a sweep of his arm. "You can't argue with this."

But Lloyd proceeded to do so, and then everyone joined in. They argued while they ate up the edibles they had brought—things in bright packages with inscrutable labels like "Deviled Ham" and "Twinkies," names that made no sense to me even after I consulted Mr. Webster. The humans dipped into my Cheezees and drank my coffee without offering me any. They stowed their equipment in cases and locked them. Ignoring army instructions, they left these in the room, along with the table and chairs. They left all of the things they had taped to the walls: the long paper with the crooked lines that made no sense to them, a series of human anatomical charts, and pictures of my vivisection. They'd drawn chalk lines from one to the other, trying to match the human organs with my highly anomalous Utorbian organs.

I listened to their footsteps retreat. I tried not to look at the photographs from my vivisection, but the human anatomical charts interested me. I studied them, memorizing the parts. I entertained myself by trying to pick out a favorite. I loved "juxtaglomerular apparatus" and "Pacini's corpuscle," but every time I thought I had found the best, another delightful specimen, such as "medulla oblongata" presented itself.

A knock at the door sent me springing to the ceiling. I heard a familiar voice.

"Martia, it's Lloyd."

I dropped to the floor. Lloyd came in and closed the door. He looked the photograph of my vivisection on the wall and shuddered. Finally, he plunked himself into a chair and spoke.

"I'm sorry. If I had known ..." His voice trailed off. "I suppose that's not much of an excuse. I thought it was my duty to report you to the government. I'm so sorry."

His voice was full of hating himself. At first he bowed his head, and then his eye made contact with mine. "I'm going to do my best to protect you, as long as you're in the Mines' custody."

Lloyd turned his head away. He was silent for an uncomfortable amount of time. I began to wish he would go. He had apologized. Did he expect me to respond in some manner?

Finally Lloyd said, "Trudie asks about you. I told her you were alive. It made her happy."

I clasped my hand over my cardiovascular ticker pump, which is located just under my chin.

Lloyd reached into his pocket. "She wanted me to give you this." He held out a small, familiar bottle. I took it and read the gold label: "*Soir de Paris.*"

27

A LADY'S TROUSERS

When the elevator returned them to the surface, Lee had to restrain herself from sprinting away from her colleagues. Their lame jokes and body odors had frayed her nerves, but she still had to endure a ride with them back to the hotel. She had tried to beg a ride from Lloyd, who had driven his car out rather than flying. He turned her down, claiming that he had forgotten something and had to go back underground.

So she was stuck in the rental station wagon with the others. She pressed herself against the door to avoid Henry's beefy thigh. He smoked and took every opportunity to reach over her to knock his ashes into the metal tray in the door handle. After he "accidentally" brushed his arm across her breasts, Lee lit her own cigarette. The next time he did it, she "accidentally" burned his arm. She apologized profusely, as was her custom.

"Oh, I'm so sorry, Henry. That must hurt. I have some ointment in my pocketbook." Lee fumbled in her purse and came up with a tube. "I carry this for just such emergencies. It takes the sting out if the burn isn't too deep."

Lee lowered her voice to a whisper. "Which it never is, the *first* time."

Henry glared at her, but quietly applied the ointment and returned the tube. Lee rolled the bottom up a bit. At one time, she would have let a man make two or three mistakes before burning him. Now it was one.

The Agency team had taken rooms in the closest town. Inexplicably named "Gnaw," it was a wind-blasted burg constructed largely out of cinderblocks and quotation marks. By way of "culture," it had a movie theatre. By way of "cuisine," it had starchy vegetables, stringy meat, and three methods of frying: deep, pan, and griddle. By way of "hospitality," it had a gauntlet of sotted and resentful men who occupied benches in front of the hardware store.

Lee couldn't wait to shut herself in her motel room. The eyes in Gnaw made her uncomfortable. Both the men and the women stared at her, gave her "the look" that said, "You're different in a way we don't like." She was familiar with that look. She wore trousers every day at a time when that was rare for a woman. She hated hearing women referred to as "skirts." The trousers were her way of saying, "I'm not a skirt, and don't treat me like the other women in your life." It pleased her that trousers offended all the right people—the nostril-flaring, pursed-lip, wind-sucking enforcers of conventional tyrannies.

So Lee had seen the "look" before but never accompanied by so much crude malice as it was in Gnaw. But if she had to live here, she might become not just malicious, but homicidal.

After she had bidden a strained goodnight to her colleagues, Lee locked her door, engaged the chain, and for good measure propped a chair under the knob. She tossed the ratty motel bedspread across the room, sat down on the thin mattress and smiled broadly.

She was more than happy to put up with this place if that's what it took. It was hard to score a decent assignment. Now one had come out of the blue. And it wasn't just any good assignment. It was unprecedented, strange, and more than a little bit wonderful. It fell into her lap like the alien fell out of the heavens.

The alien. Lee found it beautiful. Yes, the others laughed at it, but the psychiatrist in Lee was fascinated with the range of expression in its huge eyes. She could sit all day and watch how they changed. Unlike human eyes, the limbus was lighter than the iris. It had the white-gold glow of a halo. The hue of the iris varied slightly according to the creature's mood. Lee had observed the eyes carefully and noted that these color variations were partly the result of a trembling of various structures within the ocular anatomy. This motion changed the play of light across the surface of the eye.

Lee thought it laughable that the team wasted so much time trying to measure the alien with instruments like the polygraph, designed for humans while ignoring such an obvious gauge. She hadn't attempted to point this out to them yet—they would dismiss her ideas out of hand—but she was taking careful notes on which part of the ocular anatomy trembled under what circumstances. It was quite consistent. Fear set the pupillary sphincter into rapid motion. Suspicion made the dilator muscles twitch. Those eyes! They were the window to another world, another society. Did it suffer all the ills of human society or had it found cures for war, oppression, and psychosis?

Possibilities churned in Lee's head. It was late, and she

needed to relax. A regular cigarette wouldn't do. She dug in her suitcase and brought out a small, ornately carved wooden box with a brass lock. She wore the tiny key on a chain around her neck. She fished this out of her blouse, opened the box, and laid the contents out on the bed: papers and a small bag of ganja she had acquired from Jamaica. Cannabis was a mild little drug, but a pleasant one. She considered it a harmless habit beneficial to mental health and intellectual output. Lee adeptly rolled a joint and lit it. She focused her thoughts on the alien and inhaled the sweet, stinging smoke.

28

A UNIQUE PRINT

Lloyd was right, they didn't attempt to truss, splay, and incise me. Instead, they weighed me, measured me, and pressed one of my upper limb terminals onto a moist black pad and then onto a sheet of paper.

"How the hell am I supposed to get a fingerprint on this thing?" Carl asked, looking at the paper. "The webbing gets in the way and this doesn't look like anything. No arches, no loops, no whorls." He held the paper up for the rest of the humans to see. They frowned and tilted their heads.

"Almost obscene," Avery said. "It's significantly different from the print they got from the severed hand of the other alien. Hold on, I think it's in that box over there." Avery crossed the room and dug into a box stuck with red Top Secret labels. Finally, he pulled out a sheet of paper and held it up. I gasped when I recognized the graceful outline of Deyahm's limb terminal. Avery taped the two prints to the wall. "See the difference? This one has no webbing and the finger-like appendages are longer and slimmer."

Lee moved in for a closer look. "It's almost as if they came from two species. Which do you suppose was the dominant one?"

Avery nodded at me. "I bet it wasn't this guy."

Vince pulled a straight-backed chair next to me and sat down. "I'd like to get a good look inside its mouth. Open up, Duck."

I didn't want him to force my jaws apart, so I obediently opened my maw.

"Will you look at that," Vince said with surprise. "It understood what I said."

Lee looked up. "I wish we didn't have to waste time with those stupid army tests, I'd rather work on improving communication with him."

Vince peered into my mouth with a sharp little light. "It has rough ridges rather than teeth. I suppose they work well enough for masticating Cheezees, but it sure doesn't make for a dazzling smile."

The others cackled while I gagged on Vince's thick fingers, which tasted strangely sour and salty. Remembering how the humans said my proboscis "gave them the willies," I rubbed it against Vince's hand. He moved back so quickly, he knocked over his chair. I smiled at him, giving him a view of my undazzling chewing ridges. The others laughed, and this time not at me.

Vince moved to the table. He sat down to study two long sheets of paper. He chewed on a long green lozenge he had extracted from a jar labeled "Mount Olive Dill." He spoke with his mouth full. "The only difference I can see between the 1947-48 period and now is that he's turned orange—presumably from the dye in the Cheezees—and gained seven pounds. I'll get my calipers out and see exactly where he gained the weight."

"After you finish with Duck," Avery said, "Why don't you use those calipers on Lee? She's been hitting the donuts pretty hard, and I'd like to know exactly where those donuts have gone."

Lee was nibbling on a donut and sipping coffee. She straightened and slammed her mug down on the table, spilling some of the liquid. I jumped.

"Why don't you use those calipers on Avery, too?" Lee said. "There's probably less there than he would like people to think. Not more than three—"

"Enough!" Lloyd held his hands up. "Truce. We're all grown-ups and professionals here. Besides, you're making Carl blush."

Carl bent over a photograph, but I could see that his thick neck was bright red above the collar of his shirt. The room quieted down, and everyone went back to work.

Lee scowled over a box of charts and notebooks. "Those idiots. They gave him a TAT. What did they expect to learn from that?"

"What is a TAT?" Avery asked.

Lee pulled a stack of cards from the box and laid them on the table. "TAT stands for Thematic Apperception Test. The idea is to show a patient evocative images and ask him to tell stories about them. There's no normative scoring system. How do you ask an alien to tell stories about pictures of humans? A ridiculous waste of time."

"Nevertheless, we agreed to replicate all of the Army's tests," Avery said.

"But you told Crocker we don't have to send them the results, so why do we need to do the tests?" Lee asked.

Avery came over, took the stack of cards from Lee, and began to look through them. "Oh, I was playing with him. I'm going to send the Army the results. We have their alien now, no need to rub their noses in it." He laughed and held up a card, "Well this one tells a simple story." The card depicted a garmentless woman lying on a bed. A man sat behind her wearing only trousers. His head was bent and resting on his hand. "Obviously, he couldn't get it up," Avery said.

Lee gave Avery a knowing smile. "That response speaks volumes about you."

Avery slapped the cards down on the table. "Get on with it. I want to finish the Army's tests so we can begin our own."

Lee opened one of the army notebooks and read. She frowned at me. She went back to reading. More frowning. More reading.

"This is crazy," she said. "Listen to this. 'When subject was shown card number 34, he took three jumps backward, flapped his arms twice, and then scratched his hindquarters.' When he was shown card number 7, 'subject fell to the floor, rolled over four times, then began to make a honking sound through his nose.' It goes on for pages like this. Listen to this one, 'When shown card number 22, subject pointed to the ceiling light and then spat on the chair." Lee put down the notebook and came over to take a close look me. "You scamp. You were yanking his chain."

"You think it has a sense of humor?" Avery said.

Lee smiled at me. "Yes. How a sense of humor could survive all he's been through is beyond me. I wonder if he'll pull the same stunts when I give him the TAT. I'll start with the card you found so fascinating, Avery." She held it up. "Duck, what do you think of this picture?"

I had nothing to say about the man or the woman, but the bedspread was the same deep pink as the *yot* served on my favorite Utorbian holiday, *Blikix,* which marked the shortest day in the Utorbian year. The holiday *yot* was sweeter than regular *yot* and featured an additive that made our hides glow in the dark. We decorated our flocculent bloomers with a glittery spray. *Blikix* was a time of frantic limb terminal flapping and joke-telling. I laughed, remembering some of my favorite jokes. I related a couple to the humans. I thought surely they must have picked up some Utorbian by now. I overestimated them.

"Listen to him quack," Avery said. "The picture excites him. Poor bugger must be horny as hell."

Lee showed me more of the cards, which all depicted humans. I quickly grew bored because she did not become irritated or upset like the army psychiatrist.

Then something horrible occurred. Henry went into the small room with my toilet friend, Sir Cheshire. He shut the door. I immediately suspected the worst, having seen Trudie's demonstration. I went to the door, pounded on it, and told him in no uncertain terms that he was not to foul my friend.

"What the Hell?" Henry yelled, but he didn't come out.

I continued to pound on the door and yell until I heard the sound of the flush, and he finally emerged. I pushed past him to check on Sir Cheshire. A hideous stench sent me reeling backward. I fell to the floor and howled at the sacrilege.

"Good God, Henry," Avery said. "What did you eat for breakfast?"

29

UNAUTHORIZED RE-SEARCH

When they returned to the surface, the sun had set. Lee wondered if it had been a beautiful sunset. Probably. Missing it fouled her spirit almost as much as the company of her colleagues. It was the end of a long day, and she wanted to get away from them. She skipped to catch up with Lloyd.

"Can I beg a ride?"

The look Lloyd gave her wasn't friendly. "If you ride with me, it will generate no end of salacious jokes among our colleagues."

"I get that sort of joke no matter what I do," Lee said.

"I don't."

"Be a sport. If I have to spend ten more minutes with those men, I'll end up killing one of them."

"Come along, then," Lloyd said curtly.

Meanwhile, the other car was filling up. "You're not coming with us?" Avery called.

"No," Lee yelled back, "I'm riding with Lloyd."

The men hooted.

"Christ." Lloyd opened the car door for Lee, and she

climbed in. He was about to close it, when she put a hand on his arm.

"Thank you. If I hadn't been working with you, I would have never been chosen for this assignment."

Lloyd shook off her hand, pushed her door shut, crossed to the driver's side, got in, and slammed his own door. "That decision was made above my pay grade. If it were up to me, you wouldn't be here."

"I know that, too. Still, I thank you."

Lloyd had to try three times to get the car started. Lee could hear Avery having the same problem with the rental. The temperature must be in the single digits. Lloyd idled the engine to let it warm up. "Thank you," he said to Lee.

"For what?"

"You haven't given me any drugs in months."

Lee caught the bitter sarcasm in his voice. She tapped her sharp red nails on the clasp of her purse. She wanted a cigarette, but Lloyd didn't smoke. She didn't want to waste his good will on small favors because she had a large one to ask. But first she had to confess.

"I apologize for giving you drugs. I shouldn't have done it since you had a history of bad reactions. I tried to proceed carefully, with small doses. I wanted to discover what they gave you in Budapest. I couldn't because I couldn't replicate the conditions under which you got the drugs."

A grim smile twitched at the corner of Lloyd's mouth. "I suppose I should thank you for not stripping me naked, beating me with a rubber truncheon, and hanging a colleague outside my window."

Lee bit her lip. The conversation was going badly. She hadn't even gotten to her real confession. She was still trying to figure out the wording, when Lloyd spoke again.

"Look, Lee, I know you were acting under orders from Goldfarb. He passes the stuff out like candy."

Lee squeezed her eyes shut. "But I wasn't."

Lloyd gave her a penetrating look, then put the car into drive and backed out of the space. They were two miles down the road before he spoke again. "You mean you were giving me the drugs just for the hell of it?"

"I was giving them to you for purposes of research. Vital research."

"Unauthorized research."

"I'm more qualified to conduct that research than any of the men Goldfarb has authorized to do it. Do you know he's banned women from the ASPARAGUS program? They had a bad experience with some contract psychiatrist showing up at a safe house in Europe with his girlfriend, so now they throw me in the same category as her. They won't let me near anything important."

"No, nothing important. Just me," Lloyd said.

"I'm sorry. I'm not saying what I need to say. How would you like to be banned from your life's work?"

"How would you feel if someone gave you dangerous drugs because they were bored with babysitting you? Where did you get the drugs if not through Goldfarb?" Lloyd asked.

"I have a contact at Sarkara Laboratories."

"You're as devious as any operative."

Lee turned to get a better look at Lloyd. "You're not naturally devious. Not at all. Why did you choose to become an operative?"

"They recruited me because I spoke Hungarian. My mother was from Buda."

"But spying didn't come naturally to you," Lee said.

"No, but I was serving my country, not my personal preferences." Pain clouded Lloyd's face. "Maybe it would have been better if I had stuck to something I was suited to."

Lee felt herself sinking into the mire of a conversation gone south. "I'm sorry. I'm not tactful. I don't sugar-coat things."

"If you're not naturally tactful, then why did you choose to become a psychiatrist?" Lloyd asked.

"Because I don't believe in talk therapy. It doesn't work. It's like trying to talk a person out of a heart attack. I believe in a pharmacological cure. That's why I came to work here, because all the money for research into the promising drugs flows from the Mines."

Lloyd frowned. "How did you figure that out? It's a closely held secret."

"The psychiatrists under contract to the Mines aren't spies. They're self-important men who can't resist hinting that they're involved in something sexy and clandestine. It wasn't hard to figure out where the money came from. I decided to work for the source, the Mines. Now I'm shut out of ASPARAGUS."

"I don't believe we should be testing drugs," Lloyd said.

"Then why are you working for Goldfarb?"

"I'm working defense. I think we should learn all we can about the drugs and mind control techniques the Communists are developing in order to protect ourselves. I don't believe we should lower ourselves to their level."

Lee persisted in her argument. "But don't you think we should try to understand the drugs and their potential? These drugs could unlock new worlds. They could help people trapped inside their own malfunctioning brains."

"They might be a Pandora's box," Lloyd said.

"Well then call me Pandora, because when the choice is to research or not research something, I will always come down on the side of research."

"Pandora is a perfect name for you, Lee."

"Research is how humanity progresses."

"The test subjects—like me—are human, and we disagree with you."

"Test subjects don't have to be human," Lee said. They had come to the purpose behind her request for a ride.

"What?" Lloyd said. "You want to test on chimps?"

"No, they're intelligent, but not intelligent enough. I want to test on the alien, and I need your help in getting the idea across to management. I've observed him closely, and his psychology is very close to human psychology. You could call him our psychological doppelgänger. But his mind is housed in a much sturdier frame. Testing that would be dangerous and irresponsible to conduct on humans would be possible with Duck. Progress could be so much faster."

Lloyd pulled the car off to the side of the road, so he could direct a full angry stare at Lee.

"No," he said "absolutely not."

The rental car with the rest of the team caught up to them and slowed as it passed. Henry leaned out the window and whooped. He formed an "O" with the index finger and thumb of the left hand. Through this he repeatedly thrust the index finger of the right hand.

Lloyd pulled back out onto the road and wouldn't say another word to Lee.

30

LEE'S DAMN FAULT

Henry was vexed with me because he couldn't figure out my "idiot alien responses," no matter how many times he hooked me up to the curious device they called a "polygraph."

"Goddamn this thing." He pointed at me. "There's no intelligence there at all. Damned if I can tell whether he's stressed or unstressed or somewhere in between."

Lee pushed away the notes she had been writing. "You just have to look closely at his eyes. It's all in the ocular anatomy. When he's stressed, the inner section of the dilator muscles in his iris tremble. Fear makes the pupillary sphincter shake. When he finds something funny, the limbus vibrates. I've been keeping a log. For every mood, I've observed a consistent anatomical indicator."

Henry's mouth fell open. "That's the dumbest thing I've ever heard."

Avery abruptly jumped at me and yelled, "Die, alien!" He looked in my eyes and laughed. "Look at those ocular sphincters shake. Looks like we don't need you any more Henry. Good work, Lee."

"This is idiotic. It's not scientific." Henry pointed at Lee. "You're the one who doesn't belong here. You don't know what you're doing."

"Enough, Henry," Avery said. "Lee is right. The polygraph is a waste of time in this situation, so there's no need to keep you here any longer. I'm tired of your bad breath. Carl will drive you to the airport tomorrow." Avery turned to Lee. "Henry is right, too. You don't belong here, but I'm stuck with you."

The rest of the day, my new overseers glared, muttered, and smoked nasty cigarettes. I wondered that they didn't catch fire to the papers that littered the table. The Mines was not as neat as the Army. They smoked and snacked more. I was thankful for the filtering membranes that filled my proboscis.

They made no effort to restrain me during the tests. Between tests, they let me wander about and look at their things. Lee let me go through her purse, which contained many interesting items, to include cigarettes, a device to ignite cigarettes, a blue tin of Bowers Old-Fashioned Creamy Mints, a crumpled tube, a bus ticket, and a slender gold cylinder housing a waxy red substance. She helped me put some of this on my face and sternly ordered the others to shut up when they laughed.

"Don't let Jordon McAffey see that," Avery said, "or he'll accuse us of encouraging Duck's homosexual tendencies."

"Duck could be female," Lee said.

Avery squinted at me. "He's got a penis right in the middle of his face."

"It's nearly nine inches long," Lee said, "you must be dying of jealousy."

"You have an unnatural interest in that area of my

anatomy. I'm flattered. Perhaps you would like—"

"Enough," Lloyd said, blushing. "Please be professional."

※

At the end of the day, Lloyd rode with the Mines team to the surface. The elevator was a screeching beast with a heavy metal scissor gate. Designed more for freight than people, it moved too slowly for his taste. He had grown weary of his colleagues. He mentally patted himself on the back for having had the foresight to bring his car.

The elevator was about halfway to the surface when Lloyd noticed that Lee was hanging near his elbow. *Damn it, she's going to try to bum another ride,* he thought.

Sure enough, as soon as Carl had wrestled the heavy scissor door open, Lee touched Lloyd's shoulder. He looked down at her slender hand and thought of Lladró porcelain and the sound of Faye's foolish angels shattering against the wall.

Lee leaned close and whispered, "Please, Henry has been glaring at me all day. I don't want to be in the same car with him."

"Fine," Lloyd said. His voice had a not-so-subtle undertone of resignation, but he led her to his car and opened the passenger door with a courtly nod.

"You have no idea how much I appreciate this," Lee said.

Lloyd settled himself behind the wheel, wondering if politeness required him to make pleasant conversation with her. Probably. He didn't feel like it. The petty, procedural details of obtaining a divorce weighed heavily on his mind. He'd planned to spend his driving time loudly cursing out his wife. He wasn't proud that he did this, but it allowed him to let off enough steam to sleep.

"Don't worry," Lee said. "I'm not going to bring up drug testing again. Don't look so annoyed."

"I wasn't thinking about drug testing," Lloyd said. Then he mentally kicked himself for giving Lee the lead-in to the next question.

"What were you thinking about?" she asked.

Lloyd guided the car out onto the long, barren road linking the secret facility to Gnaw. He decided honesty would be the best and possibly only means to shut down the conversation. "I was thinking about my divorce, and how much I despise lawyers. I was also entertaining uncharitable thoughts toward women. I admit these thoughts were unfair. Not all women are like my soon-to-be-ex-wife. I estimate that it will be at least six months before I can even approach fairness again. That's the current state of my mind. You asked."

"I see," Lee said.

They drove the rest of the way in silence. Lee stared out the window intently as if watching something through the darkness. Now and then Lloyd could see her mouth working in a noiseless conversation. She was an odd, intense woman. Sometimes her fingers would claw at her neck, and her lips would draw back from her teeth. Then she would shake the expression from her face like a dog shedding water. Lloyd wondered about the nature of the emotion behind this demonstration. It looked to be anger or perhaps frustration or excitement. He had no desire to get close enough to her to find out.

When he finally reached his motel room, Lloyd shut the door with more force than necessary. He should never have mentioned his divorce. It was nobody's business.

With his mind full of static, sleep was unlikely. Lloyd went to the dresser, where he had stacked a good supply of reading materials. For the first thirty years of his life, Lloyd read books on history and foreign affairs. Then he met Duck and discovered the limitations of nonfiction. Now his reading included a healthy dose of science fiction, which he found oddly comforting. It helped him come to terms with Duck. He was deep into the latest issue of *Other Worlds* when he heard pounding and a shout.

"You owe me, you stupid bitch!"

Lloyd made it to the door in two long strides. Outside he found Henry, stumbling drunk, trying to force the door to Lee's room.

Lloyd grabbed hold of Henry's shirt collar and yanked him away. "What are you doing?"

Henry answered with a stream of invective directed at Lee.

"Go back to your room," Lloyd said. "Now." He pushed Henry roughly in that direction, but the man came back at him with fists raised.

"Why are *you* the only one who gets to fuck her?" he asked.

Lloyd landed a punch squarely to Henry's left eye. The polygraph examiner hit the sidewalk like a sack of sand.

Another door opened, and Avery emerged, pulling a heavy dress coat over pajamas. "What the hell is going on out here?"

Lloyd shrugged. "He was trying to break into Lee's room. I decked him."

Avery gave Henry a light kick in the side. "Wake up, asshole. Lloyd, go get some water to splash in his face."

"In this weather, that might give him pneumonia."

"That's a risk I'm willing to take."

Lloyd went back into his room and came out with an ice bucket full of tap water. He poured it over Henry's head, and the man woke up sputtering.

"Fill it again," Avery said.

"But he's awake."

"Just fill it."

Avery took the bucket from Lloyd when he returned. "What room is Carl in?" he asked.

"Fourteen," Lloyd said.

Avery walked over and banged on the door until Carl emerged blinking. "Sorry about this, but you need to be awake. You're driving Henry to the airport tonight." Avery dumped the bucket of water over Carl's head.

"You have an interesting management style," Lloyd said as they watched Carl and Henry load the car.

"So I've been told," Avery said. "This is Lee's damn fault. This is what happens when you have a woman on your team. A management nightmare."

To his surprise, Lloyd found himself defending her. "She was doing her job better than Henry was doing his. You can't blame her for his resentment."

"Of course, I blame her. Women make men crazy."

Lloyd decided it was pointless to respond. He stepped to Lee's door and knocked lightly. "Are you all right? Henry is gone. Carl drove him to the airport."

The door opened a slit, and Lee's right eye appeared.

"I'm fine," she said. "If Henry had gotten through this door, you would be reassembling his parts now. And Avery, women don't make men crazy. Men were crazy to begin with." She shut the door, and Lloyd heard the lock engage.

31

CAFFEINE

I was masticating my Cheezees one morning when Lloyd made an announcement. "I'm going to teach Duck to make coffee." He looked into my eyes and pointed to the tall silver cylinder on the table. "This is a per-co-la-tor, Duck," he said slowly. "We use it to make coffee." This footnote was unnecessary, given that I had seen them make coffee many times. Then he insulted my intelligence further by delivering a tortured explanation of how to operate the apparatus.

I had no trouble repeating his instructions. I put in the coffee, turned the percolator on, and waited for the delightful music of the bubbles. When the coffee was done, I served it out according to each individual's preferences, adding two lumps of sugar to Lee's, a splash of cream to Lloyd's, one lump of sugar and cream to Vince's, and nothing to Avery's.

"Well I'll be, Duck," Avery said, "you're twice as trainable as Lee. Too bad I won't be writing a performance appraisal for you. You would have sevens across the board. Whereas Lee is bucking for a two in interpersonal skills."

Lee's thin brows arched. "Congratulations, Duck, the coffee is now your job. It's not a good career move. Soon you'll be in charge of organizing the office Christmas party and cleaning out the refrigerator. Oh, and watch out for Avery when you bend over the percolator, he likes to pinch asses."

I felt uncomfortable. Avery and Lee were talking to me, but their meaning flew in a parabolic arc high over my head.

"Duck," Avery said, "let me tell you something about women. They come in and expect everyone and everything to change to suit them." His face grew pinched and dark. "You know what happens when women enter any field of work? The prestige disappears. The salaries go down. They degrade any job they take."

※

That night, Lloyd left the percolator on the table and took a fresh can of Maxwell House from the closet. "Here," he said, "In case you get in the mood for coffee while we're gone."

I did get in the mood. As soon as they had left, I experimented with the relative amounts of coffee and water in the percolator. I mastered the button labeled "brew strength." By morning, I had emptied the can of Maxwell House and perfected a viscous, robust brew even better than the stuff Jimmy used to make.

When Avery opened the portal the next morning, the small sound made me jump and splat myself into the ceiling with enough force to knock me breathless. I fell back to the floor and watched stars blink on and off above my head.

"What's gotten into him?" Avery said. "He hasn't jumped like that since the first day."

Lloyd picked up the empty coffee can. "What's gotten into him is a full five pounds of Maxwell House. I hope it was good to the last drop. Remind me to lock this stuff up tonight."

"We'd better postpone testing until he mellows out," Avery said. "But take a seat. We have another issue to talk about."

The team sat down around the conference table. The sound of chair legs scraping across the concrete floor set my chewing ridges on edge. I hugged myself in a vain effort to control the involuntary twitching.

Avery lit a cigarette. When everyone was settled, he began. "We're almost finished the initial testing phase. Soon we can get to something a lot more interesting, but first we have to write a report that won't make McAffey apoplectic."

"Our job is to write up our findings accurately," Lloyd said. "If they upset McAffey, that's his problem."

Avery blew a puff of smoke. "You think it's not our problem? McAffey is a font of trouble. We have to keep him happy. This report is like a pacifier—we let him chew on it, and he stays quiet. Otherwise, he'll be in Ludden's office making a royal nuisance of himself, and then Ludden will be in my office, making my life Hell. I'm not saying we write fiction here, just watch your wording. Don't dismiss McAffey's ideas out of hand."

"What are we going to say?" Lloyd asked. "Even though the creature differs significantly from Homo sapiens in terms of his skeletal, muscular, cardiovascular, respiratory, urinary, digestive, reproductive, nervous, and sensory systems, we judge that he may be a Soviet spy of

Uzbek origin."

"See, that wasn't so hard," Avery said.

"It's ridiculous." Lloyd pushed his chair back from the table. "I'm not going to write something that will make me a laughingstock."

"A laughingstock among the extremely small number of people who will actually read this report." Avery reminded him.

"Still," Lloyd said, "I have my professional pride."

Avery and Lloyd continued to argue until the door burst open. I hit the ceiling with a force that almost knocked me senseless.

Colonel Crocker strode into the room accompanied by men of assorted rank, bearing firing limbs.

Avery stood so quickly he knocked over his chair. "This is a violation of our agreement."

"The agreement is moot. The transfer of the alien to the Mines is on hold. We're kicking you guys out," the colonel said.

"By whose authority?" Avery asked.

"You'll find out when you get back to Washington."

"What does McAffey say about—"

The full bird smiled broadly. "Senator Jordan McAffey no longer has any leverage over the Army. Soon he won't have any influence anywhere. There's a movement afoot in the Congress to censure him. And this is floating around everywhere." The Colonel threw a photograph on the table. I moved to where I could get a look and saw an image of an extremely ugly female human.

Avery picked it up. "Oh my god." He held it so that the others could see.

"A transvestite," Lee exclaimed.

Lloyd looked away. "Appalling."

"Yes," Lee said. "Fuchsia isn't his color, and he's using too heavy a hand with that mascara."

"Shut-up, this isn't the time for jokes," Avery snapped.

Colonel Crocker smiled. "Well, there's nothing funny here for the Mines, but the Army can't stop laughing." He looked around the room. "I see you ignored our instructions. You were pretty full of yourself, but you're no longer in control, Mr. Stanton. I'm giving you and your team an hour to clear out this stuff or we're going to confiscate it. If you can get it done smartly, I'll promise you a slice of the alien's brain."

"You can't do this," Avery said, but I could see from his face that he knew the Army was back in control.

The Mines people packed up their papers, their equipment, and their snacks while the Army looked on holding their firing limbs.

Before they left, Avery told the army men, "I won't let you win. This is personal now." Lloyd promised me he would be back for me. Lee slipped me her lighter and whispered, "If they try to grab you, burn them."

32

A BLIND BRASS EAGLE

Back in Washington, Avery sat in the corner of a dark-paneled room, waiting for his turn to speak. Above his shoulder, a blind brass eagle perched on a flagpole and passed silent judgment on the posturing and bluster. The handful of Mines officials with access to HALFSHEEP could not come to an agreement.

In the wake of Jordan McAffey's fall, the Army had petitioned the president to regain full control of the alien. They succeeded in blocking its transfer to the Mines while the president considered the matter. Army doctors still harbored hopes of taking a scalpel to the contents of the creature's skull. They produced a one-hundred-thirty-two-page document entitled "Alien's Brain Could Unlock Secret to Life." The Mines had to come up with a demonstrably better use for Duck or they would never see him again.

Fortunately, the very length of the Army's document bought the Mines time. The president's staff returned the tome with a scribbled note: "Provide one-page gist." The primary drafter had a heart attack. Not a figurative heart attack, but a literal coronary infarction that landed him in Walter Reed.

At the Mines, the meetings and arguments stretched on for weeks, then months. Meanwhile, the Army was assembling an alien dissection team and building a dedicated alien dissection facility at an undisclosed location. Both tasks were completed well before the one-page summary of "Alien's Brain Could Unlock Secrets to Life" was ready for delivery to the president.

So far, all the Mines had produced was a single paragraph:

> We urgently appeal to the president to transfer to the Central Intelligence Agency full custody of the alien creature now in the possession of the US Army. The Agency alone possesses the depth and breadth of expertise, the intellectual and institutional creativity, and the technical resources necessary to exploit the creature in the manner that would most enhance our national security. The existence of the alien represents a unique opportunity, one which has been squandered by the Army over the past decade with a series of tests producing no useful result. Now the Army proposes to terminate the alien in the interest of one more test of dubious value. We suggest the following course of action, which we believe will yield a tangible increase in national security while preserving the alien creature for future exploitation.

It was a killer paragraph, full of gravity and nuance.

Unfortunately, before they could write the next paragraph, someone had to make a decision. How exactly would one exploit an alien in a manner that would increase national security?

They had no shortage of ideas, which ran the gamut from creative to "creative" in big blinking quotation marks. Every man defended his own scheme with the ferocity of a badger.

Naturally, only men were in attendance. Women appeared occasionally to warm their coffee, brush away their pastry crumbs, or take dictation. Lee, however, had managed to insert her idea into the room by planting it in the head of Vince, who planted it into the head of Avery, who was the only member of the original Agency team with a lofty enough rank to share a room with these high officials and their blind brass eagle.

Avery had adopted the idea with such fervor, he now believed it to be his own. He formed an alliance with Sigmond Goldfarb, head of the Human Ecology Staff. Through some mysterious alchemy involving a fusion of testosterone, tobacco, and sloe gin, Goldfarb now also believed himself to be the originator of the idea. Their alliance was fraying under the stress.

On the debate team at Groton, Avery had learned that a well-timed pause, a slightly raised eyebrow, or an adeptly-turned rhetorical flourish could carry more weight than reason. As much as it rankled Goldfarb, he had to admit that Avery was best equipped to present their argument.

Now was his moment. Avery stood and crossed to the far fringe of the carpet, turned, and raised one shapely hand ornamented with a Princeton class ring and a scar from a Weimaraner bite. He intoned the marvelous words

"Psychological doppelgänger." He paused, letting each intriguing syllable sink in.

"There are striking differences in physiology between humans and the alien. But in terms of psychology, he is remarkably like us. He reacts in a similar manner to stress. He laughs when someone makes a joke. He becomes bored when a test is repeated. He is frightened by loud noises. He is irritable before he's had his coffee.

"Furthermore, all of these emotions are accompanied by very consistent changes in his eyes. I noticed it one day when we were giving him a TAT—that stands for Thematic Apperception Test." Avery tossed off the name with a studied nonchalance. "Different emotions make parts of his eye—or ocular anatomy—vibrate. For example, when he's frightened, his pupillary sphincter trembles."

"His what?" Ludden asked.

"Pupillary sphincter," Avery said slowly.

"Eye asshole?" another official said.

"Exactly, his eye asshole." Avery smiled. "His anatomical responses are very consistent. I carefully noted what each one means, so we can easily gauge what he is feeling at any given moment without the necessity of a polygraph machine."

"That's brilliant," Ludden said. "Good work, Avery."

"Thank you, sir." Avery managed a modest blush. "In addition to his other advantages, the alien is virtually unbreakable. He survived the fiery crash of his spacecraft. He withstood vivisection. He walked away from a double vehicle collision that would have killed any human.

"But what does this mean?" Avery paused to look into each man's face. "What it means is that our alien is the optimal subject for the testing of mind control drugs. He is unlikely to succumb to any mistakes, and if he does, his relatives are on the other side of the universe. Think what it will mean if we can avoid the ... disadvantages of human testing."

Avery regretted immediately the small pause he had inserted before the word "disadvantages." He saw how eyes darted away, stared into corners, or hid behind eyelids. It was too soon after that regrettable incident with Fred Ogden, the unwitting dose of LSD, and the tenth-story window. Ludden scowled. Goldfarb gave Avery a look of malevolent ferocity.

Avery felt sweat bead on his forehead. How could he have made such a rookie error? He should have known that to refer even obliquely to the embarrassing fatality in the testing program would only antagonize his listeners. He should have let them make the connections in their own minds. Instead, he had rubbed their noses in it.

Avery stood tongue-tied until Goldfarb said, "Why don't we take a break. When we get back, I'll continue the presentation. Mr. Stanton has another meeting to attend."

33

TRICK OR TREAT

Things went back to the way they had been before, with an eye at the observation window and a tinny speaker telling me I belonged to the United States body and soul. I ate little and fell into morbid contemplation of my scheduled dissection. Would they kill me first or not? Then one day the door opened, and there stood Avery and Lee, along with Colonel Crocker and a pair of privates. I saw that one of them carried my black traveling costume under his arm. Avery and Crocker were arguing.

"The Army has been doing this since 1947," Crocker said. "We have well-established procedures for safely transporting the alien. We have a dedicated and specially-equipped vehicle, along with support vehicles ready to carry out this operation."

"Thank you, sir," Avery said, "but we'll handle it."

"I have to protest," Crocker said. "It's my responsibility to ensure the safety of the public during the transfer. If the CIA can't understand that—"

Lee laughed. "Duck is afraid of his own shadow."

It was true, I'd seen my shadow back in the desert

in 1947, and I didn't trust it. We didn't have these persistent, furtive bastards on Utorb, where the thick atmosphere diffused the light of our local star.

"Miss Ogilvie," the colonel said, "your opinions are unnecessary. I would think that, as a woman, you would be grateful for the protection."

"It's Dr. Ogilvie," Avery said, "and I'll thank you to treat my team with respect."

Lee looked at Avery with surprise. He winked at her, and her brows shot up.

"I insist that you follow our procedures," Crocker said.

"You have no further authority to insist." Avery pointed to me. "He belongs to Elliot Ludden now. He's a Mines employee. His name is Douglas A. Leon, and he's a GS-5 clerk typist assigned to the Office of Human Ecology." Avery pulled a card out of his pocket. It was attached to a silver chain. "Here's your Mines tag, Doug."

He handed me the item, and I was delighted to see my image staring back at me in lovely glowing orange. Across the front of the tag was not my new name, but letters and numbers: AL313. I turned the thing over. On the back it said, "If found, please drop in any US mailbox."

"Congrats, Doug. You're one of us, but I'm going to have to ask for your tag back now. We're not allowed to wear them outside Mines' facilities." Avery tried to take my comely tag back, but he had some difficulty in untangling the chain from my limb terminals, because already I loved the thing, which said I belonged somewhere, which is the same as saying that I was not, indeed, an alien. Rather I was an "employee," which is exactly what I was back on Utorb. "You'll get it back when we get there," Avery assured me as he finally pried it loose.

"If you refuse to take advantage of the Army's offer of

transportation, how do you propose to move the alien?" Crocker asked.

"In the back of a Chevy station wagon," Avery said.

An unpleasant expression overtook Crocker's face. "I can't allow that. You'll use the convoy provided."

"How am I supposed to make this move in secrecy with a goddamn seven-vehicle convoy?"

"As I said earlier, the Army has been doing this for a decade.

"Right," Avery said, "and the whole country is speculating about an alien."

"An alien found in Roswell, New Mexico. No one knows about the actual landing site," Crocker pointed out.

"They shouldn't know there's an alien, period," Avery said. "That Roswell diversion wasn't half as clever as you think. No, we are not going to have an army convoy arriving at the gates of an unacknowledged Mines facility. Period."

Crocker clenched and unclenched his jaw. "So you think you can drive an alien across the country in the back of a station wagon and keep it secret?"

"Why do you think we arrived on Halloween?" Avery said. "We have a costume custom made for him by our disguise team and a bag of candy. Tonight the countryside will be full of station wagons with bizarre, three-foot tall creatures in the back. Dr. Ogilvie and I will look like another set of parents with their greedy offspring in tow. Who's going to notice?"

The costume Avery brought me was nothing like the traveling costume the Army had supplied. No, the Mines had made me what they referred to as a "Dumbo the Elephant" costume. Since Avery had supplied the disguise team with very precise measurements taken with Vince's calipers, it fit perfectly. The elephant feet slid comfortably over my limb terminals, the body did not squeeze my protuberant belly, and the length of the trunk correlated to the length of my proboscis. The mesh at the end of the trunk allowed me to breathe easily while holes in the eyes allowed me to see straight ahead, although my peripheral vision was limited. The only awkward parts of the costume were the ears, whose number, size, and placement did not correspond to Utorbian equivalents. Moreover, they were quite heavy and stuck out so far that if I leaned my head too much in one direction, I fell over. Avery had to take hold of one upper limb terminal and Lee the other so that I could successfully walk.

I put my *Soir de Paris* in the pocket of my Dumbo costume. Lee carried my dictionary. We took the long ride up in the horrible squealing elevator and went outside with the full bird still squawking behind us. Because of the Army's approved method of storing and transporting me, I hadn't seen the open sky since my unpleasant excursion to the Proving Ground. Tonight, the single local moon was full and had attained an orange coloring as bright as mine. It hovered near the horizon. It seemed dangerously close. I tried to stop, but Avery and Lee merely lifted me up, so that my lower limb terminals just scraped the ground.

"Come along, Doug," Avery whispered, "let's get you out of here before they dissect your brain." When my pods touched the ground again, I was more than willing to hurry.

We approached a vehicle that in no way resembled

anything I had seen in the Army. It was long and shiny—pale blue on the bottom and white on the top. Inside, I was surprised to find a long, comfy seat instead of steel cages.

"Let's blow this joint," Avery said. The motor roared, and the vehicle took off so fast I was thrown back against the seat. I pulled myself up to the window and peered out through my Dumbo eyes. I watched as we left the army and its dully-clad humans and vehicles behind. Then we were out on the open road with the local moon and stars hanging still and peaceful in the sky. I looked down at the place where the tracker was embedded in my skin, hoping to see a citrine glow. Nothing.

Lee finally broke the silence. "Thank you for standing up for me back there."

Avery continued to stare straight ahead. "Don't take that as a sign that I've changed my opinions on women. I haven't. I'm siding with the Mines over the Army."

"I wish we knew what course of action Ludden decided on in terms of testing," Lee said. "You don't have a clue?"

"No. Goldfarb shut me out of the decision loop. Whatever it was, it convinced the president to give us the alien."

While they talked, I sat back and noticed a large paper bag on the floor behind the seat. I picked it up and saw on the front of it a round orange face with black eyes and mouth. I thought this was a crude caricature of my unattractive physiognomy, although the proboscis was wrong. I reached up and tapped Lee on the shoulder. She turned, and I pointed at the orange face and asked her why they would insult me in such a way.

Of course, she couldn't understand a word of what I

said, but I nevertheless felt the need to express my hurt at the offense. I pointed at the orange face emphatically.

"That's a jack-o-lantern, Duck—I mean Doug," she said. "A jack-o-lantern is a hollowed out fruit with a face carved out of it and a candle inside. It's a holiday decoration. If that's what you were asking."

That wasn't what I was asking, but her explanation convince me that I was not looking at a cruel caricature of myself. I sat back.

Lee turned and peered back over the seat. It was dark in the vehicle, but I could see the outline of her face against the sky. Her nose twitched. "Avery, did you say that there was candy in that bag?"

"I told the disguise team to put some in there, in case anyone stops us," Avery said.

"I wonder if there's any chocolate." One of Lee's slender limbs crossed over the seat. "Doug, could I see the bag, please?" I handed it over. She dug through it. "No chocolate, just that awful orange taffy. This would never pass for a real Halloween bag. Any child who had been trick or treating would have a large variety of candy. Certainly there would be chocolate."

"I'm sure we won't get stopped," Avery said.

"You're driving this station wagon like a T-Bird. Getting stopped is a distinct possibility. If a policeman should happen to look into this Halloween bag, he would find it highly suspicious. The next thing you know, he'd be asking Doug to take his mask off."

Avery turned to look at Lee. "Having a bad chocolate craving, are we?"

She let out an extended exhalation. "I would kill for a Baby Ruth."

"So you want to take him trick or treating?"

"Just one street."

"Good God, woman, I was joking," Avery said.

"I'm not." Lee's voice was sharp. "This Halloween bag was compiled in error. We have to rectify it, or his disguise will be dangerously incomplete."

Avery gave Lee a protracted look, which ended only when the car began to veer toward the side of the road. He corrected course. "I can see that this trip will be unbroken misery if I don't comply. So, one street it is. If we ever get to a town."

We were driving through an area with few lights or other signs of habitation. Soon, however, we began to see houses.

"Here?" Avery asked.

"Three houses? That's not enough. Keep driving. There's a science to picking the right place to trick or treat. I know, I take my nieces and nephews. You don't want a neighborhood that's too poor because all you get is candy corn. But neither do you want the best neighborhood in town. The most affluent neighborhoods tend to be inhabited by couples whose children are grown and out of the house. They keep their lights off because they're too stingy or fearful to open their doors. Besides, their houses are on larger lots, so there's more walking for less payoff. The best neighborhoods are the Levittown type, where the yards are small, and all the houses look alike. Those places are full of children, and everybody participates in Halloween. My little nieces and nephews come back with bags so full they can barely carry them."

"And how do they keep their Aunt Lee from stealing their candy?" Avery asked.

Lee sat up straight and pointed to a well-lighted hillside of small, closely spaced erections. "That's it! Perfect!

Stop there!"

Avery made a left turn, drove up the hill, and parked the vehicular station wagon. He got out and went around to open the door for Lee, a gesture that seemed to surprise her.

"Since when are you a gentleman?" she asked him.

He took her arm. "I'm not only a gentleman, tonight I'm your loving husband, Frank Miller. You're my wife, Ellen." He opened the back door. "And this, my dear, is our firstborn, little Frankie Junior, who suffers from a bad speech impediment. Let's go get the little scamp some candy."

Avery and Lee each took one of my upper limb terminals. Lee whispered, "Don't say anything."

They led me up to one small erection after another. Looking straight ahead, which was my only option, I saw little but a series of human shoes that bore no resemblance to the footwear I had observed in the Army. Lee and Avery kept yelling that curious phrase, "Trick or Treat." A number of humans called me "adorable." They dropped paper-wrapped edibles into my orange bag. Then Lee and Avery said, "thank you," and we walked, arrived at another door, and repeated the procedure.

I thought of all the snacks the humans had consumed at the underground facility. Is this how that food was obtained? How curiously inefficient. With longing, I remembered the convenient *yot* nozzle in my hexicle.

My bag was growing heavy, and my limbs tired. I was unaccustomed to continuous perambulation. My gait slowed.

Avery said, "I think this is enough."

Lee aimed a flashlight into the bag. "Wait, let me see what we've got."

"Do that on the road. We'd better get moving, we have a long trip ahead."

I surrendered my candy to Lee when we got back to the car. She foraged noisily and finally yelled the incongruous phrase "Baby Ruth!" Was it yet another codename? Lee unclothed an edible and popped it into her mouth as Avery pulled back out onto the highway.

"Mmmm," she moaned.

"Oh come on," Avery said, "it's not that good."

"Oh yes, it is."

"This is what I hate about women."

Lee's laugh bounced around inside our vehicle. "Someone isn't better than chocolate, I see." She resumed her excavation of the bag, still chuckling. "Hmmph, candy corn. Cheap." A small plastic bag of candy flew over the seat and hit me in the head. "It's orange. You might like it, Doug."

It had been a very long time since I had tried to ingest anything other than coffee and Cheezees, but it was a magical night, and I was feeling audacious. I pushed up my elephant head enough to uncover my mouth. I popped the candy in and chewed.

"Did you take the plastic off first?" Avery asked. "It sounds like you're chewing plastic."

I fished the bag out of my mouth.

"Put it in the ashtray, Doug." Lee reached back and pointed to a shiny metal concavity on the vehicle's door. "I have more. I'll take them out of the bag for you." Lee's arm disappeared, and then shortly returned with the fingers tucked into a fist. "Open your mouth wide." I did so, and she tossed in the candy. I chewed. The taste was sweet with a slight chemical tang. I didn't detect any dangerous nutrients.

Lee continued to survey of the bag. "Drat," she said, "I hate licorice."

"I'll take those." Avery stretched out his hand.

For the next fifty miles, we worked our way through the orange bag. Lee ate everything with chocolate. Avery ate everything with licorice. I ate everything else, to include a small Bit o' Honey, five butterscotches, a couple of jawbreakers, eight Jolly Ranchers, four Laffy Taffies, one package of cinnamon red hots, and a great deal more candy corn. My favorite thing, however, was a set of wax teeth. Lee told me that these were Vampire teeth and that they were not for eating. I had always wanted teeth.

An hour later, we were crossing an astounding linear body of water when my stomach began to vociferate.

"What's that noise?" Avery said. "Look back and see if Doug is all right."

Lee turned around. I had pushed my Dumbo head off. My own head was lolling.

"Stop the car, now! I know that look. Our little orange alien has turned green."

Fortunately, there were no other cars on the bridge, for Avery brought the station wagon to a sudden halt. Lee was out of the car and had my door open before I realized what was happening. She yanked me out of the vehicle, hoisted me up, and held my head over the railing. I began to regurgitate lustily until all five chambers of my stomach had emptied themselves. Lee set me down on the ground.

"Is that it?"

I nodded.

"Are you sure?"

I nodded again.

Lee wiped my face with a tissue and then tossed it over the bridge railing. "No more candy for you. Get back in the car and put your Dumbo head back on. Avery's driving may yet get us stopped by the police."

When we were back in the car, Avery said, "Doug, a little geography. That thing you just threw up in is the Mississippi River, the greatest river in the whole United States. Your putrid alien vomit will travel a few hundred miles south and eventually turn some alligator's stomach in Lake Pontchartrain before it spills into the Gulf of Mexico. What do you think about that?"

Not much. Tired from the vomiting, I nodded off to sleep and awoke some time later when Lee and Avery raised their voices in argument.

Avery had one hand on the wheel while the other stabbed the air. "Not jobs that can support families. Not jobs that require foreign travel. Not jobs where one person's incompetence can put other people in danger."

"And you have no incompetent men in the clandestine service?" Lee asked.

"Of course we do, but we can get rid of them without anybody bursting into tears. Face it, women aren't fit for the job."

Lee drew herself up. "One, I've been in the Agency for four years and never burst into tears. Two, I've often been assigned to work with men who weren't fit for the job in one way or another. You're vaunted clandestine service is chock full of alcoholics, child beaters, depressives, and others who can't take the strain of doing one job that is secret and another that is not." Lee gulped air and continued, "And three, you never get rid of the misfits, tears or no. The clandestine service protects even the worst of its own, as long as they're men. Don't tell me that women are weaker. My mother lost two brothers in the war. She gave birth to five children and lost one baby to a miscarriage and another to Polio. Her husband beat her and then abandoned her to raise three girls alone. She put me through college working two or three low-paying jobs at a time. My mother, with all of that, never became an alcoholic or a child beater or a depressive. So don't give me any of that tired 'weaker vessel' argument. I'm serious. I won't stand for it. I won't listen to it."

A long silence ensued, and then Avery said, "All right."

No one said anything more for a long time. I lay on the back seat and watched strange erections flash by, followed by miles of nothing but wires that traveled up, intersected thick poles, and traveled down again in a rhythm that was like music. I fell asleep to the sound of an old Utorbian ballad playing in my head.

34

MARY ETHEL OWENS
WORTHY HALL

Lee woke me when Avery stopped the vehicular station wagon. It was still dark. She opened my door and helped me out. "The guards at the gate aren't cleared to see you, so you have to hide." I reeled from sleep and the awkward weight of the Dumbo head. Lee pulled it off.

The moist night air swallowed me. I felt slippery and queer all over. For the first time, I was not in a desert. I blinked and tried to decipher the dark, crowded landscape. Living things seethed all around. Their tiny noises commingled into an eerie, atonal symphony. Green things crept along the ground. Something brushed against my limb. My muscles seized and sent me springing toward the stars. Without a ceiling to stop me, I attained an alarming altitude before falling to the ground, quivering.

"Jesus Christ, what a basket case," Avery said. He picked me up and carried me to the back of the vehicle. His flashlight caught a sign by the side of the road. It read, "County Ovine Disease Research Center: Authorized Personnel Only."

Lee opened the back of the vehicular station wagon

and uncovered a concavity occupied by a Brobdingnagian black donut. Avery pulled this out and threw it to the side.

"Hey, this is a rental. You can't throw out the spare," Lee said.

"They'll never notice." Avery stuffed me into the concavity and pushed the cover down on me, bruising my proboscis. "Don't make a sound," he said, "or I'll pickle your entrails."

"Do you have to threaten him?" Lee asked.

"Yes."

They got back in, and the motor started up. We didn't travel far before we stopped again.

"Names, social security numbers, and tag numbers," said a male voice.

Avery and Lee responded. We started moving again. We went up a steep hill, around a bend, then down a steep, short road. The vehicle stopped, and Avery opened the back door and pulled away the blanket. Fearing that he would pickle my entrails, I didn't even blink.

Avery pulled me out of my hiding place and hoisted me over his shoulder. We went through a door, and along a long hallway strung with bare light bulbs. The space had the damp, hollow feeling of being underground, and that comforted me. Eventually, we came into a large room.

Lee said, "All the time they had to prepare a facility, and this is where we end up?"

"The facility that was supposed to be ours was taken over by another component," Avery said. "If you leave a space empty for five minutes in this goddamn agency, someone will grab it. I'm appealing the decision to Ludden."

Lee pointed me to a rather strange-looking bed. "You sleep now, Doug. We'll see you in a few hours. We all need sleep."

They left and closed the door. I heard the sound of a lock engaging.

Suddenly, I was wide-awake and anxious to explore my new quarters. Unlike the places the Army stored me, this one was full of interesting things.

Along one wall were three white metal cylinders, standing on four legs each. My cardiovascular ticker pump quickened. I loved cylinders. We slept in them on Utorb. These were taller than me by the width of a limb terminal. A red word was inscribed on the front of each: Maytag. I climbed the side of one. On top was a metal lid, which, when removed and dropped to the floor, made a thunderous sound. Two of these lids, clapped together, made an even better sound.

Nearby, I found a square sink, large enough that I could climb in. I tried the faucet, and it gushed a great stream of water. I stuck the stopper into the drain and took a bath, splashing lustily. Afterward, I continued my tour of the room. In one corner sat several soft, floppy, flowered chairs, of a type I hadn't seen since leaving Trudie's house. I sat in each, leaving behind wet blotches. Then I pulled the chair cushions off onto the floor, piled them up, and jumped on them again and again.

I visited the corners of the room, and then I opened the door to a small bathroom. Remembering the foul fate of Sir Cheshire, I resolved not to get attached to this toilet. I returned to the bed, which was actually two beds, one atop the other. Next to it sat a desk and wooden chair.

Lee would later explain to me that we were in a former women's college that had been converted into an unacknowledged Mines training facility. "This was where rich southern girls learned to ride horses, read poetry, and paint on the back of glass," Lee told me. "It's stretching a point to call it a college." This room had been the laundry area of a dormitory called Mary Ethel Owens Worthy Hall.

Lee had left my dictionary, my *Soir de Paris*, and my most excellent wax vampire teeth on top of the desk. I put on a dab of perfume before tucking my treasures in a drawer. Suddenly, I was extremely tired. I crawled onto the bottom part of the bunk, but it didn't seem right. I crossed the room and grabbed the lid of the Maytag. I crept into the cylinder and pulled the lid closed. I fell asleep immediately.

35

EARTH'S SUPREME OVERSEER

The sounds of the search finally woke me. Avery's voice rose above the scrape and thump. "Where is the filthy bastard? Ludden will be here in half an hour."

I poked my head out of my cylinder and said "Good morning" in Utorbian.

Avery bashed his head on the underside of the bottom bunk, and Lee clasped the white stones that circled her neck.

"Doug! What are you doing in there?" Lee rushed over to help me crawl out of my cylinder. "We thought you had escaped!"

Avery stood up slowly and brushed down his clothing. I had never seen them like this. Their faces were tired, but their garments were abnormally fine. I admired the yellow-striped harness around Avery's neck and Lee's pronged shoes. Her curls, which had thrashed in the wind the night before, had been called into tight formation. Her lips were such a bellicose red, they seemed to hover in a space in front of her face.

"We're going to have a very important visitor in just

a few minutes," Lee said. "We have to get this room in shape. What have you been doing? There's water everywhere. The chairs are wet—what if he wants to sit down?"

"I never knew you were such a pig," Avery said. "You're going to help us clean. The high muck-a-muck himself is coming. He holds your miserable life in his hands, so snap to. Lee, make the bed. I'll mop up the water. Doug, close all those drawers and put the cushions back where you found them. Do it fast, or I'll pickle your alien entrails and put them on display in the lobby."

We briskly rectified the room, and then Avery turned his attention upon me. "Lee, do you have a comb? His wool looks moth-eaten. Doug, try not to move your trunk, it gives people the heebie-jeebies." Avery turned his head this way and that. "Could you try smiling?"

I tried.

"God, no, don't," Avery said. "That is one unappetizing smirk."

"Avery, stop it. He looks fine," Lee said.

"And you," Avery said, "Do you own a skirt? Where did you get that lipstick? I thought Montezuma red went out of style when the war ended."

The sound of footsteps silenced their argument.

"He's here," Lee said. She and Avery drew themselves up straight.

Meanwhile, I was feeling bad about my moth-eaten wool, my heebie-jeebie proboscis, and especially my unappetizing smile. I had a thought, which startled me with its brilliance. I turned back toward the desk.

Avery hissed, "Doug, turn around!" and opened the door.

I turned proudly, for I had inserted my comely wax vampire teeth into my mouth. I executed a dazzling smile.

Elliot Ludden stood between two other men in gray. The lines of authority flowing from him were almost visible in the air. The sacs on either side of my proboscis filled as I held my breath.

Earth's Supreme Overseer puffed on a pipe as he quietly regarded my moth-eaten bloomers, my heebee-jeebee proboscis, and my most excellent wax vampire teeth. Then Ludden removed the pipe from his lips and laughed with a great open mouth and closed eyes and a sound that broke the stillness into small, sharp bits. Air rushed from my proboscis sacs, from Lee's delicate nostrils, from Avery's thin nose.

Ludden pulled a handkerchief from his pocket and wiped at his face. "Those goddamn teeth were a stroke of genius!"

Avery and Lee, who had not yet had the pleasure of viewing my excellent vampire teeth in my mouth, now turned to look at me.

"Good to see you, Avery," Ludden said. "Introduce me to your lovely assistant."

Avery cleared his throat. "This is Dr. Lee Ogilvie, who performed the psychiatric testing and more recently aided in the transfer of the alien to this facility."

"Nice to meet you, dear." They shook hands, but instead of a quick grip and release, Ludden captured Lee's hand in both of his own while he looked into her face. I could feel her discomfort from across the room. He laughed low in his throat and said, "Wear a dress next time, dear."

Ludden approached me. I put my upper limb terminals behind my back, fearing he would try the same stunt with me, but he merely crouched down. "Let me get a closer look at our queer little friend. I understand he has a new name and position?"

"Yes, sir," Avery said. "Douglas A. Leon, GS-5 clerk typist assigned to the Human Ecology Staff."

Ludden nodded as he looked me up and down. "Excellent, but buck him up to a GS-15. You can use the extra money for incidental expenses. Cuts down on the paper trail." Ludden laughed again. "Douglas A. Leon. That doesn't sound like an Uzbek name, now does it?"

"No, sir," Avery said.

Earth's Supreme Overseer straightened up. "Now that McAffey's disgraced, we don't have to pretend he's an Uzbek. What a benighted wreck of a man. He did prove to be useful, however." A glint came into Ludden's eye. "I spoke to Goldfarb. I've approved the drug testing, but before you begin, I want to get some real intelligence from our queer friend. He arrived on a spaceship from the other side of the universe. He must know something about rocketry—a subject vital to our national defense. He's full of knowledge we've been unable to access. Your report says that he's able to understand English and execute simple commands. Is that correct?"

"Yes, sir," Avery said.

"And he can read?" Ludden asked.

"We think so. He spends hours staring at the dictionary," Avery said.

"He should be able to give us a higher grade of intelligence than he has thus far." Ludden bent to look me in the face. "Why are you holding out on us?"

Lee moved closer. "He's not holding out, sir. He simply lacks an effective way to communicate. Due to the structure of his mouth, throat, and vocal chords, he's unable to make human sounds."

"Then teach him to type, dear," Ludden said.

A strange look came over Lee's face. I thought she was about to speak, but she shut her red lips tight.

The man on the left side of Ludden tapped him on the shoulder and pointed to his watch. The high muck-a-muck nodded and spoke to Avery.

"After she teaches him to type, I want you to interrogate him on all aspects of interplanetary travel and the science behind it. I'll have a set of questions sent from HQ. I want monthly status reports.

As soon as the door closed, Lee fluttered her fingers through her curls, dismissing them from their tight formation. Then she began to pace, her pronged shoes clicking on the floor. "Since when am I a goddamn typist? I didn't go to medical school to become a typist. I don't know how to type. And how is Doug supposed to type with those pods?"

Avery's brows shot up. "You can't type? Are you kidding me?"

"No, if I need something typed, I have a secretary do it."

"Well, you don't have to type sixty words a minute, just explain sounds and letters and show him how to hit the keys. If nothing else, he can hold a stick in his pod and hit the keys."

"You do it," Lee said.

"Are you refusing?"

"Yes."

Avery curled his fingers into a bony knot and brought it down on my innocent Maytag, producing a hollow metallic boom that made me jump. "Wonderful," he said,

"I'm going to have to call Lloyd in earlier than I planned. At least I know he can type. He's more of a woman than you are." Avery ran his fingers through his hair. He walked up to Lee and stood close to her. I could see she wanted to back away, but she didn't. "Tell me, Dr. Ogilvie," Avery said, "can you do anything a normal woman can do?" He turned and walked away. "Would it be too much to ask for you to talk to logistics about the trainees still living in this building?"

"I'll get right on it," Lee said.

When she had left, Avery sat down on one of the flowered chairs. He jumped up immediately and glared at me. "How did you manage to get everything wet? And get those stupid teeth out of your mouth."

I took my excellent vampire teeth out and stowed them in a drawer. Avery was not well disposed toward me at the moment, but I was not so well disposed toward him either. I had looked over the entire room and not found so much as a single Cheezee, much less a percolator. I hadn't had anything to eat since the candy, and that I had regurgitated into the Mississippi. My stomach rumbled.

Lee would have understood right away, but Avery was not so perceptive. I waddled over and pointed to my mouth.

"I see you got rid of the teeth. You want a medal?" he said.

I shook my head and pointed to my belly.

"What? You want a belt?"

I pointed to my mug wart.

"Ah, you want coffee?"

I nodded enthusiastically. While my intelligence might be considered average on Utorb, on Earth I was a genius if Avery was any indication of the general aptitude.

"I suppose you want Cheezees, too?" he asked.

I nodded.

"Well, we ordered Cheezees and coffee. I wonder where logistics put them." Avery looked around half-heartedly. "Come to think of it," he said, "I haven't had anything to eat either." He checked his watch. "The cafeteria closes in thirty minutes. I need breakfast. I'll bring you a cup of coffee and then we'll see about those Cheezees. How's that?"

That was not satisfactory, but Avery was out the door before I could protest. I heard the lock engage. I judged the chances of him remembering to bring me anything were infinitesimal. I yawned and crawled back into my cylinder to sleep.

"Doug, are you asleep?" It was Lee. I heard a delectable crinkling sound. I poked my head out of the Maytag.

She had six large bags of Cheezees. She dropped one of them on the floor on her way to the desk, where she deposited the rest. "I apologize. I just realized that you haven't eaten. Logs was supposed to put the Cheezees in here, but they locked them up in a closet in the next room. I had to go get the key from them. Your coffee and your percolator are in there, too. I'll be right back."

I scrambled out of my Maytag and fell upon the bag Lee had dropped. I ripped it open and thrust my proboscis deep into the heavenly orange vermiform dinguses. She returned to find me on my back, pouring Cheezees into my mouth and chewing lustily.

"Slow down, or you'll get sick. God knows I don't want to deal with any more alien vomit." She shuddered. "I'm going to put your percolator over here on the end table if I can find an outlet." While she was unpacking and assembling the machine, I finished off the bag of Cheezees. I was about to open a second when Lee held up her hand and said, "Not yet. Digest those properly before you open another bag. I'm going out to get the coffee, and there had better be five unopened bags of Cheezees in here when I get back."

Lee returned shortly with a can of Maxwell House. She was about to brew a pot when I tugged on her sleeve and motioned to indicate that I would prefer to make the coffee myself.

"Why thank you, Doug," Lee said, "that's very considerate of you. But please don't make it so strong."

It wasn't considerate of me. While I liked Lee, I had little regard for her skill with the percolator. I suspected she had adopted Jimmy's old strategy: "If you don't like doing something, do it badly, and people will eventually quit asking you to do it."

"Doug, I worry that you're too obliging." Lee sat down and crossed one leg over the other. Her eyes began to follow something that was not in the room. "If you're too obliging, they take advantage of you. I learned that the hard way. It seems little girls and little aliens were raised to please people. That's not always a good thing. It pleases people when you agree to do the gritty, boring, mindless things they don't care to do for themselves. But once you start doing those things, they won't let you stop. They start to think of *you* as gritty, boring, and mindless. After a while, you think of yourself that way."

Lee got up and began to pace. "I lied to Avery when I told him I couldn't type. I'm an excellent typist."

Lee turned suddenly and stared into my face. Her

voice softened. "You have a mother somewhere. Do you think of her much? I try to remember that you have a mother, too."

Actually, due to the fact that controlled hyper-evolution had mucked up our relevant organs and left female Utorbis unable to harbor fetuses, I was grown in a tube. So I did not have a mother, per se, although I retained a fondness for cylinders.

"I bet you miss her," Lee said. "I love my mother. She's so smart. She told me not to learn to type. I did anyway. Then I took a research job at a university. All I did was type up case studies day in and day out. After two years, I quit and came to the Mines. When they asked me how many words per minute I could type, I said twelve."

I listened carefully, mulling over her words.

"Doug," she said, "you're too obliging." She took a long sip of coffee and closed her eyes. "I worry what will happen to you if you learn to type. At first they'll be interested in the answers you give to their questions, but it won't be that long until you've typed out everything they want to know. Then what? Will they decide to dissect your brain? Or will they turn you back into a GS-5 clerk typist and make you do nothing but type. It ruined my mother's hands. I used to rub them with warm sweet oil at night. It's twentieth-century slave labor. Besides, this idea of theirs is a stupid waste of time."

Lee put down her cup and came to where I stood. She got down on her knees, put her hands on my shoulders, and looked straight into my eyes. "Doug, listen to me. Lloyd is going to come here to teach you to type." Her fingers tightened on my shoulders. "Don't learn." Lee shook my shoulders so that a bit of hot coffee spilled from my mug wart onto her hand. "And guard your secrets. Don't type them out for everyone to see. Once your secrets are out, Lord knows what will happen to you. Do you understand?"

I nodded, for I understood completely. Her words reminded me of something Jimmy had said: "If it was me, I wouldn't tell 'em anything."

The blank moon of ignorance had set behind my eyes.

36

QWERTY

Avery was threatening to pickle and jar my anomalous alien entrails. Lloyd had taken to pacing and rattling the coins in his pocket until Avery threatened to pickle his entrails likewise. Only Lee was calm. Sometimes she smiled at me behind their backs.

They had brought me a bright blue Royal typewriter. I had to conceal my enthusiasm. In addition to its great beauty, it touched a spot in my memory. I'd seen a similar apparatus in a museum on Utorb. The typewriter offered a rudimentary way to communicate with the rudimentary humans. It tempted me, but I remembered Lee's and Jimmy's warnings.

I'd never had a problem failing lessons on Utorb, particularly Physics, but the lessons taught on Earth were farcically simple. Lloyd's tortured explanation of how a different sound corresponded to each letter on the keyboard was an utter knee slapper for someone who had memorized Webster's Dictionary. I could barely suppress my effervescent Utorbian laughter. Once or twice it bubbled forth despite my efforts.

"Sounds like a duck having an orgasm," Avery said.

"Please don't tell us how you know what that sounds like," Lee said. "I know you served in some remote locations—"

"Enough," Lloyd said. He leaned toward me with an earnest expression on his face. "Let's try this again. Concentrate. Take your name, Doug. If I wanted to type it on this typewriter, then first I hit this key, which is a 'D.' It makes the 'duh' sound in Doug."

I leaned forward and sniffed the typewriter. I stuck out my tongue and delicately tasted the 'D' key.

"No, no, no," Lloyd said. "You hit it like this." He demonstrated, pressing his finger down on the key. The type bar hit the paper, and I hit the ceiling, feigning terror.

Lloyd shook his head. "I could have sworn he was smarter than this. He used to understand every word I said. Maybe the coffee is eating his brain. Nothing is working."

"Well make something work," Avery said. "I need to write my report to Ludden."

Lloyd took a deep breath. "All right, Doug. Press down on the 'D' key and see what happens."

I reached out and was about to retract the webbing between my phalanges. Jimmy was the only human who had ever seen me do it. I hesitated, suspecting they would find it disgusting. Then it occurred to me that my webbing offered the perfect excuse. I left it in place, reached out, and pressed down on the 'D' key. My webbing caught between 'D' and 'F' and 'R'. The effort to disengage myself resulted in a painful tear.

"Oh dear," Lee said. "Let me look at that." She held my upper limb terminal and gently touched the rip. "Maybe I should go get some mercurochrome."

"Don't bother," Avery said. "He heals fast."

After that, Lloyd tried to teach me to type by hitting the keys with a pencil. I sniffed the pencil, then stuck it up my proboscis.

Lloyd turned away. "That's disgusting. I don't think I can teach him to type. Teaching him longhand would be even more difficult. Maybe we could try alphabet blocks?"

Lloyd and I sat on stools at a table covered by wooden blocks with colorful letters on the sides. Lee had whispered to me that I should accomplish just enough to keep Avery from pickling my entrails. So in the middle of the table, I spelled out "DOUG" with the blocks.

"Look!" Lloyd shouted. "He did it!"

Avery scowled. "Eureka. After only a few weeks of steady labor, we've managed to teach him to spell out his own four-letter name. What a fucking genius." Avery knocked the blocks off the table with a vicious swipe of his arm. "The little bastard is holding out on us. Time to stop playing kindergarten and conduct a real interrogation."

Avery pulled up a stool and sat with his dimpled chin inches from my face. He reached into his shirt pocket and pulled out a packet of cigarettes. "I know you can feel pain because you whimpered like a puppy when you hurt yourself on the typewriter." He shook a cigarette from the box without taking his eyes from me. He pulled out a silver lighter and clicked it. The flame made me jump, even though I'd seen these devices in operation many times.

"Perhaps we should experiment to see how much

pain you can feel?" Avery lit the cigarette and blew a puff of smoke into my face. I felt a sneeze coming on but managed to suppress it. Avery took the cigarette in his other hand, holding it in two long, tapered fingers with the fiery end pointed in my direction. "Do burns bother you?"

"No," Lloyd said loudly, "we're not going to do that."

Lee crossed the room and snatched the cigarette from Avery's hand. She threw it on the floor and stomped on it with her pronged shoe. "Asshole," she said.

"I was just trying to scare him. I should have known you ladies would interfere." Avery got up and paced. He stopped in front of me, reached down swiftly and grabbed a fist full of my wool and yanked until I cried out.

Lee and Lloyd started to come to my aid, but Avery held up a hand. "Back off." Without releasing my wool, he turned to me and said, "You will take those frigging blocks and spell me a word with more than one syllable, or I'll stuff every last one of them up your nose."

I was scared, but also angry. I began to shuffle blocks with speed and dexterity. Then I stood back to show him the two-syllable, compound word I had spelled: ASSHOLE.

Lee doubled over with laughter. Lloyd's shoulders shook. Avery grabbed a block from the floor, whirled, and flung it swiftly at my head, but I ducked in time.

37

WHISKEY SOUR

Lee wanted to smoke some ganja and go to bed, but the day didn't end when they secured the alien's quarters and went upstairs.

The Mines team had two suites on the fifth floor of Mary Ethel Owens Worthy Hall. Each suite had two bedrooms with a bath in the middle. Avery and Lloyd shared one suite. Lee occupied one bedroom of the other suite. They used the remaining bedroom for strategy sessions and communications with Headquarters. Logs had installed a secure phone.

Strategy sessions my eye, Lee thought bitterly. Once again, the evening had degenerated into watching Avery drink and listening to him mutter curses. He was a different man than he was during the daytime, when he generally maintained an air of pleasant nonchalance, even when delivering a nasty remark. Darkness called out darkness. He was angrier than usual tonight and resisted any suggestion that they retire. Lee and Lloyd didn't bother to stifle their yawns.

"Excuse me," Avery said and went into the bathroom.

It annoyed Lee that Avery used her bathroom and sprinkled on her toilet. Lloyd, on the other hand, always used the facilities in his own suite. He was a gentleman.

"Do you think this will be the end of it?" she whispered to Lloyd. "Surely we can get on with the drug testing now."

Lloyd glanced toward the bathroom. "Avery doesn't give up easily."

"There's a bitterness at his core," Lee said. "I don't understand how such a wealthy, privileged man gets so bitter."

"I'll tell you later," Lloyd whispered.

Avery came out of the bathroom, turned to Lee, and said, "I will continue to urinate on your toilet seat for the duration. I flushed your prissy note. Don't try to change me, Dr. Ogilvie. As you keep reminding me, you're not my wife. Thank God."

Avery sat down heavily on the bottom bunk and placed a government-issue tin ashtray on the floor between his feet. When he reached down to flick his ashes, sometimes he hit the tray and sometimes not.

Lee had to bite her tongue to keep from making a rude comment about Avery's poor aim both in smoking and urinating.

Avery stared at a spot in the mid-distance between himself and his colleagues across the room. "The little bastard is holding out on us. He's intelligent. He could communicate if he wanted to."

Lee felt a tinge of guilt for discouraging Doug from cooperating. She dreaded Avery's reaction should he ever discover what she'd done. She kept her eyes down and pretended to scribble in her notebook.

Avery railed on, his voice rising to a wail. "After all I

went through to obtain that bastard!"

Lee lit a cigarette, wishing it were ganja.

A burst of youthful laughter from across the hall brought Avery to his feet. They were sharing the building with young analyst trainees. Their fresh faces and loud voices infuriated Avery, even on a good day.

"Sit down," Lloyd said. "They're working on it. The class will end Tuesday, and then we'll have the floor to ourselves."

Avery sat slowly. "We can't let anything threaten our work here. It's too important."

Lee desperately wanted to go to bed, but this session was likely to last until Avery had drained the venom from his system. She went to the dresser, which she and Avery had converted to a bar. She plucked a few cubes from the ice bucket and made herself a rum and Coke.

"Whiskey sour," Avery said.

Lee clenched her teeth. Suppressing her sharp tongue made her stomach hurt. From across the room, Lloyd gave her a pleading look.

Fine, Lee thought, *I'll make the drink.* She prepared a whiskey sour and handed it to Avery, being careful not to get too close. He got grabby when inebriated. Moving backwards to keep her posterior out of range, Lee retreated to the opposite side of the room to nurse her drink.

"We've been too nice to that creature," Avery said. "You treat him like a pet. Don't get attached. He's not a cuddly little pet. He's an alien who is withholding information that could be valuable to our national defense." Avery took a long swig of his whiskey sour and blinked. His face took on a blank look of confusion and exhaustion. He abruptly rose and staggered from the room. He left the stub of his cigarette, still burning, on the floor next to the ashtray.

When the door had closed, Lee stomped out the butt. "So, why is he so bitter? You said you would tell me."

"You're not too tired?"

"I am, but I can't sleep yet. I have a bad feeling. I need a distraction."

"I have the same feeling." Lloyd stood up to pace and jangle the change in his pocket. "I shouldn't be telling you this, but you have a need to know."

Lee picked up Avery's ashtray, lit her own cigarette, and sat down on the bed to listen. She scooted back until she was leaning against the wall and hidden in the shadow of the upper bunk.

"You seem to know a lot of things you shouldn't know," Lloyd said. "Do you know about the operation in Albania?"

"I know it was a failure," Lee said softly. "But I've only heard the outlines."

"There are all types of failures," Lloyd said. "Failures in concept, in execution, in follow through. Albania was a failure in every respect, and Avery was instrumental in making it so. He infiltrated hundreds of Albanian expats into the country. They were all either killed or captured."

Lee considered what such a thing would do to a man. "Why, if he failed so badly with Albania, did they put him in charge of an important thing like HALFSHEEP?"

The uneven terrain of Lloyd's face broke into an ironic smile. "In the Mines, a catastrophic failure can cripple a man's soul, but it rarely hurts his career."

Lee thought back on some of the failures she had witnessed and the men associated with them. "You're right. Why is that?"

Lloyd shrugged and resumed pacing. "I don't know.

Maybe because the willingness to take a risk is valued above all else. Or because the men in charge all signed on to the operation. Or because the Mines takes care of its own. In Avery's case, it may be that he's a friend of Ludden and half of the other important men in Washington."

Lee yawned, even though she found Lloyd's story fascinating.

"Ready to call it a night?" Lloyd asked.

"Almost. One question. Why did you tell me that?"

Lloyd sat to get a better view of Lee. He spoke slowly, with a didactic tone she found irritating. "Because Avery is a hornet's nest, and you shouldn't jab at him."

Lee crushed her cigarette into the ashtray. "You're right. Time to turn in. Goodnight."

Lloyd hesitated with one hand raised, as if on the verge of continuing his lecture. Then he merely nodded and said, "Goodnight. Sleep well."

Lee went to the bathroom to brush her teeth. She wanted to fall straight into bed, but she remembered her mother's words: "The small routines keep you together when everything is falling apart."

"Yes, Mom," Lee said. She swiped the toilet seat with Lysol. She took off her blouse and added it to the laundry bag in the corner. She washed her face and slathered it with Ponds cold cream. In the bedroom, she changed into silk pajamas and cut off the light. She was about to climb into bed when she heard something in the other room.

Lee crept back into the bathroom. She could hear someone stumbling about. It must be Avery. She detected the sound of a number being dialed. Moving slowly, Lee took a water glass from the sink, gently placed it against the door, and put her ear to the rim. She heard the phone cord slide across the floor as Avery dragged it to the other side of the room. Then the radio clicked on. Avery turned up the volume enough to mask his conversation. Lee gave up trying to eavesdrop and returned to bed. She lay awake for a long time. No good could come of phone calls in the night.

"Without pain, there can be no desire to escape from pain. Without the threat of punishment, there can be no gain."—Levrenti Beria

38

BOOTS

They were late. Fortunately, they had left the percolator in my room. I emptied my mug wart twice before I heard the tumblers of the lock spin.

Coffee burbled in my stomachs when I saw them. Avery's brows pinched his nose. Lee's sharp-pronged shoes thwacked the floor without mercy. Lloyd's eyes mourned.

They had been arguing, and I was the unhappy subject of their dispute. I saw no point in picking sides. I always lost no matter who won. I crept to a corner and curled into a ball, covering my sensitive aural organs.

Avery would have none of it. "Get over here, Dick Face. I want you to hear what I have to say." I uncurled and shuffled to the center of the room. His next words were chillingly familiar. "You belong to us. We own your orange hide and we can do whatever we like to it. Nobody in the universe can help you. You're going to start communicating with us, real communication. Do you understand?"

I looked down.

Avery pointed at me. "Do you see that? Despite everything, he still has an underlying contrariness. That's the crux of the matter, learning how to destroy that. If we can do that with Doug, we can do it with foreign spies."

"What do you plan to do?" Lloyd asked.

Avery turned his pointy finger on Lloyd. "You have no right to question me."

"Of course we do," Lee said. "We're part of this team. You would be foolish disregard our opinions."

"Then call me foolish, but I'm not listening to you idiots. We're going back to Headquarters today to debrief Ludden. Pack your things. I'm not sure when we'll be back."

"What about Doug?" Lee asked. "We can't leave him by himself."

"I've taken care of that," Avery said.

"How?" Lee asked.

Avery walked up to Lee, put his face close to hers, and said, "None of your damn business."

Lee didn't flinch. "Who will take care of Doug?" she asked.

"An associate of mine named Boots."

"What kind of name is that?"

Avery stuck a finger in his ear and to indicate that Lee's voice was reaching a pitch he found unpleasant. "No more questions. We have to get on the road. We're briefing Ludden in four hours. Another peep out of either one of you, and I'll have you fired."

Then they were gone. I fixed myself a nice, strong pot of coffee. I hoped Boots would be the sort of human who could be persuaded to increase my daily ration of Maxwell House.

I stared at the closet where the Maxwell House was stored. Lloyd kept it locked so I wouldn't drink too much. A frightening thought arose in my mind: suppose he had taken the key with him? I tried the door and discovered it was open. I looked inside to see my Maxwell House, my Cheezees, and a variety of things that evidently dated from the time when this was an educational facility, including a stack of large, heavy books.

I poured my mug wart full. Then I hoisted the top book off the stack and hauled it over to a flowered chair. I read the title: "The Meekins College Beacon, Class of 1945."

It was a curious volume, filled entirely with black and white images of female humans. During my tenure with the Army and the Mines, I had only met a few females. I had calculated the ratio of males to females on Earth as eighty-six to one. Now here was a book filled with nothing but females with faces unvandalized by age.

What did this mean? What had happened to them?

There was a time when my happy, ignorant mind would have devised a benign conclusion, when I would have said, "They're probably living joyous lives elsewhere." That was before Deyahm told me about cycles and beheadings, before the overseers stuffed me into a rocket and fired it across the universe, before humans subjected me to vivisection, blast testing, and solitary confinement. Now my mind filled with less happy thoughts.

Had the beheadings begun on Earth? I had concluded that humans were at an earlier stage of evolution than Utorbis and that the future trajectory of their evolution would be similar. I had noted many items, such as the typewriter, similar to things found in our museums.

Had the beheadings begun with Earth females? On Utorb, the overseers beheaded roughly equal proportions of males and females, according to Deyahm. The criteria for selection were based on the quality of genetic material, not on gender. To do otherwise would cause problems with reproduction. Of course, after the eleventh cycle on Utorb, artificial methods of reproduction replaced natural ones, which came to be considered too random and unsanitary. But that had not happened yet on Earth, as far as I could tell.

Then I remembered some of the things Lee had said, and it occurred to me that the females might be off typing. Lee had called it slave labor. Were they all slaves? Were they locked away like me?

I turned the slick pages and gazed at pictures of unfamiliar human social constructs to include field hockey teams, glee clubs, and honor societies. I saw females reading books, walking under trees, and eating at tables. Then I came to a picture that froze my heart because it was taken in the very room where I sat. In this picture, the flowered chairs were full of females. More lounged on the floor. Their hair was adorned with cylinders that made their heads appear gigantic. They were smoking cigarettes and looking at books. Garments hung on strings above their heads. I looked more closely at the photograph and discovered that their books were like the one I held. I read the words printed beneath the photograph: "The laundry room of Mary Ethel Owens Worthy Hall is *the* place to gossip. Worthy girls giggle over last year's *Beacon*."

Heebie-jeebies crept up my back. I pulled out other books, all similar to the first, but with different numbers on their covers. I paged through them and found more females. Females who had washed their garments in my Maytag and hung them up to dry on strings.

Where were they now?

I resolved never to let the humans know I was female. I slept poorly that night.

When I woke the next morning, I poured the rest of my coffee into the brew basket. Even after drinking the entire pot, I didn't feel restored. I crawled back into my Maytag, closing the lid over my head. I resolved not to come out to meet Mr. Boots when he arrived. I fell asleep and didn't hear the door open.

A churlish voice said, "Hey, alien, get your green ass out here."

The humans nurture a number of unfortunate stereotypes concerning aliens, the most persistent of which is the belief that we are all small, green, and anxious to insert probes into their apertures. We are small, yes. But we are not green, and I believe I speak for all Utorbis when I say that we would find the idea of inserting probes into apertures rebarbative. I was already poorly disposed toward Mr. Boots, without having set eyes on him. I elected to ignore him.

I heard him walking heavily about the room. After a short time, a series of fearsome bangings commenced. This suggested a predisposition to violence against inanimate objects. I wondered nervously whether this extended to animate objects such as myself. The banging grew thunderous. It occurred to me that if Mr. Boots was indeed predisposed to violence against animate objects, then I, as the only available animate object, was in a feces load of trouble.

I made myself small and still inside the Maytag. My stomach began to growl, and I remembered that I was now dependent on Mr. Boots for nourishment. The longer I stayed hidden, the angrier he would become. I decided my best hope for survival lay in revealing myself immediately. Then I heard a thunderous banging from the direction of the closet and I stayed put.

Heavy footsteps approached. Light flooded in on me as he lifted the lid from my machine. I shut my eyes and was surprised when he set the lid back down gently. Then a deafening crash of metal against metal, taking place directly above my head, sent my muscles into spasm. I sprang out of the Maytag and stuck to the ceiling.

It took some time for the echoing crashes inside my head to stop. I became aware of a cruel laughter.

"Get your orange ass down here." A threat throbbed at the bottom of his voice. I understood in my head that the most prudent course would be to do as he said. My head was unable to communicate this wisdom to my carcass, which clung more tightly to the ceiling.

The heavy steps moved away from me, but I barely had time to exhale before a sharp object struck me. My cry of pain was met with a cackle of laughter. Then I was struck again and again by alphabet blocks. I briefly mislaid my consciousness and fell back into the Maytag. My head was down, and my pods were up, and the vast majority of my bodily components stung mightily.

A shadow fell over me, and I looked up to see a frightful physiognomy framed by the round rim of the Maytag.

"If you ain't the butt-ugliest thing I ever seen," the beast said. Yet his own countenance was considerably less aesthetically pleasing than a human posterior.

Indeed, I'd never seen a face so extensively vandalized. The nasal bones had been shattered, leaving haphazard creases across the wide bridge of the nose. One nostril had split and healed askew. White scars formed an X across the forehead above the right eye, and a small circular dent was visible high on the frontal bone. One ear appeared to have melted to his skull. At least three teeth were missing from the ghastly smile. The point of the chin was unaccounted for. A thick, oval scar marked the spot where it should have been. An eager, gleeful expression lit this extraordinary physiognomy.

"Avery made me promise not to kill you," the beast said, "but that don't mean we can't have us some fun."

I suspected that his definition of fun in no way resembled mine, nor the one provided by Mr. Webster in his excellent book.

"Let's see what we got here." A Brobdingnagian hand clasped my right lower limb and yanked me from my cylinder, scraping my hide against the rim. The beast held me upside down while he examined me. Then he abruptly let go, allowing me to fall on my head.

As I lay on the floor, he leaned over with his great paws resting on his knees. "My name is Boots. They call me that because I got big feet and I like to kick the shit out of people." Throughout this introduction, he kept the smile on his face.

I entertained the vague hope that this smile meant that Mr. Boots was being facetious. Throughout my acquaintance with him, I grasped such straws to keep myself from shrieking. If I started to shriek, I wouldn't be able to stop. I have no doubt Mr. Boots was sincere when he said he liked to kick the feces out of people. The only reason he didn't kick the feces out of me is that Utorbis don't commit excrement. Mr. Boots must have found this frustrating. Near the end, his frustration reached such a peak, that he briefly quit smiling as he kicked me.

On that first day, he never stopped smiling. He was giddy with joy as explained the breakfast game he had devised. "I'm gonna take one of these Cheezees, and put it on the head of this tennis racket I found in the closet. Now I'm going to hold the racket here while you move your orange ass over there." He pointed to a spot four feet away, and I obediently took my place, hoping that cooperation would improve my situation. "Look sharp. I'm gonna flip this racket, soes the Cheezee falls. You catch it in your mouth before it hits the floor, or I hit you over the head with the racket. Ready?"

Having concluded that it didn't matter whether I was ready or not, I nodded. Mr. Boots turned the racket over, and the Cheezee fell. I lunged for it but missed. Before I could right myself, the racket swung round and walloped me on the head so hard I saw stars, not onrushing stars such as I had seen on my trip or peaceful stars such as I had seen on Halloween night, but stars that wandered drunkenly through my field of vision, fading in and out.

Before I fully recovered, Mr. Boots placed another Cheezee on the racket. I missed this one, too, and received another wallop. The third time, I determined not to miss. I stood on the designated spot with my eyes trained on the Cheezee. When the racket flipped, I timed my lunge perfectly and snapped it out of the air. I felt the salty cheese on my tongue just as I hit the floor. Then I heard the swoosh of air as the racket swung around and walloped me on the head.

Mr. Boots cackled. "You see," he said, "that's the funny part. If you miss the Cheezee, I hit you with the racket. And if you catch the Cheezee, I hit you with the racket." He shrieked with laughter.

I hoped he would grow bored with this a simple-minded game, but "simple-minded" was exactly the sort of game that entertained him most. We "played" until he broke the racket over my head. Breakfast was over, even though I had only consumed four Cheezees. I considered picking up the Cheezees I had missed, but Mr. Boots saw my eye roll in that direction and stomped them into dust.

I needed coffee. I wondered whether Mr. Boots would allow me to make a pot without devising some dastardly game around it. I glanced toward the table and discovered, to my horror, that the percolator was gone. My eyes scanned the room, and for the first time I realized the extent of the damage wrought by Mr. Boots. He had overturned chairs, pulled the drawers from my desk and broken them against walls, ripped pages from Mr. Webster's excellent dictionary, and kicked in the closet door. Then I spotted the most devastating damage of all. My comely percolator lay on the floor, dented almost beyond recognition. I understood then that this was what Mr. Boots had used to make the crashing sound on the lid of the Maytag.

"I'm going to get some shut-eye," Mr. Boots announced. "Beating aliens makes a body tired." He fell onto the bottom bunk, threatening its structural integrity. Before long his mouth fell open in a ghastly crenelated grin and a moist, nasal grunting issued forth.

I remembered my *Soir de Paris*, which had been in the top drawer of my desk along with my dictionary. I crept about in search of it. I found something that frightened me truly: a bag of garments. Their size and aroma indicated they belonged to Mr. Boots. Next to this sat a large box of food: jars of Vienna sausages, Melba toast, cans of beans and SPAM. I found a box filled with bottles. Lifting one, I read the mysterious words "Ron Zacapa."

Avery, Lee, and Lloyd had never brought such things to the room. They slept upstairs and took their meals in the cafeteria. I had sustained myself through this miserable day by anticipating that Mr. Boots would do the same. I came to a terrible conclusion: Mr. Boots might not leave the laundry room at all.

I allowed misery to soak my being. From the corner of my eye, I caught a glimpse of something blue on the floor near the desk. It was my *Soir de Paris*. Miraculously, the bottle was unbroken. I opened it and dabbed a touch of the delightful perfume under my proboscis. It helped to mitigate the smell of Mr. Boots.

My existence improved somewhat after I abandoned hope. I gave up trying to stay clean and allowed myself to wallow in the filth left by Mr. Boots. I quit hiding because he always found me. I let the blows rain unchallenged upon my head and the kicks unimpeded upon my butt. I resigned myself to the "feeding" games. Invariably, these games also involved punishments—such as punching, kicking, or plucking the wool from my flocculent butt—and rewards—such as punching, kicking, or plucking the wool from my flocculent butt. This joke never ceased to amuse Mr. Boots.

I shudder to say that he did not exercise the nicety of closing the bathroom door. The sounds and smells that issued from that room disturbed me in the extreme. After he had clogged the toilet with pages of my dictionary, which he utilized for wiping his butt after running out of the thin paper on rolls, the fetor worsened significantly. Sometimes he urinated in the Maytag cylinders.

When Mr. Boots drank from the Ron Zapata bottles, he would become even more violent.

I ceased to think and took to wandering dull and insensate about the room, kicking at empty Cheezees bags. Then I settled into a corner and waited for death.

39

HOW THE WORLD WORKS

I drifted to a faraway planet, many cycles past, and stood in the line to the beheading machine. An exquisitely sad poem floated into my mind. I reached for a stone to scratch it onto the wall. I scrabbled but found only air. The poem drifted beyond reach.

Footsteps sounded dull, heavy, sharp, and hollow.

"Oh my God."

"What in the hell happened here? Boots, get up."

I felt a touch on my shoulder and flinched, but the hand was soft. "Doug, are you all right? It's Lee. Open your eyes so I know you're all right." With effort, I hoisted my lids and saw a blurry Lee. "His eyes are colorless. He's alive, but barely. Lloyd, get him some coffee, quickly."

"The bastard smashed the percolator," Lloyd said.

"Damn your Neanderthal hide, Boots, what have you done?" Avery kicked at a quilt-covered hillock.

Mr. Boots' voice rose thick with alcohol. "Hey, stop it. You told me not to kill him. I didn't. You wanted me to break him, and he's broke."

"You're an idiot," Avery said.

"You hired me."

Lee strode up to Avery, eyes sparking. "Exactly, you're the idiot who hired the idiot. What were you thinking? Do rich boys ever consider consequences?"

Lloyd crossed the room to stand protectively next to Lee.

Avery's face turned red, then the color drained away. He turned and kicked Boots again. "Get out of here. You're on your own. Get out of here now or I'll let certain parties know where you are."

Boots stared back at him. His scars stood out white against the deepening red in his face. Boots was frightened. Then he was gone.

Accusations and recriminations flew back and forth over my head. They wrapped me in a blanket and carried me up a narrow back stairway. I misplaced my consciousness again. When I found it, I was being lowered into a tub full of bubbly, sweet-smelling water. In the background, I heard a percolator.

"Can you drink some coffee, Doug?" Lee said.

I'd almost forgotten the taste of it. I nodded. Lloyd approached and poured the brew into my mug wart from a brand new Universal percolator. I took a long sip.

"Don't drink too fast," Lee said. "Your stomach isn't accustomed to it yet."

We were crowded into a small bathroom. Lee was on her knees by my tub. Avery sat on the closed toilet seat. Lloyd leaned against the sink.

I nibbled on Cheezees as Lee rubbed shampoo into the wool that Mr. Boots hadn't plucked out. With gentle hands, she examined and cleaned the wounds on my body. I'd been too weak to gather the energy or desire to heal myself. My emaciated carcass was a mass of cuts, abrasions, and bruises. The water soothed me and made my flesh sting.

"You poor thing," Lee said sweetly. She directed a searing glance over her shoulder. "What kind of idiot hires a homicidal maniac to care for a defenseless creature like Doug?"

"He didn't cost the Mines a cent. We needed to provide him sanctuary. At the time, it seemed like a good solution to have him soften Doug."

"Soften?" Lee snorted. "Give me your hand, and I'll rub some lotion into it," she said to me. As she slathered on the fragrant substance, she berated Avery. "Didn't cost the Mines a thing? The Mines spent years trying to get Doug away from the Army, and you almost cost us his life. What if Ludden found out that his precious alien was nearly beaten and starved to death by a criminal 'babysitter' during a six-week Bacchanal featuring bootlegged rum from Guatemala?"

"All right," Avery held up his hands. "I erred. I admit it." He seemed unnaturally subdued.

Lee pushed on. "And why did this Boots person need sanctuary?"

"You don't have a need to know."

She whipped around and splashed a handful of water into Avery's face. "I have a right to know. I'm the one who's had to clean the filth off Doug, and I'll be the one who has to nurse him back to health. You caused all of this and you're perching on that porcelain throne doing nothing. You'd better give me an explanation of why this happened, or you can scrub your own damned alien."

Avery wiped the water from his face with a hand towel. I studied his drawn features and was shocked to realize that he had been severely shaken by my near demise. When he spoke, his voice was flat. "Fine," he said, "If that's the way you're going to behave. I'll tell you with the understanding that this information goes no further than this room. Certain gentlemen, or I suppose it would be more accurate to call them assassins, are after Boots. Because this is the result of contract work he undertook for the Mines, we felt obliged to offer him sanctuary. Up until this point, he has always been competent and conscientious in his work."

"A reliably violent thug, in other words," Lee said.

"Are you going to continue to interrupt me?"

"No, go ahead."

"Thank you. I will admit that I erred in trusting Boots with this assignment. I wanted to eliminate that underlying contrariness in Doug. It might have worked if Boots hadn't brought the rum."

"And just how did a semiliterate thug end up with a case of the best Guatemalan rum?" Lee asked. "Never mind, I don't want to hear any more. Hand me a towel." She pulled the plug from the drain. I leaned forward and sadly watched the water disappear. Lee wrapped the towel around me, and Lloyd lifted me from the tub.

"Come on, Doug, let's put you to bed."

Lee tucked me into a bunk bed just like the one downstairs. The small room also contained a desk, three wooden chairs, and a dresser. Closed blinds covered the window.

"This is your new room," Lee said. "My room is through the bathroom. Lloyd and Avery have rooms on that side." She pointed. "Right now there are other people staying downstairs. They don't know anything about you, so you have to stay quiet and whatever you do, don't go out into the hallway."

Avery fixed me with a glare. "If you take one step outside, I will remove whatever portion of you breaks the plane of the door."

"If you threaten him one more time," Lee said, "I will knee whatever portion of you breaks the plane of the urinal."

"Woman, do you have any concept that *you* work for *me*?" Avery asked.

Lee narrowed her eyes. "Do you have any concept of how many security violations you committed by allowing an alcoholic thug into a compartmented operation? The man left the place unsecured for weeks, it would appear. We're lucky no one else went down there or that Doug didn't escape. You're going to have to provide an explanation for the state that area is in."

"No, I won't." Avery's face hardened. The shock had faded, and the old Avery had returned, bitter as ever.

"When logistics comes to clean it up, they're going to have to make a report," Lee pointed out.

"Logs isn't going to clean it," Avery said, "We're going to do that ourselves."

"We?" Lee's voice rose. "Exactly who do you mean by 'we'?"

"You and Lloyd. You certainly don't expect me to do it, do you?" Avery's thin brows arched high into his forehead.

"You have no concept of personal responsibility, do you?" Lee said.

"On the contrary, I have a very strong ethic of service to my country." Avery drew himself up straight. "*Noblesse oblige*. To he whom much is given, much is required. It's been my family's motto for generations. I've risked my life for the United States of America. I've parachuted behind enemy lines, fought with the French resistance, and dodged enemy spies."

"You also partied your way across Europe, drank the best wines, and slept with the most beautiful women. Your reputation precedes you. You've never cleaned up behind yourself. You sent hundreds of partisans to their deaths, without so much as getting a reprimand. You hatched a doomed operation and strolled away whistling."

Lloyd turned pale. He reached over and gripped Lee by the shoulder, but she shook him off and took two steps toward Avery. "I say clean your own clogged toilet, I'll have no part of it." She came back, sat down on the bed, and adjusted my covers. "I'll be busy taking care of Doug."

Avery's eyes narrowed to slits. "Do you want to risk your career on this issue? I'm a personal friend of Elliot Ludden. Who are you? A woman who went to a state college. You have no connections, and that is a serious deficit in this business."

"I'll tell you who I am," Lee said, "I'm someone who is in no way to blame for that mess downstairs. Lloyd is in no way to blame. Let me ask you this, why is it that the one person in this room who is most definitely to blame, thinks he shouldn't get his hands dirty?"

"Because I'm the boss. That's how the world works. Now go clean that room," Avery said.

Lee continued to paint my cuts with mercurochrome while Lloyd began to write in a small notebook.

Avery watched them. "Fine." He picked up the phone and dialed one number. "Connect me to logistics." He waited a moment. "Hello, this is Avery Stanton. We've had a spill in the north basement area of Mary Ethel Owens Worthy Hall. Some toxic substances from our experimentation have been released." He listened briefly, "No, absolutely not. It's not safe to go in there even with protective gear. Seal the north basement room from the outside. You'll need to caulk all the openings, and then build a frame against the doors and pour in concrete ... At least thirty years, so try not to do a half-assed job. And I need you to clear everyone else out of this building. No more excuses ... Of course, you can. I can get Elliot Ludden to make the request ... Somehow I didn't think it would be necessary." Avery hung up the phone.

40

PROJECT HALFSHEEP

I had such a happy time recovering from Mr. Boots that I allowed myself to heal slowly rather than use the green energy. I lounged in bed with Lee, Lloyd, or Avery waiting on me. One would look after me while the others traveled.

It was best with Lee. She came back from Jamaica and brought me a delightful percussion instrument made from a coconut. She also unpacked small brown bags, which she hid high in her closet.

Lee left, and Lloyd arrived. He spent most of his time reading and didn't allow me to play my coconut percussion instrument. He brought gifts from Trudie—a stack of books and a fetching chapeau, which he advised me not to wear around Avery. "I don't know if you can understand these," he said as he set the books on my dresser. "But I promised Trudie I would give them to you." The best was *On the Origin of the Species* by a Mr. Charles Darwin. It confirmed my observation that humans had a more passive attitude toward evolution than Utorbis. Lloyd also brought a Bible. He told me I would find comfort there.

I started to read and got as far as the part where Adam and Eve are launched out of their lovely garden. I cried for the rest of the day. I put the book away and didn't open it again.

Then Lloyd left, and Lee returned. This time she'd been to Switzerland. She brought back chocolates for herself and a fluffy embroidered towel for me. From a hidden compartment in her luggage, she removed white bags labeled "Sarkara Laboratories." She put these in the top of her closet with the brown bags from Jamaica.

I took lots of baths in Betty Bubbles. Lee dried me with my embroidered Swiss towel. She replaced my destroyed dictionary with one from the government supply room. She added to that a book of English verse. Best of all, she brought a record player and played me classical music, such as Harry Belafonte singing the *Banana Boat Song*—my personal favorite. She taught me to dance, after a fashion. Utorbian limb terminals are not optimal for executing the Lindy Hop.

Fortunately, Avery only came to take care of me once. He didn't bring me any presents. When I ran out of Maxwell House, he didn't bother to buy me more.

I didn't question anything. I sipped coffee, perused my favorite reflexive verbs and sonnets, and became mildly addicted to Betty Bubbles. I didn't ask why they were treating me with such solicitude. I assumed that they were feeling guilty about what had been done to me, but that was not the case.

They were feeling guilty about what was yet to be done to me.

Lee led me through the bathroom to her own room. "Don't make any noise. It won't be for long." She sat on the bed smoking, while I examined her possessions, tentatively touching a bit of silk or a pronged shoe.

Lee helped me try her make-up. She applied powder to my face with a soft brush to give me "a lovely porcelain complexion." Then she picked up her tubes of lipstick one by one. "Red wouldn't work with your coloring, and I only have cool pinks. You would need a warm pink with that orange. I do have a tube of Tangee. It's supposed to change color to complement your complexion, but it never did much for me." She painted my lips and waited. Dismay clouded her eyes. "My God, your lips are turning blue. I've never seen Tangee do that." She held up a mirror. I clapped my hands in approval. "Well, as long as you're happy," she said.

I was more than happy. I was beautiful.

We heard a knock at the door. "All done in here ma'am," a man shouted.

Lee went into the bathroom and closed the door. After a couple of minutes, she was back. "All clear, we have to go back to your room while they work on mine."

I returned to my room and saw that I had a new piece of furniture. It was a tall, heavy black filing cabinet of sorts with a shiny dial on the top drawer.

"What do you think of the new safe?" Lee asked.

I disliked its black color and overbearing size. I saw other changes. My wooden door had been replaced by a heavy metal one with a combination lock. Later, I would find a similar door had been installed in Lee's room so that the two-room suite was now a "vault." A box protruded from the lower half of my window while the blind covered the upper half.

"Look, Doug. They gave us an air conditioner because they had to nail our windows shut. Let's try it out." Lee pressed a button and a whoosh of air issued from the box. She lifted her arms above her head and twirled in the chilly current. "Heavenly! I get one in my room, too. Meanwhile, the boys are still sweating."

That evening, Lee transferred all of the little white and brown bags to the bottom drawer of the safe.

The next day, Avery, Lee, and Lloyd all showed up at once.

"Doug," Avery said, "as much as we adore waiting on you hand and foot, all good things must come to an end."

Neither Lee nor Lloyd would look at me. Lloyd turned his back and opened his briefcase. He took out a black and white photo and tacked it to my wall.

I squinted at the image of humans seated in a gallery. Some looked off to their left. Others looked down at their notes, and one, dressed in a uniform, peered directly into the camera with suspicion. The one who caught my attention sat front and center. He wore a plain black suit and round white collar. His eyes were empty, like the eyes of the screamer after he splatted himself against the wall.

An awful consequence filled Lloyd's voice. "This was Cardinal Jozsef Mindszenty before the People's Court in Budapest. He was broken. The Communists turned him into a human tabula rasa and inscribed their own words on his mind. If we don't discover how they did this, we leave America vulnerable to an incomprehensible evil. I want this image to serve as a reminder. Some of the projects have turned into travesties. We can't let that happen."

Lloyd's face glowed. We weren't used to seeing him

like this. Avery called him a chilly fish, a saturated blanket, and a party defecator.

We were awkward and quiet as we stared at the photo, then Lee said, "Thank you, Lloyd. My sentiments exactly."

Avery nodded. "You're right. Project HALFSHEEP must succeed." He clapped his hands together. "Let's get this show on the road."

Now Lee came to my bedside and knelt down. She took one of my upper limb terminals in her hands. Her voice was earnest, and its intonation reminded me ominously of the high language. "Doug," she said, "we have something very important for you to do for your country."

"His country is on the other side of the universe," Lloyd said.

Lee's expression grew more intense as she squeezed my limb terminal. "America is your country now, Doug. You want to serve it bravely. Don't you?"

I didn't want to disappoint her, but I had to shake my head. I was proud to serve my country by eating Cheezees, taking bubble baths, and lounging in bed. I fervently hoped more would not be required.

"Doug," she said, "you don't want to sit back while we're all under threat, do you?"

I vigorously nodded yes, keeping my head down as I did so. If there was one thing I had learned, it was not to make contact through the eye when the high language was being spoken.

"It's a dangerous time for our country," Lee said. "We have a great enemy, the Soviet Union. It's an evil country that treats its own citizens horribly. It's trying to take over the world."

As she talked, I looked down at her white hands and the smooth, shiny ovals of her fingernails. They were red, a color highly prized on Utorb. The first time I saw Lee's fingernails, I thought they were stones set into her hand. I concentrated on her fingernails and tried not to hear her words, which were about iron drapes, and show trials, and labor camps. Indeed, those things sounded disagreeable, but I was a small alien, and the Soviet Union was a big country, and I didn't see how it fell to me to do something about it.

Lee's slender, perfect hands contrasted sharply with my hideous limb terminals. While the rest of my body had turned orange, my limb terminals remained a motley gray. Avery described them as "a cross between an umbrella clothesline and a dead bat." Unlike a human hand, which features four digits of unequal height lined up against an opposing thumb, Utorbian limb terminals have seven identical and egalitarian *raliymi,* or phalanges, arranged radially around a *liyma,* which is similar to a human palm, but with a membrane-covered aural organ in the center. Our hands are strong and dexterous. They can crush stones and manipulate the most delicate tools. But in terms of beauty, they are as Avery described. I couldn't take my eyes away from Lee's lovely hand pressing my hideous limb terminal.

I didn't want to hear what she was saying or how her silvery voice pronounced the high adjectives: brave, noble, proud, patriotic, and selfless. These were things I was not. The humans' battles were their own, and I didn't want to share them. I wanted to tell them: "I come in peace."

"I would be so proud of you, Doug, if you volunteered for this," Lee said.

I heard the word "volunteer," and a hot electric current shot through me. I can't explain what happened next. I lost motor control. I lost my mind. I lost something I shouldn't have lost. And I looked up. My eyes made contact with Lee's, which were almond-shaped and green and deep. Sly, also.

"Thank you, Doug." She gave me a radiant smile and removed her hand from mine. When she returned it to me, it was balled into a fist. She opened it slowly. A small white pill sat in the middle of her pink palm.

"All you have to do is take this. Put it in your mouth and swallow it."

After all of her speeches, this was all I had to do? I obediently took the pill and swallowed it.

Lee said to Lloyd, "Thirty micrograms of lysergic acid diethylamide-25 administered to subject at 0800."

Lloyd didn't turn around. He sat at my desk straight shouldered and businesslike. He wore a jacket and tie. He didn't do this every day, but he approached the beginning of Project HALFSHEEP with solemnity, formality, and sadness. At Lee's words, he bent over a yellow pad and began to inscribe neat, black words on its surface.

Lee put her hand over my limb terminal and pressed. "Doug, this is going to make you feel ... strange, but don't worry. We'll be with you. I hope you have the same wonderful reaction to it that I did."

Avery turned sharply. "You've taken it? What was it like?"

"Transcendent, indescribable." Lee's face glowed. "Even when I was a little girl, I knew I wanted to be a scientist. When I took this, I saw my chosen path ahead of me. It wasn't an abstraction; it was a path I could walk. The view was astounding—a city of the future. I picked up glittering treasures and turned them in my hand ... It was glorious—it was science, but so much more."

It wasn't appalling at first. For a while, nothing happened. I gazed at the humans, and they gazed back at me. We felt awkward. Lee pointed to the government clock she'd hung above the safe. "It will be about fifteen or twenty minutes before you feel anything—when the big hand gets to the three or four."

I looked at the clock. I still didn't understand its purpose. I heard the seconds tick, but couldn't fathom why anyone would want to dice time so finely. My eye caught on the knives slicing round and round through time, which is a sea and not sliceable. I focused on each part of the clock in turn: the big black hand, the small black hand, the point where they all met, the numbers—one ... two ... three ... four ... five ... six ...

And then the clock revealed its true nature. The hands and numbers began to float on the rippled surface of time. Some numbers grew, and others shrank. The hands spun round and churned up water and sliced the floating numbers into strips. The hands spun faster, and the waters formed a vortex that sucked the number fragments down. The hole in the middle of the vortex was deep and cold. Numbers became points of light, then stars that first rushed away and then toward me. The stars expired, and I understood time completely.

I shook. Lee again put her hand on my limb terminal. I looked down and saw the perfect ovals of her fingernails, but they were brighter than before, so burning bright they leaped from her fingers and began to crawl all over me. I shook myself to be rid of them, and Lee took her hands away and the red ovals flew up and disappeared.

I looked more closely at my limb terminals. I saw that

some of the red ovals were still in my palm. I closed my strong phalanges over them and ground them. When I opened my phalanges, the crushed bits of red arranged themselves into a radial pattern. As I continued to open and close, extraordinary flaming yellows, singing blues, mourning purples and other colors such as I had not previously encountered congregated and began to make music and bloom. Each flower was lovelier than the last, a singing bouquet of exquisiteness.

"How long do you think he can sit there staring at his hand?" Avery asked. He yawned. I peered into his mouth and saw a great rosy cavern with gleaming white stalagmites and stalactites. He snapped his mouth shut.

Lee stood. "I'd like to see how the drugs affect his reaction to music. I have a record player in my room."

"Sounds like a party," Avery said, "let's go."

We walked through the bathroom and into Lee's room. Avery spied a silky red garment with fluffy feathers around the neck hanging on the back of the door. He reached for it. "Perhaps you should change into something more comfortable."

Lee snatched the garment away. "Sit in that chair and keep your paws off my clothing. Doug, you sit on the bed." Lee began to sort through a stack of records. She held one up. "He loves this one."

Lee set the needle down, and such extraordinary sound came out! I'd heard *Banana Boat Song* many times, but hadn't realized the profundity of its lyrics. I stretched my limb terminals toward the machine so that I could hear it better. "Day, day, me say day, me say day, me say day ..."

What else would anyone need to say?

"Look at what he's doing," Lee said. She watched me

for a moment and then jumped up and took my limb terminals in her hands. She pulled me to her bedside table, clicked on a lamp, and held them under the light. "All this time I've been looking all over his head for ears, and they're on his hands." Lloyd and Avery came over to look. "See, they're covered by a sort of membrane. If you look closely, you can see how it vibrates with my voice."

"I'll be damned," Lloyd said.

I wanted more *Banana Boat Song*. I pulled away, went to the record player, and set the needle back on the beginning.

"For God's sake give him something else to play," Avery said. "Once a decade is enough for that."

Lee reached for the needle, but I pushed her hand away. She let me listen again. I danced as I stretched my limb terminals toward the music.

"He's got to be the worst dancer in the universe," Avery said. "This is painful to watch."

I grew thirsty dancing, and they gave me the best coffee I'd ever tasted. It danced in my mouth. I stared deep into my mug wart and saw red stars twinkling in the dark liquid. I gazed into a sea on another planet in another universe.

***

The next day, Lee came into my room singing the *Banana Boat Song*. Her lips glowed vermillion, and she radiated joy. Lloyd and Avery arrived while she worked the combination on the safe. They were less colorful, less sweet-smelling, and radiated something that was not joy. According to habit, each carried a newspaper. They didn't get along well enough to share one.

Avery looked Lee up and down. "Feeling pretty this morning, are we?"

"Feeling productive," Lee said. "I got up early and worked up new protocols. The LSD-25 experiment was a roaring success. Doug reacted just as a human would. It could have gone so wrong … but it didn't. So, I think we're ready to launch into full-scale testing." Lee pulled her notebook from the top drawer of the safe and passed Lloyd his. She sat down at the desk. "First I'm going to do a survey, testing him with a range of drugs. I'll compare this to the data compiled on human subjects. We'll select the most promising drugs for in-depth study. We can afford to push these tests further than we would with human subjects and still avoid the pitfalls that have tripped up other ASPARAGUS teams."

"Pitfalls like accidentally killing the subject?" Lloyd asked.

"Yes, like that." Lee opened her notebook and began to write.

"Speaking of the dead …" Avery unfolded his newspaper and pointed to a headline: "Mutilated Body Found." "The past finally caught up to Boots."

Lee allowed her pen to fall to the desk and roll away. She grabbed the paper and began to read. "How do you know it's Boots?"

"Keep reading," Avery said.

"Six foot four inches tall … covered in scars. My God, this is gruesome. He was stabbed, burned, and beheaded. They dumped his body by the Ovine Disease Center sign." Lee looked at Avery. "You knew this would happen. When you kicked him out, you knew it would happen."

"So?" Avery said. "We had no more need for him. I tried to do him a favor, and look how it turned out. He deserved what he got. Save your sympathy for the good people we've lost. Boots doesn't deserve it."

"You're an amoral ass," Lloyd said.

All the joy had drained from Lee's face. She put the paper aside. "There's nothing we can do about this now. Let's get back to work. Lloyd, please look in the bottom drawer of the safe and bring me the white bag on the top labeled "lysergic acid diethylamide variant number one."

41

THE STORK

Trudie sat down by the beehive fireplace. Earl had burned *Out of Africa*. All that was left was the cover, which he had torn off and left on the hearth so she would know what she had lost.

"I had a farm in Africa at the foot of the Ngong Hills," Trudie said as she ran her finger over the stork on the cover. She wished she had memorized the whole thing. No book had done so much to help her come to terms with the barren grandeur of her life as this tale of a Danish woman and her coffee plantation.

She raised her eyes to the window. She could see Earl out by the barn, dressing down John, their best hired hand. Two men had already quit because they couldn't stand the rain of abuse. "Try sleeping in his bed," she had wanted to say when they came to her to complain.

Trudie had found another lawyer, but he told her the same thing as the first. "You won't get out of this marriage without losing everything. You have no grounds for divorce." But she would eventually lose everything whether she left him or not. She had considered walking away but what would she do then? Beg from her brother? She was smart enough to know that her rough life had formed her into a shape that would fit nowhere else. Besides, this place was not her father's anymore. With much effort, she had made it her own. It was her job to protect it.

Trudie went to the window to get a closer look at the argument. She saw Earl stumble a bit as he waved his arms. He was drunk—unusual for this time of day. Even drunk, he should know better than to risk having another hand walk off the job. Trudie began to assemble the clues in her mind: the trips into town, missing items from the house, increased drinking and anger. He was gambling again. She should have picked up on the signs earlier, but she had fallen into the habit of shutting Earl out of her thoughts whenever possible. How much of their money had he lost this time?

She knew better than to confront Earl when he was drunk, in the heat of an argument, and in full view of the ranch hands peering from the windows of the bunkhouse. He couldn't bear the affront to his manhood. She knew better, but she didn't care. Should she wait until he was in a good mood? No. She was tired of deforming herself to fit around the edges of his anger. She saw John walk off with the finality of a man who had just given notice.

Trudie went out through the window, breaking into a run when her feet hit the ground. She felt elated as if flying off a cliff. She was a child running in the sunshine, oblivious to consequences. Taunts and accusations tumbled from her mouth. She saw the look in his eye, saw that huge, muscular arm swing round, but she didn't alter her course.

Trudie tasted salt and blood. Glass cut into her cheek, and her horn rims flew into the air and landed in the dust.

42

CANNABIS WEEK

After lysergic acid diethylamide week was over—and truthfully, I don't remember it well—we were scheduled to start the following Monday on various recipes of an earth vegetable called "marijuana." Lee said I would get to try cannabinol, tetrahydrocannabinol acetate, and synthetic cannabinol. On Saturday night, Lee and I sat on her bed, listening to Harry Belafonte. Avery had gone back to Washington for the weekend, and Lloyd had been called to New Mexico for an emergency.

"This is like a pajama party." Lee reached into the neck of her red feathered robe and pulled out a key on a fine silver chain. "Want to watch me roll a joint? I learned how in Jamaica from the experts." She used the key to open a carved wooden box. She took out a small paper and a bag of a fragrant substance. She showed me how to roll a joint of a type unlike any listed on anatomy charts.

"The first one is for me," Lee said, "because I have to test it before I can give it to you." She lit the joint and took a puff, which she informed me was called a "toke" when executed on ganja and a "drag" when executed on tobacco. The smoke smelled sweeter and earthier than tobacco. She took two more tokes, and then carefully snuffed the joint in an ashtray. "I'll save the rest for later." She laughed low in her throat. "God bless America and the Mines. What other employer would pay a girl's way to Jamaica to buy ganja?" She made two more joints and then closed the box. "We'll put these aside for Monday. Now we're going to make a different kind of cigarette for later in the week. You stay here while I get some synthetic THC and a syringe."

Actually, we didn't *make* these cigarettes, we merely altered cigarettes from a package. Lee took the syringe and drew up liquid from a tiny bottle. "Doug, hold the cigarette. Don't squeeze it too hard. It's not supposed to look like it's been tampered with." Lee carefully stuck the needle into the end of the cigarette, pushing it in about an inch. She depressed the plunger of the syringe as she drew the needle out. "I want to distribute the liquid along the cigarette," she explained, "but I don't want it to stain the paper." She examined the finished product with satisfaction. "Not bad. It will smell just like a regular cigarette. I'll put this on the dresser to dry. Now let's make some more."

On Sunday morning, Lee came into my room wearing a hat, gloves, and pronged shoes with a dress. Lee wrinkled her nose. "Sniff, Doug, do I smell like ganja?"

I came over, took a whiff, and nodded solemnly. She wore perfume, but it didn't cover the strong scent of the delightful vegetable.

"I shouldn't have smoked it in my room. All of my clothes reek now." She considered a minute. "But I'm not going to skip services. What would Mom say? I'll park a few blocks away from the church and maybe I'll air out while I'm walking. Besides, nobody in this cow town will recognize the smell. You be a good alien while I'm gone. I'll pray for you."

43

THE ONLY OUT

Trudie was in the hospital in Las Cruces. The doctor wouldn't describe the injuries over the phone. He would only say she was in serious but stable condition and had requested Lloyd's presence. He flew out immediately.

Lloyd arrived with an armload of periodicals from the newsstand. The nurse at the station looked familiar. He glanced at her nametag: Jane Alvarez. They went to school together in El Claustro.

"I'll take those for you, Lloyd," Jane said. "She can't sit up to read yet. I'll hold them at the desk."

Lloyd relinquished the materials reluctantly. Now he would have nothing to bring his sister. "What happened?" he asked. "Was she in an automobile accident?"

Jane gave him an odd look. "No, Earl beat her up. He got in a few punches and a kick before the ranch hands subdued him. He broke her nose and two ribs and bruised her spleen. She'll recover. He'll be in jail for a while. You ought to come home more often."

Lloyd swayed on his feet, and his hands curled into fists. For a moment, he was torn between staying at the hospital and rushing out to confront his brother-in-law. He shook off the thought of leaving. He had to see Trudie.

Seeing the expression of shock on Lloyd's face, Jane took his arm and led him down the hall, leaving him alone with Trudie. He approached the bed hesitantly. She turned her blue eyes on him. Without her glasses, her eyes looked uncharacteristically small in her swollen and purple face. She squinted. "Lloyd?"

"I'm here, Trudie. How do you feel?" He felt stupid asking that question.

She answered slowly. "I feel great."

"What a time for sarcasm," Lloyd said gently.

"Not sarcasm. Give me something to wet my tongue."

Lloyd poured from the pitcher on the table. He unwrapped a paper straw and guided it to Trudie's mouth. She took several swallows. "Enough. I can talk now. I needed to clear my mouth. He broke a tooth."

"I'll kill him," Lloyd said.

"No, you won't," Trudie said. "We're done with him. I can get a divorce now."

"How long has he been beating you?" Lloyd asked.

"This was the first and last time."

"Doesn't matter. I'll kill him."

"No, you won't. It's not entirely his fault."

"Don't say that." Lloyd felt tears in his eyes. "I can't believe you would blame yourself. Don't ever say that you deserved this."

Trudie managed a chuckle. "I knew he was going to hit me and I ran right into it."

Lloyd shook his head. "Why would you want to get beaten up?"

"You're such a big intelligence expert, can't you figure it out?"

Lloyd pressed his palms to his temples.

"Migraine?" Trudie asked.

"Not yet. The answer to your question is no, I cannot for the life of me figure out why you did this."

"Would you like a catalog of all the ways a man can humiliate a woman?"

Lloyd knew Trudie would tell him everything if he asked, but he couldn't bear the knowledge. He shook his head.

"There were a lot of days when I felt less than human, but I didn't have grounds for divorce." Trudie's voice was calm, but her hand, below the tubes, clawed at the sheet. "I couldn't stand it anymore, so I screamed every insult in the book at him and ran right into his fist."

"You goaded him into it?" Lloyd said.

"I stood up for myself. I challenged his judgment. I acted like a woman in full possession of her humanity. And that's what he couldn't bear. If you want to call that 'goading him into it,' then go ahead." Trudie managed a smile, which revealed the chipped tooth. "Early on, the bitterness of living with Earl almost killed me. I took the Daddy's pistol with me out to the veranda and lay down. I wanted to die looking at the stars. Then I saw the lights of Martia's crash."

"What?" Lloyd said. His mind raced back to 1947 and the charred crash site. "You never told me you saw the crash. Are you sure that's what you saw? What direction was it from the house?"

"Due north." Trudie's eyes took on a dreamy look. "Couldn't have been anything else. It was a light show like nothing I'd ever seen, even on the fourth of July. The timing was right—a few weeks before you found her. That odd little creature saved my life."

Lloyd sat back in his chair. "Why, in all these years, haven't you discussed this with me? We could have found a better way out than this."

"Thank you, but I got myself into this mess and I prefer to climb out of it myself."

"It's not right, Trudie."

"What in this whole situation was right? Nobody handed me any good choices."

Lloyd shut his eyes and choked back a wave of nausea. "I've been negligent. I allowed this to happen. I'll stay as long as you need me here."

"Not necessary," Trudie said. "I have good hired men. They saved me, you know. I'm looking forward to running things without Earl's interference. A couple of the men who quite because of him have already come back. You go back and look after Martia. Tell her hello for me."

"Of course," Lloyd said quietly. "Whatever you want."

"Whatever I want," Trudie said with a dreamy smile. "And what do you want Lloyd? Have you thought about that?"

"What I want?" Lloyd said in surprise. "I suppose I want what I've always wanted."

"Are you sure? Things change, Lloyd. You may have set Faye free, but you're still stuck in a place you should have left long ago. Think about it."

Nurse Alvarez appeared. "You should go now, Lloyd. We don't want to tire Trudie."

"Trudie's fine," Lloyd said, "but I need something for a headache."

44

INGREDIENTS

By noon on Monday of cannabis week, I finished my Cheezees. They'd never tasted so exquisite. I lounged in bed, toked up, and read the list of ingredients, consulting my new dictionary on the meaning of each one. In a fit of gratitude, I composed an ode. It was the first poem I'd ever written, either in English or Utorbian, and its lyrical beauty left me gobsmacked. I thought it the finest poem ever conceived. Looking back now, I think perhaps not.

**Ode to the
Constituent Components of Cheezees**
*By Beyal Piyat Martia Plug
Duck Doug A. Leon*

We commence with cornmeal with its golden
    grit.
Cheezees would disintegrate if not for it.
Vegetable oil to make them slide down.

> Oil of sunflower, soybean, or corn by the pound.
> Whey, the dregs left after the curd.
> Sodium chloride or salt, use either word.
> Cheddar cheese made of ingredients fine,
> To include cultured milk, salt, and enzymes.
> Then for a blander gustatory foil,
> Partially hydrogenated soybean oil.
> Maltodextrin's a powder starchier than sweet,
> Polysyllabic component of my favorite treat.
> If it is Cheezees that you are baking,
> Disodium phosphate will keep them from caking.
> Sour cream imparts a touch of tang
> To give your taste buds a flavorful twang.
> If that's not enough to savor,
> Add some artificial flavor.
> To make your treat taste truly great
> Toss in monosodium glutamate.
> Number 2 Red and Number 6 Yellow
> Will make your alien a tangerine fellow.
> And just a dollop of citric acid
> Will keep your Cheezee from going flaccid.

I wished all of my alphabet blocks hadn't been lost in the Boots disaster. I wanted to show the poem to the humans. I made a pantomime of "writing" with blocks.

"What's he doing?" Avery asked.

"He's pretending to spell words with blocks," Lee said.

I smiled, pointed at Lee, and nodded my head. Then, moving my upper limb terminals across the bed garment, I mimicked walking. I pointed, in turn, to the invisible blocks, to Lee, and then to myself.

"I think he wants you to go out and buy him more alphabet blocks," Avery said.

I clapped my limb terminals with glee, pointed to Avery, and nodded. I pointed to my stomach and pretended to chew.

Lee rose. "And more Cheezies. Thanks to that field promotion from Ludden, he does outrank me, so I'd better fetch them."

Avery pulled out his wallet and selected a few bills. "While you're at it, buy more whiskey. The priciest stuff they've got. We could use a cooler. Don't stint, Doug just got paid."

When Lee returned, she had a dozen family-size bags of Cheezees, along with the alphabet blocks, cooler, ice, drinks, and other snacks. Avery helped, but it took them several trips to haul everything into my room. At last, Avery dumped the blocks onto the floor. He turned to me. "You had something to say?"

The blocks were inadequate in number to spell out my poem. Moreover, I had lost my enthusiasm for sharing it. I spelled out two words and turned them around to show Avery: "NEVER MIND."

"Dick Face," he said.

※

While cannabis lacked the technicolor thrill of lysergic acid diethylamide-25, it imparted a hunky dory mellowness. I felt cool smoking it. It's one thing to be considered a hideously butt-ugly alien. It's another to be a bad-ass alien toking up. I loved the fiery-sweet burn of the smoke curling through my six lung-like organs.

"Exhale, Doug. Don't forget to exhale," Lee said urgently.

I exhaled as they watched. It surprised them how much smoke I could hold inside. I became quite adept at blowing it out though my prehensile proboscis to form rings.

"Watching you move that thing like that—with smoke coming out of it, no less—is disturbing in a way I can't begin to express," Avery said.

At first it had bothered me when they stared at me and took notes. I no longer cared. Nothing bothered me, except the fear of running out of Cheezees.

"This is incredibly boring," Avery said. "He was more fun to watch under the influence of LSD."

"This is fascinating," Lee said. "My education prepared me for this. It's the most exciting thing happening in psychiatry today. We have access to the latest drugs, we have the perfect test subject, and we have all the money we need. This is nirvana. If you're bored, go out.

By the end of the week, my six lung-like organs were sore from the ganja smoke. Lloyd returned, quiet and morose. Lee's mood sagged, and she complained about never seeing the sunshine. She went to the window and peeked out the blind above the air conditioner.

Avery quickly crossed the room and slapped his palm flat against the blind.

"Oh, come on," Lee said. "No one can see in."

Avery pushed his face into Lee's and said, "We're on a hill. Who knows who might have line of sight to this place? It might spell the end of the Mines if this got out."

"Lloyd says we're doing God's work here," Lee said.

Avery glanced toward the ceiling. "Only if God deals in dangerous drugs with unknown side effects. No, the general public would not think of this as God's work. They don't understand the threat. Keep your hands off the blinds."

Lee went to the safe. She glanced at the clock and recorded the time next to her initials on a narrow sheet of paper. She opened the top drawer, removed Lloyd's notebooks, and handed them to him.

"Are you ready, Doug?" she asked.

I nodded.

"So what's on the menu at *le Cafe Pharmacologique*?" Avery asked.

"Cigarettes laced with THC or tetrahydrocannabinal acetate." Lee held the lighter while I puffed. I preferred the taste of the ganja, but I couldn't complain. These cigarettes also improved the flavor of my Cheezees. Between mouthfuls, I talked until my throat hurt. As a cloud of Cheezee dust settled around me, I told them about my planet and its cycles. Describing Deyahm, I began to cry. Tears soaked my Cheezees.

Lee frowned. "It certainly loosens the tongue, but it also makes him weepy. He's usually so cheerful. That's not good for operational purposes. We don't want something that causes noticeable changes in personality."

She went to the dresser, where she'd left her untainted cigarettes and lighter. Avery, meanwhile, sidled up to me. "Perhaps I'll sample one of Doug's cigarettes."

"No," Lee and Lloyd said in unison.

"I wasn't asking permission." Avery lit up. Lee and Lloyd exchanged looks of concern. Suddenly I found it all hilarious. Because we were smoking a mixture of tobacco and tetrahydrocannabinol acetate, I wondered whether we were taking drags or tokes. Maybe drokes? I laughed until I fell off the bunk bed and rolled on the floor.

Avery began to bloviate. He spoke of philosophy, opera, bureaucracy, Central European cuisines, and finally settled into a long diatribe on polo, a strange game involving mallets, chukkers, and a great number of vehicular horses. At one point, Avery sat down companionably next to me, which he'd never done before since he found me "borderline repulsive." Enough cannabis will make even a Utorbi look presentable.

"Alien O Alien," Avery said as he clapped me on the shoulder. "Pass the Cheezees."

I passed the bag reluctantly. He took a *huge* handful. Then he took off talking again at high speed. "You know, Lee, there are times when I want to fuck you until you scream, but some days you remind me so much of my wife, it shrivels the scrotum."

Lee's face froze. Lloyd bent over Avery and whispered, "Quit talking *now*."

Avery pushed him away. "Nobody tells me when to talk. Allow me to expound on the similarities between Dr. Ogilvie and my wife, Elizabeth. They both like to insist on things. I suspect Dr. Ogilvie is, like Elizabeth, frigid, which is why I've never made a serious effort to snag a piece of her ass."

"A wise decision," Lee said. The growl at the back of her voice should have been a warning for Avery. Evidently, cannabis had blunted his sense of self-preservation.

He said, "At one time Elizabeth did a great deal of insisting, but she's given up on her attempts to improve me, enslave me, or whatever she was trying to do." Avery reached into my Cheezees bag and withdrew another huge handful.

"Why did you marry her?" Lee asked.

"I couldn't ignore her qualifications." Here Avery stopped to swallow and wipe the orange dust from his lips. "First of all, she's beautiful—one of those dark gold blonds, not the cheap bottle type. Superb bone structure. I love high cheekbones and high color in a woman. I used to love her eyes, but I don't like their expression anymore. Her breasts could be fuller, but her ass and her connections are top notch: Wall Street, Capital Hill, the White House, and the European banking community. She has an uncle or a cousin or an old roommate's brother here, there, and everywhere."

"I suppose she's rich." Lee perched atop the desk, smoking an unaltered cigarette.

"Flush," Avery agreed.

Lee took another drag. "So what went wrong?"

"Damned if I know," Avery said. "You couldn't find a woman more qualified in every particular. But the sum of the whole isn't equal to the parts. Elizabeth is a wonderful hostess, witty conversationalist, and a great cook. She took lessons from Julia Child, an old OSS colleague of mine." Avery crunched Cheezees while he considered the question. "But she looks at me like I was an errant little boy. The sex went sharply downhill after the honeymoon. We don't bother anymore. She says its 'unappetizing' thinking of all the other women I've slept with."

"Will she come to her senses and leave you?" Lee asked.

"No. We enjoy entertaining together. We have a brilliant set of friends and wouldn't care to divide them up. We give fabulous parties and then go our separate ways. It's all very modern. As long as we don't attempt anything tricky, like sex, it should be durable."

Lee had kicked off one shoe. Her foot kept time to some inner music. She appeared fascinated with Avery's confession. Meanwhile, Lloyd was holding his head the way he did when it hurt.

"What about children?" Lee asked.

"We have one. He's at Groton now and doing an excellent job. We both find one child sufficient."

"You've arranged your life nicely," Lee said.

"I have," Avery agreed.

"Then why do you think you drink so much?" she asked. Lloyd looked up sharply and mouthed the word "no." Lee ignored him.

The usual phalanx that stood guard over Avery's face—irony, cynicism, mockery—vanished. To my horror, he began to cry with a rhythmic, wheezing and sucking noise. Lee put down her notebook. We all looked away from Avery as we waited for the crying to stop. It went on until he had trouble catching his breath. He walked over to the air conditioner and drove his fist through the front of it. Then he sank to the floor and resumed crying. Lloyd bandaged his hand while Lee fixed him a whiskey sour. Lloyd put the drink into Avery's good hand and led him away to his room.

45

GRIEVANCES

On Monday, mescaline topped the menu. "Peyote is another name for it," Lee said as she poured coffee into my mug wart. "It's a type of cactus."

I leaped to the ceiling and hung upside down to empty the liquid. I'd had nothing but foul experiences with cactuses—to include being impaled on one and regurgitating parts of another.

"Come on, Doug," Lee purred, "mescaline has effects similar to LSD, and that was fun, wasn't it?"

I dropped to the floor. Lysergic acid diethylamide-25 was indeed diverting.

"I know you'll like this one, too."

Meanwhile, Avery lounged on the floor reading his paper, and Lloyd sat at the desk with his pen poised above the paper. The air conditioner no longer functioned, so he'd taken off his jacket. This gave us a view and a whiff of the spreading damp patches under his arms.

Lee began to dictate. "I'm administering subject 200 milligrams mescaline at 0830. It has a bitter taste, so I'll put it in his coffee." She put a pinch of brown powder into my coffee. "It will take longer for the mescaline to take effect than the LSD. It may be as long as twelve hours." Lee chose a psychiatric journal from the stack on the dresser and plunked herself down on my bed.

Avery let his newspaper drop. "Twelve hours? We have to simmer in this hot box for twelve hours? Why don't we move to your room? Your air conditioner works."

Lee settled her back against the headboard and stretched out her legs. "Sometimes mescaline causes diarrhea. We'll stay here. You could go into town. One less sweaty man in this room would be a godsend." Her eyes lit briefly on the damp stains under Lloyd's arms. He reddened.

"Excuse me, I'll go take another shower," he said.

"Thank you," Lee said.

"And what would I do in town?" Avery asked Lee, "Hang out at the filling station with the locals whittling or whatever it is they do around here for intellectual stimulation?" His voice was whiny. We all found it difficult to be around him when he behaved this way.

"Avery, why are you even here? I know chemicals, drugs, and psychiatry. Lloyd is helping with record-keeping, research, and analysis. What's your function?"

Avery scowled. "I'm your boss. Why do I have to remind you every ten minutes?"

"Do you think we can't do our jobs without supervision?" Lee asked.

"I provide invaluable insight," Avery said. "Also, this is the hottest project in the Mines right now. Psychedelic drugs and an alien? I have to be here." Then Avery proceeded to offer up his notion that I was a Holy Grail that imparted special powers to whoever possessed it.

"Really?" Lee gave Avery a long, searching look.

"Stop looking at me like that. In the Mines, you always derive power from proximity to the most urgent—and most secret—projects," Avery said.

"I see," Lee said.

"Don't use that tone of voice with me. I'm your boss."

Lloyd returned, and they fell silent. I could hear the ticking of the clock. To escape the awkwardness, I picked up Mr. Webster and turned to the Q section.

Lee threw aside her journal. "Avery, you think you're doing the agency a big favor by working here. *Noblesse oblige.* There's more than a touch of contempt in it."

"You have something there," Lloyd remarked. "You and I are grateful to the Agency for hiring us and paying us. We respect the rules."

"Actually," Lee said, "if I had any respect for the rules, I would be vacuuming some man's livingroom. Don't lump me in with you. You resent Avery because he's privileged, but you don't realize that you're privileged, too."

Lloyd's pale face flushed. "How am I privileged? I come from a hard-working family. Nobody handed me a trust fund and an Ivy League education."

"But I bet your family supported you when you went to school. Your professors didn't pull you aside to say you shouldn't be taking up a seat that should go to a 'serious student.' You didn't have to beg to be admitted to a school, even though your grades were excellent. And now, you don't have to prove yourself every time you walk into a room. Because of that dangly thing between your legs,"—Lee pointed, and Lloyd blushed painfully—"people listen to you when they don't hear me speaking. So quit complaining that you don't have any polo ponies." Lee ground out her cigarette.

"Somebody is on the rag," Avery said.

Lee shot him a hot look of irritation. "Are you going to write that on my performance appraisal?"

"No," Avery said. "While I don't approve of women in the clandestine service, I'm professional about it. As a boss, I treat you just as I would if you were a man."

Lee gave Avery a charming smile. "If I were a man, I'd be *your* boss."

Avery's brows shot up. "How did you come up with that bizarre conclusion?"

"Enough of this discussion," Lloyd said.

Something unpleasant crept across Avery's face. "You should be careful, Lee. You have the potential to become a bitter, whiny woman, nursing every real or imagined grievance."

Lee's laugh spiraled to the ceiling. "Whiny woman! That's delicious, coming from such a non-stop complainer."

"Surely you don't think women have a bigger complaint than, say, the Negro?" Avery asked. "I don't see women subject to lynchings and the other atrocities that southerners have inflicted on the Negroes."

"'That southerners have inflicted on the Negroes,'" Lee repeated. "No responsibility assumed there."

"Why should I assume any responsibility?" Avery said. "I like Negroes. My favorite servant growing up was a Negro."

Lee collapsed back on the bed laughing.

"I don't see anything funny," Avery said. "Have you been sampling the wares?"

I'd been listening intently and could contain myself no longer. I told them what it was like being an alien on Earth. I wasn't sure what lynching was, but it couldn't be a great deal more unpleasant than vivisection or being subjected to Mr. Boots or being tethered next to a nuclear blast. Then there was the underground incarceration, the experiments, and being treated like I was an idiot—not a Utorbian idiot, but an Earth idiot, which is a stupid creature, indeed. I spoke vociferously and at length.

They sat watching me. When I'd talked myself out, Avery said, "What do you suppose he was quacking on about?"

The conversation petered out, and we lapsed into boredom. This was the day I discovered that a bored Mines officer is a dangerous Mines officer.

Lloyd left to use the toilet facilities in his own suite. Lee sloshed coffee on her blouse and retired to select another.

Avery gave me a sly smile and said, "I'm going to try my own experiment." Moving quickly, he went to the bottom drawer of the safe and removed the mescaline. He slipped some into Lee's iced coffee and Lloyd's orange soda. He paused a moment, then sprinkled some into his own drink. He returned the bag to the drawer, looked at me, and said, "Don't give me away or I'll have your alien entrails pickled and put on display in the lobby."

46

THE DUPLICITOUS CACTUS

Lloyd backed his chair into the corner. He grew sullen and depressed as he waited for the alien to show the effects of mescaline. Lee had hurt his feelings. Was it just the nature of men to become sexually interested in any woman in their proximity? Certainly he and Lee had little in common beyond work, but he couldn't deny his growing attraction. He thought of the temporary insanity that led Trudie to marry Earl, and himself to marry Faye. They both should have known better, but loneliness and flattery were a dangerous mix. They were trapped before they knew it.

It was a struggle for Lloyd to keep his eyes off Lee as she sat reading. It was hard not see the charm in her intensity or the grace in her hands as she turned the pages. He must not let her guess his feelings. Lloyd wrenched his gaze away and settled it on Doug. The little alien was showing signs of agitation. The scaly hide of his neck twitched. Different parts of his eyes quivered in rapid succession.

"Lee," Lloyd said, "I think something may be happening with Doug."

She looked up from her book. "Doug, do you feel funny?"

The alien flinched as if she had screamed at him. He sprang to the ceiling and clung there shivering. He launched into a keening and discordant crying jag. His body grew limp, and he fell to the floor. Lee started to go to him, but he let out an unearthly sound and scuttled under the bed. She brought her fingers to her lips and her eyes widened. "He's never had a reaction like this."

Her voice triggered renewed crying. The alien trembled, and his ragged howling continued for over an hour until nerves frayed and tempers grew brittle. Lloyd feared a return of his old demons. He took a few deep breaths to steady himself.

Abruptly, Doug fell silent. Avery, who was the closest to him, leaned over to get a better view. He put a finger to his lips and mouthed the words, "He's asleep."

Lloyd closed his eyes and let the tension drain away. The circling demons departed. He slept for a while in the chair, with his shoulder propped against the wall. When he woke again it was to a new sound, human sobs this time, so soft he wasn't sure he heard them until he opened his eyes to see the tears running down Lee's face.

She sat in the upholstered chair hugging her chest with her arms. She stood up and began to turn in slow circles, scanning the room with anxious eyes. "Look at this place! Crumbs everywhere. The bed clothes are filthy." She stared into the small mirror above the dresser. She ran a finger under her eye, wiping off a bit of smeared mascara. "Look at us. We're sweaty and dirty, and we look debauched. This isn't professional. If we're going to do this, we have to be professional or we lose control."

The alien howled again. Lee snatched her bag and pulled out a pack of cigarettes. Her hands trembled as she lit one. She took a couple of drags and then began to cry again.

Lloyd and Avery both moved toward her, but Avery got there first. He placed a hand on her shoulder. "Lee," he said, "don't go female on me now." He couldn't have dried her tears more quickly if he had used a blowtorch. Lee's body went rigid, her eyes fixed on Avery's hand, and she changed her grip on the cigarette.

"Remove that hand from my shoulder or I'll burn it," she said.

Avery complied, backing off several steps.

Lloyd felt a surge of pride in Lee. Here was one woman who wouldn't be led astray by a handsome man.

"Lloyd," Lee said. He caught his breath. "You're right. Maybe we shouldn't be doing this. It's going to deteriorate like the other tests. Turn into a farce."

"No," Avery said sharply. He swept his hands through his hair. Lloyd detected nervousness in his boss. No, something stronger, an incipient panic. "Don't listen to him," Avery said. He pointed angrily at Lloyd. "He's a coward. Don't forget how important this is. Look at old Cardinal Mindszenty up there on the door. Our freedom is at stake. Our minds. We don't have a choice. How do you think it made me feel when I lost every last man I sent into Albania? Do you really think I laughed it off? We had to make that effort no matter the cost. If I have to sacrifice a good night's sleep, or a clear conscience, or my sanity, by God I'll do it. I won't let the Communists win. I'll pay them back for everything."

Lee grew unnaturally still as she listened. Then she drew herself up straight and turned on Avery. "Don't you lecture me about the seriousness of this. I know damn well how serious it is, but this thing could get away from us. Look at this room, how filthy it is."

"There's a janitor's closet down the hall," Avery said, his voice full of a counterfeit cheer. "I'll go get a broom and dust cloth. We'll tidy up. It will help us get our minds in order." Lee looked unconvinced. "Buck up," he continued. "Why don't you put on some music while we clean. It will drown out that godawful alien caterwauling. Anything you like. Even Calypso."

Lee's face relaxed a bit. "Harry Belafonte always makes things better. My god, I need to feel better right now."

Avery left, and Lloyd helped Lee move her record player into the room. They bumped shoulders as they set the device up on the top bunk, and Lloyd's vision momentarily blurred. Everything felt off, Lee's behavior, Avery's behavior, even his own physiology felt off.

Lee put on the *Banana Boat Song,* and it had the effect of calming the alien. He stopped crying and listened quietly.

The song was still playing when Avery got back to the room. He smiled at Lee and began to dance with the broom. She watched him until she could no longer suppress a smile. "Well, that's not Calypso dance, but it's a creative guess."

Avery tossed the broom to the side. "If this isn't it, baby, then show me how it's done."

Lee kicked off her espadrilles and engaged in the rhythmic, seductive movements of Calypso. Doug flattened himself against the wall, and Lloyd's eyes widened.

"Where did you learn to do that?" Avery asked.

"Trinidad."

"Trinidad? I thought you got the cannabis in Jamaica."

"Trinidad was a vacation."

"So you were dancing down in Trinidad with some half-naked buck?" Avery asked.

"I was dancing with my mother. That's where I took her for her birthday. If you lived in a drafty little house in upstate New York, you would think it was pure paradise." Lee stumbled a little and stopped in the middle of her dance. Her fingers rushed to her face, and her voice came out in a wail. "I'm doing it again. I'm not being a professional. I'm messing up. This is the biggest opportunity I've ever had, and I'm messing it up. What's wrong with me? Why am I feeling so panicky …" A look of astonishment passed over Lee's face, her legs buckled, and she sat down hard on the bunk. "Shit, the damn walls are covered with bugs. You gave me something."

Then Lloyd felt it, too, a crawling in the veins, a slipping of the mind, the rush of solid ground retreating beneath his feet. His mouth fell open. He looked at Avery and screamed, "God damn you."

The alien began to howl again. Lee backed away from the bugs. Lloyd pushed over a lamp that threatened to bite him. The strain in Avery's face blossomed into panic. He poured himself a drink.

47

THE MORNING AFTER

I woke to find my old eyelids gone, replaced by new ones made of a heavy, translucent substance filled with pulsing red light. The effort to push them off my eyeballs exhausted me. I went back to sleep. When I awoke later in the day, my head had doubled in size. With effort, I lifted it enough to look around. I expected to see total devastation from the night before, but, to my surprise, the room was intact. The screaming overseers, headless Utorbis, and raging cactuses of the night before were gone without a trace.

I smelled something loathsome, however. I pushed myself up until I had a view of the floor. I saw Avery, lying in a pool of a malodorous substance I took to be human vomit. I had an urge to wake him up to point out that human vomit was no less putrid than alien vomit—despite what he told me—but then it occurred to me that he might have expired. I watched him for a moment and detected no movement, but I didn't care enough get up and make sure. I lay back, pulled the cover over my head, and fervently wished that someone would remove him before he began to decay.

I awoke to the sound of the toilet flushing. The bathroom door opened, and Lee emerged with great hollow eyes. She wore her red silk robe with the feathers, and her hair stuck out in all directions. She glanced with concern in my direction. I nodded to let her know I had survived. She responded with an attenuated smile, and then stumbled to Avery. She nudged the body with a toe and spoke in a moist growl. "You'd better be dead, you filthy bastard, I haven't got the energy to kill you."

Avery moaned. Lee went to the cooler and dipped a glass into the ice melt that had collected in the bottom. She poured it over Avery's head.

He woke up sputtering and cursing. I heard an exclamation, then a banging from under the desk. Lloyd crawled out, blind without his glasses. He sat up blinking.

Lee snatched the glasses from the floor and gently slipped them on Lloyd's nose. He blushed deeply. He must have felt the heat in his face because he tried to explain it by mumbling something about the effect of drugs.

We were all aware that Lloyd had grown stupid over Lee. The humans would call it love, not stupidity, but the symptoms were identical from my vantage point: inarticulate speech, diminished awareness of social signals, impaired decision making.

Avery, meanwhile, sputtered as he struggled to extract himself from the vomit and stand up. He made it to his feet and uttered the word "shower."

"Not in my bathroom," Lee said. Taking advantage of his wobbliness, she took him by the elbow and shoved him into the hall, being careful not to touch any vomit-covered body parts. She shut the door and engaged the lock. We heard a bellowing outside. Lee dismissed it with a shrug. "It will be hours before he's in any shape to work the combination." She fetched a towel from the bathroom and threw it over the vomit. "I'll clean it up later. I can't face it until I've had some coffee."

Feeling better, I got up and motioned for her to sit while I made the coffee. I was in no mood for Lee's foul brew.

"Thank you," she said and collapsed into the upholstered chair.

Lloyd was on his knees, making painstaking preparations to stand.

"Don't," Lee said, "you'll just fall over."

Lloyd sank back down, shaking. "Is it going to start again?" he asked. "The after effects?"

Lee gave him one of her intent, unblinking stares. "I don't know. Avery gave us too much. I've taken mescaline before and didn't feel like this. Don't get anxious. It will only make things worse. I'll help you get through it if it happens."

While I made the coffee, Lloyd went to the bathroom, and Lee sank deeper into her chair. I filled their cups. Nobody spoke as we drank. When we were done, we were still bone tired. I crawled into bed and dropped off to sleep.

When I awoke again, the noxious human vomit was gone. Lee and Lloyd were presentable if somewhat haggard.

"What are we going to do about him?" Lee whispered.

I thought she was talking about me, so I pretended to sleep.

"We have to change the combination lock so he can't get to the drugs," Lloyd said.

"Logistics will give him the combination."

They were talking about Avery, not me.

"I'll pick up a few lockboxes at the hardware store," Lloyd said. "We can store the drugs in the boxes inside the drawer. I'll have keys made for both of us. We can wear them around our necks."

Lee rubbed her eyes. "Avery will scream bloody murder. Probably call Ludden."

"Let him," Lloyd said.

Lee shuddered. "Underneath that glib exterior, he's weak and wounded. Just the type of person who shouldn't be exposed to these drugs."

"Like me?" Lloyd asked.

"No," Lee said. "You're not weak. You're quite strong. You were given the drugs under extreme circumstances. That's why things went wrong."

Lloyd stared down at his hands. "But Avery and I are alike in our guilt. We're both responsible for other men's deaths."

Lee leaned forward and put her hand over Lloyd's. "Yes," she said, "but you've acknowledged your guilt and allowed it to change you. You let yourself feel the pain. You'll never get over it, but you've grown strong enough to live with it. Avery put all of his energy into trying to be the same shallow golden boy he was before Albania. He drinks whenever he feels a twinge of pain." Lee withdrew her hand, and Lloyd watched it go sadly. "You were right. I should never have thrown Albania in his face. I didn't realize how fragile he is. I'm a psychiatrist. I should be more perceptive."

"You're remarkably perceptive."

"I'm more perceptive than you think."

Lloyd blushed.

48

LINES OF AUTHORITY

I awoke when metal crashed against metal.

"Do you idiots not understand that you work for me?" Avery yelled. He was standing over the open drawer of the safe holding up a dented metal lockbox. He struck the box against the side of the safe.

Lloyd and Lee stood together nearby, calm in the face of his fury.

"You gave us drugs against our will," Lloyd said.

Avery shoved the box back in the drawer. He approached them and stood too close, as he did when he wanted to intimidate. Instead of stepping back, Lee took a step forward. I had the momentary impression she held a knife, but she didn't.

"Do you know the damage you could have caused?" she said. "You gave us too large a dose. One more incident like the Ogden affair, and drug testing will be suspended." Avery backed up, but Lee moved in again. "And what about Doug? He was reacting horribly to the mescaline, and no one was in any condition to take care of him. No, you gave us drugs and drank yourself insensible. I'm not letting you anywhere near these drugs again. If you go running to Ludden, I'll tell him what I just told you."

Avery retreated to the other side of the room. The lines of authority that radiated from him grew tangled and frayed. "Fine," he said, "I can't deal with you right now. It gives me a headache. Get going with the testing. We have to submit another report next week, and I want results to put in it."

"Doug needs time to recover from the mescaline reaction," Lloyd said.

Avery came and leaned over my bed. I tried to avoid breathing his foul breath. "He looks fine to me," he said. "We're going ahead. Or rather, you are. I'm going back to bed. When I wake up, you better have results to show me." Avery stumbled out, and Lee locked the door behind him.

"I don't want to subject Doug to more tests right now," Lloyd said.

"Certainly not hallucinogens but there are other drugs," Lee said.

"Can't you stand down for a few days? What is this compulsion you have for testing?"

"You still think we should stop all testing?" Lee asked.

I could see Lloyd didn't want to argue with her because he was miserable with love. He didn't want to argue but he did so for my sake. "The testing has killed people, made them suffer."

A tightness puckered Lee's mouth. "People suffer and die every day for lack of cures. The mentally ill suffer as much as those with physical maladies. Maybe more, and what can we do for them? If we don't test, it's a sin of omission. If we don't test, the Soviets and Chinese get the upper hand."

Lloyd stared at me sadly. "I wish we didn't have to

test on Doug."

"He's not human. Would you rather run these tests on humans?"

The words caught me off guard. I knew I wasn't a human, but I hadn't realized it made such a difference to Lee. I sat up and leaned against the wall. I didn't trust the objects around me. Occasionally something inanimate would begin to crawl or scream or melt again without warning. I still felt the cactus drug in my system. It lay hidden among my anomalous organs and occasionally hiccoughed in technicolor.

Lee came over and sat on the bed. "Still feeling funny, Doug?"

"Funny" seemed a hilariously inadequate word.

"Would you like some Cheezees?"

I shook my head. Lloyd had spent the night shrieking about crawling orange caterpillars, and I no longer found Cheezees appetizing.

"As much as I hate to say it, I think Avery's right. He's fine," Lee said.

Lloyd sat down next to me and looked me over closely. Not the way he would look at a human, but the way I once saw him examine his vehicular horse. I fervently hoped he would not attempt to pry open my maw and look at my chewing ridges. It occurred to me that it would be easier to deal with the humans if I had something in my system. Not the cactus drug, but something more palliative like cannabis.

"Doug," Lloyd said, "Would you be willing to try more drugs today? Not mescaline, but something milder?"

It was rare that the humans divined my needs with such accuracy. I reached up and patted Lloyd on the neck, a form of positive reinforcement I had seen him employ with the vehicular horse. He seemed confused by the gesture, so I nodded vigorously.

"We could start with barbiturate and amphetamine cocktails," Lee said. "They have enormous promise for use in interrogations." She went to the second drawer of the safe and took out needles. I protested. I had been stuck with needles before.

"Please, Doug, hold still," Lee said. "It really won't hurt that much. Lloyd, can you help me?"

"I hate this," Lloyd said. "Do we have to do this against his will?"

Lee stepped back. "I have an idea." She went to the dresser that served as a bar and selected a bottle.

"Kahlúa? What are you going to do with that?" Lloyd asked.

"Watch. Doug, I have something that might put you in a better mood. It's like coffee, only better." She poured the liquid into my mug wart. I sniffed, took a sip, then drank the rest of it so quickly, Lee didn't have time to ask me to slow down. I shrugged my mug wart vigorously to request more.

"Not yet," Lee said, "it's not good for you to drink it so fast."

I gazed pointedly at the bottom drawer of the safe, then at Lee. This woman had been feeding me dangerous drugs for weeks, and she was going to decline my request for more of the marvelous Kahlúa because it might not "be good for me?" I expounded at length upon the logical fallacies and internal contradictions inherent in that statement.

"We're quacking up a storm this morning, aren't we?" Lee said. "I wish I knew what was going through your little orange head."

I narrowed my eyes and pointed to my mug wart and called her an obscene word in Utorbian.

"My, that was a funny quack," Lee said brightly. "Okay, I'll let you have more, but drink it slowly. We don't want any more alien vomit, now do we?"

I could have killed her cheerfully.

She filled my mug wart, and I sipped calmly as she stuck in two needles. Lee's voice grew happy as she talked about her beloved drugs. "I'm putting in two lines. One for methedrine and one for sodium Amytal. The sodium Amytal reduces inhibitions, but it makes him sleepy. The methedrine loosens his tongue. With two lines, I can manipulate the dosage more quickly. When he starts quacking nonstop, we'll know we have the right balance."

I sipped my Kahlúa as Lee played with the tubes in my arms. First I felt sleepy, then energy surged through my body, and I had a great desire to talk. I began to tell them from the beginning about the Cycles and how unintended surprise consequences spiraled into unintended surprise consequences into more unintended surprise consequences, until everything was, as they used to say in the Army, FUBAR.

"Bingo," Lee said.

49

TRUFFLES

Sins of omission, sins of commission. The words stuck in Lloyd's brain. He mulled them over until their meaning evaporated. He was tired of judging Lee. Maybe if he quit judging her, he could come to understand her better. He wanted to understand her, to know everything about her.

No, he did not.

Lloyd sat up in bed and reached for his glasses. He poked himself in the eye on his first attempt to put them on. He turned the clock so that he could see the lighted dial. Six a.m. He'd been awake at one, three, four a.m. He reminded himself again that his interest in Lee was a product of proximity and lack of opportunity. He was divorced, lonely, and filled with an inconvenient lust. He'd been holed up for weeks in a former women's dormitory with a drug-addled alien, an obnoxious alcoholic, and Lee. He supposed he had to fall in love with one of them.

She had guessed his feelings and she'd given him enough subtle encouragement to destroy his sleep.

No, he probably imagined it. If there was one thing

Lloyd knew about himself, it was that love destroyed his judgment. It made him see things that weren't there. It was like drugs that way.

No, this wasn't love, it was lust and proximity. He had to remember that. Besides, how could he ever get over the fact that she was the one who sat with him when he was helpless and beset by demons? She gave him drugs, and that was unforgivable.

Avery had left for Washington the day after the incident with the mescaline. He'd been gone for eight days, leaving Lloyd and Lee alone. Lloyd didn't think he could take another day of it without throwing himself at Lee's feet.

I have to get away from here. The thought brought a wave of calm. Why not? He could make an excuse to go to Washington for the day. The drugs they were testing now did nothing more than make Doug talkative. It would feel good to drive for a few hours. He could stop in at his favorite bookstore and refresh his supply of reading material. He could look at other women and see that there was nothing special about Lee Ogilvie.

The thought allowed him to catch an hour of sleep.

When he woke, Lloyd had lost his enthusiasm for leaving. The idea of another day with Lee and without Avery was too pleasant. He showered and dressed quickly. He was late, but she might still be in the cafeteria having breakfast.

The cafeteria was located in the basement of Agnes Winters Hall. The Agency hadn't altered it much since it had served grits and bacon to budding southern ladies. Indeed, most of the former staff had kept their old hairnets, obtained low-level clearances, and now served starchy vegetables and stringy meat to a predominantly male clientele of Mines personnel. Lloyd smiled to think how vehemently Lee hated the food. If you got her started on the subject, she would go on a diatribe accompanied by the most comical facial expressions.

As soon as Lloyd walked in the door, he spotted her near the coffee urns. She sat alone at a small table animatedly talking to her food—evidently reaming out the eggs for being too runny or the biscuit for being too dry. Lloyd wanted to sit down immediately but remembered that he should get some food and pretend to eat.

He got a tray and grabbed a biscuit and a pat of butter. He gave a number to the lady at the end of the counter so the food could be charged to the proper office.

As Lloyd approached her table, Lee gave him a brilliant smile. She was dressed entirely in white—capris, a crisp blouse, and a band that held back her dark hair. Her complexion glowed against the white. No, she was not entirely in white. Lloyd caught a glimpse of her shoes: espadrilles with a red and white striped upper. The cherry red of the stripe matched her lipstick.

"Nothing to drink?" Lee asked, glancing at his tray. "If you try to eat that biscuit without something to wash it down, you'll choke. Sit down, I'll get you some juice."

Halfway into his chair, Lloyd felt a weakness in the knees that made him bobble his tray. He sat down heavily and wondered what Lee meant by fetching him juice. She wasn't the sort of woman to fetch anything for a man. Perhaps she didn't think of him as a real man. Maybe that was why she'd bummed rides from him at the underground facility. She felt safe with him because she didn't think of him as a man. Lloyd wanted to sink through the floor.

Lee returned with his juice and sat down.

Lloyd's voice came out shaky, "Would you mind ..."

"Mind what?"

"Would you mind if I took a day trip to DC? I have business there. I'll be back this evening."

Was that disappointment he saw in Lee's face? Just a flash before she smiled again? No. He saw what he wanted to see.

"I wouldn't mind," she said. "Doug and I will be fine."

"Is there anything I can bring back for you?"

"No, but promise me one thing," Lee said. "Go to a nice restaurant for lunch and remember every bite, because you're going to describe it to me in detail when you get back."

Lloyd cursed himself all the way to Washington.

⁂

During the barbiturate and amphetamine trials, Lee had concocted many excellent recipes for me employing sodium pentothol, Benzedrine, desoxin, and other ingredients with delightful names. Her cooking today, however, was sub-par. I experienced no buzz, no floating, no pleasant deviation from reality. I didn't even feel like talking, and talking was the whole point of the current exercise.

Lee shook her head. "Let's call it a day." She removed the needles from my limbs and stowed the drugs and paraphernalia in the safe. "I'm in a foul mood, too. Tell me, Doug, do *you* like my new outfit?" Lee touched her white sleeve.

I shrugged. I would have preferred a color.

Lee's eyes wandered the room. "I need to feel young and irresponsible. Want to listen to music?"

I nodded enthusiastically. The record player still sat

on my upper bunk. Lee went through the stack of records and came up with one we hadn't listened to yet. "This one is old," Lee said. "I loved it in high school. Are you in the mood for Glenn Miller?"

She set the needle down. It was a lively song, but instead of dancing, Lee sat with a sad and distant look on her face. When it was done, she slipped the record back in its jacket and closed the lid on the player.

"I'm sorry, Doug. It didn't make me feel young. It made me feel old. So many things have happened since that song came out. We've had a world war and a cold war. Rosie the Riveter died of boredom in the suburbs. My knuckles are raw from knocking on closed doors. You were my big opportunity, Doug. I'm thirty-six, approaching that age when women become invisible and even more powerless than they were in youth." Lee got up and went to the window. She touched the blind that Avery had duct taped fast to the wall. "Bastard," she said. "Take away the view and you lose all perspective. It's stupid sitting in a dark room, but I can't rip this tape away because he could destroy my career. He might have already done it. Who knows what he's been up to at Headquarters for the past week."

※

Lloyd returned before dinnertime. Lee's face brightened when she saw that he carried a large basket. He smiled shyly at her. "I thought you might be getting tired of the cafeteria food," he said.

"Tired of shit on a shingle?" Lee laughed. "What have you got in there?"

"Patience," Lloyd said. He pushed furniture back to

clear a space in the middle of the floor. He took a red-and-white-checked cloth out of the basket and spread it out. He slipped off his shoes and sat cross-legged next to the basket.

Lee kicked off her shoes and sat down next to him. "Where were you today?"

"A French bakery and fromagerie in Georgetown, a wine shop, and another shop that shall remain secret for now." Lloyd handed Lee a foil-wrapped disk.

She held it to her nose and inhaled. "Oh my God, Camembert."

Lloyd put a cylinder in Lee's hand, and she broke into a grin. "*Saucisson sec*! Did you get any mustard?"

Lloyd retrieved a small round jar, and Lee clapped her hands with delight.

It occurred to me that Lloyd must be trying to extract some sort of favor from Lee. Of all the humans I had known, she was the one most keenly interested in food. Lloyd had filled the basket with items that appealed to her sense of taste and smell. What was he after? It must be something pertaining to myself. I hoped he wasn't going to attempt once more to get Lee to give me a vacation from the drugs, as I had developed such a strong fondness for them that it might almost be described as addiction.

Lloyd pulled out a bottle and two glasses.

"Cabernet!" Lee clasped her hands over her heart. "I've never seen you indulge in alcohol."

"I enjoy an occasional glass of wine," Lloyd said. "But don't like to drink around Avery." He poured two glasses and handed one to Lee. He held up his glass and blushed deeply. "To a brilliant and beautiful woman unlike any I've ever met." He touched his glass to hers.

I hadn't seen this sort of behavior from the humans

before. Having developed a keen interest in anthropology, I quietly shifted my position on the lower bunk so that I might observe them while appearing to sleep.

Lee sipped her wine and then gave Lloyd an atypical smile. Her usual smiles were bright but brief. This one included all parts of her face, particularly the eyes. It lingered. It had an astonishing effect on Lloyd. All signs of intelligence and discernment abandoned his face, to be replaced by a look of the most blank stupidity. Lloyd had apparently lost any advantage he had gained over Lee by offering her tasty food items.

They began to eat. Lee made small sounds of pleasure, but Lloyd might have been eating cardboard. He put things into his mouth and chewed mechanically, without taking his eyes from her.

Evidently as a result of the wine, their conversation was inane and not worth repeating. At least not until Lee pushed away the remainder of the cheese and said, "What's for dessert?"

Lloyd's eyes never left her face as he reached into the basket and pulled out a small box wrapped in gold paper and tied with a red velvet ribbon. "Chocolate truffles," he said.

"Oh my God!" Lee tore off the ribbon and opened the box. "Look at them, so perfect and beautiful." She held up a truffle. "Open your mouth, Lloyd."

"But they're for you," he protested.

"Don't eat it just hold it in your lips." Lee placed the truffle in Lloyd's mouth, and he held it carefully. I had to restrain myself from laughing at the sight. Then Lee leaned forward and took a small bite out of the truffle. Lloyd's eyes grew wide. Lee took another bite, then a sound at the door made them both sit up straight. Someone was working the combination lock.

"Shit," Lee said. She snatched the remainder of the truffle from Lloyd's mouth with her fingers and popped it in her own. She stood up, still chewing. Lloyd looked about with a panicky expression in his eyes. He made a move as if to clear away the picnic items, but stopped, evidently realizing the effort was futile. He stood.

The door opened, and Avery stepped in. "Oh my," he said as he scanned the room. "What have we been doing here? Lloyd, I underestimated you. It seems as if you were in the process of exploiting Lee's weakness for chocolate. You should both wipe your lips. It's a dead giveaway."

Lloyd turned crimson. He took out his handkerchief and rubbed vigorously at his mouth. Lee's tongue shot out and swiped the last traces of truffle from her lips.

"I should have never left you two alone. Mind if I have something to eat? I'm starved." Avery didn't wait for an answer. He sat down on the picnic cloth and began to paw through the leftovers. He popped a piece of cheese into his mouth and watched the play of color across Lloyd's face. He swallowed and said, "You gingers are spectacular at blushing, but it looks like nothing happened here tonight. I must have interrupted your plans. Sorry about that, but I stayed away for more than a week. How much time do you need for foreplay? Dr. Ogilvie, pass the sausage."

Lee picked up the remaining *saucisson sec* and threw it at Avery's head. He managed to duck in time, and then he lay back on the floor and laughed. "You'd better accelerate your pace, Lloyd, celibacy is making her mean."

"What news do you have from Headquarters?" Lloyd asked. He began to clear away the picnic things.

"Marvelous news." Avery stood and brushed the

crumbs from his trousers. "A marvelous surprise."

Lee and Lloyd exchanged looks of concern. I shrank against the wall. No one liked Avery's surprises.

"A surprise from Goldfarb himself," Avery said dramatically.

"Just tell us," Lee said.

"Don't look so sour. You will like this surprise. How could you not?" Avery spoke in a deep, portentous voice. "Dr. Ogilvie, I have brought you the flesh of God."

Lloyd frowned, but Lee's face registered eagerness and joy. "Psilocybin?" she asked.

"Exactly," Avery said.

"Synthetic or the actual mushrooms?"

Avery glowed with satisfaction. "Genuine mushrooms from Mexico."

"Oh yes!" Lee cried. "I've been trying to get my hands on some for months. She turned to Lloyd. "I've heard astounding things about psilocybin. It's used in religious ceremonies. That's why they call it the flesh of God."

"The Mines' answer to transubstantiation," Lloyd said with irony.

Avery gave Lloyd a pitying look. "And you just got her a box of chocolates."

Lee's face abruptly clouded over. "Avery, where are the mushrooms?"

He smiled in a way that gave me a chill. "They're in a lockbox in my room." He reached into his collar and pulled out a chain with a key. "I control access to them."

※

Lloyd didn't sleep that night. Images assaulted his brain: Lee's red lips dusted with cocoa, a checked cloth, and a key on a chain. He wanted go into the next room and strangle Avery. That would solve so many problems.

No, Lloyd admitted to himself, it wouldn't. Perhaps Avery had done him a favor by preventing that kiss he had been so close to enjoying. What was he doing going after someone like Lee, that minefield of moral ambiguity? She was the last woman on earth who could give him what he wanted.

Then he remembered Trudie's question. "And what do you really want, Lloyd?"

He sat up in bed. The question had struck him as odd when Trudie asked it. It never occurred to him to examine that musty catalog of personal desires to see if it wanted updating. The images were as vague and confused as the ones that had been assaulting his brain all night.

Lloyd got up to pace. The oppressive heat and humidity had returned along with Avery, and the room was unbearably close.

"What do I really want?" Lloyd said out loud. He had no idea. All his life he had borrowed his wants from elsewhere. First from his big sister. Trudie longed for an east coast education and foreign travel, so Lloyd had wanted those things, too. He went to Georgetown and then overseas.

When he married Faye, he had a clear image in his mind of a two-story house, a station wagon, and three kids, but where did that image come from? Lloyd focused on it, and after a minute found himself humming a bright little tune. A familiar tune. With a bitter laugh, Lloyd realized it was the jingle for a laundry soap. That image of marital bliss was from a soap commercial. Odd that he never made the connection before. No wonder his marriage failed. Faye hated doing the laundry.

Would he be happier with a woman who liked doing the laundry? Probably not. He didn't mind doing his own laundry. What about that two-story house? He had it during his marriage. He had hated painting it, mowing its yard, and gluing patterned paper to its walls. He sold it after the divorce.

What did Lloyd Pilcrow really want?

He wanted to set fire to all of the glossy, saccharine, fake, borrowed, bought, and sold images that had served him so poorly. He went out into the hallway. On bare feet, he slipped past Avery's door, then Doug's. He stopped in front of Lee's room and rapped softly. She must have been awake because the door opened before he could have second thoughts.

50

THE FLESH OF GOD

I didn't want the flesh of God, for the only Earth edibles I trusted were Cheezees. Lee insisted. I chewed the mushrooms without enthusiasm. They were tasteless—devoid of salt, monosodium glutamate, and other fine ingredients present in a Cheezee.

But then the flesh of God showed me all the cycles of Earth, those past and those to come. I saw the dinosaurs more glorious and horrifying than those depicted in books. They had scintillating scales in colors so brilliant it hurt my eyes to look upon them. Then came the swirling, smoking, sparkling ice to cover them. I saw the short, brutal, blood-spattered lives of the cavemen. Then the images accelerated. Incas gouged the hearts from living bodies. Lions tore into human flesh. Puritans covered women with stones until air and spirit left their bodies. I saw gas chambers, frozen labor camps, and asylums full of vacant stares. Then I saw the future and shrieked until Avery held me down while Lee administered a sedative.

After the alien had fallen asleep, they sat awkwardly. Lee smoked. Avery nursed a whiskey sour. Lloyd sat unnaturally still, his head turned away from the others.

Is he thinking about last night? Lee wondered. *What a grim expression. He's probably thinking about Doug and what we're doing to him.*

"I should have tested the drug on myself first," Lee said. "Poor Doug, he's had a spotty record with hallucinogens."

"Like me," Lloyd said.

Lee bit her lower lip. *What a stupid thing to say. I sound like a shallow idiot.* She went to Doug's bed. He slept fitfully. The enormous eyes moved behind their lids. Now and again his limbs jerked. As a child, Lee had suffered from nightmares that made her scream and brought her mother running. "If I could yank those nasty things out of your head I would," her mother used to say.

During her medical training, Lee had thought of those words often. She began with the high idea of yanking the nasty things out of peoples' heads—the obsessions, depression, and neuroses turned the brain into Hell on earth. But those things were more stubborn than she had imagined. You couldn't talk them away. But drugs? Drugs, used correctly, could set the brain free, destroy the obsessions, unleash the creativity …

A fresh wave of spasms broke across the scaly terrain of the alien's face.

I put those nightmares in Doug's head, Lee thought. *What does that make me? Not a distinguished research scientist. More like a damned Nazi doctor.*

Lee shivered, despite the warmth of the evening. She wanted Avery to leave so she could take Lloyd to her room. Unlikely Lloyd, the sort of man she never dated.

She wanted to curl up with him and talk. Sure, he suffered from self-delusion just like any other human being, but there was an honesty at the core of him that she longed for now.

"We don't need to watch Doug sleep," she said.

Avery balled up a candy wrapper and threw it across the room toward the trashcan. He missed. "If I want to watch the fucking alien sleep, I'll watch the fucking alien sleep. But you two lovebirds feel free to retire for a romp. I promise not to listen."

Lloyd turned crimson and stood up to pace.

"If you jangle the change in your pocket, I will murder you," Avery said.

Lloyd sat down again.

Avery got up to make himself another drink. His demeanor alarmed Lee. He kept a smile on his face: a cold, lopsided, joyless smirk that made her skin crawl. His eyes wandered the walls and didn't fix on anything.

"Avery," Lee said, "How much psilocybin do you have left?"

"I thought you didn't want do give Doug any more."

"I don't. He doesn't react well to it, but if there are any mushrooms left, I would like to add them to our inventory."

Avery reached inside his collar and pulled out the chain with the key. He looked down at it, but Lee saw his eyes weren't focusing. "Nice try, but I own the magic mushrooms. Don't be greedy. You have all the other drugs. There's something irritatingly female about that need to have all of the goodies under your control, like a mommy who keeps the cookie jar on the highest shelf."

Under her breath, Lee cursed an agency so willing to keep damaged, dangerous men in positions of authority.

Avery finished making his drink and sat down at the foot of the alien's bed. This proximity made Lee uncomfortable. Drunk and bored, Avery might reach out and perform some small act of cruelty upon the creature, like using his thumb and middle finger to flick Doug's sensitive trunk.

"Don't disturb him," Lee said. Then she realized she'd only made it more likely that Avery would do it just to spite her. She saw him put his thumb and middle finger together and reach toward Doug's head. Without thinking she lunged toward Avery and crushed the burning end of her cigarette on the top of his hand. He jerked away, curled his wounded hand into a fist, and drove it into Lee's face. She staggered backwards and hit the wall, stunned and bleeding from a cut on her brow. By sheer determination, she remained on her feet.

Lloyd grabbed Avery by the collar. He had the dual advantages of a heavier frame and sobriety.

"Don't hit him," Lee yelled. "Don't hit him or I'll never touch you again. Get him out of the room." She stumbled to the door and pulled it open. Lloyd shoved Avery into the hallway and watched as he windmilled his arms in a vain effort to stay on his feet. He sat down hard on the floor and began to laugh. Lloyd slammed the door. Lee engaged the lock, then propped a chair under the knob just in case Avery could manage the combination.

Lloyd came to Lee and put his hand to her face, stopping short of touching it. "Are you all right?"

"It's just a cut."

Lloyd fetched gauze, bandages, and Mercurochrome from the bathroom—supplies left over from Doug's recuperation.

Lee sat on a straight-backed chair and allowed Lloyd

to dab at her eye. His hands trembled. She had gone stone-faced and limp. She didn't flinch at the pressure of the cloth or the sting of the Mercurochrome. When he was done, Lloyd stepped back. Confusion and then comprehension played across his large features.

"This isn't the first time you've been hurt like this," he said.

"Not the first and not the worst." Lee managed a grim smile. She had never told anyone about the first time. Pride, humiliation, and pain had all played a hand in her silence. Now she found it surprisingly easy to tell Lloyd. Her voice was so light and matter-of-fact, she might have been reciting a fairy tale.

"My father broke my jaw when I was nine. I had to have it wired shut for weeks."

"How could a father strike his daughter?"

Lee shook her head, wondering how a grown man could say such a thing. "It happens all the time. My case was not unusual, so get that pitying look off your face."

"I truly don't understand how such things can happen."

Lee turned to study Lloyd's face. "That's what I like about you. You truly don't understand."

"How many times did he hurt you?" Lloyd asked.

"He only hit me once, but he beat my mother regularly. He probably wouldn't have hit me at all, except that I deliberately burned him with a cigarette. He was sitting in his favorite chair, smoking. He put the cigarette in the ashtray while he unfolded his newspaper. I took it from the ashtray and pressed it into the tender part of his arm, and held it as long as I could. Then his other arm came around, and he knocked me across the room. It was much like what just happened with Avery, except that my father was a heavier man and my bones were more delicate back then."

Lloyd pressed his palm to his forehead. "Why would you do that?"

"Because I couldn't watch him beat my mother anymore. I knew that no matter how bad he hurt her, she would never leave him because he supported her children. She stayed with him for us. I reasoned that if he hurt one of us, she would leave. I was right. It worked. We went from being comfortable to being dirt poor, but it was better than seeing my mother crash into the bookcase."

"There must have been another way."

The dreamy expression on Lee's face disappeared, and she looked Lloyd straight in the eye. "No, there was no other way. When you're powerless, you have to use your powerlessness. It's the only thing you have. You can die trying or die not trying."

Lloyd closed his eyes and covered them with his hand.

"I didn't hate my father," Lee said. "He could be funny and kind when he wasn't out of control. He gave me my first look at mental illness. I knew that something was broken in his mind. If I could have fixed it, we would have had a wonderful life. But I had no capacity to fix it, so I burned him with a cigarette." Lee reached for Lloyd's hand and squeezed it. "There's a selfish reason behind my enthusiasm for testing. I am my father's daughter. I have periods of depression and blind anger. They'll grow worse as I get older, judging from what happened to him. I'm trying to save myself. Does that make me evil?"

"We're all trying to save ourselves," Lloyd said. "I pray we don't hurt Doug too badly in the process."

Lee's eyes drifted to the little alien sleeping fitfully under a frilly bedspread intended for a college girl. "As

Avery would say, nobody should sign on to the Mines expecting to sleep well at night. I don't. Do you?"

"Not since Budapest."

"Well, if neither one of us can sleep, then let's go to bed. I need to be held."

Lloyd reached for her, but she stopped him. "Know that this is just for now," she said. "Don't ever think there's a future with me. I am my father's daughter."

"Then what is this?" Lloyd asked.

Lee took Lloyd's hand. "A distraction," she said.

51

LAUGHTER

Grains of laughter, dry as yeast, lay dormant in Avery's gut. A substance—dry but smelling of damp earth—entered his system and made his juices flow. The grains swelled, bubbled, and rose to seek the light.

The laughter rushed upward through the vertical cavern of Avery's throat, through the reek of alcohol and lemons, past white teeth ground down by bruxism. It pushed out into the muggy, buzzing air.

The laughter pealed out in crazy loops and spirals. It bounced off the walls. It was now a liquid, now a gas. It frightened Avery and thrilled him. At first, he ran from it, bursting into the hallway, sprinting to the window, and crawling out onto the fire escape. Then, in the silvery light of summer's last full moon, he leaned far out over the railing and breathed in the night. Cicadas took up residence in his lungs. They tickled. He surrendered himself to elation and laughed. The laughter would soon eat away everything inside his brain, including the dark and heavy detritus he had pushed to the far corners.

Insanity nullifies responsibility. He had no idea whether those words were his own or whether the Almighty had whispered them into his ear. Avery couldn't shed the belief in a higher power, but he couldn't bear the idea of a judgment day. But those words, "insanity nullifies responsibility," gave him an out.

Avery spoke between gassy gulps of laughter. "Thank you, God." All he had to do was let the laughter destroy the last vestiges of rational thought.

Two more words drifted to his ear: fucking Communists. Insanity could lead to salvation or the most abject vulnerability. He had to fight off the laughter so he could keep his wits about him and fight off the Communists.

The fucking Communists were behind everything. Goldfarb put the mushrooms into Avery's hand, but who put them into Goldfarb's hand? They came from Mexico—Trotsky's haven, Rivera's canvas, and a hotbed of incipient Communism.

"Fucking Communists," Avery screamed through choking laughter. He ran back to his room, opened his top dresser drawer, and pulled a loaded gun from under a stack of underwear. His paramilitary training told him to seek higher ground. Avery ran to the stairwell and went up one flight to the door that led to the attic. He disabled the flimsy lock with a small tool he kept on his key chain.

Laughter settled into wheezing as Avery stood in the door and waited for his eyes to adjust. The long attic was expanding and contracting like a lung. A thin thread of panic wove itself into the laughter, but the laughter itself never faltered. It found broken, dust-coated dressers, boxes of copper pipe, and tubs of sealant. It bounced off the objects and returned to Avery, becoming a sonar that enabled him to negotiate the space without stumbling. He came upon a faintly luminescent rectangle on the floor.

Light radiating from wood. He knelt down and pressed his lips to it. Then he looked up to see a window, and the enigma of the phenomenon vanished. Avery swiped the floor dust from his lips and stood. Boxes, containing something solid and heavy, made it an easy climb. The awning window stuck at first, but Avery forced his weight against it, and it gave. He crawled onto the roof. Here the laughter could expand into the darkness. It carbonated the cloudless sky. The laughter grew stronger, and Avery had to shout to be heard over it. "Fucking Communists!"

His had thought they were over there, behind an iron curtain, but they were here, inside the Mines. How else could they have found and executed every single partisan he sent into Albania? There had to be a fucking Communist mole. It could be Goldfarb or Lloyd or Lee.

"I'll destroy you fucking Communists," he shouted.

His slick-soled shoes had little traction on the slate roof. With his back against the dormer, he slid down until he was sitting. He removed his shoes and socks and watched as his long toes moved like fresh dug worms, writhing and panicked. The sight of them slowly filled him with horror. He inched his way down until his legs dangled over the edge of the roof, and he could no longer see his toes. Now he could also see the approach to the building clearly. He should stop laughing. It would give his position away. But he couldn't stop, even though it was becoming difficult to breathe. What was that moving by the path? It was an *ushanka*, a damn Russian fur hat on the head of a goddamn Cossack crawling through the periwinkle. Avery took aim.

The laughter played around the edges of Lee's consciousness as she slept, but it wasn't until it rained down on her from above that she opened her eyes. It was a struggle to slough off the sleep that had descended less than two hours before, but something told her she must try. At first, she didn't identify the sound as human laughter. She thought some bird had fallen to an owl. She tried to go back to sleep, but the sound persisted and then formed itself into the words, "fucking Communists." She sat up and listened until she recognized Avery's voice. She gripped Lloyd's shoulder.

"Wake up."

⁂

Lloyd smiled as he opened his eyes, but the smile quickly faded. Even in the dim light of the room, he could see the fear in Lee's face and feel it in her touch. A high shriek of laughter reached his ears. He sat up and froze, listening.

Lloyd stumbled out the door on legs still rubbery from sleep. Lee followed him to Avery's room, but it was empty. The laughter grew louder.

"It's coming from outside," Lloyd said. He leaned out the window and twisted his torso to look up. He saw Avery's bare feet dangling over the edge of the roof. The sight banished the last remnants of sleep. What was the pitch of that roof? *About thirty degrees*, Lloyd thought.

"Fucking Communists," Avery screamed. Laughter looped through the air, rising, keening, falling, and ending with a gunshot.

In the silence after the shot, Lloyd gripped his chest and struggled to breathe the thick air. Lee sobbed. She grabbed Lloyd around the waist and pulled him back into the room. Lloyd expected to see Avery's dead body fall past the window.

Then the laughter began again, more manic than before. "Take that, fucking Communists!"

"He's roaring drunk," Lloyd whispered.

"Not drunk," Lee said. "He's hallucinating. He ate the mushrooms."

"I'm going up there."

Lee held tight to Lloyd's arm. "No, he'll think you're a Communist—or a giant lizard—and shoot you."

"I can't let him kill himself." Lloyd shook her off and kissed her on the forehead. "Talk to him, keep him distracted. Tell him Communists are in the rose garden. Tell him whatever you need to, just keep your head inside the window." Lloyd left.

Another gunshot made Lee sink to her knees. Not enough time had passed for Lloyd to have reached the roof. Had Avery shot himself?

She went to the window and called out. "Avery, do you hear me? It's Lee."

"Lee!" He broke into a rhythmic child's chant, interrupted by bursts of laughter. "Lee's not really a woman ... Lee plays with fire ... Lee sleeps with Lloyd ... Lee's a Communist spy! Where are you? Uncle Avery is going to shoot your sweet little ass."

She heard Avery scrabbling about on the roof. Would he try to climb down into her room? She picked up the desk chair, holding it with the legs facing out, and crept to the window. If he tried to climb in, she would push him out again. She calmed herself with the notion that he couldn't climb and hold a gun at the same time. He would have to put it down to have both hands free. The gun would fall. He would probably fall. He wouldn't have much to hang onto, but a few Virginia creeper vines that had made it all the way to the fifth floor. His coordination would be impaired. Lee put the chair down and tried to think clearly.

She didn't notice the small figure that crept into the room, paused, then slipped out the door.

"Avery," she said, "What are you doing?"

"I'm not going to tell you, fucking Communist."

In a shaky voice, Lee said "Avery, do you see something moving in the rose garden?"

"Think you're clever don't you? The Communists aren't down there. I should have known. There was always something wrong about you and Lloyd Pilcrow. No wonder you're sleeping together. I hope you had fun because you'll both be dead before this night is over."

Lee began to shake. Avery would shoot Lloyd as soon as he saw him. Merely talking to Avery wasn't going to be enough to distract him. He would kill Lloyd without batting an eyelash. Lee was willing to lure Avery to his death to prevent it.

Lee made her tone mocking. "Avery, you're too scared to climb down here. You can't get me."

Avery gasped for breath between shrieks of laughter. Where was Lloyd now? He must be almost to the window. The thought that a shot might come at any second made it hard for Lee to breathe. She looked around the room. She spied a broom leaning in the corner and grabbed it. She pushed the dresser to the window, ignoring the bottles that fell to the floor. She climbed on top and pushed the upper window sash down. She leaned out and saw Avery's bare feet hanging over the edge of the roof. She braced her back against one side of the window and her right foot against the other. She leaned out again and reached up with the broom, jabbing at Lloyd's feet. "Fall, goddamn it," she said under her breath.

He kicked, swore, and pulled up his feet, but he didn't fall. Again she heard him scrabbling about. She watched the edge of the roof. Avery's hand appeared holding a gun. He blindly pointed the barrel toward the window. Lee threw herself backward into the room as the shot rang out.

※

Lloyd reached the dormer window in time to see Avery face down on the roof, head just above the edge, legs pointed toward Lloyd and splayed for greater stability. He entertained the hope that he could sneak up on Avery and pull him away from the edge. Then, in a state of paralysis, he saw Avery reach down and fire his gun. Lloyd screamed, "Avery!"

Lee's voice came from below. "He'll shoot you."

"She's right," Avery said.

Lloyd climbed out onto the roof as Avery adjusted his position, pivoting on his belly so that he could take aim at this new threat. "I always knew something was wrong about you," Avery said. He tried to hold the gun steady despite his awkward position and the laughter that was beginning to choke him. "Think you're quite a man, don't you? Bedding Lee. Coming out here unarmed to protect her. Think it will get you laid? It will get you laid out on a granite slab."

Lloyd stood with one hand holding onto the window. He wasn't phobic, but he had a healthy distaste for high places with bad footing. Now that the gun was aimed at him rather than Lee, he could take a moment to think.

"You're under the influence of drugs. You're not yourself," Lloyd said softly, kindly. "You don't want tonight to lead to a lifetime of regret."

"A lifetime of regret!" Avery screamed. His laughter grew louder, wilder, and he scowled with the effort of trying to keep the gun steady. It appeared to Lloyd as if the man were being shaken by some invisible hand.

"Let me help you back inside," Lloyd said. He sat down much as Avery had earlier, sliding his naked back slowly down the face of the dormer--he had left Lee's room wearing only his boxers. Meanwhile, Avery turned his body to face Lloyd more squarely. He rose up onto his knees. He aimed the gun with both hands, but he shook so hard he couldn't keep it steady. Lloyd almost felt sorry for the man as he watched him struggle to gain control of his laughter and shaking. If Lloyd approached Avery slowly, as he had been planning to do, he would be shot as soon as he grew too close for Avery to miss. Nor would Avery let him retreat back through the dormer window. In his state, he would have no qualms about shooting a man in the back.

"Let's go inside," Lloyd said. "You can go back to your life if you don't fire that gun."

Avery fought to get the words out between bursts of laughter. "And why ... would I want ... to do that?"

Pick a moment, Lloyd thought, leaning forward a bit. *Sooner or later he's going to shoot whether he can steady the gun or not.* Lloyd would have to move fast. Fifteen feet of roof lay between them. But how could he tackle Avery without sending them both tumbling five stories? Lloyd let out his breath, pushed his back up against the dormer again, and searched his mind for anything he could say to the man that would cut through the drug haze.

Lee knelt on the floor next to the bullet hole. She looked up through the window, but could no longer see anything but the edge of the roof. She heard Lloyd's voice, low and soft, in the interstices of Avery's laughter. Of course, Lloyd would try to talk him down. *There's nothing you can say that will make any difference,* she wanted to scream. She still gripped the broom. The only thing she could do now was to try to distract Avery again and hope that Lloyd would use the time to get away. Lee climbed back up on the dresser, leaned as far out as she could manage, and banged the broom on the underside of the eaves.

"Knock, knock. Who's there?" Avery called.

"The whole damn Politburo, half the Red Army, and a few assorted Young Pioneers from Omsk," Lee said. "Come and get us, you cowardly capitalist dog."

"You're precious, Dr. Ogilvie. I'd love to come down, but I have to shoot comrade Pilcrow first. Hold still, Tovarishch Pilcrow."

Lee collapsed at the sound of the shot. Sudden silence, after all the ungodly laughter, took her breath away. She looked up and prayed, "Dear God, don't let me see his body fall."

She saw liquid falling from the slate roof. Perhaps it was the scientist in her that made her seek confirmation that it was blood. She grabbed the nearest piece of cloth, a white shirt. Stretching her arm out the window, she held it under the drip, then pulled her arm back in the window and lowered herself down from the dresser. In the gunmetal and ash lambency of the full moon, she couldn't confirm with her eyes that it was blood, but she could smell it. She crossed the room and flicked on the light. The garment in her hands was stained bright red.

"He's dead," Lee said. A clinical chill washed over her. Then she shook off the paralysis and tore out of the room still clutching the shirt, which might be used to bind a wound. She raced up the stairs and through the open door of the attic. Then she cursed herself for having turned on the light in her room, because now she was blind in this dark space. She kept going, though, knocking into things, slowing to a walk, and feeling her way forward with trembling hands outstretched. She came upon the same glowing rectangle on the floor that Avery had knelt to kiss. She climbed the boxes to the window, sobbed once, then stuck her head out.

She saw Lloyd first. He peered up at her from where he sat at the base of the dormer.

"Don't look. Go back inside. I'll handle it."

Her eyes had adjusted enough so that she could see that he was whole and unharmed. A sudden release of tension left her shaky and almost in a mood to laugh herself. "You idiot. I'm a doctor."

"He's dead," Lloyd said. "He doesn't need a doctor."

Then Lee saw Avery. He had fallen backward with his head near the edge of the roof. The side of his skull was missing.

"He committed suicide?" It wasn't really a question, so she was shocked to hear Lloyd's answer.

"No," he said softly. He slowly stood up, pressing his body close to the dormer. Lee feared he would lose his balance. She reached down and gripped his shoulder, digging her nails into the bare flesh. She bit back her questions and waited until he was ready to speak.

"He pointed the gun at me. He was about to pull the trigger. Then Doug came up behind him and grabbed his arm. They struggled, and the gun went off."

"Doug?" Lee looked around. "Did he fall?"

"Doug," Lloyd called. "It's all right."

Lee heard a rustling, then saw Doug's pod-like hands appear at the edge of the roof. In a second he pulled himself up and sat hunched, his huge eyes full of silver coruscations.

"Come here, Doug. It's all right," Lloyd said.

The alien was so clumsy on a flat surface; it surprised Lee how easily he negotiated the slant of the roof. When he reached Lloyd's feet, Doug made himself small, curling his body into an orange sack.

"We left the vault door open," Lee said.

"He must have crawled out the hall window and climbed along under the eaves. He arrived at just the right time," Lloyd said.

"Thank you, Doug," Lee said. Her tears began to flow freely.

Doug looked up at her and nodded. His eyes briefly scanned the heavens, and the pupillary sphincters trembled.

"Let's go back inside," Lloyd said. "I'll call Security."

52

THE INVESTIGATION

Two days after Avery's death, a federal investigator, a dour and self-important man named Charles Doherty, arrived to conduct a probe. He would have come sooner, but for the need to obtain special clearances, submit to a polygraph, and fill out a raft of forms. These delays intensified his natural sourness, so by the time he found the County Ovine Disease Research Center sign, he had puckered from mouth to anus.

His Agency handler, Fred Caldwell, greeted him at the gate. A senior official from the Office of Security, Caldwell was an old friend and schoolmate of Avery's, a fact he had no intention of disclosing to Doherty. Caldwell had a firm handshake, Alice blue eyes, and a direct, genial gaze that inspired trust. He assured the investigator that he would have access to everything—although he deeply regretted that he could not talk about the work Avery had been doing at the time of his death. Then, in the most engaging manner possible, Caldwell steered Doherty away from those things about which he had no need to know, like the existence of Doug, Project ASPARAGUS, Project HALF-

SHEEP, and a safe full of mind control drugs.

First, Caldwell took Doherty up to the roof of Mary Ethel Owens Worthy Dormitory. Following behind on the stairs, Caldwell noted that Doherty had an exceptionally narrow ass, one that matched his narrow mind. He had taken a strong dislike to the man within seconds of meeting him, another fact he must keep to himself. No problem, he would ramp up his bonhomie another notch, and the man would never know.

It delighted Caldwell to note that Doherty had a fear of heights. The man wouldn't admit it of course, but Caldwell could see the cold sweat collect on his forehead as he gingerly lowered himself from the dormer window down to the roof. He noted that the hand gripping the window ledge was as fine-boned as a bird's, and had to resist the temptation to slam the window on it.

"I can get a rope to tie around your waist if you're worried about falling," Caldwell said.

"Of course not," Doherty said. "Heights don't bother me."

Caldwell chuckled to himself. He'd made a number of parachute jumps during the war, when he served on a Jedburgh team codenamed Clove. He was a nimble man who moved easily and fearlessly on the roof, walking to its very edge without hesitation. He pointed out the chalk outline drawn on the slate shingles. Avery's body had fallen in an odd position, with the head near the edge of the roof and the legs oddly bent. Caldwell watched Doherty sketch the outline in a notebook. His hand shook and he had to pause twice, presumably to let the dizziness pass.

Next came a thorough search of Avery's room. It wasn't Avery's real room, however, but another room on the third floor of Mary Ethel Owens Worthy Dormitory.

Caldwell didn't want Doherty coming across anything he shouldn't see, so he and Lloyd had moved Avery's things two floors down, omitting only the lockbox of Psilocybin mushrooms and some pornographic materials that would embarrass Avery's family, should they ever come to light. Caldwell was scrupulous in photographing Avery's old quarters and arranging the new room precisely so. Wearing gloves, he laid out the objects on the shelf above the bathroom sink: a shaving mug containing a half-used puck of cup soap; a horn-handled shaving brush sitting upright; and a narrow leather manicure case of German manufacture with a missing nail file.

Caldwell hovered over Doherty's shoulder as he made a careful note of the missing nail file and underlined twice the fact that the manicure kit was German made. He followed Doherty into the bedroom and watched as he got down on his knees and went through a trashcan full of empty whiskey bottles and lemon rinds.

"Hmmm, a heavy drinker," Doherty said at last. Caldwell shook his head at the lame deduction. Later that evening he wired a message to Ludden, "Don't worry. Investigator idiot."

The next day, Caldwell took Doherty to the local morgue to view Avery's remains. From the ostentatious way the investigator scowled at the wound and nodded, Caldwell guessed the man had no expertise in forensic pathology. While Doherty took notes, Caldwell stood on the undamaged side of Avery, more out of respect for his old friend than squeamishness. He gave the corpse an inconspicuous salute and sent him a silent message, addressing him by an old school nickname: *Happy to do you one last favor, Sunny. You were a magnificent fellow, before Albania.*

Before they left the morgue, the coroner opened a refrigerator and pulled out a cloth-wrapped object. A sheepish look came over his face as he tipped the contents onto a slab: a dead and staring raccoon. "I felt silly keeping this thing, but Mr. Caldwell said you should see all of the evidence. It was found in a bed of periwinkle in front of the dormitory. It had been shot with a bullet from Mr. Stanton's gun."

This prompted furious note-taking by Mr. Doherty. "Is it a male or female?" the investigator asked.

Caldwell and the coroner exchanged a glance that was extremely brief, but full of meaning.

"Feel free to look," the Coroner said.

Doherty raised the tail with such a look of dour consequence on his face that Caldwell had to turn away and cough.

The next day, Caldwell sat in as Doherty interviewed Lee and Lloyd in the lounge area of Mary Ethel Owens Worthy Hall. He had coached them on their stories the evening before. Sitting pale and prim on opposite ends of a flowered davenport, they told a sanitized version of the truth that excluded any mention of drugs, mushrooms, or aliens.

"I don't know why he went to the roof," Lloyd said in response to Doherty's question.

"You have no idea?" Doherty said, injecting his voice with skepticism and surprise. It was how he responded to everything Lloyd and Lee said. It was tic of his, a particularly annoying one, but thus far they had not become defensive.

"I was asleep at the time Avery went upstairs, so I have no idea why he went up there," Lloyd said calmly.

"And you?" Doherty turned to Lee. "Do you know why he went up there?"

"I was also asleep at the time," she said.

Doherty pointedly looked Lee up and down. "You're an attractive woman. Surely you were having an affair with the deceased?"

Lee's expression of polite interest didn't change. "Surely I was not," she said.

Good girl, Caldwell silently instructed her, *don't let him rile you.*

"You can't tell me that there was nothing going on. I know how it is with so-called career women." Doherty let his eyes slide down her body, stopping with obvious distaste on her light summer trousers.

"I'm sure I can't tell you anything," Lee said with a slight smile, "but I was not having an affair with Avery Stanton."

Doherty continued with his line of questioning for another five minutes before moving on. It was abundantly clear to Caldwell from the complete lack of interaction between Lee and Lloyd, that they were the ones having the affair. Not that he cared, because he had concluded they had nothing to do with Avery's death. He did find them an odd couple. The lovely Lee had a combative intelligence that struck sparks off surrounding surfaces. Lloyd was thoughtful and plodding.

Doherty stayed another two days, trying everyone's patience, but ultimately he ruled the death a suicide. The only fingerprints he found on the gun were Avery's own. He saw the strange marks left by Doug's pods, but could not fathom their origin.

53

SEALED WITH BLACK TAPE

With an almost obsessive neatness, Lee set about the task of packing her materials and notes into boxes. Lloyd sealed them with black tape and stacked them on a cart to be taken to the archives. The alien watched from the corner. He had been subdued and uncommunicative since the night of Avery's death. He ate little, hugged the wall on the opposite side of the room from the window, and suffered nightmares.

"I never thought it would end so bitterly, so barrenly," Lee said as she conducted a final inventory of her drugs. She counted out five tablets and sealed them in an envelope. She printed the amount and name of the drug on the front in small block letters and placed it in a file box arranged alphabetically. She met Lloyd's eyes. "You knew how it would end all along, didn't you?"

"I had strong misgivings."

"Yet you chose to participate in the program when you could have opted to do something else. Why?"

Lloyd ran his hand along a stretch of black tape, pressing it over the seam of a box. "Because it would have happened whether I was there or not. I didn't want Doug to go through it alone. I felt an obligation to him. Now I owe him my life."

They both turned to look at the alien, who sat on the bottom bunk with his back pressed against the wall.

"He was happier in the basement," Lee said. She took a deep breath and finally asked out loud the question that had been plaguing them for days. "What happens to him now?"

The decision lay with Elliot Ludden. Shortly after they finished archiving their materials, Lloyd and Lee got word that they would be allowed to submit a recommendation on the final disposition of the alien. They quickly came to an agreement on the basic idea. They wrote up it up with hefty doses of scientific jargon and hard-assed, anti-Communist boilerplate designed to disguise the fact that they were proposing the kindest and most comfortable situation possible for Doug. They labored for days, second guessing every clause and comma. Then Lloyd drove the recommendation to Washington to deliver it personally to Ludden.

Then they waited.

54

THE ARCHIVES

The humans would call it murder, but I meant no offense to Avery. I peeked over the edge of the roof and saw him aim the gun at Lloyd's chest. He would have fired, but I didn't have to kill him. I could have pushed the barrel straight into the Bitter Sharp. In the sliver of a second before the gun went off, I realized I couldn't leave Avery alive and suffering. I pushed the barrel to his head. His skull burst, and his pain dissolved in a red mist.

It took me a long time to recognize in Avery the same thing I saw in Deyahm when he said, "Death I would have sooner preferred." It wasn't until we had moved upstairs, and the humans took to imbibing in my room in the evenings, that I saw how he was moving from alive to "alive." A part of him was broken that could not be fixed with all the healing green energy in the universe.

The mushrooms told Avery to kill the wrong man. If they hadn't whispered in his ear, I'm sure he would have come to the right conclusion and put the gun to his own head. He was grateful to me for what I did because he came to me in a dream and said, "Thank you, Dick Face." I said, "You're welcome," because I am nothing if not polite. After that dream, I perked up and began to eat again.

※

One night a few weeks after Avery's death, Lloyd and Lee came into my room with a large bottle. Lloyd twisted its neck, and the head popped and flew to the ceiling, startling me and causing me to fly to the ceiling likewise.

They burst out laughing.

"I'm sorry, Doug," Lloyd said. "We didn't mean to frighten you. This is a celebration. We brought champagne. Hop down and try it."

I dropped to the floor. I sincerely hoped that champagne was alcoholic because weeks of sobriety weighed heavily on my spirit. They poured the bright and gassy substance into my mug wart, and I took a tentative sip. It was not as good as Kahlúa, but it was alcoholic.

"We have good news," Lee said.

I glared at her. I'd had enough of the humans' good news.

She smiled broadly. "Ludden approved our recommendations. You don't have to take any more drugs."

This was not good news. While I wouldn't miss the mushrooms or mescaline, I had grown quite fond of cannabis and lysergic acid diethylamide-25.

"He doesn't seem happy," Lloyd said.

Lee poured more champagne into my mug wart. "Cheer up. We're taking you to a new place soon. A place with no windows. Won't that be good?"

I had no desire to see again the stars that had witnessed Avery's murder. Nor did I want to see the Earth moon, sad in its singularity. I'd had enough of the Bitter

Sharp.

Then Lee and Lloyd proceeded to make more promises, which I didn't take to heart. "You'll be working in the archives. You'll be perfect for it because you can't tell our secrets."

"I'll have a brass nameplate made for you," Lloyd said. "It will have 'Douglas A. Leon' engraved in fancy letters."

I shook my head. I reached for the notebook and pen, which lay on the desk. Lloyd and Lee gaped as I retracted the webbing on my limb terminal. Utilizing the perfect cursive hand taught to me by Jimmy, I wrote, *I would prefer to be called Alice Webster.*

Lee's voice shook as she said, "Don't ever let anyone else know you can do that."

I nodded.

I have been here for a long time. I love the archives and I'm honored to share the same esteemed profession that Deyahm once practiced. His remains are here, in a box high on shelf 34 of section G. I visit once a week.

I still get visits from Lee and Lloyd. They are growing old now. They are sometimes together and sometimes separate. When they come separately, they tell me that they will never be together again. When they come together, they say they will never be apart again. Together or apart, I sip my coffee and frown as if I were paying close attention. The story of Lee and Lloyd is too complex for my alien brain.

I have only left the archives once. After much conniving and preparation, Lloyd sneaked me out and took me to his home. Trudie was there, visiting from New Mexico. I thought my cardiovascular ticker pump would burst from joy. We hugged and then we sat on Lloyd's sofa together, and she told me all about her life. She was still on the ranch, but she said it was much improved since my visit. She had turned it into a "the best paint breeding and training operation in the state." Paints are vehicular horses with spots. Trudie told me they were originally bred from quarter horses. I assume this was done by fragmentation, a form of asexual reproduction we had tried unsuccessfully on Utorb. I was astounded that humans had devised a way to slice a vehicular horse to produce four more horses. All we had managed to do was ruin quite a few innocent Utorbis. Deyahm had told me all about it.

I wanted to hear more about the vehicular horses, but Lloyd kept asking Trudie about Joe. Joe had been living with Trudie for many years. Joe had called Lloyd and asked him to help convince Trudie to marry him. She said she didn't require a ring because she was happy enough to rupture anyway. She and Lloyd talked about this a great deal, but I found it boring and fell asleep.

Trudie asked me to go back to New Mexico with her. Lloyd said he could make it look like I had escaped from the archives on my own. I had to turn her down. Just talking to Trudie about her spacious ranch made me long for my windowless archives. As I said before, I have no desire to see the stars again. Certainly I have no desire to travel.

All the many cycles of evolution on Utorb fitted me perfectly to my work in the archives. I don't need a ladder to move among the boxes. My latest supervisor, Vic, is a delightful fellow who is as pleased as I am to have a job that limits his contact with humans. He reads and drinks a lot of coffee. We play chess. He seems satisfied with my work, although he doesn't know that I sometimes switch labels just for fun, and sometimes I ignore his directions altogether.

Now and then the order will come down to retrieve things for destruction—all the boxes related to Project ASPARAGUS, for example. When that happens, I first memorize the contents of the boxes to be destroyed. Then I take some of the most important papers and tuck them into other boxes where they will be safe. Someday the third mission may come, *Uyiquiti Ri Bo*. Or perhaps some human will pause in his arrogance and pay heed to my story. I think it would be instructive for the humans to discover that they are not the center of the universe.

The other day two old men came to paw through the archives. I got impatient waiting for them to find my boxes and pushed one off the shelf. It frightened them, and I had to suppress my effervescent Utorbian laughter. They sat on the floor and read about me for hours. I hid nearby, waiting to hear what wisdom they would extract from my history. Finally, the one with unpigmented hair stood and said, "What the hell do we do with this shit?"

The other human considered this question as light bounced off his curiously hairless pate. At last he said, "We do nothing. We put these boxes back on the shelf and pretend we never found them. I don't care what the boss wants. I'm not going to be responsible for turning the Mines into a joke."

His colleague nodded. "You pack this stuff up. I'll go get the tape."

About Susan Hasler

Susan Hasler spent twenty-one years in the Central Intelligence Agency. She began her career as a Russian linguist and moved on to become a Soviet analyst, speechwriter to three Directors of Central Intelligence, and finally a counterterrorism analyst. She served in the CIA Counterterrorism Center before, during, and after 911. In 2013, Hasler appeared in the Emmy-winning HBO documentary *Manhunt: The Search for Bin Laden*.

Ms. Hasler's work has appeared in literary journals, magazines, and anthologies. She lives with her husband in Virginia.